Praise for *Too Little, Too Late*

'A winning combination of food and romance ...
Caddle will have readers laughing and crying along
with the heroine every step of the way'   *Irish Times*

Praise for *Shaken and Stirred*

'An engaging warm slice of life with which all women
will be able to identify'   *Books Magazine*

'A warm and engaging read about five colleagues in a
Dublin marketing company'   *Heat*

'A warm and funny novel perfect for that sunny beach
or a rainy day read'   *ri-rá*

Also by Colette Caddle

Shaken and Stirred
Too Little, Too Late

About the author

Colette Caddle is the author of *Shaken and Stirred* and *Too Little, Too Late*, a No.1 bestseller in Ireland. She lives in Dublin with her husband and son.

A CUT ABOVE

Colette Caddle

CORONET BOOKS
Hodder & Stoughton

First published in Great Britain in 2002 by Hodder and Stoughton
A division of Hodder Headline

The right of Colette Caddle to be identified as the Author
of the Work has been asserted by her in accordance with the
Copyright, Designs and Patents Act 1988.

A Coronet paperback

2 4 6 8 10 9 7 5 3 1

A CIP catalogue record for this title is available
from the British Library

ISBN 0 340 79287 6

Typeset in New Baskerville by Palimpsest Book Production Limited,
Polmont, Stirlingshire

Printed and bound in Great Britain by
Clays Ltd, St Ives plc

Hodder and Stoughton
A division of Hodder Headline
338 Euston Road
London NW1 3BH

For Tony & Peter,
with all my love

A CUT ABOVE

Prologue

Monday morning, 21 August 2000

Toni threw the notebook on to the table in front of her and flopped back in her chair. The conservatory was her favourite room in the house and, with the early morning sunshine streaming in, it was even lovelier than usual. But it was useless trying to work. She just couldn't concentrate. Though, God knows, there were plenty of issues at the Blessington Clinic that she should be addressing: staff problems, a fall in business, ethical issues – life in cosmetic surgery was never dull.

Alice Scully put her head round the door. 'Would you like a coffee, Toni?'

'I just made a fresh pot, Alice. Sit down and I'll pour you a cup.'

The housekeeper shook her head. 'I won't, thanks. It's such a lovely morning I thought I'd get the bed-clothes washed and out on the line.' She hurried off.

Toni sighed. The woman was supposed to be taking it easy but there was no slowing her down.

Chloe appeared in the doorway. 'Oh! Why aren't you at work?'

She brightened at the sight of her stepdaughter. 'I thought you could use some company.'

'There's still no sign of the postman. How come he's always early with bills and junk mail and late with the important stuff?' She started to pace the room nervously.

'It's only ten o'clock – he should be here soon,' Toni said. Chloe had been a bundle of nerves all weekend, knowing that the first offers of college places had been posted. 'Tell me, are you worried in case you don't get a place or in case you do?'

Chloe flopped down into a chair. 'It would be kind of nice if I got UCD and not Trinity. That would solve all of my problems.'

'And if you get both?'

Chloe made a face. 'I suppose I'll have to try to persuade Dad to let me go to UCD.'

'I hope you've given this enough thought, Chloe. Deciding on a college because that's where your boy-friend's going isn't a very good reason. You're going to be studying medicine for a long time. Don't dismiss Trinity on a whim.'

'Dad's asked you to try to get round me, hasn't he?' Chloe scowled.

Toni shook her head. Theo and she were way beyond having a reasonable discussion about Chloe's future. 'No, I just want to make sure you realise what you're doing.'

'I'm going to call Mark and Ollie to see if they've got any news yet.' With that Chloe flounced out of the room.

Toni hadn't intended to say anything to Chloe about college. It was enough that it was the main topic of conversation – or argument – between the girl and her father. But she was afraid that Chloe would turn down Trinity purely to spite Theo. It was a difficult time for her and it wasn't going to get easier. Toni was trying to work up the courage to talk to her but kept finding reasons to put it off. It would have to happen soon, though.

There was a thump in the hall as the post hit the floor. Toni got up, went outside and scooped up the letters, among them two official ones for her step-daughter. 'Chloe,' she called.

Chloe appeared at the top of the stairs with the phone still in her hand. 'Oh, Ollie, it's here! Look, I'll call you back in five minutes. Wish me luck.' She flew downstairs and took the envelopes Toni was holding out to her. 'This is it, then.' She tore open the first and squealed. 'Yes! Medicine at UCD.'

'Congratulations, love.'

'Thanks.' Chloe opened the second envelope. 'It's Trinity.'

Despite Chloe's earlier remarks Toni heard a note of pride in her voice. 'Now you're in a position to make a decision,' Toni said gently. 'Think long and hard, love, and don't let anyone influence you one way or the other.'

Chloe gave her a quick hug. 'I'd better phone Ollie back,' she said, and charged upstairs.

'You'd better phone your father, too,' Toni called after her. 'He should be at the hospital by now.' She went back into the conservatory and sat down. Okay, it was time. Once Chloe had decided which college she was going to accept, Toni would tell her. And she'd make sure that Theo was there when she did. They had to do this together.

Moments later Chloe was back again, looking miserable. 'Mark didn't get an offer.'

'Oh, the poor boy. Is he devastated?'

'I've told him he's sure to get something in the second round.'

'And is he?'

'Yeah, I'd say so. I suppose Dad will be thrilled.'

Theo French had never approved of Chloe's boyfriend.

'Of course he won't,' Toni said, with more conviction than she felt.

'What has he got against Mark? Is it just because he's Daniel's son?'

Mark was the son of Daniel Wheeler, the chairman and managing director of the clinic where Toni was director of administration and Theo was a non-executive director. The two men had different views on cosmetic surgery and their relationship was polite but distant.

'No, I think he's just being a possessive dad who has realised his only daughter is growing up.'

'He can be a terrible old fuddy-duddy,' Chloe stated. 'Why on earth did you marry him, Toni?'

'Chloe! What a question!'

'Well, it can't have been his looks, so what *was* the attraction?' Chloe was right, Toni knew. Theo could never have been described as handsome – his nose was too hooked and his face too narrow. But there was something arresting about him. She remembered the awed silence that descended on the administration department in Sylvester's whenever he'd dropped in. She had been a lowly secretary in those days and he'd never noticed her. But she had noticed him: he was hard to miss, striding around as if he owned the place. He practically did – Theodore French had been the top surgeon and Sylvester's was the largest general hospital in Dublin. He was tough with his staff but they put up with it because he was such a brilliant surgeon. She remembered how the nurses used to joke about the French God. It had been suggested that he probably walked on water in his spare time and could turn a fish supper into a feast for thousands.

Toni had admired him from afar. But it had been a different story on the day he had first walked into the clinic.

She'd been standing in Reception, flicking through the appointment book when he'd approached.

'Excuse me, do you work here? I've an appointment with Mr Wheeler.'

She looked up into piercing blue eyes and was lost for words.

'Theodore French. I've an appointment with Mr Wheeler,' he repeated. 'Mr Daniel Wheeler?'

Toni realised he was looking at her as if she were a moron and pulled herself together. 'Of course, Mr French. Please, follow me.' She led the way to the meeting room, conscious of his eyes on her back. Flustered, she introduced the two men and took her seat at the conference table.

Daniel saw Theo's questioning look. 'Mr French, this is my colleague Toni Jordan. She's in charge of administration.'

Theo turned his gaze on Toni once more. 'Really? How interesting.'

Daniel had watched, amazed, as his normally self-possessed manager flushed like a schoolgirl.

'He was so different from any man I'd ever met,' Toni said, finally answering Chloe's question.

'So it wasn't his sexy body, then?'

Toni laughed, and Chloe thought how pretty she was despite her boring clothes. Her stepmother lived in functional business suits and never wore makeup to work – not that she needed any. With her natural dark colouring, high cheekbones and large hazel eyes she always looked good. On the rare occasion that she left her wavy hair loose around her shoulders, Chloe joked that Toni could pass for her big sister. The only time Toni made anything of her appearance was when she went out in the evening and then she could look stunning. As she watched her stepmother now, Chloe wondered for the hundredth time what had brought Toni and her dad together. They had nothing in common and there were nearly twenty-four years between them. In fact, Toni was closer in age to Chloe.

'He was very attractive in his own way,' Toni was saying, 'but it was more his presence and power that did it for me. I was incredibly attracted to him.' *Like a moth to the flame.* 'I couldn't believe it when he asked me out.'

Chloe nodded sagely. 'You were flattered.'

'I suppose I was.'

'Not a great reason for getting hitched.'

Toni looked up sharply, but Chloe was plaiting her hair absently. 'There was a bit more to it than that,' she protested lightly.

'Whatever. I'm just glad you *did* marry him. Before you moved in this house was like a mortuary. Sometimes I felt like we'd all died with Mummy. But when Dad married you it was like we'd been given a second chance.'

Toni took her hand and held it tightly.

Chloe was startled to see tears in her eyes. 'Toni! What's wrong? I'm sorry, I didn't mean to upset you!'

Toni gave a shaky laugh. 'You didn't. I'm just remembering how sweet you were when we met.'

Chloe arched an eyebrow. 'Fooled ya, didn't I? Look at the monster I turned out to be.'

'The honey monster, maybe,' Toni said gently.

'You must have been the only couple ever to take a kid on your honeymoon!'

'We couldn't possibly have left you behind.'

'It was a wonderful holiday,' Chloe said wistfully. 'I'm definitely going back to California someday.'

Toni blew her nose. 'Yes, it was nice.'

'Nice? It was the best! I never thought I'd see Dad on the back of a horse. And once he was up there he thought he was John Wayne.'

'He was sore for days,' Toni remembered.

Chloe snuggled up to her like a child and breathed in her musky perfume. 'Maybe if we took him back there he'd lighten up a bit.'

Toni stroked her hair. 'He's under a lot of pressure.'

Chloe snorted. 'Yeah, work, work, work—'

The sound of the phone ringing in the hall inter-rupted them. Chloe jumped up. 'That will be Ollie. Oh, I hope she got a place in DCU. She'll be crushed if she didn't.'

Toni stared out into the garden. How weird that Chloe should start questioning her about her marriage now – just when it was about to end.

Chloe came back into the room. 'It's Dad's secretary. She wants to talk to you.'

'To what do I owe the honour?' Toni said drily, as she went into the hall. Emma Dunphy called her only if she had to. And if Toni rang Theo, Emma treated her with cool disdain – how dare she disturb the Master?

'Yes, Emma?'

'Toni. Sorry for bothering you' – Emma sounded anything but sorry – 'but do you know where Mr French is?'

'He was in Oxford for the weekend,' Toni said, 'but he was due back on the first flight this morning.'

'Yes, I *do* know that. I made the booking,' Emma said shortly. 'But he hasn't arrived yet. I thought he might have gone home first.'

'I'm afraid not. The flight must have been delayed. Have you tried his mobile?'

'It's switched off.'

'Of course it isn't,' Toni said dismissively. Theo never turned off his mobile. 'He must be out of range.'

'Then I'll just have to keep trying. Thank you, Toni. Goodbye.'

Toni hung up and went back into the conservatory.

'I thought Dad would have been on the phone by now,' Chloe said.

'It looks like his flight has been delayed.'

'Well, I'm going to call Ollie to see what the news is.'

'And I'd better go to work.'

An hour later Toni parked outside the Blessington Clinic and ran up the steps. 'Hi, Sandra. Everything okay?' she asked, as she crossed Reception to her office.

'Eh, not really,' the receptionist whispered, hurrying after her. 'Mrs Phillips is early but she won't sit in the waiting room.'

Toni stopped in her tracks. 'Why not?'

'Little Mindy Norton and her mother are in there,' Sandra mumbled.

'The old bitch!' Toni exploded. A dog had savaged Mindy, and her right eye was the only recognisable part left on her face. 'Where did you put her?'

'In your office. Sorry, Toni, there was nowhere else.'

'That's okay, Sandra. You did the right thing. Now, why don't you make Mrs Norton a nice cup of tea and give Mindy a lollipop? I'll see to Mrs Phillips.'

Sandra heaved a sigh of relief. 'All right, then. Oh, before I forget, Mr French's secretary called. She says he hasn't turned up yet.'

Toni frowned. Where on earth had Theo got to? 'Thanks, Sandra.' She threw open the door of her office and looked with distaste at the woman sitting on the small sofa. At well over sixty, Cora Phillips was dressed in a skirt shorter and tighter than the one Chloe wore when she was out to upset her father. Toni wondered which bit of her was getting tucked or nipped this time. She pasted a professional smile on her face. 'Good afternoon, Mrs Phillips. I'm afraid I'll have to ask you to wait outside for Mr Perkins.'

The woman put down her magazine and levelled cold eyes on her. 'I'm staying right here. You people charge enough. The least you can do is provide a decent waiting room.'

Toni resisted the urge to grab the woman by the scruff of her expensive suede jacket and throw her out on her ear. 'We do, Mrs Phillips. It's right over there.'

'Well, there should be a separate one for Mr Perkins' patients.'

The stiff smile faded from Toni's face. 'Now, look here—'

'Mrs Phillips! How lovely to see you!' Robert Perkins strode in, his arms outstretched. 'Why don't you come with me? Did someone get you some coffee? No? See to it, would you, Toni?' He shepherded the woman outside.

'No sugar,' Mrs Phillips barked over her shoulder.

Toni banged the door after them and buzzed Reception. 'Sandra? Would you get Mrs Phillips a coffee? With three sugars.' She sat down behind her desk and hurled a biro at the door. What a great day this was turning out to be. Bitches like Cora Phillips really pissed her off. How on earth could she look at someone like Mindy and feel anything other than pity? And how could Robert Perkins tolerate it? But she already knew the answer to that. Money. Daniel Wheeler had been right in his reservations. He should have kept the practice small and not allowed the likes of Robert to muscle in. Since he'd joined the Blessington it had seemed more like a beauty salon than a clinic. But if it wasn't for the money that the cosmetic end of the business brought in, they would probably have gone under years ago. Daniel was too easy-going when it came to chasing up patients who hadn't paid their bills. Often he had taken on bad cases knowing that he wouldn't be paid – but he couldn't turn them away, especially if they were children. She had thought it a good move to expand. It had been Theo's idea and, in those days, she had thought all of his ideas were brilliant.

Thinking of Theo reminded her of Emma's message. Where the hell *was* he? It was so unlike him not to get in touch. He was a stickler for punctuality and if he was going to be late for an appointment, he always called. She rang his mobile number. 'The customer you are calling may be out of range . . .' Toni hung up then called the hospital. 'Emma? It's Toni. Has Mr French turned up yet?'

'I'm afraid not.' Emma sounded agitated. 'And I've checked with the airport. His plane did land on time.'

'Then he must have missed it. Did you call his hotel?'

'Yes . . .' Emma hesitated.

'And?' Toni prompted. It wasn't like Emma to be reticent.

'It's a bit odd, actually. He never checked in.'

'Sorry?'

'He didn't stay at the hotel, Toni. Does he have friends in Oxford? Someone he could have spent the night with?'

Toni ignored the implication. 'He has some colleagues, of course, but none he'd stay with. Could you ring round, Emma? Maybe call the conference organisers, some of the delegates—'

'I already have. He didn't attend the conference either.'

'This is ridiculous, Emma. He can't have just disappeared off the face of the earth.'

There was a short silence at the other end of the phone. Then Emma's voice, unconvincing: 'No, of course not. I'm sure there's a reasonable explanation.'

Chapter One

Sunday, 7 May – three months earlier

Toni zipped up her shorts, pulled on an old white T-shirt and dragged her hair under a battered baseball cap. It was a beautiful day and she'd decided it would be good for body and soul to do a bit of gardening. It might clear her head, if nothing else. She wandered downstairs and was just filling the kettle when Theo arrived with the Sunday papers. 'Morning.' He sat down at the table and began to scan the headlines.

Toni yawned widely. 'Hi.'

'You got home very late.'

Theo's voice was even and he didn't raise his eyes from the paper in front of him, but Toni could smell an argument in the air. She groaned inwardly. *Not today, Theo.* She was too hung-over for this. Usually she only had a couple of drinks when she went out with Jade, but last night she'd felt like another. And then another. She sighed. Sometimes her nights out with her friend were all that kept her going. 'Sorry if I woke you,' she said now to Theo, her tone conciliatory.

'Where did you go?'

'Just to the Chinese. Jade likes it there,' she added lamely. *Why are you apologising? Normal people eat Chinese food. Normal people think it's okay to eat after nine at night. Normal people have a life!*

Theo snorted. 'I'm surprised the woman eats at all. She's ridiculously thin.'

'She has a high metabolic rate and she works out,' Toni replied calmly, as she made a large pot of tea. 'Shall I make you an omelette?'

'You'd only burn it. I'll just have toast and orange juice.'

Toni made a face at him, put bread in the toaster and went to the fridge for the juice. After setting the table she rummaged in the press for some pain-killers.

Theo watched as she swallowed them with a mouthful of tea. She met his gaze steadily, daring him to comment. 'I think the toast is ready,' he said, and she turned in time to see smoke rising from the toaster.

'Shit!' She extracted the blackened bread gingerly and threw it into the bin. 'I'll make some more.'

'Don't bother. I'll have brunch at the golf club. Where's Chloe?'

'She's gone to a study group at Ollie's house.'

Theo's brow wrinkled in annoyance. 'That's an excuse if ever I heard one.'

'That's not fair, Theo. Chloe's been studying hard.'

'Maybe, but these so-called study groups are just a way of getting together to discuss boys or pop groups. There won't be a tap of work done.'

Toni smiled. She must remember to ask her step-daughter who her favourite pop group was. 'I'm not sure I agree. I think brainstorming sessions can be quite useful.'

'You would,' Theo said dismissively.

Toni rolled her eyes. The man could be so bloody archaic at times. He didn't have a clue how to talk to Chloe, always rubbing her up the wrong way. But why did that surprise her? He couldn't communicate with a thirty-three-year-old so what hope did he have with a teenager?

Theo drained his glass and stood up abruptly. 'I'll leave you to recover from your hangover.'

'Don't hurry back,' Toni murmured, as the front door slammed. She sipped her tea and began to relax. A day alone in the sunshine and fresh air would do her good. It would revive her and prepare her for the week ahead.

She thought back to when Sunday mornings had been special, full of laughter and love. That was when she had been with Ian. Usually after much arguing and tickling, he would clamber out of bed to make breakfast. He would arrive back, grumbling that she just used him as her sex slave and gofer, and they'd sit side by side munching toast and chatting companionably. Sometimes after they'd finished, they'd make love among the crumbs, dress lazily then stroll down to the pub in time for opening. How different things were with Theo. In her six years of marriage, she couldn't remember them ever staying in bed all morning. In fact he was usually gone seconds after the alarm went off. As for cosy, boozy afternoons in the pub, he would be shocked at the idea of wasting his time in such a way. And as for drinking—

Toni jumped as the dog next door yapped. She put her mug into the sink and went out to the shed to get her gloves and trowel. She knelt down beside the flowerbed and began to weed. It was only ten o'clock but the sun was intense on her back.

Later, she clipped the hedge and mowed the lawn. She was red-faced and sweating by the time she'd finished. After she put away her tools, she went to the house to get a beer from the fridge, brought it outside and flopped down on the grass.

'It's all very well for some,' Chloe remarked, when she emerged from the house to find Toni stretched out on the lawn, the empty bottle beside her.

Toni shaded her eyes and looked sleepily at her. 'What are you doing home? What time is it?'

'It's just gone one. I came home early. The gang was more interested in sunbathing than studying. Bloody weather!'

And this was the girl Theo thought he had to keep tabs on! 'Why don't I make us some lunch and then you can study in the conservatory?' Toni suggested. 'It'll be nice and cool in there.'

Chloe stretched out and closed her eyes. 'Sounds good. Call me when it's ready.'

'Yes, my lady! Of *course*, my lady!' Toni stood up and went inside to prepare a salad. Even she could manage that. When the cooker wasn't involved, her food was quite edible. Of course, it helped that Alice always left the fridge well stocked with cold meat and smoked fish.

As she worked she thought about Chloe, the one element of her marriage that had been a success. Chloe had added so much to her life. And she felt she'd been a welcome addition to Chloe's. Toni had always tried to be open with her, answering her questions honestly, however embarrassing. But Chloe had become more secretive in the last few months and Toni was sure there was a boy on the scene. About time too, she thought privately. Thanks to Theo, Chloe's life revolved around school and success, and she needed some fun. Toni felt a little hurt that Chloe hadn't confided in her about her lovelife – but, then, she was probably terrified that her father would find out and put a stop to it. No, she was right to play this one close to her chest. Good luck to her! She poured sparkling water into two glasses and went to call her. It would be nice to have a relaxing lunch, just the two of them. And afterwards . . . well, afterwards she'd find something else to take her mind off her problems. She must be one of the few people in the world who looked forward to Mondays.

Monday, 8 May

'Now if you select that column there,' Jade said patiently, 'and press the "sum" icon, it will automatically total the figures and put the amount in the next field.'

Sandra Tomkins, receptionist at the Blessington Clinic, looked blank.

Jade sighed. Why was she doing this? She was a nurse, for God's sake, not a teacher, and Sandra could be a particularly obtuse pupil. 'Here, let me show you again.'

As she started to type in some figures the phone rang, and Sandra rushed thankfully to answer it. 'Good morning, Blessington Clinic, can I help you? Oh, hello, Mr French. No, no, he's not in yet – yes, I'll get him to call you as soon as he gets in. Of course – thank you. Goodbye, Mr French.' Sandra wrote down the message and trotted off to Robert Perkins' office with it.

'You could have handed him the message when he came in,' Jade pointed out when she returned.

'No, I might have forgotten, and Mr French would have been very annoyed.' Sandra shuddered.

'He's only a man, Sandra,' Jade said, irritated.

'Well, he scares the hell out of me. I don't know how Toni could have married him.'

I won't argue with you there, Jade thought, but said nothing.

'Maybe it was because he was her boss,' Sandra mused. 'Some girls are into that.'

'But he's never *been* her boss, Sandra.'

Sandra sighed, with exaggerated patience. 'Well, not as such, no. But he brought her into the clinic, didn't he? It's the same thing.'

'He didn't. In fact, if anything it's down to Toni that Theo got involved with the Blessington.' *But we won't hold that against her.* 'You've got to remember, Sandra, that originally this was just a consulting room. Daniel Wheeler inherited the building from an uncle and transferred his private rooms here from Sylvester's. He brought Toni with him as his PA. She'd been working in the admin area at the hospital for, oh, it must have been five years. After a year or so Daniel hired me when he started to carry out minor procedures here and needed a full-time nurse.'

Sandra nodded. 'Oh, I see.'

'Theo only joined as a non-executive director when Daniel needed extra investment.'

'Gosh, I thought Theo had started the Blessington.'

'I'm not surprised, the way he throws his weight around.' Jade laughed. 'But this is and always has been Daniel Wheeler's clinic. Robert Perkins came on board when Daniel expanded the clinic to encompass cosmetic surgery. Robert, God bless him, was the one who hired dear Vicky.'

Sandra grimaced. 'I don't know what I ever did to that girl but she's always really bitchy to me. And what about those boobs? They can't be real!'

'I suppose it makes her a walking talking advertisement,' Jade said.

'I like Daniel the best of all the directors,' Sandra confided.

'And what about Toni?'

'Oh, she's great too, but I never think of her as a director. She's my boss.'

'I think that's sexist or something,' Jade said drily.

'Oh, I didn't mean it to be.' Sandra looked worried. 'The place would fall apart if it wasn't for Toni.'

'Daniel is a bit scatter-brained,' Jade acknowledged.

'But he's so nice and all his patients adore him. I'm surprised he ever went into business with Mr French and Mr Perkins. They're so different from him.'

Sometimes Sandra hit the nail on the head without even realising it, Jade thought. Daniel would never have chosen either Theo or Robert as partners: they were a necessary evil, the price he had to pay for having rooms in such an old house – it needed money sunk into it regularly. Money that Daniel didn't have and Theo French did. Theo had brought in his old buddy Robert, who specialised in bums-and-boobs because that was the kind of surgery that brought in real money.

Jade had taken an instant dislike to Robert and had considered leaving.

'Please, Jade,' Daniel had entreated, 'I'd be lost without you. We'll be hiring another nurse soon and she can work for Robert if you dislike him so much. But I'm sure you're too professional to let personal feelings get in the way.'

Jade had bristled at this, but she stayed.

'And I don't know how Toni could have married the man.' Sandra repeated, breaking in on her thoughts.

Jade concentrated on the screen. Sandra was too fond of gossip for her liking and she wasn't going to encourage it.

But Sandra wasn't put off by Jade's silence. 'I mean, he's so much older than her, what could they have in common?'

'I really don't know, Sandra.'

'Was your husband older than you, Jade?' she asked hesitantly.

'Three years,' Jade said shortly.

'Oh, that's the perfect gap,' Sandra said, relieved. 'My mam always says—'

Jade stood up. 'Sorry, Sandra, lesson over for today. I've got to get to work. See you later.'

Jade made her way up to the little office she shared with Vicky Harrison, stopping to get a coffee on the way. There would have been plenty of time to show Sandra a few more functions of Excel, but she couldn't face the girl's attempts to glean information about her personal life. It was hard enough trying to fend off her questions about Toni. And at the moment Jade felt protective of her friend. Toni had seemed particularly glum on Saturday night, drinking a lot more than usual. It was surprising that she had suggested going out at all. They never usually met at weekends, which were strictly reserved for family in the French household. Though that hadn't seemed to be the case lately. Chloe was studying for her Leaving Certificate, and Toni didn't spend much time alone with Theo. Jade sipped her coffee thoughtfully. She hated to admit it but she agreed with Sandra. What *had* Toni Jordan seen in Theodore French? And how could she have let someone as gorgeous and funny as Ian Chase slip through her fingers?

Jade had had plenty to say on that at the time, but once Theo's ring was on Toni's finger, she hadn't uttered another word. Yet she missed Ian. He was a nice guy and good company, and they'd had some great nights out as a foursome. Jade's husband Aidan had taken to him immediately. Usually he hated being dragged along to hospital dos because half the time he didn't know who they were gossiping about and didn't much care either. But Ian had made him laugh with his impressions of the hospital hierarchy – although Aidan didn't believe they could possibly be as mad or as bad as he made out.

'They are,' Jade had assured him. 'Complete nutters, most of them.'

'But Ian's one of them,' Aidan argued.

'I suppose he is.' Jade had looked surprised. Ian had been consultant anaesthetist at Sylvester's for some time. 'But he's not like the others.'

Aidan had laughed. 'You can say that again. The man's almost normal!'

If only it were possible to turn the clock back, Jade thought. She often wondered if Toni would like to do that too but it was a question she couldn't ask.

Chapter Two

'There was a mix-up with the appointments so only three operations are down for today.'

Toni sighed. Vicky was always having a go at Sandra but it didn't help when the receptionist made cock-ups like this.

'The ear surgery at two,' Vicky was saying, 'the birthmark at three and the nose job at five.'

'Rhinoplasty,' Daniel corrected automatically.

Vicky yawned and flicked her blonde hair over her shoulder. 'Whatever.'

'Morning, everyone.' Robert breezed in ten minutes late and took his place opposite Daniel. Since the day he had joined the Blessington he had been late for meetings. Jade maintained that it was his way of demonstrating how important he was. 'So where are we at?' he asked as he ran an eye down the agenda in front of him.

'Good morning, Robert,' Daniel said equably. 'We were just going through my appointments.'

'Oh, yes. Did I mention I've had to bump your ear surgery? I have an urgent eyebrow lift.'

'There's no such thing as an urgent eyebrow lift,' Daniel said drily.

23

'Oh, but there is! She's flying out to the South of France next week.'

Daniel laughed at his colleague's consternation. 'Well, I'm terribly sorry to upset the lady's plans, but I've got a kid whose parents have been saving for months so that he could have this surgery.'

'You must reconsider, Daniel.'

Daniel didn't raise his eyes from the agenda. 'No, Robert, I must not. The paediatric anaesthetist is booked and I have no intention of cancelling him. Now, Vicky, would you like to continue?'

Robert snorted angrily and helped himself to coffee. Vicky flashed him a sympathetic smile then said, 'Daniel, you have six consultations tomorrow afternoon and surgery on Wednesday morning at Sylvester's. That afternoon you have ward rounds. On Thursday you have a clinic here for return visits, and five operations that afternoon at Sylvester's, starting at two. On Friday you're operating here all morning and the afternoon is given over to first consultations.'

'Where's my list?' Robert interrupted. 'I thought *I* had the theatre on Friday.'

'No, Robert,' Jade interrupted smoothly, 'you asked me to switch you to Thursday.' She caught Toni's eye and winked.

Toni buried her face in her notes. Robert had switched days to avoid working with Jade. Or, to be more accurate, to ensure that he'd be working with Vicky. Though 'work' probably wasn't the correct word, Toni thought, remembering the day she had walked in on them in the kitchen. Robert had had Vicky pressed up against the fridge, his tongue half-way down her throat, and Vicky's left leg had been practically around his waist. Toni had considered coughing discreetly but decided that in the interests of a relaxed working environment it would be more diplomatic to withdraw quietly.

'That's nothing,' Jade had scoffed, when Toni told her. 'I caught them at it in the recovery room one night.'

Toni shuddered. 'Oh, don't! Even the thought of it makes my stomach churn. How can she?'

'She's mesmerised by the colour of his money,' had been Jade's caustic reply.

Toni smiled inwardly at the memory.

'Oh, did I? Yes, right, of course,' Robert was muttering now. 'Are you on duty that day, Jade?'

She flashed him a brilliant smile. 'Afraid not. Vicky will have to look after you.'

Robert eyed her suspiciously over the rim of his glasses but Jade gazed back at him innocently.

'Let's move on.' Toni broke in. She turned the page and the others followed suit. She nodded to Vicky, who ran through Robert's list without further interruption.

'Anything else?' Daniel asked Toni.

'Just one more item. Our costs are up five per cent on last month.'

Daniel stroked his beard thoughtfully. 'That's quite a lot, isn't it? Do we know why?'

'No idea,' Toni replied lightly, 'but Jade is going to do a stock-take tomorrow so we'll know more after that.'

'Couldn't Sandra do the stock-take? It's ridiculous that a nurse has to do it,' Daniel complained.

'Sandra can take care of general office stuff but I'd

prefer someone who knows what they're doing to deal with the medical supplies.'

'Tomorrow is a very busy day,' Robert said. 'Why not let Vicky check the stock on Wednesday?'

Jade and Toni exchanged glances.

'That makes more sense,' Daniel agreed. 'Well, if that's everything?'

Toni nodded, and everyone stood up.

'Robert, have you got a minute?' Daniel asked, as the others filed out of the room. He watched the older man settle back in his chair. He'd rather have faced a lengthy and difficult surgery any day than deal with Robert Perkins. Normally he avoided the man, leaving Toni to deal with him, but he couldn't this time. He had kept his head buried in the sand for far too long. But things had been brought to a head when Toni had come to see him a couple of weeks ago . . .

'Daniel, I don't want to worry you but I'm a bit concerned about some of Robert's cases,' she'd said, her beautiful face grave.

The absent-minded smile had faded from Daniel's face. 'What is it, Toni?'

'I don't have all the details . . .'

'Just tell me, Toni,' Daniel had said flatly. They'd known each other too long for pussyfooting. And if Toni was worried enough to bring it to him, then Daniel knew he had a problem.

Toni had taken a deep breath. 'Some of the operations he's carried out lately weren't, in my opinion, necessary and there were a couple that weren't . . . wise.'

'Are you saying he put patients at risk?'

Toni shrugged unhappily. 'I'm not qualified to answer that. But from an administrative point of view, I *can* say that our legal position wouldn't be strong.'

'Jesus! What the hell has he done?'

He had become paler and angrier as Toni read details of seven cases from her notebook, among them a liposuction case on a forty-three-year-old woman, who was a heavy smoker and extremely overweight, and a breast reduction on a young mother suffering from post-natal depression. Daniel winced. He was against plastic surgery for vanity's sake but there were often serious reasons why people were prepared to undergo such an ordeal. It was the surgeon's job – no, his duty – to ensure that each patient was doing it for the right reasons *and* had thought it through.

Now, his eyes flickered over the man in front of him with barely concealed distaste. He noted the greased-back hair, dyed a ridiculous blue-black, the shiny, manicured nails and flamboyant Paisley bow-tie. Daniel couldn't abide or understand such vanity in a man.

Robert smiled confidently. 'Can't stay long. I've a patient in twenty minutes.'

'I'll be brief,' Daniel said curtly.

'Is it about my advertising proposal? Have you reconsidered?'

'No, I haven't.'

Robert looked annoyed. 'I must say, Daniel, you're being terribly old-fashioned about this. Advertising in magazines like *Cosmopolitan* and *Tatler* would bring in a lot more custom. I had eight patients from the UK last month alone. Eight!'

'And you know what my feelings are on that,' Daniel retorted. 'It's bloody ridiculous. These patients are treating our clinic like a holiday resort. "Will I go to Greece this year? No, maybe Turkey would be nicer. Oh, no, I'll go to Ireland instead and get the fat sucked out of my stomach!"'

'That's the world we live in, old man,' Robert responded. 'Everyone wants to look perfect and it's cheaper for them to come here, with the exchange rate as it is. And there's the added bonus of telling their friends that they were in the Emerald Isle for a little holiday.'

'But it's wrong, Robert.' Daniel was pulling at his beard agitatedly. 'They aren't taking the proper amount of time to consider the seriousness of the surgery. They're jumping right in and, I have to say, I don't think you're doing much to discourage them.'

'If they want to spend their money who am I to stop them? Anyway, if I turn them away they'll just go to someone else. And that's their prerogative, Daniel. They're adults, for God's sake.'

'Not always.' Daniel's expression darkened. 'What about that eighteen-year-old girl from Manchester who I found sobbing in the waiting room a few weeks ago? She'd had her consultation and breast enhancement within two weeks, for God's sake! She didn't know what she was doing and she ended up even more self-conscious than she had been when she was flat-chested.'

'That operation was a complete success,' Robert

argued, 'and we shouldn't have to reverse an operation just because a patient changes her mind.'

Daniel took several deep breaths in an effort to calm himself. 'Robert, you have carried out liposuction on three patients in the last month who should have been refused the operation.'

Robert's eyes narrowed. 'That's not true.'

'Yes, it is, and your quarterly report showed an alarming increase of twenty-five per cent in these operations. How do you account for it?'

Robert laughed. 'It's spring. The women want to get rid of the flab before they don their bikinis.'

Daniel clenched his fists. It was exactly this sort of flippant comment that made him regret having agreed to Robert's appointment in the first place. 'But these women in particular were not suitable candidates,' he pointed out, struggling to keep his voice calm. 'Two were very overweight and one had diabetes.'

Robert looked at him coldly. 'A mild form, I assure you. I don't take risks, Daniel, and I resent your implication that I do. These women are looking for a miracle cure and I try to give it to them. Of course, if they're obese, I send them away.'

'They don't have to be obese to be at risk,' Daniel persisted, despite Robert's rising colour and the angry glint in his eye.

'Not one of my patients has had problems after surgery because of a weight problem.'

'Not yet,' Daniel flung at him. 'You've been bloody lucky.'

'Lucky? How dare you?'

Daniel ignored Robert's outrage. 'I dare because the

patients of this clinic come first. Now, I've decided to bring in a new rule to reduce the risk of unnecessary operations taking place. From now on, the first consultation must take place at least three weeks before the operation and the second within ten days of the procedure.'

'But that's ridiculous! We'll lose all our UK customers if we do that!'

'If we do, so be it.'

Robert stood up and glowered down at him. 'You're overreacting, Daniel, as usual. You know you can't bring this in without putting it before the board first.'

Daniel's eyes were cold and determined. 'Then that's what I'll do.'

Robert muttered something under his breath, stalked out of the room and slammed the door behind him.

Daniel sank back in his chair and massaged his temples. He was fairly sure he would win this one. The board consisted of Toni Jordan, Theo French, Robert and himself. He would have Toni's backing for sure – anything to keep Robert's 'cosmetic drive-thru' under control. And he believed he could count on Theo's support too, not necessarily because he would agree with him but because Theo was terrified of the clinic being sued for malpractice. Yes, his new system would get board approval and that would slow down Robert Perkins. For a while, anyway.

Something's going on,' Jade said, without preamble, when they were in the privacy of Toni's office.

'But what?' Toni asked. She was a little distracted –

Daniel was probably confronting Robert at this very moment. 'What could Vicky possibly be up to? What's in it for her?'

'Dunno, but Perky is either involved or protecting her.'

Toni nodded thoughtfully. 'His behaviour was a bit odd.'

'Though Daniel didn't seem to think so,' Jade added.

'For goodness' sake, Daniel wouldn't notice if there were flashing neon signs all around him saying, "Warning, something fishy's going on here."' Toni set down her mug of coffee and looked at Jade with a twinkle in her eye. 'How do you feel about a bit of detective work, Ms Peters?'

A smile spread slowly across Jade's face. 'Tell me more, Holmes.'

'Okay, here's the plan. We'll let Vicky go ahead and check the stock on Wednesday.'

'And?'

'Then *we*'ll do it again.'

Jade nodded enthusiastically. 'Great.'

'I'm afraid it'll mean working late.'

'No problem.'

'It'll be safer if we do it after hours. It would ruin everything if Vicky realised what we were up to.'

Jade's perfectly plucked eyebrows went up an inch. 'Don't worry about that. Her three brain cells will be worn out after a real day's work.'

'You're so cruel.'

Jade grinned. 'So, if we find any discrepancies, we confront Vicky on Thursday?'

Toni shook her head. 'No, I don't think so. I think

we should just keep an eye on her for a while. Try to figure out what's going on and if Robert is involved. We can't go making wild accusations.'

'I suppose you're right,' Jade agreed reluctantly, disappointed that she wouldn't get the chance to pin the other nurse up against a wall and shine a bright light in her eyes.

'Of course I am. Okay, then. We'll meet here on Wednesday night, say about seven?'

'Okay, boss. I'll wear my mac, trilby and dark glasses. What's the secret password?'

Toni laughed. 'You do know you're certifiable, don't you?'

Later that evening, Toni stood in her kitchen and studied the contents of the fridge. She was eating alone tonight as Chloe was playing basketball and Theo was out – she couldn't remember where. The fridge was packed with food but nothing took her fancy. It was all too damn healthy! All the things Theo liked, thanks to his devoted housekeeper. She shut the door and went into the garden. To hell with it! She'd order in later *and* open a bottle of wine.

It was a beautiful evening and the sounds of summer filled the air. Toni listened to laughter and glasses clinking in a neighbouring garden and smelt the unmistakable aroma of barbecuing steak. She had foreseen such evenings in the French household, but casual wasn't Theo's thing. Place-mats and linen napkins were more his style. No paper plates, cold beer and children munching burgers with tomato sauce dripping down their chins. She wandered round the flowerbeds checking her plants then settled in a large garden chair to enjoy the last of the sun.

She tried to relax but her mind was working overtime. She was dying to know how the meeting with Perky had gone, but Daniel had been tied up all day and there hadn't been an opportunity to ask. Maybe she'd call him at home: it would certainly be easier to talk. She went in search of the phone – that was the problem with these cordless jobs: you put them down and forgot where. She finally discovered it in the sitting room under Chloe's maths book but by that time she'd decided it wouldn't be fair to disturb Daniel at home. She'd leave it till morning.

Instead she dialled for a curry, opened a bottle of wine and carried her glass out to the garden, remembering to bring the phone with her. She sank back into her chair and closed her eyes. It was nice to have the place to herself, though she'd been looking forward to telling Theo about Perky's latest behaviour. She knew her husband would not be impressed – finally, an issue they could agree on. That made a pleasant change.

She sipped her wine and thought about the mystery rise in the clinic's costs and Robert enthusiastically volunteering Vicky to do the stock-take. It was very strange. Daniel would be really cheesed off if Robert was involved in anything remotely dodgy but she wasn't going to mention it until she and Jade got to the bottom of it. Thank goodness for Jade, always happy to turn her hand to anything. She was adept on the computer and Sandra had benefited greatly from her tuition, her skills improving daily. Which was just as well, because Perky and Vicky were always looking for reasons to complain about the girl. They'd like nothing better than to see Sandra fired. But Toni and Jade would do everything they could to make sure it didn't come to that. Sandra needed her job.

She was an only child whose father had died many years ago. Her mother – now sixty-three – had contracted multiple sclerosis shortly afterwards. The symptoms had been mild for the first few years, but in recent months Valerie Tomkins had deteriorated rapidly and sometimes had to use a wheelchair. Toni, realising the extra burden on Sandra, had offered to put her on a three-day week, but the girl had been horrified. 'This job is the only thing that keeps me going, Toni,' she had said, her eyes filling with tears, 'and – and we need the money.'

Toni had been shocked that she hadn't seen the signs earlier. She'd just taken Sandra's cheeriness at face value. She had assured Sandra that her job was safe and that she could work whatever hours suited her best. If Perky knew, he'd be horrified but it looked as if Sandra was going to be with them for the long haul. She belonged at the Blessington with the rest of the motley crew. The two anaesthetists they used weren't based at the Blessington and were never in the building longer than they had to be – Toni doubted they even knew the names of her staff. The contract cleaners were middle-aged women who seemed to spend most of their time giggling and whispering about the clinic's patients and the funny operations that went on. Vicky Harrison, the voluptuous, backbiting nurse, was determined to get a rich man – and if he was under eighty it would be a bonus. Slippery Robert Perkins was obsessed with money, and younger, well-endowed women. And Jade Peters, while attractive and funny, was almost obsessively secretive about her private life. As for herself, Toni laughed aloud: her problems and idiosyncrasies were too numerous to mention. In fact, Daniel Wheeler was probably the only normal person in the clinic. Just as well the patients didn't know that.

Chapter Three

Wednesday, 10 May

Jade closed the door as quietly as its age would allow, collected her post and crept up the stairs.

'Mrs Peters? Is that you? Yoo-hoo.'

Jade slumped resignedly against the banisters. 'Yes, Mrs Stewart, it's me.'

A wizened little woman in black leggings and sequined top, with a cigarette hanging out of her mouth, tottered into the hallway. 'Come on down, love. I'll make a cup of tea and we can have a nice chat. I've hardly seen you all week.'

'Sorry, I've been busy.' It was no lie, and doing the stocktake after a long, difficult shift had exhausted her.

'You got a letter. I think it's from the bank.'

'Really?' Jade said, through gritted teeth. One of the downsides of living here was that her landlady always had a good nose through the post. 'Look, I'll pass on that tea, Mrs Stewart, if you don't mind. I just want to go to bed. I've a bit of a headache. Night.' She hurried on up the stairs.

'Please yourself,' Patsy Stewart muttered, went back into her sitting room and poured herself a gin.

Jade hurried up to her room, kicked the door shut after her then flung her bag and the letter on the bed. After plugging in the kettle carefully – the flex was frayed and the plug loose – she spooned two teaspoons of coffee into a large, cracked mug and went over to the tiny fridge to inspect the contents.

Four yoghurts, two days past their sell-by date, a carton of milk, half a tub of cream cheese and an egg. Nothing appealed. There were two chocolate biscuits left in the press. What the hell? She'd push the boat out and eat both of them. She took out the milk – there was only a drain left – and poured it into her coffee.

She carried her 'dinner' over to the threadbare armchair and turned on her tiny portable TV. She flicked through the stations until she found BBC's *Changing Rooms*. Her favourite. She often thought about writing to them. Now, this room would be a *real* challenge.

She thought wistfully of the beautiful house she'd left behind. It stood in a leafy cul-de-sac just off Collins Avenue, and was the house she'd thought she would end her days in. The huge garden where her grandchildren would play – no! *Stop it!* She tried to concentrate on the shelves Handy Andy was erecting but her heart wasn't in it. Her eyes flickered to the letter on the bed. It would be a polite reminder of the debt remaining and an offer to renegotiate her payment plan. The civility of the whole thing irritated her. She didn't want letters or phone calls or cosy chats with one of the bank's advisers. She just wanted to pay them the damn money and be done with it. Another couple of months would do it and then she'd be able to breathe again. She could have asked Toni for an advance on her salary to clear the debt and she had no doubt that Toni would have agreed, but then she would have had to tell her the whole sorry story. Of course Toni knew that when she and Aidan had separated they had sold their house in Glasnevin. 'Too many memories,' Jade had explained lightly, when Toni asked why she was giving up her home. Now her friend was under the impression that she lived in a plush new apartment and Jade had not disillusioned her. It was bad enough having to live in this hellhole with a pathetic old drunk for a landlady without the whole world knowing about it.

The shrill sound of the doorbell startled her. After a few moments, the caller rapped the knocker long and hard.

'Hey! Stop that,' Patsy Stewart shouted, as she made her way down the passage. 'I'm coming, I'm coming.'

Jade held her breath as her landlady opened the door, straining to hear the conversation. After some discussion, the front door was shut again and she could hear her landlady's step on the creaking staircase. There was a rap at her door. 'Mrs Peters? There's a man wants to talk to you.'

Jade opened the door a couple of inches. 'Tell him I'm not in, will you?' she pleaded.

Patsy eyed her warily. 'Are you in some kind of trouble? Cos I don't need that in this house. I don't want all sorts of shady characters coming knocking on my door—'

'It's my husband,' Jade cut through her tirade. 'And I assure you, despite his appearance, he's . . . a decent man.'

Patsy's pencilled eyebrows went up an inch. 'I see. You two separated, then?'

'That's right,' Jade muttered.

Patsy nodded sympathetically. 'Fair enough, love, but you're going to have to talk to him. I don't want him coming back at all hours and banging the door down. So you put him straight, there's a good girl.'

Jade sighed. 'Well, okay then, but not up here.'

'You can use my front room,' Patsy said graciously.

And you'll be in the next room with a glass against the wall, no doubt, Jade thought grimly. 'Thanks, Mrs Stewart,' she said.

Patsy led the way downstairs and stood watching as Jade opened the front door. 'Come on in, Aidan.' She led the way into Patsy's shabby sitting room and closed the door firmly in Patsy's face.

'Hiya, love. How are you?' Aidan smiled nervously.

Jade sat down on a hard-backed chair. 'I asked you to stay away from me,' she said dejectedly. She'd already moved twice in an effort to get away from him.

'I just wanted to see you.'

Jade gazed sadly at his bent shoulders, shabby jeans and battered trainers. It was hard to believe that this was the smart, handsome architect she'd married nearly twenty years ago.

'How's work going?' he asked.

'Fine.' *Why do we have to go through this every time, Aidan? Why bother with the small-talk? We both know why you're here.*

He rubbed his tobacco-stained hands together, and Jade noticed that his nails were bitten. 'What do you want?' she asked. The sooner he left the better. It broke her heart to see him like this.

'If you could just lend me a few quid,' Aidan said, his eyes pleading, 'whatever you can spare.'

'I can't spare anything,' she told him bitterly. 'I'm still paying off your debts, remember?'

He looked away. 'I know, love. I'm sorry. I've let you down terribly. Not a day goes by that I don't think about it. I failed you. I was a lousy husband.'

'Not always,' Jade reminded him. She couldn't stand it when he started down the road of self-pity.

'No. Not always,' he repeated quietly.

'Are you still going to the meetings?' Jade asked.

'When I can.'

Jade laughed bitterly. 'Ah, yes. It must be hard to fit them in between all the jobs you've got on.'

Aidan flinched. 'Ah, don't, love.'

Jade watched him angrily. 'I'm not giving you more money.'

'Just fifty quid – twenty, even.'

Jade saw his desperation and weakened – as she always did. 'Wait here.' She ran upstairs for her purse. She knew without checking that she had only thirty pounds. She took twenty and went back down to him. 'It's all I can afford.'

'Thanks, love.' He stuffed it into his pocket and turned to leave.

'Aidan?'

He paused, his hand on the door handle.

'I don't want you to come here again.'

'But, Jade—'

'I mean it, Aidan,' she said, her voice quiet but

determined. 'I don't want to see you again. You're going to have to stand on your own two feet from now on. I can't continue to support you.'

'I understand. Thanks for this. Take care of yourself, love.'

Jade shut the door quickly. She couldn't bear to watch him walk away. Her sweet, kind, charismatic husband. Where had he gone?

She hurried back upstairs before her landlady realised he'd left. She knew that if Patsy Stewart questioned her about him she was likely to lose her temper and tell her where to go, and however much she hated living here she couldn't afford to move. In the privacy of her room she curled up on the bed and let the tears come. It might be two years since she'd thrown Aidan out, but it still hurt as if it were only yesterday.

She remembered the day well. She had been enjoying a day off from the clinic, catching up on all the things she'd been putting off, including a letter to her sister, Anita, in Australia. When she'd finished she'd gone into Aidan's study in search of a stamp. He was out working on a large new property in Delgany. She'd admired the drawings spread out on his desk. He was such a great architect and she was so proud of him. She resumed her search and, after a fruitless rummage through the drawers, she decided to try his filing cabinet. Maybe he was more organised than she thought and filed them under S. The smile had died on her lips as she came across the stack of crumpled envelopes wedged at the bottom of the drawer. It was the Telecom logo that first set off alarm bells in her head. That, and the stark red line across the top of the page. It was a final notice and it had arrived two weeks ago.

'Oh, dear God.' Jade had started to go through the other letters with trembling hands. The electricity bill, their joint credit cards and – dear Jesus! – a note from the insurance company saying that the motor and household policies had lapsed.

'Oh, Aidan, what the hell's going on?' she'd groaned. She'd dialled his mobile. 'Aidan? It's me. You have to come home.'

'What's wrong, love? Are you sick?'

'No, nothing like that.'

'Then what is it? I'm really very busy—'

'I don't care how bloody busy you are! Get your ass back here now!' She'd hung up and gone out to the kitchen to get a drink.

When Aidan had arrived home, she had been sitting at the kitchen table with a large vodka and the pile of bills in front of her. His face fell. 'I can explain.'

'You can try,' she'd said grimly.

'It's just a cash-flow problem. I didn't tell you because I didn't want to worry you.'

'You'd prefer me to get arrested for driving without insurance,' she had retorted scathingly.

'Don't be silly, of course you're insured. I took care of that last week.'

'How kind.'

Aidan ignored her sarcasm. 'Look, Jade, this has been a difficult time for me. Brown's haven't paid their bill yet and Seamus Phelan is about to declare bankruptcy. I'll be lucky if I get a tenth of what he owes me.' He had sat down at the table and put his head in his hands.

Against all her instincts, Jade chose to believe him and they had talked long into the night about what needed to be done. Aidan would go to the bank manager the next morning to discuss a temporary loan and Jade would call the ESB, Telecom and the credit-card companies to agree a payment plan. 'But you mustn't keep problems like this to your future, Aidan,' she had warned.

He'd looked suitably chastened. 'I know, love. I'm sorry.'

And that had been the end of that – or so Jade had thought. They were on the breadline for a while. There were no Saturday nights down at the pub, no eating out and certainly no foreign holidays. But they'd coped and life had carried on as usual. Until the day that Jade had bumped into Seamus Phelan on O'Connell Street.

They had made awkward conversation for a few minutes, until Jade could stand it no longer. 'I was very sorry to hear about the business, Seamus,' she had blurted out.

Seamus had given her an odd look. 'I beg your pardon?'

'Aidan told me you had to declare bankruptcy.'

Seamus had laughed. 'Then he's having you on, Jade. Unless, of course, he knows something I don't.'

Jade had laughed, too, although it hadn't been easy. 'I must have got it wrong. Sorry.'

'Don't worry about it. Listen, I'd better be going. Take care of yourself, Jade, and tell Aidan I'll be in touch about the new apartment complex in Swords.'

'I will. 'Bye, Seamus.' Jade had walked back to work in a daze. Aidan had lied to her. There was no way he could have made such a mistake. Seamus Phelan was responsible for more than fifty per cent of his business. *Why* had he lied? Seamus had paid him and he'd spent the money. But on what? What could be so expensive that he hadn't paid any of their bills?

She'd confronted Aidan again that night, but this time she was ready for him. She'd spent a quiet half-hour at the clinic making phone calls and her worst fears had been confirmed. Aidan was also behind on the repayments for his car and – the most shattering piece of news – the mortgage. The building society was threatening to repossess their beautiful home.

She had prayed that Aidan would have a reasonable explanation, that he'd persuade her it was a temporary glitch and there was nothing to worry about. But her hopes were in vain and no one was listening to her prayers that night.

Jade got up, went over to the tiny sink in the corner and doused her face in cold water. Then she took a small bottle of vodka and a glass from her kitchen press. Her emergency supply. She'd never liked the idea of drinking alone – it would make her as weak and pathetic as Aidan – but sometimes even she had to break the rules. She sat down on the narrow bed, stacked the pillows behind her head and sipped her drink. Maybe she should find somewhere else to live. She wasn't sure she could trust Aidan to stay away. But the thought of notifying the clinic of yet another change of address was not appealing and it was unlikely she'd find somewhere as cheap. No, if Aidan came back again she'd just have to be more forceful. Maybe if she threatened to tell his mother the truth about their separation that would do the trick. But she wasn't sure she could do that. Because at the end of the day, Aidan Peters was the love of her life and hurting him went against every fibre of her being. She stared blankly at the TV and drank the vodka diluted with her tears.

Chapter Four

Monday, 22 May

'So we're agreed?' Daniel Wheeler looked at the other three directors.

Theo gave a curt nod.

'Absolutely.' Toni smiled.

'Bloody ridiculous,' Robert fumed.

'Robert,' Theo said warningly. He looked at his watch. 'If there's nothing else?'

Daniel shook his head and managed to smile at the only non-executive director. 'No. Theo. Thank you for your time. It was good of you to come at such short notice.'

Theo glanced briefly at Robert. 'Not at all. We don't often have emergency general meetings.'

'Thank goodness,' Toni said, under her breath. Two weeks had passed since Daniel had tackled Robert and the atmosphere in the clinic ever since had been electric.

'Come along, Toni. I've booked Chapter One for lunch.'

Toni looked crestfallen. 'Oh, sorry, Theo, I can't.'

'Nonsense,' Daniel said jovially. 'You go and have a nice lunch. Treat her to a glass of wine too, Theo. She's been working very hard lately.'

'I've noticed,' Theo said drily, holding the door for his wife.

Toni smiled wanly at Daniel and preceded her husband out of the meeting room. 'I really can't afford to take a long lunch, Theo,' she tried again.

'Oh, for God's sake, Toni. You're not indispensable. Anyway, I have a consultation at three. You'll be back behind your desk by two thirty at the latest.' He strode across Reception and held open the front door for her.

'Well, okay, then,' Toni agreed reluctantly. She hadn't expected this. It had been a long time since Theo had suggested lunch. In the early days they had always gone out to lunch or dinner after a board meeting, and Toni had enjoyed sitting over a good bottle of wine, discussing the clinic with him. She had felt then that Theo respected her opinion.

Now she noticed the grim set of his jaw as they got into his Mercedes. This was going to be fun. Not. 'Chapter One,' she said brightly, as she strapped herself in. 'It's ages since we've been there.'

'You were supposed to be there three weeks ago,' Theo reminded her, 'but you were otherwise engaged.'

Toni remembered the row they'd had when she'd refused to cancel a night out with Jade. Theo had been furious. 'You see that woman every bloody day and Nigel is only in Dublin for one night.'

'And you knew your ex brother-in-law was coming but neglected to mention it,' she retorted.

'I've been busy.'

'Well, maybe you should get your secretary to check with me in future,' she'd snapped, and had gone to meet Jade.

'The meeting went well,' she said now, determined

to make an effort. Surely they could manage a couple of hours without arguing.

'I'm not sure Robert would agree.'

'No. We've certainly upset his gravy train.'

'You're being a bit unfair, Toni. You wouldn't see anything wrong with someone in another profession trying to make some money.'

Toni was incredulous. 'Some! The man is loaded! And you're right, I think this profession *is* different. He's capitalising on people's feelings of inadequacy and lack of confidence.'

'Are you saying cosmetic surgery should be outlawed?' Theo countered.

'Of course not, but there should be tighter controls. You must agree?'

Theo inclined his head in acknowledgement. 'There is room for improvement and there are definitely some questionable practitioners out there, but' – he shook a finger at Toni – 'Robert isn't one of them.'

'I know that, Theo,' she relented, 'but he could be a bit more . . .'

'Humble?' Theo suggested, with a wry smile.

'That would be a start.'

'He has his faults but he's a good surgeon.'

Toni said nothing. She didn't want to spoil the almost pleasant atmosphere that had developed. Maybe lunch wouldn't be such a trial, after all.

'You do know that Daniel's new rules will seriously affect the Blessington?'

Toni frowned worriedly. 'Certainly the number of our UK clients will fall.' However, Daniel had seemed unconcerned when she'd warned him of this.

Theo pulled into a parking spot on Parnell Square. 'Your Irish patients may be affected as well. A lot of new clinics have popped up in the last eighteen months and not all of them are run by people with Daniel's morals.'

Toni sighed: Theo was always having a go at Daniel. Mind you, Daniel wasn't much better. They tolerated each other but no more than that. It wasn't always easy being in the middle. Especially because she usually agreed with Daniel.

They were seated quickly in a quiet corner of the restaurant and Theo ordered – without consulting her – a bottle of Sancerre. Toni picked up the conversation again. 'It seems we're caught between a rock and a hard place. Daniel's new system will save people unnecessary pain and money, but it will piss them off too. They won't agree to wait that long for an operation if the clinic down the road will do it in half the time.'

They paused as the waiter poured their wine and took their order – steak and salad for Theo and duck in a rich sauce for Toni. She ignored his look of disbelief as she ordered a portion of fries on the side.

'So you don't actually agree with the new system,' he said.

'Oh, I do! But with my administrator's hat on, I can see it might cause financial problems.'

Theo smiled sympathetically. 'It's not easy balancing money and conscience, is it? Excuse me a moment, I just need to check in with Emma.'

Toni watched him thoughtfully as he went outside to call his secretary. She had forgotten what it was like to conduct a normal conversation with Theo. At times like this she caught a glimpse of the man with whom she'd fallen in love. Authoritative and opinionated, but incisive and wise too. She'd respected him so much in the early days of their marriage, even excusing his patronising ways. It was only natural that such a well-educated man would find fault with her simple reasoning.

Theo returned to the table moments later and sat down, laying his white napkin carefully in his lap. 'You know, Daniel should get out of private practice and stick to the hospital,' he said, dispelling any warmth she'd felt towards him in the last twenty minutes.

She waited until their food had been served before she replied. 'Why on earth would he do that?'

Theo sliced a minute piece of fat off his steak. 'It's not a business for the faint-hearted, Toni. And make no mistake, it *is* a business.'

Toni watched him eat with concentrated precision and tried to imagine him digging into a bag of chips. She failed. 'Daniel isn't in it for the money.'

Theo looked amused. 'Very admirable.'

Toni flushed angrily. 'Yes, it *is* admirable, Theo, to me and to all the people he's helped.'

Theo nodded, with mock enthusiasm. 'The man should be canonised.'

Toni looked at him curiously. Then her face slowly broke into a smile. 'You're jealous.'

'I don't think so,' Theo said witheringly.

'You are!'

Theo put down his knife and fork and pushed away his plate. 'Don't be so bloody juvenile, Toni.'

Toni bit into a chip, enjoying his discomfort. 'It's

because his patients love him, isn't it? Your patients admire and respect you but they don't love you. They're too scared of you for that.'

'Ridiculous.'

Toni shook her head emphatically. 'No, it isn't. They're *all* scared of you, the patients, the doctors, the nurses, and that's the way you like it. But occasionally' – she was almost talking to herself now – 'you'd like to be on the receiving end of a look of pure trust and love from a sick child, a grateful parent or—'

Theo threw down his napkin and stood up. 'Spare me the amateur psychology, please.' He stormed off to the gents'.

She'd struck a chord, Toni thought. Interesting that on occasion Theodore French could show vulnerability. At least in his professional life.

There was no sign of any such weakness at home. Theo saw himself as the head of the family and expected his wife and daughter to accept this without question. Over the years Toni had learned to handle it – following her friend Dotty's excellent advice – by ignoring him. Chloe sometimes got her way by wheedling, cajoling or just plain begging. But as she got older she was becoming rebellious and Theo's draconian attitude didn't help. These days he did nothing but harangue Chloe about her studies and question her suspiciously about her social life. But it was his constant instruction as to how her future should develop that would eventually drive her away. Her mother, Marianna, had left her a small trust fund that she would receive on her eighteenth birthday and Toni wouldn't be surprised if she used it to buy a flat.

'Would you like some tea?' Theo asked stiffly, resuming his seat.

'Cappuccino,' Toni replied. *I never drink tea after a meal. You'd think he'd have noticed after all these years.*

Theo beckoned the waiter over and ordered coffee for her and tea for himself. 'And could you bring the bill, please?'

'To get back to these new procedures, Theo. Why did you agree to them if they're going to be bad for business?'

'I agree that some steps should be taken to safeguard the patient, and it makes sense from a legal standpoint.'

Toni rolled her eyes.

'You may mock, Toni, but a nasty court case could put the Blessington out of business for good. Anyway, as I was saying, I believe Daniel's idea is a good one but he will probably have to compromise on the time-scales. We can see how it goes, then reassess the situation in a few weeks.'

Toni looked at him suspiciously. 'Did you say that to Robert?'

Theo gave a small, smug smile. 'I suggested that he might be as well to sit back and let the problem sort itself out.'

Toni shook her head in disbelief. 'I just don't believe you! You're as bad as he is!'

Theo's smile disappeared. 'Look, Daniel has got exactly what he wanted and I'm sure if it proves to be a non-starter he'll be the first to admit it.'

'And everything will go back to the way it was,' Toni added.

'If it's what your customers want.'

'They're patients!'

Theo leaned across the table and took her hands in a firm grip. 'No, Toni, they're customers. They're not sick. They don't need surgery. They're doing it out of choice. Paying to get their bodies carved up in the name of vanity!'

'You don't approve?'

'Of course I don't approve!'

'I never realised. Robert's your friend. And you were the one who wanted the clinic to branch into cosmetic surgery.'

Theo sighed irritably. 'Because it's a business. A lucrative one.'

Toni was bewildered. 'But how can you reconcile that in your mind? You don't approve of something but you give it your backing in order to make some money?'

Theo gave her a pitying look. 'You are so incredibly naïve, darling.'

'Maybe I am. I have nothing against cosmetic surgery where it will clearly benefit the patient psychologically. What I object to is Robert – and surgeons like him – operating on anyone who comes through the door with cheque book in hand. It's not medicine and it's not business. It's exploitation and it's dangerous.' Toni picked up her bag and stood up. 'And now I'd like to go.'

'Certainly, my dear.' Theo followed her out of the restaurant.

Toni stood beside the car, taking deep breaths to calm herself. 'I'll walk back.'

'Oh, don't be ridiculous. Get into the car.'

'No, I need the air. See you tonight.'

Chapter Five

Friday, 26 May

Mark kissed Chloe tenderly then propped himself up on one arm so that he could see her properly. He never tired of looking at her. She was so beautiful, with her silky dark mane, startling blue eyes that looked into his very soul, and a body that had the most incredible effect on him. 'Had you any problems getting out?' He stroked her cheek.

'No. Dad was working late and I told Toni I was staying over at Ollie's.'

'I don't see why we have to do all this creeping around,' he complained.

'It might be easier if your surname wasn't Wheeler.'

'For God's sake, we're not Romeo and Juliet.'

'It will be okay once the exams are over,' Chloe promised. 'Dad doesn't believe in me doing anything except studying, eating and sleeping at the moment.'

'But you have to take a break sometimes,' Mark protested.

Chloe giggled as she ran her fingers over his chest. 'I'm not sure this is the sort of break he'd approve of.'

Mark pulled her closer so that he could feel her

bare skin along the length of his body. 'Maybe not,' he murmured, and bent to kiss her again.

'I should be going,' she said half-heartedly.

He kissed her throat. 'What's the rush? They're not expecting you home.'

'I'm not staying *here* all night! It's freezing.' She shifted slightly to avoid the spring that kept digging into her back. They were in his mother's car, which was parked in the garage beside his house. 'Anyway, what if someone comes out?'

'It's after midnight, Chloe. Mam and Dad will be in Dreamland by now. Just stay for another little while,' he pleaded. 'I'll keep you warm.'

'How are you going to do that, then?' Chloe asked coyly.

'I'm sure I'll think of something.'

Later, Mark smoked a cigarette and watched as Chloe buttoned her shirt and pulled up her jeans. 'I wish you wouldn't watch,' she said.

'I like watching.'

'Tough!' She pushed him out of the car and fiddled with her zip. Getting dressed in the back of a car was sordid and Mark watching made it worse. She combed her fingers through her hair, jumped out and kissed him lightly. 'I've got to go.'

Mark pulled her back for one more kiss before he opened the garage door quietly.

Chloe peered out anxiously from behind him. 'Are you sure no one's around?'

Mark patted her hand reassuringly. 'Will you relax?'

But as they stepped out into the driveway, the garage door slammed and Chloe jumped as a high-pitched alarm went off and lights flashed.

'Shit!' Mark glanced anxiously at the house. 'Dad's put the bloody alarm on! Quick, hide in the garden! And, for God's sake, be quiet.'

'It's a bit late for that.' Daniel was at the front door, tightening the belt of his dressing-gown. 'I think you two had better come inside.'

'What are we going to say?' Chloe hissed, as they followed Daniel into the house. 'Dad will kill me *and* you if he finds out about this.'

'Don't worry. It's cool,' he said, with more confidence than he felt. 'Dad won't tell him.'

'What is it, Daniel?' Meg Wheeler called down.

'Just a cat, love. Go back to sleep. I'll be up in a minute.'

Mark smiled gratefully. 'Thanks, Dad, sorry about that. I'll just take Chloe home—'

Daniel glared at him. 'Not so fast, young man. You have some explaining to do.'

'We haven't done anything wrong,' Mark protested.

'Really? And I suppose you're going to tell me that Chloe here has a passion for cars – particularly 1994 Micras – and couldn't wait until daylight to get a look at your mother's?'

Chloe went as red as a beetroot and prayed for the ground to open up and swallow her.

'Dad, you're embarrassing her. Look, we just wanted a little privacy. It's not like there's any in *this* house.'

Daniel looked at him thoughtfully. 'Privacy, eh? Does your father know where you are, Chloe?'

Chloe shook her head mutely.

'I see. So where does he *think* you are?'

'At my friend Ollie's. That's where I'm going now, I just stopped by to say hello . . .'

Daniel looked at his watch. 'Really?'

'Oh, Dad, come on! You were young once, remember?' Mark pointed out.

'I hope I showed my lady-friends a bit more respect. If I remember rightly, we used to go to the cinema or to a dance.'

Chloe bent her head, and her hair fell across her face to hide her burning cheeks.

'Dad!' Mark was pleading now.

Daniel relented. He wouldn't prolong the poor girl's agony. 'I'll say no more about this now but don't ever put me in this position again. Apart from anything else, Chloe, I have no intention of deceiving Toni and your father.'

'Oh, please don't tell them!' Chloe begged. 'I promise, Mr Wheeler. We won't do it again.'

'Then we'll leave it at that. Now, Mark, ring for a cab. Goodnight, Chloe.'

'Is everything all right, love?' Meg asked sleepily, as Daniel climbed back into bed beside her.

'Fine, pet. You go to sleep.' He turned over on his side and wondered if he needed to have strong words with his eldest son. He was a responsible lad – well, most of the time – but messing around with Theo French's daughter of all people! He hoped Mark had remembered to use a condom. If he hadn't the possible consequences didn't bear thinking about.

Ollie stood at the corner of her road, shivering. She wished she'd listened to her mother and worn a jacket, but it would have looked naff over her gorgeous new red hipsters and clingy black cropped top. Goose pimples stood out on her bare white midriff, and her feet in their skyscraper platform sandals were like blocks of ice. She hopped anxiously from one foot to the other. Chloe should have been here ages ago. She craned her neck eagerly as she saw a taxi approach then heaved a sigh of relief as it pulled in beside her and Chloe jumped out. 'Jeez, Chlo! Where the hell have you been? I was worried and Mum's going to be wondering where we are. I swore we'd be home before two.'

They began to hurry down the road. 'Stop fussing, Ollie! We're only ten minutes late,' Chloe said.

Ollie snorted. 'You can talk! Your dad would go spare if he knew you were out at all.'

'I know. It's a real pain. I can only get him to agree to me going to Old Wesley if your mum's picking us up.'

Ollie frowned. 'But Mum never picks us up.'

'*He* doesn't know that.'

'Weird.'

'What are we going to tell your mum?' Chloe asked, as they turned into the Coyles' driveway.

'Oh, that the first taxi-driver looked shifty and we waited for another one. She'll think we've been so responsible.'

Chloe was impressed. 'You're *really* good.'

Ollie gave a small bow before putting her key in the lock. 'Learn at the feet of the master!'

Mary Coyle heard the front door close and the whispering and giggling in the hallway. She turned over to look at the clock. They were a bit late, but nothing to get excited about. She always worried when her wild, headstrong daughter was out partying but it gave her some comfort if Chloe French was with her. She was a steadying influence. Mary hated it when Ollie talked about leaving home and getting a flat. But she'd have peace of mind if her daughter moved in with Chloe. She heard steps on the stairs then Ollie's door closing softly. She shut her eyes contentedly. Now she'd be able to sleep.

'So, tell me?' Ollie looked expectantly at her friend curled up in the opposite bed.

'Tell you what?' Chloe asked, sleepily.

'You know what, come on, Chloe,' she wheedled. 'I'd tell you.'

'So what happened with Alan Pearson, then?'

'He's history. I wouldn't have done it with him if we were the only two people on a desert island.'

'It didn't look that way last week. You were all over each other like a rash.'

Ollie shrugged nonchalantly. 'That was last week. It's important to experiment. It adds to your wealth of experience.'

'Or your reputation as a tart.' Chloe was only half joking. She was a bit worried that Ollie was getting a name for herself. She seemed to have dated half the boys in Wesley. She yelped as Ollie tumbled into the bed beside her.

'Stop avoiding the issue,' her friend ordered. 'You're not going to sleep until you tell me everything.'

Chloe sighed. She'd have to come up with something to satisfy Ollie. Otherwise she'd never get any sleep tonight. 'We didn't do it,' she muttered reluctantly.

'Get out of here! You were in the back of his mum's car in a garage, all alone, in the dark and you're telling me you didn't *do* anything!'

Chloe was glad it was dark and Ollie couldn't see her face turn crimson. She didn't want to talk about Mark. He was special. 'We did *do* things,' she admitted, 'we just didn't go all the way.'

Ollie's eyes narrowed. 'Are you sure?'

'Of course I'm bloody sure!'

'Did he use a condom?'

Chloe felt her cheeks get even hotter. 'He didn't have to.'

'Maybe,' Ollie said mysteriously. 'Did he put it in and tell you that he got it out in time?'

'Olivia Coyle!' Chloe turned away angrily and stared at the wall.

'Oh, okay. There's no need to sulk.' Ollie went back to her own bed.

'Sorry. Night.'

'Night.'

Chloe pulled up the duvet to her chin and closed her eyes. No doubt Ollie would begin the whole discussion again tomorrow morning. Deep down, she figured her friend was jealous. She'd never gone out with a guy for more than a few weeks, and Chloe and Mark had been together for almost a year. He was the only boyfriend she'd ever had. They'd known each other for years, often bumping into each other at the clinic. Chloe had always secretly fancied him. He had the same dark red hair as his dad but he was much taller and had an amazing smile that showed off almost perfect white teeth. And those beautiful blue eyes – she sighed, hugged the duvet to her and remembered the warmth of his body against hers. She hadn't lied to Ollie. They hadn't actually 'done it', though she'd been tempted. With the tight rein her dad kept on her, it was the best opportunity they'd had yet. But, at the last moment, Mark had paused and looked deep into her eyes. 'Are you sure this is what you want?' he'd asked softly.

And Chloe, although disappointed, had realised that he must really love her because he was willing to wait. God, she loved him! And she was glad now that they hadn't done it. When it did happen it should be something special, not a furtive romp in his mum's car. No, Chloe dreamed, it should happen somewhere beautiful. Because their love was special and she knew she would never love anyone the way she loved Mark.

Ollie lay staring into the darkness, her mind racing. She thought of the look on Chloe's face when she talked about Mark. The girl had it bad and she didn't even know if he was any good in bed yet. Ollie thought Chloe was nuts to tie herself down to one guy when they hadn't even finished school. 'We've got so much living to do,' she would say. 'There's so many guys out there just waiting to be jilted by us!'

To Ollie's eternal exasperation, Chloe just laughed. A knowing laugh that meant 'You don't know what it's like to be in love.' Well, Ollie didn't want to know! She was too young to limit herself to one guy. Chloe was a bit strait-laced like that. She was good fun after a few drinks but she laughed at any guys who came on to her.

'You're putting them off,' Ollie would say crossly. 'They think you're a tease.'

'That's their problem,' Chloe would say carelessly. 'I'm just being friendly.'

Ollie could not understand why the girl didn't realise that when she smiled at a bloke he thought all his birthdays had come together. She didn't seem to have a clue how gorgeous she was. She was one of those sickening girls who could look good in a sack. She didn't even have to comb her hair to attract the guys: they were like moths to a flame. It would have pissed Ollie off if Chloe hadn't been her best friend. She snuggled down under her duvet and wondered whether the guy she'd snogged tonight call her tomorrow like he'd promised. 'Probably,' she murmured, and closed her eyes.

Chapter Six

'Theo, we have to talk.' Toni rehearsed the words, keeping her voice level. It was important that she remain calm: she got upset easily and Theo loved it when she did. He would give her that cold, superior smile and tell her that they would discuss the matter calmly when she was over her little tantrum. It drove Toni nuts. But it wasn't going to happen tonight.

She'd been waiting three hours to talk to him. He had told her he'd be late but she'd stayed up anyway. She wasn't going to put it off any longer. Things had deteriorated speedily and Toni wondered if Chloe had noticed that, when the three of them were together, Theo directed all his conversation at his daughter. When there was only herself and Theo conversation was clipped and banal. Or Theo ignored her.

She was dying for a drink but was afraid that if she started she wouldn't stop. She paced up and down the large dining room, its gloom reflecting her mood. Theo insisted on dining in here but when he was out Toni and Chloe ate in the kitchen or, on a nice day, on the patio or in the conservatory. The dining room wouldn't have been so bad if Theo would allow her to redecorate it in brighter colours. But he'd vetoed that. 'You have a rather individual style, dear,' he'd said drily. 'Don't inflict it on the rest of us.'

At the time, Toni had thought he was reluctant to change things because of Marianna and that he was worried it would upset Chloe. She laughed now at her stupidity: Theo hadn't been remotely sensitive about his first wife. And he didn't show much consideration for his daughter either. There was no doubt that he loved her, but in a detached sort of way. And, Toni realised, it was the same with her: she was no more to him than a possession that had disappointed him.

She jumped when she heard the front door slam and the unmistakable sound of his steps in the hall. He went straight to the kitchen where she imagined him removing his covered plate from the fridge and pouring himself a large glass of water. Moments later he appeared in the doorway, tray in hand. 'Why are you still up?'

For an instant, Toni thought she saw a flicker of pleasure in his eyes, but then the impassive mask was back in place. She felt a wave of sadness engulf her. She watched him settle himself at the table and pour half a glass of the burgundy she'd opened. He hadn't even bothered to say hello. 'We need to talk,' she said, taking the seat at the opposite end of the table.

'What about?' Theo ate the chicken salad Alice had prepared for him. It was always salad when Theo was late. He wouldn't eat anything heavier after nine o'clock. Toni had teased him about it when they were newlyweds and often tried to tempt him with Chinese take-away or fish and chips. Even then he had given her a tight-lipped, tolerant smile and refused.

Toni sat watching him now, her hands clasped tightly in her lap. When her family and friends had tried to persuade her not to marry him, she'd told them that age didn't matter. But it did. Theo treated her like a child, to be indulged, spoiled and punished on occasion. Now he was waiting for an answer, a bored look on his face.

'This isn't working out, Theo,' she said clearly.

He continued to fork salad into his mouth. 'What isn't?'

'Our marriage. And I think it's time we admitted it.'

'Well, don't let me stop you.' He shot her an amused glance.

'Theo, I'm serious.'

He put down his fork and lifted his glass to his lips. Then he said, 'I realise that, Toni. What do you propose we do?'

Toni stared at him. It was as if she'd just suggested they buy a new car. 'I want a divorce.'

Theo threw back his head and laughed.

Toni was startled. She'd prepared herself for a number of reactions but she hadn't expected that. 'You think this is funny?'

Theo wiped the corners of his mouth on his napkin. 'Well, yes, I do actually.'

'May I ask why?'

'I just can't believe you've even asked!' His expression darkened and his eyes were cold and hard. 'I won't give you a divorce, Toni. Not now, not ever. If you want to leave, then leave. You *do* realise we'd have to be separated for years before you actually *got* your piece of paper, don't you?'

She met and held his gaze. 'There's no rush and I

don't want to do anything until Chloe has finished her Leaving Cert.'

'How noble of you,' he sneered. 'You know she's going to hate you for this?'

Toni dug her nails into her palms. 'She's an intelligent girl. I'm sure she's sensed that something's wrong. She'll understand.'

'You think so, do you?' Theo stared oddly at her. 'It was hard when she lost her mother, but she was young enough to get over it. You came into her life when she was at a very vulnerable age, and now it's "Thank you very much. It's been nice – but I've had enough of being a stepmother."'

'That's not fair! I love Chloe, I'd never desert her—'

'No, just me,' he flung back angrily.

It would have been easy to reel off all the reasons why he'd driven her to this, but it would get her nowhere, so Toni stayed silent.

'Hell, you just don't give a damn how much you hurt me, do you?'

Toni was astonished. If she were an innocent bystander, she'd be feeling sorry for Theo right now, convinced that he was the injured party. The man should be on the stage. 'This wasn't an easy decision, Theo. I didn't make it lightly. Now, can we just sort things out between us? Decide what has to be done? I don't want lawyers turning this into a sordid mess.'

'You've already talked to one, haven't you?' he said, almost to himself.

'I just made a few enquiries.'

He moved closer, his face just inches from hers. 'You scheming bitch! I suppose the two of you were trying to figure out how much you could squeeze out of me. Playing "Let's stitch up the surgeon"!'

Toni forced herself to stand her ground. 'I'm not interested in your money.'

Theo bent and placed a gentle kiss just under her ear-lobe. 'That's good to hear, darling, because you won't get a penny out of me.' He strode from the room, slamming the door behind him.

Well, at least he hadn't hit her, Toni registered. Mind you, it might be easier if she had some bruises to show people. But Theodore French was too controlled for that. And why use your fists if you could do a better job with your tongue?

She carried her glass and the wine bottle out to the conservatory. It was nearly eleven and she had an early start tomorrow but she knew that a night's sleep was unlikely. She'd just ended her marriage, for God's sake. She'd told Theo it was over, after years of living with his sarcastic jibes. She still had a vivid memory of the first time he'd humiliated her in public. They had been having dinner with Francis and Dorothy Price. Francis was a heart surgeon at Sylvester's and one of the few people to whom Theo looked up. Conversation, as usual, had centred on the hospital and Toni had been phasing in and out of it when, out of the blue, Theo asked Dorothy what she thought of his wife's outfit. Toni had been wearing a simple white shift dress with shoestring straps. Before she could answer, he'd continued, 'Bit young for you, darling. You should get Dorothy to bring you shopping.'

Toni had stared at him. She wasn't thin-skinned but his comment had hurt.

Dorothy, who had been listening to Theo's barbs all evening and was heartily sick of them, gave him a cool look before she said kindly, 'Actually, I think she looks beautiful. If I had a body like that, I'd show it off too.'

Toni had been surprised to find an unexpected ally and smiled gratefully at the older woman. It was the beginning of the only real friendship she had developed with any of Theo's set. Dorothy Price – 'call me Dotty' – was quick-witted, charming and funny, and Toni was always playing around with table arrangements so that they could sit together at the many dull functions they had to attend. She liked Francis, Dotty's husband, too. Perhaps because he was nearly a decade older than the others and close to retirement, he kept out of their political wrangles.

'He used to be just as driven as Theo,' Dorothy had confided, 'with an ego the size of a small planet, but he's mellowed with the years, bless him.'

Toni had only been married to Theo a year when Dorothy had imparted this snippet of information and it had made her feel slightly sick.

When she saw the look on Toni's face Dorothy had smiled. 'It will be different for you, dear, you're young and clever. You'll keep him young too. Just don't let him turn you into something you're not.'

Now Toni gazed up at the stars and wondered if Theo had succeeded in doing exactly that. She was only thirty-three but, apart from her nights out with Jade, she lived the life of a nun. Which reminded her of the other problem with her marriage: on the rare occasions they made love there was none of the closeness Toni craved. Theo didn't believe in snuggling up together or pillow-talk. Foreplay was predictable and mechanical, and his technique left her feeling as if she'd been attacked by the lord of the manor.

Leaving the empty glass and bottle in the kitchen, she went upstairs. She moved silently past Chloe's room, glanced briefly at Theo's door and carried on into her own sanctuary. They had always had separate bedrooms. Toni had been shocked at first but Theo pointed out that it made sense, given the size of the house and the odd hours he worked. After a while, Toni came to like it. Initially it was quite exciting each time her door opened softly and Theo slipped into bed beside her. It was almost as if he were a forbidden lover – very Mills and Boon. After a while it dawned on her that he was always the one in control. He decided if and when they would make love while she just lay there wondering and waiting like an expectant, hopeful mistress.

Maybe that was the point, she mused, as she undressed. Maybe he considered himself still married to Marianna and she had always been the Other Woman. It was a pity that that wasn't the case. Then she would have been able just to walk away and not worry about separation or divorce. She laughed bitterly. If she managed to get herself out of this mess, she just might go and join a convent. Life would be a lot simpler.

Chapter Seven

Tuesday, 6 June

Jade sat in the restaurant, a glass of water in front of her, and waited for Toni. She'd suggested they meet here rather than the pub because Toni was often late and it wasn't easy to sit in a bar for long without buying a drink. But in the China World restaurant she could read the menu undisturbed until her friend turned up. Dinner and a bottle of house red would cost sixteen quid each, and Jade would save money by walking home – it only took twenty minutes. Toni thought she did it for the exercise. That was a laugh! She'd always hated any form of exercise but Toni must have forgotten that.

It amazed her that her friend never asked why she always wanted to eat in the same restaurant – set dinner menu, nine ninety-five – but then, being married to Theo, she was probably just glad to have the opportunity to eat some ethnic food. Mustard on his steak was about as adventurous as Theo got. The waitress passed the table again and flashed her a friendly smile. We're probably their best customers, Jade thought, chuckling to herself. Over thirty quid a week – sometimes nearer forty when Toni insisted on buying an after-dinner drink. Jade double-checked her purse. Twenty-three pounds and some loose change. She'd have about eight quid to see her through the rest of the week if she was careful. It would mean she'd be walking everywhere but she was used to that. And living in the city meant she was near to the clinic. Life would be easier financially if she didn't meet Toni so often, but if she gave up their dinners she'd lose the plot. Sitting alone in that bed-sit night after night was heavy going: there was nothing to do but go over her past and wonder if she should have handled things differently. If she had, would she be still living in her nice house? If they'd had a child, would Aidan have been more resilient?

'Jade! Sorry I'm late – or are you early?'

'You're late as usual.'

Toni settled herself in the seat opposite. 'Well, you looked like you were deep in thought. Who were you mentally assassinating?'

'Perky, of course,' Jade lied smoothly.

Toni smiled her thanks as the waitress handed her the menu. She didn't need to read it – she knew it off by heart. 'But Robert hasn't done anything – lately.'

'Pity,' Jade murmured. 'I was so sure he and Vicky were on the fiddle.'

'Me too, but we were both wrong.'

When Toni and Jade had carried out the second stock-take their results were exactly the same as Vicky's. Even worse, when Toni had gone back to check her figures again it transpired that Sandra had made a typing error. Vicky had got a lot of mileage out of that one. Sandra had been miserable for days.

'I still don't trust either of them,' Jade was saying. 'But let's not talk about them now. They'll only put me off my food.'

Toni closed the menu. 'The usual?'

'Why not?'

The waitress approached and Toni gave the order. 'Two spring rolls, one chicken curry, one kung po prawn, both with fried rice and a bottle of the house red. And this is on me,' she added, when the waitress had left.

'No, Toni—'

'Yes, it is,' Toni insisted. 'I've had you working some ridiculous hours lately and doing all sorts of things that are way beyond your job spec. I owe you one.'

Jade smiled broadly. 'Okay, then, thanks.' She'd be sixteen quid richer this week. She'd be able to treat herself to a take-away some evening, maybe even buy another bottle of vodka . . .

'No problem.'

'So, how are things?'

'You don't want to know.'

Jade frowned at the dark shadows under Toni's eyes. 'Try me.'

Toni waited for the waitress to pour their wine. 'Last Friday I told Theo I wanted a divorce.'

Jade's eyes popped. 'I didn't know things were so bad.'

'They're not, really. He doesn't beat me or anything like that.' She gave a small, nervous laugh. 'And he's not seeing anyone else. It's just—'

'There's nothing there any more?' Jade suggested.

'There hasn't been for a long time,' Toni admitted.

'I've tried to ignore it – I mean no marriage is perfect – but it's just wearing me out. There used to be good times and a few bad times. Now it's all bad times. I can't remember the last time we made love.'

'You're not sleeping together?'

Toni laughed. 'Oh, we've never done that.'

'Sorry?' Jade looked puzzled.

'We've always had separate bedrooms.'

'Weird.'

'I can see that now. But when Theo suggested it I thought he was being thoughtful. He had a lot of early starts and if he was feeling stressed he used to go out driving at night.'

Driving?' Jade looked bewildered.

'He says it relaxes him.'

'You mean he still does it?'

'Oh, yes. Usually it's the night before a difficult operation.'

'Well, I suppose we all have our own ways of dealing with stress. But separate bedrooms?'

'I thought – when we first got married – that it was for Chloe's sake. She was only eleven, after all, and seeing another woman in her mother's room might have freaked her out.'

'But you don't believe that now?'

'Theo isn't that thoughtful or sensitive.'

'So has he agreed? To the divorce, I mean.'

'No chance.'

Jade patted her hand. 'That's probably just a knee-jerk reaction. He'll come round.'

'I'm not so sure. But I don't understand why he'd want to stay with me. We haven't been happy for a long time, and now he knows I want to go, why would he want me to stay?'

'Maybe he doesn't think it's that bad,' Jade suggested.

'But we can barely exchange two words without it turning into an argument.'

'Isn't that what marriage is all about?'

'God, I bloody hope not! What a depressing thought. Anyway, look at Daniel. He's got a happy marriage.'

'True,' Jade acknowledged. 'Anyone else?'

Toni made a face.

'So how did you leave it?'

'He said he'd never agree to a divorce, that I could leave if I wanted to but he'd never give me a penny. I can't believe he thinks I'm just after his money.'

Their starters arrived and Jade tucked in hungrily. 'You should just leave. The sooner you separate the better.'

Toni shook her head. 'I can't do that to Chloe, not while she's doing her exams. When they're over, I'll go.'

'How do you think she'll take the news?'

'Theo says she'll hate me but I don't believe that. It might take a bit of time but I hope she'll get used to the idea.'

'Well, I'm sorry it's come to this, but I think you're doing the right thing.'

'I always believed in the "till death us do part" bit,' Toni said, 'but I was never the kind of wife Theo wanted and, if I'm honest, I just married an image.'

Jade flinched at her brutal honesty.

'You warned me I was making a mistake,' Toni reminded her. 'I just wish I'd listened.'

'I get no satisfaction from being right, I can assure you,' Jade said. 'All sorts of strange couples make it work. I was hoping you'd be one of them.'

'Why did you and Aidan break up, Jade?' Toni asked suddenly. 'You seemed the perfect couple.'

'Just like you and Ian,' Jade shot back.

'Sorry?' Toni stared at her, a mixture of hurt and surprise in her eyes. Jade hadn't mentioned Ian in years.

Jade sighed. 'I'm sorry, Toni. That was below the belt. I don't know why I brought it up.'

Toni didn't reply, just pushed her food around her plate.

'So, what are you going to do now?'

'I wish I knew. Theo's barely talking to me. I just hope Chloe doesn't notice.'

'Have you spoken to a solicitor?'

'I just made some enquiries.'

Jade rummaged in her bag for a pen. 'Here, ring this guy.' She scribbled a name on a napkin and handed it to Toni. 'He looked after my sister's divorce. He was good and not too pricy.'

Toni looked at it doubtfully. 'I don't know.'

'You need to know your rights. Trust me, Toni, I've seen what Karen went through.'

'How come you haven't divorced Aidan?'

'I . . . we . . . never got round to it.'

'Maybe you'll get back together.'

'That's not going to happen.'

Toni saw the closed expression on Jade's face. 'What did he do that was so bad?'

'Look, I don't want to talk about it, okay?' Jade's voice was cold and hostile.

'But I'm telling you *my* problems—'

'You volunteered the information,' Jade pointed out.

'Yes, you're right. Sorry.'

Jade's smile was impersonal. 'No problem. Where the hell are those main courses? I'm starving.'

Chapter Eight

Thursday, 8 June

'Okay, Mam. I've fed the cat and watered the plants. Is there anything else you want me to do?'

'No, Sandra. Let's have dinner. You must be tired after your day's work.' Valerie was glad she was going into the MS care centre in a few weeks: it would give Sandra a much-needed break.

Sandra dropped a kiss on her mother's hair. 'I'm fine, Mam. You concentrate on getting over this attack.'

'I'm not sure I will this time,' Valerie Tomkins said, in a rare moment of disillusionment.

'You will. You always do.'

Valerie watched her daughter worriedly as she served their meal. Sandra always refused to talk about the possibility of her not recovering from an attack, so Valerie did her best to get better. Follow the bloody diet, take her starflower oil capsules – she had been taking evening primrose oil, but apparently these were better. Not that Valerie could see any evidence of it.

'Now, eat up.' Sandra set the poached chicken and steamed vegetables in front of her.

Valerie stared at her plate dejectedly. 'I'd prefer steak and chips.'

'Now, Mam . . .' Sandra said. She poured two glasses of water and they started to eat.

Valerie picked clumsily at her food. Sandra pretended not to notice when a pea flew off the table, followed closely by a piece of carrot. 'Bugger!' her mother muttered angrily.

'Here, let me,' Sandra said gently. She cut the chicken into even smaller pieces and mashed the vegetables together. 'There, how's that?'

'It looks like baby food,' Valerie said, but obediently took the spoon Sandra offered her. 'Thanks, love.'

'Have you written me a list of what you want from the shops?'

'Yes, if you can read it. There's nothing much.'

'Still,' Sandra chuckled, 'you know what my memory's like.'

'You'd forget your head if it weren't screwed on,' her mother observed, 'but you'd better remember to look after my plants while I'm away.'

'I will,' Sandra promised. Valerie's greenhouse was her pride and joy. Sandra knew she'd have to leave home if she forgot to water the plants and check the temperature every day. She couldn't see the attraction herself. If her mother had grown a few roses or lilies or something, well, that would have been understandable. But no, Valerie went for unusual, tropical plants. Sandra couldn't begin to remember their names even.

'And don't you come visiting me every day,' Valerie warned. 'Your Auntie Barbara will be dropping in and no doubt Mrs Byrne will come to see me too. She's very kind and she makes the nicest scones I've ever tasted.'

'You shouldn't be eating scones,' Sandra said mildly. She wasn't sure her mother's diet made a blind bit of difference but she would never say so.

Her mother smiled her wide, beautiful smile. 'A little of what you fancy does you good.'

Sandra started clearing away the plates. 'True.'

'I'll do those.' Valerie pulled her walking frame towards her and stood up slowly.

'You look steadier today,' Sandra remarked.

Sandra washed and Valerie dried, and they spoke of the garden, the neighbours, what was on television later and the latest gossip from the clinic. 'Have you got the hang of that computer yet?' Valerie asked.

Sandra had always been terrified of computers, but now she was even more so since she'd made that mistake on the stock control. Everyone else could use the system, no problem – even that cow Vicky – but Sandra just couldn't figure it out. And as for the printer! 'I'm getting there,' she said brightly.

'That's good. You've done so well in this job, much better than in that auctioneer's office.'

'Yes,' Sandra agreed lamely. She'd been let go from her last job after she'd deleted the payroll file and, to add fuel to the fire, hadn't run the backup program correctly the night before. 'I just don't understand it,' her manager had said, scratching his head. 'No one has ever managed to do that before. It's a secured file.' Sandra thanked her stars that he'd been so desperate to be rid of her he'd given her a reference.

'You are happy at the clinic, aren't you?' Valerie asked anxiously.

'Oh, yes, Mam! It's great. Mr Wheeler's lovely and Toni's really nice. Jade's great too. But Vicky – she's an awful bitch.'

'There's always one. What about that surgeon who used to give you a hard time? The one with the head dyed off him?'

Sandra giggled at her mother's description of Robert Perkins. 'I try to keep out of his way. I don't think he likes me. But when he's with the patients – especially the women – he's as nice as pie.'

'There's a surprise,' Valerie said drily.

'And he gets on well with Vicky too,' Sandra added thoughtfully. Strange, that. No one else got on well with Vicky. Mind you, no one liked Mr Perkins much either.

'Well, keep on the right side of him, love,' her mother advised. 'Don't answer back or give him any reason to fault you.'

'I won't,' Sandra said obediently. 'Now, why don't you go inside and put on the telly? *Emmerdale* will be starting soon. I'll bring in the tea.'

'Thanks, love.' Valerie shuffled into the living room and settled herself on the sofa. She lifted up her legs, then fixed pillows under them and behind her back. It took a long time to get comfortable, these days. She'd have a cup of her special tea before she went to bed. That would relax her and dull the pain.

Sandra carried in a tray and put it down on the table next to her mother. 'Here we go. I've brought you a Jaffa cake.'

'Is it my birthday?'

'Like you say, a little of what you fancy . . .'

'Speaking of which, why don't you arrange a couple of nights out when I'm away?'

Sandra's eyes were on the TV screen. 'I'm not bothered.'

'It's not right. A girl of your age should be out several nights a week, not stuck in with her mother.'

'I'm just as happy here.'

'You need company of your own age. Why don't you give Caroline or Susan a call?'

'We've sort of lost touch,' Sandra mumbled.

The last time she'd gone out with her friends, it had been a total disaster. Caroline, hell-bent on getting drunk, had chatted up every guy in the pub then wanted to go clubbing. Susan had stared morosely into her drink and confided that her husband was having an affair.

'You're better off single,' Caroline had told Sandra bitterly. 'Just look at me and Suze. Old before our time, we are. Dealing with screaming kids all day and cranky husbands at night. If I could live my life over again I'd never get married!'

Susan had sniffled into her drink. 'I would. I love Dave. I'd do anything for him. But he doesn't find me attractive any more, I know he doesn't.'

Sandra had looked helplessly from one friend to the other. This was not the image of marriage she had cultivated. When – if – Mr Right came along, he would love and cherish her always. He would remember her birthday and their anniversary and be kind to her mother. He would be attractive, not handsome – Sandra was realistic – and have a good, sensible job.

'Well, I think that's a mistake,' her mother was saying.

'It's important to hang on to your friends. You never know when you might need them.' She blew her nose and gave her eyes a surreptitious wipe.

Sandra patted her hand. 'Don't worry, Mam. I'll be fine.'

'I'll always worry about you. Aren't you my daughter?' She winced and eased her hand out from under her daughter's.

'Oh, Mam, did I hurt you?'

Valerie smiled. 'No, love. I'm grand.'

Chapter Nine

Tuesday, 13 June

'Chloe? Come on, you'll be late.' Toni walked back into the kitchen and sat down.

'What is it today?' Theo asked, without looking up from his newspaper.

'Biology.' Toni buttered a slice of toast.

'She'll sail through it.' Theo's voice was smug.

Toni sighed. It was exactly this kind of comment that had shredded poor Chloe's nerves.

'Dad thinks I'm going to get straight As in everything,' she'd said tearfully, only the previous night, 'when I'll be lucky to scrape a pass in German. Oh, God, why can't the Leaving Certificate be as straightforward as A Levels? Then I'd only have to do my three science subjects and I could forget about poxy German!'

Toni smiled. 'Well, I'm sorry, but this is the Leaving Certificate and you have to do seven subjects. You'll do just fine, Chloe.'

She had slipped a comforting arm around the teenager's shoulders. 'Don't be too hard on your dad. He's just trying to encourage you.'

'Well, I wish he wouldn't. Why can't he be like Ollie's

parents? They just tell her to do her best. *They* don't expect her to get the highest marks in the class.'

Toni had silently applauded Olivia Coyle's parents. She didn't agree with all this pressure over examinations and points.

Moments later, Chloe wandered into the kitchen and sat down. Toni jumped to her feet. 'Will I make you some toast? Or would you prefer cereal?'

'Just coffee.'

Theo lowered the paper and gave her a disapproving look. 'Coffee isn't going to keep you going for three hours. Have some cereal.'

'I don't want any bloody cereal, okay?' Chloe jumped up again and ran out of the kitchen.

Theo went back to his newspaper. 'Nerves are good.'

Toni glared at him and went after her. Chloe was sitting on the stairs, her head in her hands. 'Are you okay?'

Chloe blew her nose loudly. 'Yeah, fine. I'm just dreading this paper. Is Dad furious?'

'No, he says nerves are good.'

'They don't feel it,' Chloe muttered. 'I think I'm going to throw up.'

'Come on. Have some toast. It'll make you feel better.'

'If I go back in there he'll start preaching again.'

'Then I'll bring it up. You go and look over your notes.'

'Thanks, Toni.' Chloe dragged herself upstairs and Toni went back into the kitchen.

Theo threw her a scathing look. 'There's no need to mollycoddle the girl. She's going to have to get used to taking exams. The Leaving Certificate is a piece of cake. Wait till she starts medicine.' He stood up, drained his coffee cup, tucked the newspaper under his arm and collected his keys. Then he ran up to see Chloe. 'Good luck, darling. You'll do fine.'

'Thanks, Dad.' She smiled shakily at him.

He blew her a kiss, ignoring Toni, who had just walked in with a tray, and was gone.

Toni hoped Chloe hadn't noticed the snub. 'There, you see? He never even mentioned an A.'

'Let's see if he's as light-hearted when the results come out,' Chloe said darkly.

'You're not really worried, are you?'

'No. I know I'll probably do okay. I just don't know if I can live up to his expectations.'

Toni sat down on the bed and took Chloe's hands. 'Now, you listen to me. Your dad will be proud of you no matter what your results are like. He might nag you a bit, but it's for your own good. He just wants the world for you. Every dad does.' Toni hoped she sounded convincing. The truth was that she was sure Theo would take it as a personal affront if Chloe didn't get enough points to do medicine. In fact he'd probably be quite upset if his daughter wasn't in the top five per cent of her class.

Chloe's face relaxed. 'Yeah, you're right, Toni. Sorry. I'm a bit hyper this morning.'

Toni patted Chloe's hand and stood up. 'I'd better get my act together or I'll be late.' She went into the bathroom and turned on the shower. She felt guilty about the lies that had just tripped off her tongue, but what else could she have said? Chloe needed reassurance.

She showered quickly, hurried into her bedroom and was buttoning her white shirt when Chloe tapped on the door. 'I'm off.'

Toni hugged her. 'Best of luck, love. Drop in when you've finished and let me know how it went. I'll treat you to lunch.'

'I'll be too upset to eat,' Chloe moaned.

'Then I'll eat yours too,' Toni said cheerfully. 'Now, scoot! You'll be late.'

''Bye.' Chloe ran down the stairs and out of the front door.

Toni put on her sandals and tied back her damp hair in a tight ponytail. Theo hated it when she wore her hair like this. As if she cared, she could hardly bear to look at him these days. If they brushed against each other in a doorway or their fingers touched across the dinner table, she had to stop herself flinching. It was obvious that Theo wasn't any happier than she was. He'd wanted her to turn into a clone of his first wife, but Toni knew that she and Marianna were opposites.

Marianna had been a primary-school teacher but she'd given up work as soon as she and Theo had married. She'd been the perfect mother, housewife and hostess for Theo. She had cooked, baked *and* taught Chloe to play the piano at the tender age of three. In fact, Toni reflected, the only area where she outperformed Marianna was in the garden. Her cooking was mediocre, she was bored silly by all of Theo's pompous colleagues and their stuffy wives, and she was tone deaf. In the garden, though, she was in her element. It had been an overgrown mess when she'd married Theo, but in the evenings and at weekends she'd weeded and dug, planted flowers, herbs and vegetables. Even Alice had been impressed. Theo thought that pruning the odd rose tree or flower arranging would have been more suitable tasks for a surgeon's wife, but when he'd ventured this opinion, Toni had laughed and kept digging.

In the early days, when Theo had asked tentatively how she felt about children, she'd assured him that she was content to be stepmother to such a lovely child. This had pleased him. But then again, had it? Toni could never be sure *how* Theo felt about the possibility of being a father again. Any time she'd tried to get him to open up on the subject he'd made light of it, joking that he was probably better qualified to be a grandfather than a father. She was happy enough to leave it at that – possibly even relieved. She just couldn't imagine having a baby. *Or not Theo's baby,* a little voice said. She jumped up, grabbed her bag and ran downstairs. There was no point in going down that road.

Alice was letting herself in the back door just as Toni was putting on her jacket. 'Oh, good morning, Toni. I thought you'd be gone by now.' The tone was disapproving.

'I'm running a bit late. I was talking to Chloe. She's worried about her exam this morning.' Toni wondered why she was explaining herself to the woman.

'She'll do fine,' Alice said firmly. 'She has her father's brains and I lit a candle for her on my way in.'

'Oh, well, that should do it, then.' Toni grinned.

Alice looked up sharply.

'Got to go. See you later.' Toni escaped out of the back door.

Over an hour later, she swung into the car park as Daniel was carrying a stack of files up the steps. She locked the car and ran to hold open the door for him. 'Morning, Daniel. How are you?'

'Thanks, Toni. I'm grand. Lovely morning, isn't it?'

'It always is when the exams are on. Poor kids.'

'Biology this morning. Mark's a nervous wreck.' Daniel's eldest was hoping to get enough points to do computer science.

'Chloe's the same.'

'The best days of their lives, eh? Cobblers!' He strode down the corridor, whistling.

Toni went into her office. It was a pity Theo wasn't as laid back about the exams as Daniel.

'Morning, Toni.' Sandra came in carrying a mug.

'Hi, Sandra. Thanks.' Toni eyed it dubiously. As always, the tea was too strong and too milky. That was the way Sandra liked it, so that was the way she made it for everyone. Unless Toni managed to sneak into the kitchen without Sandra noticing, she'd be forced to drink it. Either that or the busy lizzie in the corner would be the unfortunate recipient.

'It's a busy day today. Mr Perkins has eight operations this morning.'

'Has the first patient arrived yet?'

'She's in the waiting room and looks as if she just stepped off the cover of *Cosmo*.'

'Why do they do it?' Toni murmured.

'Asked me for camomile tea, she did,' Sandra continued. 'I ask you! I think some of them think they're in the Mayo Clinic, the airs and graces of them.'

'Has Daniel got a nine o'clock?'

'Yes. It's that little boy with the gammy hand.'

'Jamie Michaels?'

'That's the one, poor little fella.'

Jamie was only three but had been a regular visitor since he was six months old when his hand had been crushed in a car accident. This would be his fourth operation but hopefully his last. 'Is he here yet?'

'Daniel just called him.'

Toni looked at her watch and smiled. It was only eight forty but Daniel didn't believe in hanging about. 'And is Perky—' She stopped short. Damn Jade for coming up with that bloody nickname! 'Is Mr Perkins in?'

'I just brought him in coffee and the newspapers.'

And that, Toni thought wryly, summed up perfectly the difference between the two men.

Her phone rang. 'Hello? Jade, hi. Come on up.'

Sandra went to the door. 'I'll leave you to it. Now, drink your tea before it gets cold.' As she left Jade walked in.

'Hi, Jade. I didn't think you were on duty today.'

Jade perched her slim frame on the arm of a chair and rolled her large green eyes dramatically. 'I wasn't supposed to be, but Ms Harrison has one of her headaches.'

Toni grimaced. Vicky had more sick days than she had hot dinners. 'I'm beginning to think that girl should be a patient not a nurse.'

'Lord, imagine having to nurse *her*! Now, let's have a look at the work roster for next week. I want to make her pay for sticking me with Perky today.'

Sandra finished the letter she was typing, pressed the save button, then the print button and looked expectantly at the printer. It remained silent.

'Hi, Sandra, how's it going?' Chloe bent down to look over the receptionist's shoulder. 'You forgot to press "okay".' She hit the button and the printer sprang into action.

Sandra smiled at her gratefully. 'Thanks, love. I'm so useless. I can never get the silly thing to work.'

'You're not useless,' Chloe told her irritably. Then she added more kindly, 'Some people are just more technically minded than others.'

'Well, never mind about me. How did you get on in your exam?'

'Okay, I think.'

'I'm sure you'll pass with flying colours. You're bound to with such a clever father.'

Chloe scowled angrily. 'What the hell has that got to do with anything?'

Sandra's cheeks reddened. 'Well, it's just that . . . All I meant was—'

'Is Toni free?' Chloe cut her off impatiently.

'Yes, love. You go on in. Do you want me to get you some tea or coffee? Or what about a nice cool drink?'

Chloe smiled apologetically. Fighting with Sandra was like pulling the wings off a fly. 'No, thanks, Sandra. I'm sorry for biting your head off. I'm a bit stressed at the moment.'

'Of course you are. Isn't it natural? I always hated doing exams. A nervous wreck, I was.'

Chloe moved quickly in the direction of her step-mother's office. 'Thanks, Sandra. I'll go on in then. See ya later.'

Toni was just finishing a call when Chloe walked in. She looked at her watch in astonishment. 'Lord, I'd no idea it was so late. How did it go?'

Chloe's face lit up. 'Brilliant, Toni, but if you tell Dad that, I'll deny everything.'

Toni smiled. *No chance of that.* 'Oh, I am glad.'

Chloe paced up and down the tiny room, too excited to sit down. 'It was incredible. Everything I revised in the last couple of weeks seemed to be on the paper. It was a miracle!'

'Well, Alice *did* light a candle for you,' Toni informed her.

'Did she? The old pet! So where are we going for lunch? I'm starving!'

Toni picked up her bag and stood up. 'How about the Indian restaurant? I fancy some chicken tikka masala.'

'Yum!'

The two walked across Reception, said goodbye to Sandra and emerged into brilliant sunshine. Toni paused to put on her sunglasses.

'Now you look like one of your patients!' Chloe laughed. 'Did you ever see anything like that waiting room? There were three women in there wearing shades *and* coats. In this weather!'

'People are self-conscious about plastic surgery,' Toni said, in her professional voice. 'Now, will we drive or walk?'

'Oh, let's walk. I've been stuck in a dark hall all morning – I could do with some air.'

'I'm not sure you'll get any here,' Toni said, as

they reached the road and the fumes of a passing bus overpowered them. They walked quickly, and within ten minutes a smiling waiter had shown them to a table by the window.

Chloe opened her menu. 'How about a drinkie to celebrate?' she said hopefully.

'Nice try, kiddo, but I'm working and you have to go home and study for tomorrow's exam.'

Chloe groaned. 'You're no fun.'

'I know. But I promise I'll make it up to you when the exams are over. We'll do something really special.'

'Who's we?' Chloe asked quietly.

Toni glanced up, surprised. 'You, me and your dad, of course.'

'Then I think I'll take a rain-check.'

Toni put down her menu. 'Chloe! Why?'

Chloe twiddled a strand of hair. 'Oh, come on, Toni. It would hardly be a fun night out with him around, would it?'

Toni looked steadily at her. 'I don't know why you say that. I'm sure we'd have a great time.'

'Please, Toni, don't lie to me. I know there's something wrong between you and Dad.'

Toni's heart skipped a beat. It would be a disaster to let Chloe know how bad things were. She had to keep up a front until the exams were over. 'It's nothing for you to worry about.'

'Stop treating me like a kid, Toni. Tell me.' Her eyes were clouded with worry.

For a second Toni hesitated. 'There's nothing to tell, Chloe. We had a silly argument. A storm in a teacup that's all forgotten.'

'What was it about?'

Toni raised her eyebrows. 'Mind your own business. You don't tell me about your love-life, do you?'

Chloe grinned. 'So it was a lovers' tiff?'

'You could say that. Now, let's order. Then we can discuss where we'll have this big celebration.'

'Well, if you're sure . . .'

'I'm sure.'

'Okay, then. Can Ollie come? It would be really nice. She's my best friend and . . .' Chloe chattered on excitedly, and Toni wondered how and when she was going to explain to her that she was divorcing her father.

Chapter Ten

Thursday, 15 June

'You can't be serious?' Toni stared at her husband, immaculate in his black dress suit.

'Of course I am. You *must* come tonight, Toni. I'm speaking at this dinner.'

'Tell them I'm sick,' Toni said dismissively, and went back to her book. She had no intention of spending the evening pretending to be a loving, devoted wife in front of Theo's yes-men.

'Don't be such a bitch, Toni. This was arranged months ago. You're expected.'

She put down her book and stood up to face him. 'Tough.'

Theo held her gaze. 'If you don't come, I'll tell Chloe right now that you're walking out on us.'

Toni's eyes flickered between him and the door. Chloe had German tomorrow – her worst subject – and had been closeted in her room since she'd got in from school. She was pale, exhausted and miserable. 'You wouldn't . . .'

'Oh, but I would, my darling,' he said silkily.

Toni knew he wasn't bluffing. She pushed past him and went upstairs to dress.

'Do hurry, *darling*,' Theo called after her. 'We don't want to be late.'

Chloe wandered in as Toni was applying her makeup. 'You going out?' She flopped on to the bed and watched.

'Unfortunately.'

'Let me guess. A spectacular night of fine wines, good food and lively conversation with Dublin's finest?'

Toni grinned unwillingly. 'Those aren't quite the words I'd have used.'

'Will Dotty Price be there?' Chloe had met her a number of times and liked her just as much as Toni did. Dotty was unimpressed with status and rank, and more interested in people. You couldn't say that about many of the hospital bunch.

Toni frowned. 'I'm not sure. She was due to go in for some tests.'

'To Sylvester's?'

'Lord, no! Dotty wouldn't let that lot anywhere near her. She was going in to the Mater Private.' She sighed guiltily. 'I really should have visited her or at least called.'

'I'm sure she's fine. If she's not there tonight some-one's bound to know how she's doing.'

Toni slipped her dress over her head.

Chloe's eyes widened and she let out a low whistle. 'You're wearing that?'

'What's wrong with it?' Toni asked defensively.

'Nothing . . . if you were going to the Oscars.'

Toni studied herself in the mirror. The dress *was* quite dramatic. She'd bought it for the Sylvester's Christmas dinner dance then chickened out of wearing it at the

last minute. But it seemed perfect for tonight's performance. Flame red, it shimmered with her every move,
the fabric clinging seductively to her body. The high
cowl neck looked demure, until she turned to reveal
the deep plunge at the back. That would show Theo
not to blackmail her!

'The men are going to get cricks in their necks trying
to see your bum!' Chloe giggled.

Toni wavered. 'Maybe I should change—'

'No way!' Chloe protested. 'It might liven things up
a bit. Go on, Toni, live dangerously.'

Toni met her stepdaughter's mischievous gaze in the
mirror. 'You're right. Now, get me my long black coat.'

'Aren't you going to show Dad your dress first?'
Chloe asked.

Toni concentrated on putting in her earrings. 'Eh,
no. I think I'll surprise him.'

Theo went to take her arm as they climbed the steps to
the Shelbourne ballroom but Toni pulled away. 'Don't
push your luck. I'm only here for Chloe's sake.'

Theo glared at her. 'What have I done to deserve the
way you treat me, Toni?'

'Well, blackmailing me into accompanying you tonight
is a good start,' she retorted, as they made their way to
the cloakroom.

'You do exaggerate so— My God! What the hell are
you wearing?'

Toni had taken off her coat and handed it to the girl
behind the counter. She looked at him calmly. 'I bought
it with your card in Brown Thomas. Don't you like it?'

She started to walk away, affording him an excellent view of her naked back.

Theo practically threw his coat at the girl and went after her. 'Now, you've gone too far—'

'Dotty!' Toni's voice and expression softened when she saw her friend. The two women embraced warmly, while their husbands shook hands.

'Toni, you look beautiful! Doesn't she look lovely, Francis?'

Francis Price's eyes twinkled appreciatively. 'Charming, my dear. You're a lucky old dog, French.'

Theo grunted. 'Drinks?'

'White wine would be lovely, Theo,' Dotty replied.

'A large Scotch, old boy.' Francis pulled out a cigar and fumbled in his pockets for matches.

'I'll have the same.' Toni turned back to Dotty.

'White wine?' Theo asked, his voice steely.

Toni barely glanced at him. 'No, *dear*, a large Scotch. Straight.'

'I'm so glad to see you, Toni,' Dotty said, as Theo gave the waiter their order. 'I've already been in to rearrange the place names.'

'Good. Now, tell me. How are you? You look well,' Toni lied. She had been shocked at how gaunt her friend had become.

'Don't bullshit me, dear, I look terrible,' Dotty said. 'The damn cancer is back.'

Instinctively Toni reached out a hand. 'Oh, Dotty, I had no idea. I'm so sorry.'

'I'm going in for some treatment. Apparently they're optimistic.' She gave a cynical laugh and turned to accept a glass from Theo. 'Thank you, my dear.'

Theo shoved a whisky into his wife's hand and turned to talk to Francis.

Toni hardly noticed, her attention focused on Dotty. 'How long is it now since you were first diagnosed?'

'More than ten years.'

'Treatment has come on in leaps and bounds since then,' Toni said inadequately.

'Of course it has. I'm sure I'll be fine. But let's talk about something more cheerful. How is that lovely stepdaughter of yours?'

Toni was happy to change the subject. She had no words of comfort for Dotty, for it was clear from her attitude and her changed appearance that the situation was serious.

'Another drink?' Francis hovered over them.

Toni drained her glass. She felt like getting drunk. 'Yes, please.'

'We should go in.' Theo's voice was tight with disapproval, his glass full.

'There's plenty of time. Same again, girls?'

Dotty beamed at her husband. 'Lovely!'

Francis squeezed her arm affectionately and went to the bar, leaving Theo to fume as the women continued their conversation.

'Chloe's exams seem to be going well,' Toni was saying, 'but she's exhausted.'

'You must throw her a huge party when it's all over,' Dotty told her.

'Time enough for parties when the results come out,' Theo said grimly.

Toni ignored him. 'I thought we'd go out to dinner and bring along some of her friends.'

'Has she a boyfriend?'

Toni's eyes darted briefly to Theo. 'I'm not sure,' she replied, with a twinkle.

Dotty's eyebrows went up in mock surprise. 'A good-looking girl like that? She must have!'

'She's not interested in boys,' Theo said coldly.

Dotty slapped his hand playfully. 'Silly man!'

Toni laughed at Theo's expression. It wasn't often his opinion was questioned and even rarer that anyone had the audacity to call him silly. She told Dotty so when they went to the ladies' to freshen up before dinner. 'Well, he'd be a much nicer person if someone put him in his place more often,' Dotty replied, in her usual forthright manner. 'I'm sorry, my dear, but he does behave as if he has a rather large poker stuck up his arse.'

'Oh, Dotty, you're terrible!'

Dotty eyed her shrewdly. 'Well, at least I can make you laugh. You don't seem to do as much of that as you used to.'

'I'm fine.' Toni was applying lipstick. She would have loved to confide in Dotty, but now wasn't the time or the place.

'You must fill me in sometime.'

'On what?' Toni asked innocently.

'On why you're dressed purely to shock your husband would be a good starting point.'

The smile faded from Toni's face as she met Dotty's candid gaze in the mirror. 'It's stupid, isn't it?'

'I have no idea, Toni. You tell me.'

Toni opened her mouth to reply, but Dotty put a finger to her lips. 'But maybe not now. We must have lunch *very* soon.' She put her arm through Toni's and led her back to the ballroom.

As Toni and Dotty threaded their way through the room in search of their table Toni felt the whisky high ebb away. Francis and Theo were sitting in front of the small dais at the top of the room.

'Hello, Toni,' said a melodious, familiar voice.

She whirled round. 'Ian! How are you?'

He ignored her question as his eyes were roaming over her body. 'That's a nice dress you're almost wearing,' he said.

'Aren't you going to introduce me?' A tiny dark-haired woman appeared at his side and slipped an arm possessively through his.

'Oh, Carla, this is Toni Jordan. Toni, Carla Doyle.'

The two women nodded coolly. Toni had seen Carla with Ian before but they'd never actually come face to face.

'Toni is married to the great Theodore French,' Ian explained, with an edge to his voice.

'And when I'm not working on my needlepoint, I run a clinic,' Toni said tightly.

Carla's eyes narrowed speculatively. 'You're married to Theo French? I'd love to meet him.'

Everyone always wanted to meet her esteemed husband, Toni thought wearily. 'Maybe later. I should go. I believe we're under starter's orders. Nice to meet you, Carla. Goodbye, Ian.' She walked away with her head held high.

Theo stood up to hold her chair as she approached. She ignored his questioning look and sat down, conscious of envious glances from the other women at the table. Silly cows! How could they be fooled by his phoney act? *You were,* she reminded herself. He sat down beside her and she was grateful that he wasn't opposite and that she wouldn't have to avoid eye contact all night. Dotty had secured the place to her right and Francis had ordered her another whisky. Toni toasted him gratefully.

Theo pursed his lips. 'Slow down, for Christ's sake,' he said, through gritted teeth.

Toni drained her glass.

'Good girl,' Francis said delightedly. 'I love a lady who knows how to drink!'

'Theo looks as if he's swallowed a wasp.' Dotty whispered in Toni's ear.

Toni giggled. 'I'd better behave myself or I'll be sent to my room when we get home.'

Theo bestowed a charming smile on the woman to his left. 'Tina, isn't it?' he asked, staring intently into her eyes.

'Tracy,' the girl breathed, 'I'm with Alan Mackey.'

'Of course. Alan's a lucky man.'

Tracy giggled and Toni and Dotty exchanged amused looks.

Tracy's partner turned a shrewd gaze on his boss. 'Evening, Mr French.'

'Alan.' Theo acknowledged him briefly.

'We were just talking about the new laser equipment the Blackrock Clinic have installed,' Alan told him. 'They say it will knock at least an hour off most operations.'

Theo gave him a mocking smile. 'Really, Dr Mackey? And who are *they*?'

Alan flushed. 'Well, the reports in the newspaper . . .'

'Ah, the *newspaper*. Then it must be true.'

Toni frowned as a couple of the women tittered. Thankfully Tony Chapman, another of Theo's staff, came valiantly to Alan's rescue. 'Actually, I know a guy working over there and he told me they're fitting in at least four extra operations a week.'

Theo buttered a slice of brown bread carefully. 'Speed doesn't necessarily spell success, wouldn't you agree, Mr Price?'

Francis let out a booming laugh. 'Ha! True enough, Theo. Too many surgeons are letting the machines take over. It will all end in tears, mark my words.'

The general conversation carried on in this vein, but Toni and Dotty talked quietly to each other. Then came the speeches. Toni looked surreptitiously at her watch and wondered how much longer it would be before they could leave. Theo had been droning on for ages and the combination of whisky and wine was catching up with her. She could barely keep her eyes open. The only amusement afforded to her and Dotty came from the redhead across the table, who chattered all the way through Theo's speech.

'Who *is* she?' Dotty whispered to Toni.

'Tony Chapman's latest – I can't remember her name. Somehow I don't think she's going to last long.' Toni watched delightedly as Theo glanced down at the woman, his hands clutching the side of the lectern in barely suppressed fury.

He had just finished and was resuming his seat to polite applause when the redhead said, quite clearly, 'Isn't Toni the image of Catherine Zeta Jones with her hair done like that? You know, the actress who's married that old guy, What's-his-name Douglas.'

There was a stunned silence at the table and Tony Chapman looked nervously at his boss.

Dotty hooted with laughter. 'You're right. I never noticed it before. Isn't that funny? And they've got so much in common too.'

Toni kicked Dotty's ankle under the table. She glanced at Theo from under her lashes, curious as to how he was taking all of this, but Theo was looking at his watch. 'Catherine who?' he asked, and a collective sigh of relief went around the table.

Chapter Eleven

Friday, 23 June

'Can I help you?' Sandra looked curiously at the man wandering around Reception. He was quite attractive in a reserved way, although he was thin and his clothes had seen better days. He certainly didn't look like a patient of Mr Perkins. Maybe he was an odd-job man looking for work.

He approached the desk. 'Good morning. Is Jade Peters about?'

Sandra was surprised by the cultured voice. 'I'll just check. Your name, please, sir?'

'Just say it's a friend.'

Sandra watched him from under her lashes as she dialled Jade's extension. Toni picked up. 'Oh, Toni, did I dial the wrong number? I was looking for Jade.'

'No, Sandra, you got the right number. I was just passing. I think Jade's in theatre.'

Sandra smiled apologetically at the man. 'I'm afraid she's not available—'

'Please, I have to see her. It's really important – I'll wait all day if I have to.'

Sandra was alarmed at the urgency and determination in his voice. 'I'm sorry, sir, but Jade is in theatre.'

Aidan leaned across the desk and stared intently into her face. 'Now, look, Miss, I don't want to cause any trouble. I just want to talk to my wife.'

Sandra's eyes widened. This dishevelled, broken man was Jade Peters' husband?

'Tell her I won't take up much of her time but I'm not leaving until I see her.'

Sandra hurried round the desk and put a hand on his arm. 'Come with me,' she said quietly, and led him into the kitchen. 'If you'll just wait in here I'll see what I can do. But if she's in surgery, Mr Peters, I can't interrupt her. You'll have to come back.'

'I'll wait.' Aidan sat down at the table.

Sandra sighed and backed out, closing the door behind her. It was unlikely that anyone would stumble on him: Daniel was in theatre, Mr Perkins and Vicky weren't in today and Mary, the new nursing assistant, hadn't come on duty yet. She hurried upstairs and peered into Recovery. Jade was just wheeling in the patient. Sandra tapped urgently on the door.

Jade stripped off her gloves and mask, dumped them in the basket and came over to her. 'What is it, Sandra?'

'You have a visitor, Jade,' Sandra whispered. 'I've put him in the kitchen.'

'Him?' Jade looked over her shoulder at the patient. 'Can you stay here for a few minutes, Sandra? Mary should be in soon but if you've any problems come and get me.'

Sandra watched her leave and wondered why she hadn't told Jade that the visitor was her husband. She looked around the room with its plain white walls and stainless steel trolleys. She hated the bare, functional look. She sniffed in distaste. She'd always hated that smell too. Thank God she worked in Reception and rarely had to come up here. She'd never have made a nurse. But then she'd had her fill of hospitals over the years. She jumped as the woman on the trolley groaned. *Please come in soon, Mary, please,* she prayed.

Jade ran down the stairs, along the corridor and stopped short outside the kitchen. It had to be Aidan. She pushed open the door.

'Hiya, love.'

'What are you doing here, Aidan?'

'I needed to see you.'

'Well, you've seen me. Now go.'

'Jade, don't be like that.' Aidan looked like a dog that had been kicked by his beloved master.

'What is it, Aidan? More money?'

He looked even more hurt. 'No, nothing like that. I have some news.'

'Oh?' Jade said tiredly, and wondered what trouble he was in now.

'It's my mother.'

'Is she sick?' Jade was immediately concerned. She'd always got on well with Betty Peters and had agreed readily to Aidan's request that they did not tell her the truth about why they had separated. It would have broken her heart.

Aidan put his head in his hands. 'She died this morning, Jade.'

'Oh, God!' Jade dropped to her knees and pulled him into her arms. Aidan held her tightly and sobs racked him. When he eventually released her, she sat back on her heels and handed him a tissue. 'What are the arrangements?'

'I'm not sure. I've left it all to Ann.'

Jade nodded: Aidan's younger sister was more than capable of organising everything. She checked her watch. 'Look, I'm off duty soon. Why don't you go over to the café on the corner and I'll meet you there?'

Aidan brightened. 'Really?'

'Of course.' She escorted him down the corridor and out into Reception. 'Now, go and get yourself a cup of strong tea. I'll be as quick as I can.'

Aidan left, and Jade hurried back to Recovery. 'Sorry about that, Sandra,' she said briskly.

'No problem.' Sandra was happy to see her back. 'Is everything okay?'

'Fine,' Jade said shortly, without looking at her.

'Good. See you later, then.'

Jade watched the door close behind her. She was sure Sandra would have been dying of curiosity about her mysterious visitor. It wasn't like her to be discreet. Jade's thoughts were interrupted by a low moan from her patient. 'You're okay, Pamela. It's all over now,' she said. She checked the woman's blood pressure, updated the chart and buzzed Mary, who came in to wheel the patient off to a private room for the night. Then she went to her office, checked her messages, grabbed her bag and ran downstairs.

On her way she put her head into Toni's office. 'I'm heading off, Toni. Everything okay?' Her voice was light but her eyes were sharp. Sandra had probably been spreading the word by now.

Toni looked up absently. 'Yeah, fine. See you tomorrow.'

Jade relaxed. Toni knew nothing. 'I'm on the bleep if Mary needs me, but I think it will be a quiet evening.'

'Don't worry. Daniel's working late anyway. Are you going out?'

'No!' Jade knew she'd overreacted – Toni was only making conversation. She smiled apologetically. 'No. Just looking forward to a quiet night in front of the telly.'

'Sounds good. See ya.'

Jade hurried across to the tiny café. 'Cup of tea, love?' Aidan stood up as she walked in.

'Coffee, please.' She nodded at the waitress, who was looking at her curiously. God, maybe this hadn't been the best venue to choose. Tongues would wag: everyone from the clinic popped in here at some time or another. *Stop bloody worrying,* she chided herself. *Sandra will have told everyone by tomorrow anyway.* She concentrated her attention on her husband and ignored the waitress hovering nearby. 'Tell me what happened.'

'She went up to bed at nine. Ann brought her a cup of tea and some toast this morning.' He shrugged. 'And she was dead.'

'Oh, poor Ann. What a terrible shock. How is she?'

Aidan looked down at his cup. 'I don't really know.'

'You mean you haven't been over there yet?'

He shook his head.

'Oh, Aidan, you have to! You're her brother!'

'Exactly!' he hissed back. 'And look at me. Hardly a credit to the family now, am I?'

Jade took in the frayed cuffs, the stains on his jumper

and the unshaven face. 'Come on. We're going to get you cleaned up and then we're going over there.'

'We?'

'Of course,' she said briskly. 'I want to pay my respects too.' She swallowed the last of her coffee and stood up. 'We'll go to Henry Street first and get you some clothes.'

'But I can't afford—'

'Don't worry. I'll pay for them.'

Aidan followed her to the door. Jade glanced up at the clinic windows as they walked past. What would Toni think if she saw them together? But that was the least of her problems. Her priority was to make Aidan look presentable as cheaply as possible.

Within minutes they were in Dunnes stores and Jade led Aidan to Menswear. She stood back and watched as he wandered among the racks of clothes. Finally, when she grasped that (a) he didn't know where to begin and (b) he didn't care, she took over. Within minutes she'd selected a pair of black chinos, a white shirt, a black tie and some black shoes. 'I'm afraid I can't run to a jacket,' she said apologetically.

'Don't worry. I still have my leather one. That will do fine.'

'You always loved that jacket.'

'Well, you spent enough on it. Why wouldn't I?'

Jade felt herself responding to the tenderness in his eyes. *No, no, no. There's no going back, Jade. Nothing's changed. You're just feeling sorry for him.* She turned away and went off to pay for his new wardrobe. Twenty minutes later, a lot poorer than she had expected, they made their way up North King Street towards

Jade's flat. 'I'm afraid you'll have to make do with me trimming your hair,' she told him, as they turned into her street.

'That would be great, Jade. Thanks.'

As they climbed the steps up to number sixty-seven, Jade prayed that Patsy Stewart would be sleeping it off in front of the TV, although the way her luck was going today that was unlikely. 'Just be as quiet as you can and if the old trout appears leave the talking to me,' she instructed. She put her key in the door. Aidan followed her silently into the dark, narrow hall.

'I hope you're not thinking of moving him in here.' Patsy had appeared beside them before they'd shut the door. 'That room's only a single, you know.' She looked suspiciously at Aidan's bags.

'Tell me about it,' Jade muttered, then smiled politely. 'He's just visiting, Mrs Stewart. He'll be gone in half an hour.'

'Oh, now, you know me, love. Very broad-minded, I am. Always willing to bend the rules. Especially for my friends. It's just that another body would add to me costs—'

'Mrs Stewart, he's not stopping.'

'If you say so.' Patsy shuffled off down the hall.

'Pleasant woman,' Aidan said drily, when they were in the safety of Jade's room.

'Oh, yeah, salt of the earth. Now sit down and let me do something with that hair.' Jade fetched her scissors and snipped away expertly. 'There.' She stood back to admire her handiwork. 'That looks a lot better. Here's a towel, soap and shampoo. The bathroom is the last door at the end of the hall. Hurry up before the old biddy realises you're using the facilities.'

Aidan shut the door quietly behind him, and Jade sat down abruptly. What had she got herself into? On the other hand, what else could she have done? He was still her husband and his mother had just died. At least now he would look reasonably presentable at the funeral – damn, they'd need to get flowers. Jade thought of her dwindling cash.

Aidan arrived back with the towel wrapped around his waist. The hairs on his chest glistened with water. Jade averted her eyes. It had been a long time since she'd seen her husband naked and it didn't help that this room was so tiny and claustrophobic. 'I'll go down and phone a florist while you get dressed.' She smiled and escaped into the hall. She ran down to the public phone by the door and picked up the *Golden Pages*. She thought of the two hundred pounds in her post-office account – all her savings. A decent wreath would set her back at least forty. And Aidan would need money to get him through the next few days. 'One thing at a time,' she muttered, and dialled the number of the nearest florist.

Two hours later, Ann Peters opened the door and threw her arms around her big brother. 'Oh, Aidan, thank God you're here! I'm so glad to see you.'

Jade watched as Aidan rocked his sister in his arms. She hoped he didn't intend to disappear out of Ann's life again. Nine years younger than her brother, Ann had been a surprise baby – but a welcome one. Mother, father and son had doted on the little girl, and when Leo Peters died suddenly eleven years later, Aidan had become even more important to Ann. But from what Jade had been able to piece together from this afternoon's conversations, he hadn't been near her or his mother in over a year.

Finally Aidan pulled back from his sister, concerned eyes searching her face. 'Are you okay?'

'I am now you're here.' She turned to hug her sister-in-law. 'And you, Jade?'

'Hello, Ann. I'm so very sorry about your mum.'

'Thanks. She was very fond of you, you know. She was really upset when you and Aidan split up.'

Jade nodded dumbly. *What the hell could she say to that?*

'Let's go inside. I'll get us all a drink,' Ann said.

Jade followed brother and sister inside. She'd thought she'd never again set foot in this house but her life had caught up with her. She'd been a fool to imagine she could just walk away.

Chapter Twelve

Saturday, 24 June

'To Chloe and Olivia.' Theo lifted his glass and smiled proudly at his daughter.

Toni raised her glass of champagne. 'Chloe and Olivia.'

Chloe grinned back at them. 'Thanks, Dad, thanks, Toni. And thank you so much for this.' She fingered the silver ring on the third finger of her right hand.

Toni looked pointedly at Theo. It had been her idea to buy Chloe a present.

'Shouldn't we wait for the results?' he had asked when Toni suggested a night out to celebrate the end of Chloe's exams.

'This isn't about grades and points, Theo,' Toni said reproachfully. 'It's to congratulate her on getting through a difficult time and to wish her success in her new life.'

'Right.' Theo hadn't been impressed. Now, though, he smiled and nodded benignly at his daughter as if it had all been his idea.

Toni quelled the irritation that was always near the surface these days. 'So what now?' she asked the two girls.

Ollie drank her wine greedily. 'Now we relax, laze and have a good summer.'

'That doesn't sound very productive,' Theo remarked, as he looked around impatiently for a waiter. They'd been here almost fifteen minutes and no one had come to take their order.

Ollie snorted. 'Won't we spend the rest of our lives being productive?'

Toni grinned. 'You're quite right, Ollie. You enjoy yourself while you're young.'

Theo scowled at her, then addressed his daughter. 'What do you think about that, Chloe?'

Chloe took a deep breath. 'I'd like to work this summer.'

Theo's face lit up. 'Excellent idea! What did you have in mind? I could probably get you a job in the hospital – maybe as a nurse's assistant. That would be good work experience.'

Chloe glanced nervously at Toni. 'I thought fruit picking in France.'

Theo's smile disappeared. 'Over my dead body.'

'Dad!'

'Theo!'

Theo ignored his wife and looked coldly at his daughter. 'I haven't forked out a fortune on your education so that you can gad about the French countryside picking fruit. Are you going, Ollie?'

'No way! That's too much like hard work for me.'

Theo waved away the waiter who'd finally approached to take their order. 'So, who else is going, Chloe?'

'No one you know, Dad,' Chloe lied.

'Look, let's discuss it later,' Toni intervened. Why

did she get the feeling that a boy was at the bottom of this? 'We're supposed to be celebrating and I'm starving.'

Chloe shot her a grateful look. 'Me too.'

'There's nothing to discuss, Chloe. You're not going.' Theo beckoned the confused waiter. 'What's the fish of the day?' he asked.

Toni smiled reassuringly across the table. The smile that said, 'Leave it for now. I'll help if I can.'

Chloe buried her head in the menu.

Ollie ordered crab claws to start then fillet steak. 'Do you have chips?'

The waiter eyed her disdainfully. 'No, but there are new potatoes and a selection of vegetables.'

'I'd prefer chips,' Ollie said obstinately.

'I quite fancy a few myself,' Toni interjected.

'Me too,' Chloe agreed.

'Maybe you could do something for us?' Toni gave the morose waiter her most charming smile.

'I'll see what Chef says,' he replied smoothly.

'And a large bottle of sparkling water, please,' Theo put in.

'And some more of this.' Chloe held up her glass. 'It's lovely.'

'Two glasses of champagne are more than enough at your age, young lady,' Theo said, his voice loaded with disapproval.

Ollie giggled. 'You should see her after a few lagers.'

Chloe kicked her friend under the table. 'She's just kidding, Dad.'

'I certainly hope so.'

'Are you planning on going away this summer, Ollie?'

Toni changed the subject.

'Oh, I'll probably head off on one of these cheap last-minute deals to Ibiza or Majorca.'

'You could get a job in a bar and stay for the whole summer,' Chloe suggested.

'Cool! I never thought of that.'

'I thought you weren't interested in work,' Theo said drily.

'Oh, well, now, that wouldn't be *real* work, Mr French.' Ollie's eyes twinkled mischievously. 'Think of all the men I'd meet if I was working in a bar.'

'I doubt your parents would approve.' Theo's face was even grimmer than his voice.

'Ollie's winding you up, Dad,' Chloe said, with a beseeching look at her outspoken friend. Ollie winked.

Toni bit her lip. Maybe bringing Ollie with them tonight hadn't been the best idea in the world. Theo would probably forbid Chloe ever to see her again for fear that Ollie would lead his little girl astray.

'Still,' Ollie carried on, as their starters arrived, 'I might come to France with you after all, Chloe. Think of all the free wine we'd get.'

Toni smothered a laugh, Chloe concentrated on her starter and Theo glowered.

'Great food, Mr French. Thanks for inviting me.'

'You're welcome.' He bit viciously into a chunk of melon.

'How are the chicken wings?' Toni asked Chloe.

'Fine.'

Toni sighed. Poor Chloe. *And poor me.* For this was yet another row that Chloe would want to involve her in.

But that wasn't going to happen. It was time to tell her the truth. And time to move out. She had put a deposit on an apartment in Clontarf. It was a bit pricy because it had two bedrooms, but Toni wanted to have a place where Chloe could stay over – if Chloe was still talking to her after the separation.

'Is there something wrong with your food?' Theo asked stiffly, as he looked at Toni's untouched smoked salmon.

'It's fine, thank you,' Toni said politely, and started to eat. *Thank God this is nearly over. I can't handle this charade any more. I can't continue to live like this. I have to get away. I'm sorry, Chloe, but you'll fly the nest soon. And I'll always be here for you if you need me.* She took a gulp of wine and swallowed her tears with it. But no one had noticed. Theo had gone back to ignoring her, Chloe was deep in her own thoughts, and Ollie was eating heartily, oblivious of any undercurrents.

Chloe chewed mechanically and planned all sorts of horrible deaths for her friend. Her dad was annoyed enough about the trip to France without Ollie winding him up. And he didn't even know whom she was going with yet. She wished she were with Mark right now in some cheap café eating tasteless pizza rather than sitting in this stiff, fancy restaurant. It was all so pretentious – a place where the staff looked down on customers who ordered the house wine or didn't pronounce things correctly. As for the menu! Rack of lamb *au jus*. Why didn't they just call it gravy when that's what it was? And of course it had brought out the demon in Ollie. Chloe could imagine her father's comments later: 'Hasn't she ever *had* champagne before?' Ollie had stuck her finger in her glass and marvelled at all the bubbles. And: 'She didn't *really* think the finger bowl was soup, did she?'

Chloe usually enjoyed her friend's sense of humour but it was a bit much making fun of her dad when he was paying.

'How's work going, Mr French?' Ollie was asking now.

Theo looked taken aback. 'Fine, Olivia, thank you.'

'It must be very interesting.'

'Well, yes, it is, my dear. I didn't realise you were interested in medicine.'

'Oh, I'm not, but all of that blood and gore appeals to me,' she replied cheerfully.

The smile faded from Theo's face. 'Really?'

'Oh, yeah. I watch all those medical dramas. You know, *ER*, *Casualty*, *A&E*.'

'I can't say I've watched *any* of them.'

'Oh, you should, Mr French!' Ollie told him enthusiastically. 'They've got some really unusual cases. Lots of gunshot wounds, too. I don't suppose you come across many of them,' she prompted hopefully.

'Not many.' Theo was relieved to see the main course arriving.

Ollie poked dubiously at the garnish on her steak. 'What's all this stuff?'

'Flat-leafed parsley, Miss,' the waiter said coldly.

'I didn't order that,' Ollie said haughtily, 'and where's the chips?'

'The *pommes frites* are just coming.'

Ollie opened her mouth to protest but shut it when

she saw the murderous look on Chloe's face.

'This is lovely,' Toni said smoothly.

Theo nodded. 'Indeed. *Bon appétit*, everyone.'

'Yeah, right,' Ollie said, as a tiny dish of limp French fries was placed in front of her. She offered it to Toni.

'No, you have them. I'll never be able to eat all of this as it is.'

'Chloe?' Ollie said half-heartedly.

'They're all yours, Ollie.'

'Cheers, Chlo.' Ollie beamed at her and scraped the fries on to her plate.

Chloe grinned back. She found it hard not to. Ollie was a bitch for stirring things up but she was fun. Tonight would have been intolerable without her. She sneaked a look at her father. He was getting grimmer by the day and Toni wasn't a bundle of laughs either. 'Have you two booked a holiday yet?' she asked suddenly.

Toni and Theo looked at each other then started speaking at the same time.

'It's very busy at the clinic—'

'I'm not sure I'll get the time—'

'Oh, guys, that's crazy! You deserve a holiday as much as anyone.'

'And, Mr French, you'd be the first one to tell a patient the importance of relaxation,' Ollie chipped in helpfully.

'Yes, Olivia, that's true. But one doesn't have to go away in order to relax. A good long walk is just as beneficial.'

'Oh, Dad, really! What about Toni? Don't you think

she'd like to be brought somewhere nice?'

'Oh, I don't mind,' Toni said quickly. 'I'm just as happy in the garden.'

'Rubbish,' Chloe scoffed. 'You love lounging by a pool with a good book just as much as I do.'

'We'll think about it,' Theo promised, in an effort to put an end to the conversation.

'Great! I'll pick up some brochures for you tomorrow. What about the South of France? Or maybe somewhere more exotic?'

'Hawaii would be nice,' Ollie said dreamily.

'Yeah, Hawaii or Barbados. What do you think, Toni?'

'I think you should pick up the brochures, Chloe, and we'll have a look. Theo, could you order some more wine, please?'

'Certainly.' Theo signalled the waiter.

'Oh, goodie!' Ollie's eyes lit up.

'A bottle of the 'ninety-five Margaux.' He levelled a stern look at Ollie. 'And two Cokes, please.'

Ollie rolled her eyes at Chloe, who shrugged. It had been a miracle that Dad had allowed them champagne.

Ollie looked at her watch. At least in Peg's nightclub she'd be able to have a beer.

Chloe was equally impatient to escape. Mark would be at the club and it would be a relief to get away from the folks. Chloe felt guilty after all the fuss they'd made over her tonight but they were proving really hard work. There was a definite atmosphere between them. She hadn't noticed it before, what with all her studying and worrying, but now she realised that things hadn't been right for a long time. It was nothing she could put her finger on, just a coolness in the air. She thought of the day in the Indian restaurant when she'd asked Toni whether there was anything wrong. Toni had dismissed it but now Chloe wondered.

'How about some dessert?' her father was saying.

Ollie patted her flat, bare stomach. 'Have to watch the weight, Mr French.'

'I'm full,' Chloe assured him.

After a decent interval Chloe announced it was time for her and Ollie to go.

Toni hugged her. 'Have a good time.'

'We will. Thanks for dinner, Dad. It was great.'

'Yeah, thanks, Mr French. It was ace.'

'Don't be too late, Chloe.'

'And make sure you share a taxi home,' Theo instructed.

'We will, Dad, don't worry. See you. 'Bye.'

And they were gone.

Toni and Theo were left looking at each other over the wine. 'That went well,' Toni said drily.

Theo remained silent.

'Look, Theo, it's time we talked to Chloe.'

Her husband stared moodily into his glass.

'It would be better coming from both of us,' Toni said gently. 'It would be easier for her.'

'Easier for you, you mean,' Theo retorted.

'I only want what's best for Chloe,' Toni said steadily.

'Then don't go,' he said simply.

'I have to, Theo.'

'Why? Because of *him*?'

Toni looked puzzled. 'Who?'

'You know who. Ian bloody Chase.'

'Have you lost your mind?' she hissed. 'I broke up with Ian seven years ago. I left him for you, in case you'd forgotten.'

'And have regretted it ever since,' he shot back.

'That's not true.'

'Isn't it? Oh, come on, Toni. I'm not stupid.'

'Yes, you are, Theo, if you think there's something going on between Ian and me. The man hates me.'

'And what about you?' Theo's voice was dangerously soft. 'Do you hate him too, Toni?'

'No, I don't. I feel guilty about the way I treated him and I'm sad that I lost his friendship.'

'Friendship!'

Toni gathered up her bag and jacket. 'Yes, friendship, Theo. And now I've had enough of all this. I'm going home.'

'Oh, sit down, Toni. Save the melodrama. I'll get the bill.'

Toni sat down obediently and sipped her wine while Theo went to the desk. There was no point in storming out of the restaurant like an adolescent. She needed to reason with Theo, get him on-side. It was important – for Chloe's sake – that this separation was as amicable as possible. She wasn't going to let him turn her into the scarlet woman. She would explain things to Chloe and make it clear that there was no third party to blame or resent. Because, as she had told Theo quite honestly, the only third party she would ever care about hated her guts.

'There's something going on with those two,' Chloe said, as she and Ollie hurried down the street towards the club.

'They've had a fight,' Ollie told her. 'It's obvious.'

'But it's not just tonight. They've been getting at each other for ages.'

'Maybe your dad's having a fling.'

'Now why do you say that?' Chloe asked irritably. 'Why couldn't Toni be having a fling?'

'Women don't,' Ollie said wisely. 'It's the men that go astray.'

'Dad wouldn't. Anyway, he's too—'

'Old?'

'Yeah.'

'He must be years older than Toni.'

'Yeah,' Chloe said again. 'All the more reason why he'd hardly be knocking around with another woman.'

'Oh, I don't know. You know the way nurses are about doctors. And he's a surgeon. The top man.'

Chloe frowned. It was true that her father was treated like a god in Sylvester's. Could Ollie be right? Could he be seeing someone else?

'Oh, let's forget about your folks,' Ollie said, as they joined the queue outside the club. 'Tonight is supposed to be about celebrating, remember?'

'Yeah. I wonder if Mark's here yet.'

'I still think it's ridiculous that you're meeting him. We'd have a lot more fun if it was just a girls' night out.'

'He's bringing all his mates,' Chloe reminded her.

Ollie brightened. 'Does that include Justin? You know, the dark guy. He's gorgeous and I'm sure he fancies me.'

'Who doesn't?'

'When are you going to tell your folks about Mark?' Ollie asked, as they edged nearer the door.

'I don't know.'

'I can't believe they haven't found you out yet. But you're going to have to come clean if you want to go to France together.'

'Maybe I'll tell Toni first. She could tell Dad.'

'That's hardly going to help if they're fighting already,' Ollie pointed out. 'He'll probably think she knew about you and Mark all along.'

'You're right. I suppose I'd better tell them together.'

'When?'

They reached the door and the bouncer stood aside.

'Soon.' Chloe moved eagerly inside the club. 'Now, forget about it for tonight, Ollie, I want to enjoy myself. Look! There's Mark.'

Chapter Thirteen

Monday, 26 June

Jade looked around the large living room at her mother-in-law's friends and wondered how soon she'd be able to slip away. The funeral had been small: many of Mrs Peters' friends and relatives had pre-deceased her. Jade saw Aidan's maiden aunt approaching, dragging a reluctant Ann in her wake. 'There you are, Jade. Lovely to see you, my dear.'

Dutifully Jade kissed Margaret Finn's heavily powdered cheek.

'You're looking well, dear, though much too thin.' Margaret's shrewd eyes scanned Jade's slim figure in the simple black dress, the short auburn bob and the perfectly applied makeup. Jade might be in her forties, but she was still an attractive woman. 'I was just saying to Ann it's wonderful to see you and Aidan together again.'

'But we're not—' Jade threw an alarmed glance at Ann, who shrugged. She was used to her aunt's assumptions.

'A fine man, he is – a credit to his mother,' Margaret continued. 'I never could understand why you left him.'

Jade resisted the temptation to defend herself. The

old biddy wanted the inside story on what had *really* happened. She had never accepted their story from the start. 'They don't get on any more?' she'd said incredulously, to Ann and her mother. 'But they're like two peas in a pod. They'd be lost without each other.'

Jade sized the woman up. She was taller and thinner than her sister had been, and her eyes were sharp. 'Good to see you again,' she said eventually, much to Margaret's disappointment. 'Now, if you'll excuse me, I think Aidan wants me.' She hurried across the room to his side. 'Margaret's trying to grill me. Look as if we have something important to discuss.'

Aidan, who'd been staring blankly at a family photo, smiled at her. 'You're more than a match for old Margaret.'

'I'm not so sure. I think I'll slip away soon.'

Aidan looked disappointed. 'Do you have to?'

'I think I should.'

He patted her hand. 'If that's what you want. You've been a tower of strength. I'm very grateful.'

'Will you stay with Ann again tonight?'

'I may as well. It's more comfortable than Gerry's sofa.'

Jade stared at him. 'You've been staying at Gerry's?'

Aidan looked shamefaced. 'It was either that or a shelter.'

Jade thought he was being a touch dramatic but this wasn't the time to have a go at him. Gerry Carson, however, was married with three children. And his home, while comfortable, could not accommodate another adult. 'You can't stay there indefinitely. It's not fair to Jean and the kids.'

'I know. She's been great but I'll have to find something else.'

Jade nodded. 'Look, I'm going now but I think we should meet up in a few days. Discuss what you're going to do.'

'It's not your problem any more, though, Jade, is it?'

'I'll call you. Say goodbye to Ann for me.' She slipped quietly from the room, let herself out of the house and walked slowly down the tree-lined road.

She could have said goodbye to Aidan and left it at that. But no, she had had to get involved again. 'Who do you think you are, Peters? Mother Teresa?' She turned the corner and strolled down Bulfin Road. As she neared the church she remembered that Sandra also lived in Kilmainham, quite near here, in fact. Maybe she would drop in and say hello.

When she'd walked into the clinic the day after Aidan's visit Jade had been amazed to find that no one seemed to know anything about it, and she hadn't had an opportunity to thank Sandra for her discretion. She checked her watch. It was only three o'clock but Jade knew that Sandra was off work today, preparing for her mother's return from the MS care centre. She turned into the street where Sandra and Valerie Tomkins lived. As she walked up the path she admired the well-tended garden and wondered how Sandra managed to do a full-time job, look after her mother and the housework, *and* keep the garden looking so lovely. She rang the doorbell and within seconds a rosy-cheeked Sandra, holding a tin of Pledge and a duster, opened the door. 'Jade! What are you doing here? Is everything okay?'

'Everything's fine, Sandra. Sorry to call by out of the blue but I was in the neighbourhood, as they say.'

'Great! Come in. I was just going to take a break anyway. I'm dying for a cup of tea.'

Jade followed her into the hall and looked around in admiration. The hall was deceptively large, painted a pretty eggshell green and a richly patterned rug covered the tiled floor. 'Oh, Sandra, this is so pretty!'

Sandra blushed. 'Do you think so?'

'Absolutely! It's so bright and cheery.'

'We like it,' Sandra said modestly. 'I got the idea from an *Ideal Homes* magazine. I thought the colours would cheer the place up.' She led the way into the equally pretty little kitchen, with its pine dresser and table and comfortable armchair by the window. 'That's Mam's,' she explained. 'She loves to look out at the garden and the kitchen chairs are too hard.'

'This house is so beautiful and tidy too.'

Sandra put on the kettle. 'I'm doing a spring-clean because Mam's coming home tomorrow so you're seeing it at its best.'

'Is your mother house-proud?'

'No, I'm the hygiene freak. Mam's much more interested in her plants. Tea or coffee?' she asked, as the kettle boiled.

'I'd love a coffee, Sandra. And would you mind terribly if I had a cigarette?'

Sandra was surprised. 'Not at all, but I thought you'd given up smoking ages ago. If Mam was here she'd probably cadge one off you.'

Jade pulled a packet out of her bag and rummaged

for the lighter. She lit up and inhaled deeply. 'I didn't know she smoked.'

'She says it helps her relax.'

'Well, whatever works for her.'

'I don't think her neurologist would agree.' Sandra handed her a mug of coffee, and they sipped their drinks in silence for a few moments.

'I wanted to come and thank you,' Jade said, and stubbed out her cigarette in the ashtray.

'Why?' Sandra looked mystified.

'For not mentioning Aidan's visit to anyone.'

'Ah, that's okay. He seemed a bit upset – is everything okay?'

'His mother died. I've just come from the funeral.'

'Oh, I'm sorry, Jade. Was it sudden?'

'Yes, she was a healthy woman.'

'Is there any other family?'

'Just Ann, his sister. His father died a long time ago.'

'They'll need each other now. I don't suppose you two—' Sandra began.

'No.' Jade lit another cigarette. It would have been too much to hope that Sandra had become the soul of discretion. But when Jade saw her crestfallen expression she felt sorry. To Sandra, life was one big soap opera. 'Sorry,' she said.

Sandra smiled, relieved. She hated it when Jade's face took on that closed angry look. 'That's okay. I should mind my own business. Mam's always telling me I gossip too much, but honestly, Jade, I'd never tell anyone about Aidan. Or about his mother.'

'Thanks, Sandra. So, tell me, have you enjoyed having the house to yourself?'

'I've been a bit bored. I'm not really any good on my own.' She laughed. 'I have to talk to myself! I'll be glad to collect Mam tomorrow.'

'How is she?'

'A lot better, thank God. The rest and the company have done her the world of good. They're so nice in there. And it was wonderful timing, too. She was getting a bit depressed because this attack was lasting so long.'

'It's hard to be cheerful all the time. I think she's been very brave.'

'Me too.'

Jade finished her coffee and took the mug to the sink. 'My goodness,' she said, looking out of the window, 'your greenhouse is amazing! I half expect David Bellamy to appear.'

Sandra groaned. 'I know what you mean. To be honest I hate it, but it's Mam's pride and joy – oh no, I forgot to check the thermostat!' She opened the back door. 'Sorry about this, Jade. Won't be a minute.'

'Can I come?'

'Of course, if you're interested. I'm not much of a plant person myself. Now, flowers I like, with lots of colour.'

'I just miss anything green,' Jade said sadly, as she followed her down the path. 'I don't even have a window-box now.'

Sandra opened the door and closed it immediately after Jade. Jade stared around her. 'Good Lord! It's like being in the botanical gardens.'

Sandra giggled. 'It gives me the creeps. I keep expecting some huge tropical spider to come out and attack me.'

'Do you know what all of these plants are?'

'No. There are some herbs down that end that Mam makes tea from, but otherwise I haven't a clue.' As Sandra adjusted the controls, Jade wandered down to inspect the herbs and chuckled as she fingered the leaves of one.

'What is it?' Sandra came up behind her.

Jade sniffed the air appreciatively. 'Your mother has interesting taste in tea.'

'What do you mean?'

'Don't you know?' Jade's astonishment was written all over her face.

'Know what?'

'These are cannabis plants, Sandra.'

'No way!' Sandra stared at the plants, her eyes like saucers.

'Your mother's manufacturing her own medicine,' Jade told her.

'Oh dear. What must you think—'

'I think your mother's trying to make life a bit more bearable,' Jade said bluntly. 'Let her get on with it, Sandra. In fact, don't even tell her you know. The less said about it the better.'

'Do you think so?' Sandra looked dubiously at the offending plants. 'Maybe I should get rid of them.'

'Don't you dare! Doesn't she deserve some respite from her symptoms?'

'She seems to sleep better after she's had some.'

'There you are, then. Leave well enough alone.'

'You won't say anything, will you, Jade?' Sandra asked, as they made their way back to the house.

'Of course not.'

Sandra smiled shyly. 'Thanks. I know Mam would be mortified.'

Privately Jade didn't think that Mrs Tomkins sounded like the type who'd care – and why should she? 'I'll never breathe a word.'

'How about another coffee?' Sandra asked.

Jade looked at her watch. She wasn't due back at work until tomorrow, and a long, lonely evening stretched out before her. 'I'd love one.'

'If you're not in a hurry, I could make us some dinner,' Sandra suggested, 'and I think there's a bottle of wine in the press.'

'That's the best offer I've had all week,' Jade said truthfully. 'I'd love to stay – but only if you let me help.'

'Brilliant!' Sandra said delightedly. She took two chicken fillets from the freezer and set Jade to preparing some vegetables. The two women chatted easily as they worked. Jade was surprised at how relaxed she felt. She would never previously have considered having dinner with Sandra Tomkins. They had nothing in common and Sandra's incessant chatter at work got on her nerves. But Jade was beginning to realise that the chatter covered her nervousness and she wasn't remotely as feather-brained as she appeared. Also in her own home she was much more confident. True, she was technically challenged – Jade could never see her getting the hang of the computer system – but she was a damn good cook and Jade told her so when they sat down to eat.

Sandra blushed. 'Oh, it's nothing special. I enjoy cooking and it's been a real challenge coming up with some half-decent menus that fit in with Mam's diet.'

'Well, this is delicious. Thank you for asking me to stay.' Jade forked roasted vegetables into her mouth. She'd been up at all hours this morning making sandwiches with Ann for the funeral reception, but she hadn't been able to eat even one. Aidan hadn't touched anything either.

'It's nice to have company,' Sandra was saying.

'Don't you ever have friends round? I would have thought you'd be partying while your mother was in the care centre.'

'I've no one to party with. I've lost touch with my old friends, not that I miss them. They were all married and any time we went out they did nothing but complain about their lives. All I wanted was a bit of fun and all I got was earache.'

'That's terrible,' Jade said sympathetically. 'You'll have to come out with me and Toni one night. We usually have a laugh.'

Sandra lit up. 'Oh, I'd like that.'

Jade visualised Toni throttling her when she heard about this invitation. 'Then I'll organise it,' she said bravely. 'Though not for a while. I'm a bit strapped for cash at the moment.' She sipped her wine and wondered what the hell it contained to loosen her tongue so much.

'I could give you a loan, if you like,' Sandra said tentatively.

Jade looked horrified. 'Oh, no! Thanks all the same, Sandra. I'm exaggerating, honestly.'

'Well, if you're sure. Now, how about dessert? I think there's some chocolate ice cream in the freezer.'

Chapter Fourteen

Tuesday, 27 June

A lice leaned across the staircase to dust the Constable that was Mr French's pride and joy. Though why he had to hang it so high up in the hall she would never understand. She could only reach it if she used the long-handled feather duster and balanced on the tips of her toes. As she completed the job and stepped back she tripped over the can of polish and fell heavily down the three steps into the hall.

Almost two hours later Toni found her still lying on the floor. 'Alice! Oh, my God. What's happened?'

'It's my leg,' Alice muttered and winced.

'Take it easy now. Don't move.' Toni ran her hands over the housekeeper who gasped in pain when Toni touched her right thigh. 'I'm going to call an ambulance.'

Alice was alarmed. 'Surely there's no need for that?'

'Yes, ambulance, please,' Toni said into the phone, then covered the mouthpiece with her hand. 'We need to get you checked out. I think you may have broken a bone.'

'Oh dear. I'm sorry to be so much trouble.'

'Don't be silly, Alice. It was an accident.' Toni gave the address to the operator and hurried back to Alice's side. 'I'm just so glad I came home early today. How long have you been lying here?'

'I'm not sure.' She looked a bit dazed. 'I'd finished peeling the potatoes for dinner and I thought I'd get a bit of dusting done.'

'Never mind.' Toni glanced at the painting Alice had been trying to clean. 'But do me a favour and leave that one to me from now on.'

Alice looked faintly shocked. 'Oh, but that's my job—'

'Your job is to look after us, which you do very well. Don't worry about some old painting. I'll go and get a blanket.' Toni patted her hand and ran upstairs. Alice was shivering – probably in shock. Toni was pretty sure that the leg was broken. The best they could hope for was a clean break. But, she thought, as she made her way downstairs with a blanket and pillow, Alice was certainly going to be out of action for a while. 'Do you want me to call anyone for you?' she asked, once she'd made Alice comfortable.

'There's no one. My sister's in Wales and there's no point in worrying her.'

'Are you sure there's no one else?' Toni felt embarrassed asking. After six years she knew nothing about Alice other than that she was a widow.

'No one,' Alice confirmed.

Toni wondered wryly what crisis would have to befall Alice before she opened up and talked to her. Clearly this wasn't serious enough. 'The ambulance should be here any minute,' she said, to fill the silence. 'I'll come with you to Sylvester's.'

'Oh, no, thanks all the same but there's no need for that.'

'Well, I'll call Theo and get him to meet you there.'

Alice was horrified. 'No! Don't do that! I'm sure I'll be well looked after – but if you could get me my handbag from the kitchen?'

'If you want to give me your house keys I'll pick up some nightgowns and toiletries for you,' Toni volunteered.

'They won't keep me in, will they?'

'They probably will, Alice,' Toni said gently. 'But there's nothing to worry about, I promise. I'll get your handbag.'

When she returned, Alice took the bag and rooted for her keys. 'Maybe Chloe could go round and get my things.'

'I'd be glad to—'

Alice shook her head emphatically. 'Thanks all the same, but Chloe knows where everything is.'

Ungrateful old bag, Toni thought. 'Okay, then, if that's what you'd prefer. Chloe should be home soon. I'll drive her round and we'll be up to see you before you know it.'

As the ambulance carted Alice away Toni dialled Theo's number. He wasn't there, of course, so she had to deal with the unhelpful Emma. 'This is urgent,' she said tersely. 'Please page him immediately and tell him to ring home.' She hung up unceremoniously.

Moments later Theo rang.

'What is it, Toni? Is something wrong with Chloe?'

'She's fine. It's Alice. She fell down the stairs and I think she may have broken her leg. She's on her way to Sylvester's in the ambulance now.'

'And why didn't you go with her, for God's sake?'

'She didn't want me—'

'Where's Chloe?'

'In town. She should be home soon.'

'Oh, for God's sake, Toni, I don't have time for this.'

'All you have to do is drop into A and E, say hello and put her mind at rest,' Toni said angrily. 'It won't take you more than five minutes.'

'I still don't see why you couldn't take care of it.'

'She didn't *want* me, Theo.'

'I suppose I can understand that,' he replied caustically.

'Will you call me when you know something?'

'If I've time.' Theo hung up.

Toni put down the phone and stared at the feather duster that lay at her feet. Poor old Alice. After years of devotion and loyalty, Theo saw her as no more than an inconvenience. Thankfully, Chloe would be more supportive.

'Oh, poor Alice! I hope Dad's making sure she's being looked after properly,' Chloe said anxiously, as Toni drove them over to Alice's little cottage.

'I'm sure he is,' Toni said, with more confidence than she felt.

'She's never been in hospital before. She'll be terrified.'

Toni found it hard to believe that anything could terrify Alice. 'She'll be fine,' she said comfortingly.

'Toni, I'm not sure she will. She has almost a phobia about hospitals. She'll hate every second of it.'

Thank God Alice opens up to someone, Toni thought,

as she parked outside Alice's home. 'I'll wait here for you.'

As Chloe hopped out and let herself in at the side gate, Toni studied the pretty little cottage. Dainty lace curtains hung at each window, the woodwork and front door were freshly painted in pale blue, and the garden was neat and lined with a border of carnations. Toni wondered where she found time to do all this *and* look after them.

Chloe emerged with a small overnight bag and locked the gate carefully behind her. 'I'll just nip next door and let Mrs Donnelly know what's happened.'

Toni marvelled at the girl's common sense. It would never have occurred to her to tell the neighbours, whom, it seemed, Chloe knew. Toni had had no idea that Chloe spent time in Alice's home. She said as much when Chloe was back in the car and they were on their way to the hospital. 'Alice used to bring me over here when Mum was sick,' Chloe explained. 'She said it wasn't healthy for me to spend so much time at home. Mrs Donnelly used to have a little terrier, Sooty, and I'd play with him for hours.'

Toni gave herself a mental rap on the knuckles for all the times she'd maligned Alice Scully. The woman had been there for Chloe when she needed her most. 'I always loved that house.' A reminiscent smile played around Chloe's lips. 'It was always such a happy, homely place. There was always a smell of baking and fresh flowers – and polish, of course! Alice tried to teach me to make scones but I made more of a mess than anything else. She didn't seem to mind.'

Toni tried to absorb all of this as she searched the

hospital car park for a space. It was hard to reconcile the woman Chloe described with the Alice Toni had come to know and hate. She pulled into a bay and Chloe sprang out. 'Do you think she's still in A and E or will they have moved her to a ward?'

'Let's check A and E first.'

'Maybe we should drop in on Dad and ask him how bad it is.'

Toni wondered if Theo had bothered to find out. 'I think he's operating this afternoon,' she said vaguely. 'Let's find Alice first.'

They made their way into A and E and a nurse showed them into a small cubicle. Alice lay on a narrow trolley, looking frail and ashen.

'Alice?' Chloe took her hand.

Alice's eyes fluttered open. 'Hello, Chloe love. Isn't this a fine pickle I've got myself in?'

'Poor you. Are you in a lot of pain?'

'No, they gave me an injection, but I feel sleepy.'

'They may have given you a tranquilliser,' Toni said.

'You shouldn't have come, too, Toni, there was no need,' Alice murmured.

'Of course there was,' Chloe said briskly. 'Toni was worried about you. Has Dad been in?'

'He came down to talk to the doctor. So good of him.'

'He'll make sure they look after you, Alice,' Chloe reassured her. 'Have they told you anything yet?'

'No. They did some X-rays but I haven't heard anything since.'

Chloe looked at Toni, who took the hint. 'I'll go and see if I can find out anything.'

She went off in search of a nurse. A man was hurrying

in the opposite direction, his head buried in a file. He crashed into her, sending her shoulder-bag flying across the corridor. 'Oh, I'm terribly sorry! Toni!'

Toni found herself staring into Ian Chase's eyes. 'Hello, Ian.'

'I'm terribly sorry.' He picked up her bag. 'Did I hurt you?'

'I'm fine.' Toni was more flustered by their unexpected meeting than the collision.

They stood looking at each other for a moment then spoke together.

'I should really—'

'How are—'

They laughed awkwardly.

'You first,' Ian said, with a slight bow.

'I was just asking how things are with you.'

'I'm surprised you care after the way I talked to you at the consultants' dinner.'

Toni's eyes twinkled. 'You were no worse than usual.'

'I suppose I deserve that.'

'What were *you* going to say?' Toni asked.

'I was going to apologise for my behaviour that night.'

Toni arched an eyebrow. 'And you're not going to now?'

'Yes, I am. I apologise, Toni. I was rude and insulting.'

'You were, but I understood.'

'Really?' Ian seemed surprised.

Toni was unable to hold his gaze. 'I've done a lot to be ashamed of, Ian, and I'm quite sure I owe you several apologies.'

'Oh, Toni, if only—'

'Hello, darling.' Theo appeared behind Ian.

'Hello, Theo,' Ian said, coolly polite.

'Chase.' Theo barely acknowledged him. 'If you'll excuse us, we have family business to discuss.'

'Goodbye, Ian,' Toni said faintly, as Theo practically frogmarched her away.

'That was very cosy,' he said, teeth clenched, as he steered her back towards Alice's cubicle.

'For God's sake, Theo, don't be ridiculous! We were just passing the time of day.'

'I don't care what you were doing. Let's stick to the business at hand, if that isn't too much to ask.' He paused outside the cubicle and lowered his voice. 'They're going to have to operate on Alice and she'll probably be laid up for some time. We need to contact a relative, someone she can go and stay with or who can move in with her.'

'There isn't anyone. Her only sister is in Wales and she's older and not in good health.'

'Then she'll have to go into a convalescent home.'

'I'm not sure—' Toni started, but Theo had already thrown back the curtain and was addressing his housekeeper.

'Hello, Alice. How are you feeling?'

'Not too bad, thank you, Mr French. Sorry to be so much trouble.'

'Not at all. They're going to take you up to the operating theatre now and sort that leg out.'

Alice's eyes expressed her alarm but Chloe held her hand tightly. 'It's okay, Alice. You won't feel a thing.' Chloe sent a pleading look to her father.

'No, of course not,' he said hastily. 'It will be over before you know it.'

A nurse poked her head around the curtain. 'We're ready for Mrs Scully now, Mr French.'

'Very good. See you later, Alice.'

Chloe kissed Alice's forehead. 'I'll light a candle for you in the chapel, Alice.'

'Good luck, Alice,' Toni added.

Alice smiled weakly at them as she was wheeled away.

'Let's go to my office,' Theo said. 'We can make a few phone calls from there.'

'Phone who?' Chloe asked.

'Convalescent homes,' Theo told her.

'Oh, no, Dad! You can't put her into one of those places – she'd hate it!'

'Chloe, she is not going to be able to manage alone and she has no relatives or friends to take care of her. There really is no alternative.'

Chloe shook her head miserably. 'She'll never agree.'

'She doesn't have much choice.' Theo nodded absently at Emma and led the way into his office. He sat down at his large desk.

'Couldn't we look after her?' Chloe suggested, perching on the windowsill.

'I thought you wanted to go to France?' Theo said.

Chloe had finally worked up the courage to tell him and Toni about Mark, although she'd played down their relationship and said nothing about how long it had been going on. Theo had reluctantly agreed to Chloe's trip although he wasn't at all pleased that Mark Wheeler was going along. Still, they were part of a much larger group of students and with a bit of luck Chloe would soon tire of her boyfriend.

'That's two weeks away,' she said now.

'Chloe, Alice is going to be laid up a lot longer than that.' Theo buzzed Emma and asked her for a list of convalescent homes in the area. 'And bring us some tea,' he added.

Toni saw her plans go out of the window. She couldn't let the poor woman go into a home – she'd been too good to Chloe. It would mean another few months with Theo but that couldn't be helped. She took a deep breath and looked her husband in the eye. 'Maybe Chloe's right. Alice will only need help with getting washed and dressed. When Chloe's in France I could probably go into work late in the mornings and pop back and check on her every so often.'

Chloe beamed at her. 'And I'm sure Mrs Donnelly would come and visit – Alice's neighbour,' she added, for her father's benefit.

'Why can't she look after her? If she lives next door it's the perfect solution.'

'She's over eighty and she's got arthritis, Dad,' Chloe said impatiently.

'But where would we put her?' Theo asked.

'We could bring a bed down and put it in the back lounge,' said Toni. 'The room is never used and it would be much more convenient.'

'Toni, you're a genius,' Chloe said delightedly.

Theo started to relax as he slowly realised the ramifications of Alice's injury: Toni would stay and Chloe would go off to France in ignorance of their problems. 'That's very considerate of you, darling. Okay, Chloe, why don't you tell Alice the good news when she gets out of surgery?'

Chloe ran round the desk to kiss her father. 'Thanks,

Dad. Alice will be thrilled.' She hugged her stepmother. 'Thanks, Toni.'

Toni returned the hug and closed her eyes to Theo's gloating expression. 'No problem.'

Chapter Fifteen

Tuesday, 18 July

Daniel and Toni sat in his office going through the financial statement that the accountant had prepared. Toni was finding it hard to keep her mind on her work. She was exhausted juggling her job at the clinic and nursing her ungrateful patient. Daniel seemed pensive. Extending the time frame between consultations and operations had resulted in a drop in profits. Robert had shot him a 'told you so' look when he'd read the figures. Daniel drummed his fingers on the large mahogany desk as he stared moodily out of the window.

'I think you may have to readdress the consultation limitations, Daniel.' Toni struggled to suppress a yawn.

'And won't Robert love that,' Daniel muttered.

'How about changing the time limit to two weeks for the smaller procedures with only one consultation unless a second is requested?'

Daniel tugged at his beard. 'I don't like it. It's open to abuse.'

'I don't think you've much choice. We're losing business to the other Dublin clinics' – just as Theo had said they would – 'and we have no UK appointments for next month. Robert has only two consultations tomorrow and he's taking Friday off because he has no operations.'

'Oh, all right. We'll do as you suggest, Toni, but only for the minor stuff. Draw up a list so that when we tell Robert the good news there are no misunderstandings.'

Toni made the note and rubbed her eyes.

'Is looking after your housekeeper a bit of a strain? Take a few weeks off if you like. As you say, it's not as if we're run off our feet.'

Toni shuddered at the thought. Things hadn't been too bad when Chloe was there, but now that she had left for France the atmosphere was taut. 'I couldn't stay at home with her all day, Daniel. I'd throttle her! But I might take an extra couple of hours here and there.'

'You do what you have to, Toni. As long as the clinic doesn't suffer I don't mind what hours you work.'

She stood up. 'Right. I'd better get going. I have to get the old dragon her lunch.'

'Don't put any arsenic in it. It'll show up in the pathology report.'

'Thanks for the tip.' Toni left Daniel's office and went down to Reception. 'Sandra, I'm heading off in a minute. I'll be back in a couple of hours.'

'Okay, Toni. By the way, I'm really looking forward to our night out.' She smiled shyly at her boss.

'Me too.' Toni collected her bag and car keys, wondering what on earth had possessed Jade to invite Sandra to go out with them. She'd been quite annoyed about it. She looked forward to her evenings with Jade but it would be different with Sandra tagging along.

'I'm sorry, Toni, but she seemed so lonely,' Jade had said.

Toni had been surprised at that. Jade didn't usually listen to sob stories. In fact, she rarely encouraged Sandra to talk at all. And what had Jade been doing at Sandra's house anyway? It all seemed very odd. Still, a night out – even with Sandra in tow – would be a welcome break from Alice Scully. The ungrateful old bag hardly said two words to her unless she had to. And she hated having to accept Toni's help. Theo didn't get involved in the care of his housekeeper at all, apart from popping his head round the door occasionally to say hello. He had been at home rarely since Chloe had left – for which Toni was grateful. When he was there the atmosphere was unbearable.

'Is that you, Toni?'

Toni shut the front door with an irritable sigh. 'Hello, Alice.' *Who else would it be?* She crossed the hall to the small lounge that was now Alice's room. 'How are you?'

'Not too bad.'

'Good.' Toni pasted on a bright smile. She glanced round the dark, depressing room. She hated its mute colours and heavy curtains but again Theo hadn't allowed her to change the décor. She felt a pang of pity that Alice had only these four walls to stare at all day. It couldn't be helping the recovery process. 'It's a lovely day today, Alice. Why don't I help you into the conservatory and I'll bring you your lunch there?'

'Well, if it's not too much trouble . . .'

'Of course not.' Toni put the walking frame in front of Alice then slipped a strong arm around her.

'Am I too heavy for you?'

'You're as light as a feather.'

Alice gave a small smile and they proceeded slowly out into the hall.

'It's a good job this is such an old house,' Toni remarked conversationally. 'The wide doorways come in handy in situations like this.'

Alice nodded but said nothing as she concentrated all her efforts on manoeuvring herself forward.

Toni watched in reluctant admiration. She was obviously in a lot of pain, but she never said a word. Her only complaints were that Toni wasn't looking after Theo or cooking him proper meals. Toni blatantly ignored Alice's culinary tips: 'Mr French loves a bit of smoked salmon with that rye bread I get in Tesco's.' Or 'Mr French enjoys a nice bit of hake – the fishmonger's in Finglas is the best.' She watched disapprovingly when Toni unpacked frozen food and TV dinners after a shopping trip on the way home from work. Toni found it hard enough to deal with Alice's meals and certainly wasn't going to worry about cooking for an ungrateful husband.

To be fair, Alice's needs were simple: a boiled egg and some toast, soup and brown bread, or cold meat and salad. Chloe had confided that she was also partial to cod and chips, and sometimes Toni stopped off at the chip shop on her way home. While Alice protested that there was really no need for her to go to such trouble, she always ate every morsel with relish.

As Alice reached the conservatory, Toni moved ahead of her to plump the cushions on the most comfortable chair. Then she moved the walking frame out of the way and lowered her down. Once Alice was settled, Toni carefully raised the injured leg on to a footstool.

Alice sank back and closed her eyes. 'Thank you,' she said breathlessly.

Toni felt a pang of pity. She looked so frail and tired. The short trip from the study had exhausted her. Even when the plaster came off it would be a while before she was properly mobile again. 'You rest there and I'll get your lunch.' Toni switched on the radio to the classical channel that Alice liked and went out to the kitchen.

When she carried in the tray of barbecued chicken and salad that she'd picked up at the local deli, Alice opened her eyes and smiled. 'Aren't you having any?'

Toni looked surprised. 'Yes, it's in the kitchen.'

'Why don't you join me? I'd appreciate the company.'

Toni nearly fell over in shock. 'Oh, right. I'll just get it.' She fetched her plate, sat down opposite Alice and started to eat in silence.

'I haven't been very fair to you, Toni, have I?' Alice said, cutting her chicken into smaller pieces.

'Sorry?' Toni kept her head down. She could hardly believe her ears. Alice had always been so hostile.

'You see, I've always felt so protective of Chloe,' Alice continued, 'and though I approved of Mr French remarrying—'

'You didn't think it should be to me,' Toni said bluntly.

Alice had the grace to look embarrassed. 'It was nothing personal. It's just that I felt Chloe needed a mother and you were – are – so young. But I was wrong.'

Toni nearly choked on her coleslaw and reached for her glass of water.

Alice was amused. 'Are you all right, dear?'

Dear? Toni nodded dumbly.

'You've been a great friend to Chloe, more like a big sister, really and she loves you.'

'I love her too.'

'I can see that now. You've brought stability and common sense into her life and been there for her when her father hasn't. He doesn't seem to understand her or accept that she's growing up.'

Toni couldn't remember Alice ever having been disloyal to Theo before. 'He thinks she should concentrate on university and a career,' she said.

'What nonsense! The girl needs a bit of fun. I'm so glad she's gone off on this trip. And Mark Wheeler is a lovely young man. He'll take care of her.'

'I agree, though I don't think Theo does. He might be happier if Mark wasn't Daniel's son.'

'Ridiculous! At least he knows the boy's from a good family. If he tries to clip her wings she'll fly the first chance she gets,' Alice warned.

Toni nodded soberly. 'I think she might move into a place of her own when she turns eighteen.'

'And gets the money her mother left her? Yes, you're probably right. You don't think she'd live with Mark, do you?'

Toni burst out laughing. 'I don't know who'd throw more of a fit – Theo or Daniel!'

'And the funny thing is that the boy would probably be a better influence on her than Olivia Coyle.'

'She's a wild one, all right.'

Alice sighed. 'I think it's up to you and me to look out for Chloe, Toni. She needs us both.'

Toni looked away. If things went as planned, she

would leave Theo when Chloe got home and Alice was on her feet again. She wondered if she should take advantage of the moment and confide in Alice.

But Alice was way ahead of her: 'You know, I have a feeling that Chloe might not be the only one thinking of taking flight.'

'What do you mean?' Toni spluttered.

'I'm not blind *or* stupid, Toni. I can see what's going on. Be honest. If I hadn't had that fall you'd have been gone by now, wouldn't you?'

Toni's voice was barely a whisper and her eyes were large in her pale, drawn face. 'How did you know?'

'I've got to see things from a different perspective since I moved in.'

'I did try to make it work.'

'I'm sure you did, but Mr French isn't an easy man.'

Toni looked at her, amazed. 'I thought you worshipped the ground he walked on!'

'I've known him a long time and I respect him, but I'm aware of his faults. He gave Marianna a tough time too, you know.'

'But – but I thought they had the perfect marriage,' Toni stammered. Hadn't Theo's first marriage been as idyllic as he'd always led her to think?

'Well, it was better for Chloe to believe that,' Alice said matter-of-factly, 'but Marianna was unhappy for a long time before she got sick.'

'I don't understand. I thought he was disappointed in me because I didn't measure up to *her*.'

'Marianna was a wonderful girl but quite human, I assure you. And she hated entertaining as much as you do.'

Toni tried to make sense of it all. 'I wish you'd told me this before.'

'What difference would it have made?' Alice said, almost philosophical.

'So why tell me now?' Toni said, angrily.

'Because I think you should leave him. You've done your best for Chloe. It's time to live your own life.'

Toni took a moment to absorb this. Was the woman serious? 'I didn't think the Catholic Church approved of separation,' she said at last.

'It doesn't, but *I* do. The priests don't have any idea of what goes on inside a marriage. It's God you'll have to answer to at the end of the day and I don't believe in a vengeful God.'

Toni rested her head against a cushion, drained. Alice had impressed, amazed, shocked and annoyed her in the space of one conversation – probably the first they'd ever had.

'I've said more than enough for now. But I just want you to know that if you want to talk, I'll be happy to listen. But I'm afraid now I need a nap.'

Toni looked at her tired face and stood up quickly to help her. 'I would like to talk again,' she said carefully, after she'd helped Alice back into bed, 'when I've had time to think. But in the meantime, please keep all of this to yourself.'

Alice looked mournfully around the empty room. 'Who would I tell?'

That evening when Toni phoned Dotty, the older woman suggested that she come over as Francis was away. Toni jumped at the invitation. She was dying to talk to someone and she wouldn't be able to confide in Jade tomorrow night, what with Sandra coming along. Anyway, it was time she saw Dotty. Their long-planned lunch had never happened because Dotty had been kept in hospital longer than she had expected. Now she stayed in bed most days. However, on the phone she had sounded like her old self.

'It's like something out of a movie!' Dotty said delightedly, as Toni filled her in on events.

Toni was finding it hard to concentrate on her problems now that she'd seen her friend, who was wasting away before her eyes.

'I must say, I'm not entirely surprised that you're leaving Theo, though I do think you're making a meal of it,' Dotty went on. She could always be relied on to speak her mind.

'What else could I do?' Toni asked helplessly. Between Chloe's Leaving Certificate and Alice's accident—'

'There are times when you have to think of yourself,' Dotty insisted.

'Oh, really? And do *you* think of yourself at all, Dotty?' Toni said bluntly.

'Of course I do. I'm a selfish old woman. All I do is stay in bed all day and watch TV.'

'You're sick,' Toni pointed out.

'I'm fine, so don't start to fuss. It's bad enough having Francis cluck over me. It took me ages to persuade him to take a break and visit his brother for a few days. But the truth is, Toni, I need it as much as he does. He's driving me mad. Eat this, drink that, take this tonic, have a nap – he treats me like a child.'

'He loves you.'

Dotty's eyes were suspiciously bright. 'I know that, but I have to deal with this in my own way.'

Toni watched as her friend drained her glass. She'd hardly touched any of the chow mein Toni had ordered for them. 'I ate a huge lunch,' she'd explained apologetically, 'but I'll gladly drink your wine.'

Dotty picked up the bottle now and reached over to top up Toni's glass.

'Actually, I wouldn't mind something a bit stronger if you don't mind.'

Dotty laughed. 'I wondered why you didn't bring the car. Well, what will you have? Francis must have every drink under the sun in this cabinet.'

'Just Scotch, please. I'll go and get some ice.' Toni walked quickly from the room. She couldn't bear to watch Dotty pour it with skeletal hands. Why hadn't Francis told her things were so bad?

'There you go.' Dotty handed her a very large glass of whisky when she came back into the dining room. 'Let's go out into the garden. It's such a lovely evening.'

Toni followed her outside, trying not to notice Dotty's skinny little ankles above the large, furry slippers.

'So, what now?' Dotty asked, when they were settled side by side on the garden swing.

Toni shrugged. 'Oh, I don't know. Alice has thrown me into a spin. Why did she decide to talk to me now, after all these years?'

Dotty studied her glass. 'Because suddenly she's feeling old, vulnerable and dependent. And the person she least expected to do so has taken control and come to her aid. You've made her think. Her saintly lord and master wanted to put her in a home, for God's sake.'

'She doesn't know that,' Toni told her.

'Don't kid yourself. You can bet she knows a lot more than she lets on.'

Toni thought back to her conversation with Alice. 'Yes, you're probably right. Poor woman.'

'I never thought I'd hear you say that.'

Toni laughed. 'Isn't it amazing how quickly things can change?'

Dotty watched the sun sink behind the trees. 'Amazing,' she murmured.

Chapter Sixteen

Wednesday, 19 July

'That was lovely,' Sandra said to Jade and Toni as they sat in the small restaurant.

'The chicken was a bit tough,' Toni complained. She caught the dirty look Jade was directing at her and felt ashamed. She'd been terrible company and ratty with Sandra, and for no real reason. Other than that she'd have loved to tell Jade about Alice and poor Dotty. She felt depressed again as she remembered the slight figure that had seen her off, one hand gripping the doorpost for support. 'I'm sorry I'm such bad company,' she said.

'You're not,' Sandra assured her. 'I'm not always in the mood for chatting myself.'

Toni avoided Jade's eyes. 'Thanks. Anyway, let's have some more wine.'

Sandra looked alarmed.

Jade grinned. 'Don't worry, Sandra. I promise we won't bring you home drunk.'

'Your mother would be shocked.' Toni giggled.

'My mother would be delighted,' Sandra told them. 'She's always nagging me to go out and have a good time.'

'*My* mother used to nag me to stay in!' Jade said.

'I bet you were a terror as a teenager,' Toni remarked.

'I don't know what makes you say that, I'm sure.' Jade pretended offence. 'Anyway, Sandra isn't a teenager.'

'It's a long time since I was,' Sandra agreed mournfully.

'So why don't you go out more?' Toni asked.

Sandra shrugged. 'I've nothing in common with the gang I used to hang around with.'

'What about men?' Jade's eyes twinkled.

'What about them?'

Jade winked at Toni. 'I think your mother's right. You should get out more. We need to find you a date.'

Sandra looked panic-stricken. 'I don't think so!'

'Jade's right,' Toni said cheerfully. 'There must be someone we know who'd be suitable. What about Johnny?'

Jade looked blank. 'Johnny?'

Sandra gasped. 'The guy who delivers the medical supplies? He wouldn't give me a second glance.'

'Oh, *him*!' Jade remembered him now. 'Yeah, he's not bad. How old would you say he is? Thirty, thirty-five? And why wouldn't he give you a second glance? You're attractive and around his age—'

'I'm sure he has a girlfriend,' Sandra said hurriedly.

'Ah, so you *do* like him, then,' Toni teased.

'He's okay but, like I say, he's probably seeing someone. Excuse me. I really must go to the loo.'

Jade's eyes were thoughtful as she watched her leave. 'I think our Sandra's a very lonely girl.'

'She's not the only one,' said Toni.

'Oh, yes?'

Toni grimaced. 'I know I'm married, but I feel lonelier in that house than I think I would if I was all on my own.'

Jade's face darkened. 'Don't bet on it.'

'Sorry, that was tactless.'

'Aidan's mother died,' Jade said suddenly. She'd put off telling Toni. She should really have told her before the funeral – Toni and Aidan had always been good friends.

'Oh, no! When?'

'A couple of weeks ago.'

Toni looked dumbfounded. 'Why on earth didn't you tell me?'

Jade felt uncomfortable. 'It was a small funeral. I didn't think—'

'No, you didn't!' Toni's eyes flashed but she said no more as Sandra returned to the table.

'I'm glad I'm off tomorrow.' Sandra eyed the full wineglass in front of her.

'Have you any plans?' Jade asked, to cover the angry silence emanating from Toni.

'Mam is spending the day with her sister so I thought I might give the house a good clean. She gets all sad if I do it when she's there.'

'Because she can't help?' Toni asked.

Sandra nodded. 'Though it doesn't stop her trying. And then I get worried and tell her to rest and she gets annoyed with me.'

'It can't be easy,' Jade said simply.

'Oh, we do okay. What about you, Jade? You've had a tough time, what with Aidan's mother and all.'

Toni's eyes reflected her surprise and Jade looked

away. Sandra carried on oblivious, her tongue loosened by the wine: 'You've been great to stand by him the way you have.'

'Indeed you have.' Toni looked at her friend reproachfully. She was furious that Jade hadn't told her about Betty Peters – Aidan must be upset that she hadn't been at the funeral or sent flowers – and flabbergasted that she had confided in Sandra.

Jade sighed, then began to explain herself. 'Aidan came to the clinic to tell me about his mother. Sandra met him then.'

Sandra sipped her wine happily. 'He was very nice. I'd say you made a lovely couple.'

'They did,' Toni snapped.

Jade's fingers tightened around her glass. 'Please, Toni, don't be like that. I'm sorry I didn't tell you before, but it was so sudden and there was so much to organise.'

'How come you were doing the organising?' Toni said. 'You're *supposed* to be separated.'

'He needed me, Toni. And there was Ann to consider.'

'Of course. Sorry. How is she?'

'Bearing up quite well, really. Though I think she may still be in shock.'

'How did it happen?'

'Her heart. It was very sudden. She was healthy up until the end.'

Sandra's eyes were misty. 'It's good she didn't suffer.'

'I think it's time we got you home,' Toni said gently, and signalled for the bill.

'Oh, but I'm enjoying myself.' Sandra wiped her eyes.

'I think Toni's right, Sandra. It's getting late.'

Sandra focused with difficulty on her Swatch. 'I had no idea it was *that* time! Mam will think I've been kidnapped.' She giggled. 'I'd love to do this again. It's been really nice.'

Jade buried her head in her bag.

'Then we will,' Toni said magnanimously.

'We will?' Jade repeated faintly.

'We will.' Toni smiled, and Jade knew she was forgiven.

'Why don't you two share a taxi?' Toni said, after they'd paid the bill.

Jade's face fell. 'Oh, eh, no need for that. If we hurry we can catch the last bus. We'd probably be waiting ages for a taxi anyway. What do you say, Sandra?'

'Okay.' Sandra smiled vacantly.

'You don't mind us leaving you, do you, Toni?'

'Go for it. See you tomorrow.'

'Yeah.' Jade bent to give her friend a quick hug. ''Bye, Toni. See you Friday.'

''Bye, Sandra. Safe home.'

Toni drained the last of the wine into her glass: no point in wasting it, and sitting here alone was preferable to going home – although Theo, no doubt, would already have retired for the night. Unless, of course, he was out on one of his solitary nocturnal drives. He could never have been called a party animal, that was for sure – his idea of socialising was a drinks party that had ended by ten o'clock. Or Sunday brunch: that way he'd have met his obligations and be rid of everyone by two.

Theo's entertaining was never spontaneous and the guest list was always carefully thought out. When Toni had suggested that Daniel or Jade or even her parents might come along he had dismissed the suggestion out of hand. 'Not their sort of thing,' he'd said of her parents. Though how would he know what her parents were into? Toni wondered bitterly. He'd never taken the trouble to find out. As for inviting anyone from the clinic other than Robert, he'd just laughed. Though it was unlikely that Jade would have accepted. The dislike was mutual. They had never gone out as a foursome, the way they had when she was dating Ian.

She sighed as she thought back to the day of Alice's accident and her chance meeting with him ... the wistful look she'd seen in his eyes. No! She must have imagined that: he had a new woman in his life and they looked very much a couple. She must forget all about Ian Chase and start planning for the future. Maybe she would even have to consider leaving the clinic. She didn't want to, and she certainly wouldn't bow to any pressure from Theo, but it might make things easier for everyone in the long run. How could she ever get on with her new life if she still had to deal with Theo regularly? She stood up to leave, thanked the waiter and wandered out on to the street. It was the first time for ages that she'd been in the city centre so late at night. Now, instead of making her way to the taxi rank on Dame Street, she walked into Grafton Street and headed towards Stephen's Green. She'd pick one up there after she'd breathed in the ambience of the vibrant city. It was after eleven but there were still a couple of hardy buskers about and she had to step aside a couple of times to avoid being mown down by passing rickshaws.

She had been waiting at the taxi rank for several minutes before she realised that the white BMW that had pulled up across the road was beeping at her. She peered across and gulped as she saw Ian gesturing to her. Talk about timing. She waited for a gap in the traffic and went over to the car.

'I thought it was you.' Ian grinned at her. 'Hop in and I'll drop you.'

'There's no need—'

'Oh, come on, Toni, you could be waiting there for ages and it's not as if it's out of my way.'

Ian still lived in his apartment in Beaumont, just ten minutes' drive from Theo's house. Now why, she mused, as she climbed in beside Ian, did she still think of it as Theo's house? It was her home too.

'Toni?'

'Sorry, what was that?' Toni busied herself with her seat-belt as he pulled back into traffic.

'I was just asking what an old married woman is doing wandering the streets of Dublin on her own at this time of night.'

'Less of the "old", please. I was out with Jade.'

'Oh, how is she?'

'Great. I think.' Toni thought of the tension earlier in the evening.

Ian glanced at her. 'You think?'

'Aidan's mother died a couple of weeks ago.'

'Oh, I'm sorry. Why didn't you let me know?'

'Jade never mentioned it until this evening.'

'You're annoyed with her?'

'Well, of course I am. I should have been at the funeral.'

'Yeah, me too. I always liked Aidan. Remember the night in the Indian restaurant on George's Street?'

'God, I'd forgotten all about that.'

'He'd been to the dentist that afternoon and the anaesthetic hadn't quite worn off—'

'And he ordered the vindaloo!' Toni finished for him.

'Extra hot,' Ian reminded her. 'And then half-way through the meal the anaesthetic started to wear off.'

Toni smiled as she remembered the sweat standing out on Aidan's red face. 'I've never seen anyone get through so much water.'

Ian chortled. 'I did try to warn him.'

'Not too hard, if my memory serves me right.'

Ian sighed. 'We had some good times with those two.'

'Yes.' Toni didn't dare look at him. Sitting so close in the dark, she could feel the electricity crackle between them. She inhaled deeply. He still wore the same cologne. The one she'd bought him.

'We had a lot of good times.' Ian laid his hand on hers.

Toni snatched it away. 'Don't.' This was ridiculous! What was he playing at? For years he'd treated her like something that had crept out of the woodwork. And now this.

'Don't what?' Ian's voice was soft and caressing.

'I think I preferred it when you were horrible to me.'

'Did you?'

'Oh, stop this, Ian. What are you trying to achieve? Maybe you've had a tiff with Carla and you're looking for something or someone to amuse you.'

Ian's fingers tightened on the steering-wheel. 'I was just making conversation. And no, Carla and I haven't had a tiff. In fact, she's probably waiting up for me. She doesn't like going to bed alone.'

Toni tried to ignore the red-hot jealousy that coursed through her.

'No doubt Theo's waiting up for you too.' Ian turned on to Griffith Avenue and pulled up with a jerk in front of the house.

Toni looked at him sadly. 'Goodnight, Ian. Thanks for the lift.'

He looked as if he were about to say something but changed his mind.

'What?' Toni prompted hopefully. She couldn't help it. She didn't want him to go like this. She wanted to grab his hand back.

'Nothing. Goodnight, Toni. Take care of yourself.'

Toni stumbled out of the car. 'Goodnight,' she said softly, as he drove off into the night.

Chapter Seventeen

Wednesday, 19 July

Jade insisted on walking Sandra to her bus-stop. She was a little unsteady on her feet and Jade felt responsible. But Sandra had enjoyed herself and had seemed oblivious to the tension. Jade plunged her hands deep into her pockets and wandered back towards her flat. It wasn't very far and walking on a beautiful night like this was preferable to sitting on a stuffy bus. The evening had gone very well, she reflected, until Aidan was mentioned. She couldn't blame Toni for being annoyed. She had thought of inviting her to the funeral but dismissed the idea: she didn't need Aidan and Toni reminiscing over a few drinks. Who knew what skeletons might have come out of the cupboard? And with the likes of Aidan's aunt around to listen in, it would have been asking for trouble. No, she had done the right thing.

But, on the other hand, Toni *was* her best friend and had trusted her with all the miserable secrets surrounding her marriage. Was she being disloyal in not returning the confidence?

Jade sighed as she turned into her narrow street. It went against the grain to talk about herself and her problems. And even though Aidan had let her

down, she didn't want other people passing judge-
ment on him. She would do anything to protect him
from that.

'Please stay, Aidan. What's the point of us living sep-
arately? Two can live as cheaply as one,' Ann said
persuasively.

'Like I say, Ann, I'm travelling a lot at the moment.
There's plenty of work in Cork.'

'Which is all the more reason for you to sell your
place in Dublin.'

Aidan scratched his head and shuffled uncomfortably.

Ann watched him speculatively. She had been convinced that he was living with another woman and that
that was why he'd stayed away so long. Their mother
had made it quite clear that she thought he was mad to
break up with Jade and he wouldn't have dared bring
home a replacement. Still, there had been no girlfriend
at the funeral – just Jade. And they had seemed quite
comfortable together. So the other woman – if she'd
ever existed – seemed to be gone. Perhaps there was
some hope of reconciliation, and especially if he was
living here at home where she could keep an eye on
him, Ann thought.

'I'm a bit nervous on my own,' she said quietly, trying
a different tack.

'Oh, love, there's nothing to be nervous about. You
have the alarm, and Caesar to look after you.' He
reached down and fondled the Alsatian's ear.

'Yes, of course. And you have your own life to lead.'

Aidan sighed. 'You're right, Ann. It makes sense for me to move in. I'll get my stuff tomorrow.'

Ann flew across the room and threw her arms around him. 'Oh, thanks, Aidan! I'll feel so much safer with you here, and it won't be as lonely.'

Aidan stroked her hair. 'You've always got me, no matter what happens.'

Toni undressed, then paused before putting on her pyjamas. She studied herself critically in the mirror. Did Ian see much of a change in her? She had put on a few pounds since they'd been together, but otherwise she hadn't changed much. Her hips were a little fleshy and slightly broader, but her breasts were still small and high. And her waist was narrow, though not as narrow as Carla's. That woman was like a tiny doll. And although Toni knew she was a few years older, she didn't look it. She probably had wrinkles under all that makeup, she thought, as she dressed for bed, then laughed at her childishness.

But when she turned off the light and curled up in bed she remembered Ian's smell and the look in his eyes, and wondered, if she'd left his hand on hers and hadn't mentioned Carla, how the evening might have ended. Would he have turned into a dark alley or asked to see her again? Did he still have feelings for her? She plumped the pillow angrily. He was living with Carla – why was she even thinking like this? Even when she did leave Theo, the last thing she needed was another relationship.

Suddenly, she felt a strong urge to talk to her mother,

which took her by surprise. Toni and her mother had grown apart since her marriage and were more like polite strangers than mother and daughter. She'd go and visit her. Toni's heart lightened at the prospect. She closed her eyes and slept.

Ian let himself into the apartment and threw his keys on to the hall table. He walked through to the kitchen to fix himself a drink, flicking the switch on the answering-machine as he passed. Carla's voice filled the room. 'Hi, honey, it's me. You said you'd call.' Her sexy voice was reproachful. 'But I forgive you. Come over tomorrow evening. We can catch up. 'Bye.'

Ian sighed as he poured a large whiskey. Sometimes he found Carla a little too clingy. She wanted him to spend every free moment with her when sometimes all he wanted to do was fall asleep in front of *Match of the Day*. He'd lied to Toni in letting her believe that he and Carla were living together. God forbid. He chuckled as he carried his glass into the bedroom. As if Toni cared. She'd made her feelings quite clear seven years ago when she'd walked out on him. He tossed back the drink, stripped naked and threw himself on the unmade bed. He was a pathetic old man still clinging to dreams that the love of his life would come back to him. He'd only stayed in this flat because, if he closed his eyes and concentrated really hard, he could see Toni floating around the bedroom in one of his shirts. Or standing beside him in the kitchen, barefoot, drinking a mug of coffee while he made breakfast. He sighed heavily. It was time he grew up. And maybe he should show Carla a bit more consideration. They'd been together for over a year now. Perhaps he should move in with her. She was quite a nice woman once you got past the hard veneer. He turned over on his side and closed his eyes. He'd call her in the morning and arrange for them to spend the weekend together. And then, maybe . . . He slept.

Sandra turned off the light in the kitchen and carried her cocoa upstairs. She was feeling decidedly groggy. It wasn't a bad feeling, just different. It had been a long time since she'd had more than a couple of glasses of wine and tonight she hadn't a clue how much she'd drunk. Either Jade or Toni had been topping up her glass whenever she looked. It had been red wine, which she never usually drank, but it had given her a nice warm glow. She tiptoed past her mother's door and went into her bedroom. It had been so kind of Jade to see her to the bus-stop. There had been no need, of course. She was a bit unsteady but that was all. Still, it was nice having someone fuss over her. It was just so weird that it should have been Jade. She had never thought they would be friends. She'd hoped she'd get on with all the staff at the clinic but hadn't seen herself socialising with them. Vicky hardly talked to her and when she did it was usually to make a smart comment or tell her a dirty joke, which Sandra didn't like. And while she did like Toni, she was still the boss. Sandra was rather in awe of Jade: she was so attractive, gutsy and clever, she seemed to have everything. *You know different now, though,* she thought, as she undressed. Jade had problems, just like everyone else. She was just better at hiding them.

Sandra considered going back to the bathroom to take off her makeup, but she was too tired and, anyway, she might disturb her mother. She got into bed and took a sip of her cocoa. Maybe it would head off a hangover. Still, that would be a small price to pay for the great time she'd had. It had been so different from her nights out with Susan and Caroline. No drunken flirting with anything in trousers. No moaning and gossiping about their partners. Though she was a bit disappointed that Toni hadn't talked about Theo French. She was fascinated by that marriage, but Toni had hardly mentioned him. Sandra hadn't found out any more about Aidan Peters either, though she thought it strange that Jade hadn't told Toni about his mother passing away. Maybe they weren't as close as she had thought. Maybe she and Jade were destined to become firm friends. She smiled as she finished her cocoa, chuffed at the thought. And it would be nice to go out regularly again. Her mother had been right. She'd talk to Jade tomorrow about arranging another night out next week.

Sandra turned off the light, closed her eyes and snuggled down under the covers.

Chapter Eighteen

Saturday, 12 August

Jade was just back from the launderette when Patsy informed her that her husband was downstairs again. The woman had hung around the hall watching curiously as Jade shepherded Aidan quickly upstairs. His visit was unexpected but Jade was surprised to realise that she was happy to see him. He sat down in her chair while she perched on the edge of the bed.

'How are you—'

'You look well—'

They broke off and laughed awkwardly.

'You first,' Aidan prompted.

'I was just asking how you were doing. And how is Ann?'

'We're okay. Ann's going through Mother's clothes at the moment.'

'That can't be easy.'

'No. Margaret offered to help but Ann wouldn't hear of it. She said Mother would haunt her.'

Jade laughed. 'She's probably right, but tell her to give me a call if she wants any help.'

'Thanks.'

Jade stood up and went to the press. 'Would you like

a drink? I'm afraid this is all I've got.' She took down the bottle of vodka and two glasses.

'I'd prefer a cup of tea.'

Jade glanced at him but said nothing. She put on the kettle, fiddling around with the plug until she was sure it was working.

'I'll take a look at that for you. It could be dangerous,' Aidan said.

'Everything in this place is dangerous,' Jade responded. She put away the vodka and took down two mugs instead.

When the tea was made, she sat down and stared into her mug. Their meetings over the last two years had been acrimonious, angry and emotional. It was strange to be sitting here now as if they were distant acquaintances.

'Ann wants me to stay.'

Jade looked up. 'And will you?'

'I may as well. I can't stay at Gerry's for ever.'

It made sense for him to go home, but Jade wondered if it would be the end of him altogether. Ann would wait on him hand and foot, and he'd probably sit in front of the TV all day and let her.

'You don't think I should?' Aidan had read her thoughts.

'It's none of my business, Aidan. You're a grown man.'

'But you think I'll just sponge off her, don't you?'

'I never said that!' But Jade couldn't meet his eyes.

Aidan put down his mug and rubbed his eyes. 'I know I've made a mess of my life, Jade, but I think this might be a chance of a new start for me. Ann thinks I'm working – I told her I travel around the country a lot.

So that's what I'm going to do.'

'Oh?'

Aidan nodded. 'There's a guy I went to college with – Dave Bell – who has his own business in Thurles. He needs someone to cover the Leinster area for him.'

'He's offered you the job?'

'It's mine if I want it.'

'But can you ... do you think ...' Jade searched for the right words.

'I'm going to try, Jade. I owe it to you, to Ann—'

'You owe it to yourself, Aidan. You have to do this for you and no one else.'

'That's what they say in the meetings.'

'So, you're still going?' Jade felt guilty. She had always been ready to believe the worst of him. But then, she reminded herself, he'd given her good cause to.

'I did miss a few,' he admitted. 'Sometimes it got on top of me. I'd lost you, my business, my family, and I didn't see the point in making an effort.'

'And now?'

'I've got Ann to think of. She needs me.'

'Ann may not be on her own for ever,' Jade warned him. 'She's a lovely girl and she won't always want to live with her big brother.'

'I'm not stupid, Jade. Of course I realise that. But right now, she needs me. I'm not going to let her down.'

Jade saw the determined set of his jaw and her eyes filled with tears. She was happy for him but she felt bitter too. He hadn't thought twice about letting her down. His wife and home hadn't kept him from going off the rails. When times had been tough, he hadn't thought of her and the effects his actions would have on their marriage. No, he'd just slunk off to the racecourse or the bookie's and lost their home and their life savings.

'I want to repay you too,' Aidan said. 'When I see you living in this dump it makes me sick. I've dragged you down to this. You should be living in luxury.'

Jade's eyes hardened. 'I should be in the house you built for us.'

'I'm sorry, Jade. What more can I say?'

Jade pulled herself together and managed a wintry smile. 'Nothing. I'm glad you're going to make the effort for Ann. I wish you the best of luck. Just don't hurt her . . .'

'. . . the way I hurt you,' Aidan finished for her. 'I haven't gambled since the day my mother died, Jade. And I hope I never will again. I'm going to try, and I'll keep going to the meetings. I can't say more than that.'

'No, you can't. What is it they say? One day at a time?'

Toni stood in Arrivals and watched the screen. Finally, the flight from Paris had landed – an hour later than it had been expected. She'd already phoned Alice to tell her to hold dinner. She'd call her again from the car when they were on their way.

'Toni?' Daniel was pushing his way to her side. 'God, it's bedlam here.'

'It always is. Is Meg not with you?'

'Lord, no. She's at home preparing the fatted calf.'

'Alice is the same. You'd think they'd been away for years instead of six weeks.'

'Still, I missed Mark,' Daniel admitted.

'Yeah. I missed Chloe too.' Toni was looking forward to seeing her stepdaughter again. But she was also dreading the conversation they would have to have.

'Here they come.' Daniel moved forward as a large group of teenagers came through the doors. There was a lot of laughing and hugging before they turned to seek out parents and family.

Toni stared at the sophisticated young woman approaching her. 'Chloe?'

Chloe put a hand self-consciously to her cropped hair. 'Do you like it?'

'Yes, I do.' Toni couldn't stop staring at Theo's daughter in her black jeans and tight black sleeveless T-shirt. The sleek haircut showed off her wonderful bone structure and large blue eyes. 'You look marvellous!'

Chloe inspected her stepmother, eyes narrowed. 'You've lost weight. Are you working too hard? Has minding Alice been too much for you?'

'Everything's fine, but I'm glad you're home. And Alice can't wait to see you.'

'Hi, Toni.' Mark came over and slipped an arm round his girlfriend.

Toni smiled at the tall, handsome young man. 'Hello, Mark. Did you have a good time?'

'Well, it was hard work. But we managed to fit in a bit of sightseeing.'

'And some socialising, no doubt,' Daniel said drily.

'We always seemed to be laughing,' Chloe told him. 'There was a great atmosphere there.'

'Well, I'm glad to hear it went well,' Daniel said, 'but

I'd better get you home, Mark, or your mother will go mad.'

Mark bent to kiss Chloe lightly on the lips. 'I'll call you later.'

Chloe smiled up into his eyes. 'Okay. 'Bye.'

Toni took command of the trolley and led the way out to the car.

'How's Dad?' It hadn't occurred to Chloe that her father would be at the airport to meet her. She knew he wouldn't have time.

'Great,' Toni replied lightly. 'Unfortunately he has to go out tonight but he said he'd try to get home a bit early to say hello before he went.'

'I'm honoured.'

Toni looked at her but there was no acrimony behind Chloe's sarcasm.

'And Alice?'

'Wonderful. She's come on in leaps and bounds since the plaster came off. And she's very good about doing her exercises. The hardest part is stopping her doing too much.'

'You two seem to be getting on much better.'

'We are. We've spent so much time together since you left.'

'So I did you a favour by going to France.'

'Maybe.' Toni stopped beside the car and switched off the alarm. 'I hope all your stuff fits in.'

Chloe had left six weeks ago with a large rucksack but seemed to have accumulated a few more bags in France. 'I went a bit wild in Paris,' Chloe admitted. 'I hardly spent any money in the country so I had a major spending spree when I hit the city.'

Toni laughed. 'That seems reasonable.'

'The shops are just amazing. And the shoes were gorgeous.' She giggled. 'It's just as well Ollie didn't come with us. She'd have spent a small fortune.'

'I'm sure Ollie could do that on a desert island,' Toni said wryly, as she crammed the last bag into the back seat. 'Okay. Let's go. I hope you're hungry. Alice has been cooking all day.'

'I promise to eat every morsel. Oh, it's nice to be home.'

'Will you be saying that next Wednesday?' Toni asked, concerned. The exam results would be out and she had thought Chloe might be apprehensive.

'You mean my results? Well, there's nothing I can do now so there's no point in worrying about it.'

Toni was surprised by her composure. 'Well, France has had a settling effect on you. Or is Mark responsible for the new laid-back Chloe French?'

Chloe blushed. 'A little of both. He's so great, Toni. It would be wonderful if we could go to the same college.'

'Let me guess,' Toni said, 'he wants to go to UCD.'

Chloe nodded glumly. 'I don't suppose Dad's changed his thinking on that score, has he?' Theo was adamant that she follow in his footsteps and go to Trinity.

'We haven't discussed it,' Toni replied honestly. She had hardly seen Theo in the last few weeks, let alone talked to him.

'Well, maybe I won't get enough points to go to Trinity.'

Toni glanced sharply at her.

'Look, Chloe, you're very young, and if you seriously

want to do medicine you have to give it your best shot. Even if you and Mark attend the same college you're not going to be able to spend much time together. It's going to be hard work.'

'Yeah. That's what Mark says.'

'Well, thank goodness he's being sensible about it.'

'Oh, Toni, don't nag. You know what I'm saying. If we were in the same college we could have lunch together, meet for coffee. But if I'm in the city and he's all the way out there we'll never see each other.'

'Don't be so dramatic,' Toni said briskly, as she turned on to Griffith Avenue. 'And if you want to persuade your dad to let you go to UCD, you'd better come up with a better argument than that.'

'Speak of the devil,' Chloe murmured, as Theo's Mercedes turned into the driveway in front of them. 'Daddy!' she cried, jumped out of the car and ran to greet him.

Toni grinned as she watched Theo hug his daughter. 'Now, *that* kind of behaviour will get you a lot further, Chloe!' she murmured to herself, as she climbed out of the car and started to unload her stepdaughter's bags.

Chapter Nineteen

Tuesday, 15 August

Sandra hummed happily as she went through the morning post. She had always been a morning person and the sun streaming into Reception added to her good mood. She smiled as Jade walked through the door. 'Morning, Jade—' She broke off to answer the phone. 'Hello, Blessington Clinic, can I help you?'

Jade flashed her a smile. 'Morning,' she whispered

'Jade?' Toni stuck her head out of the office. 'Have you got a minute?'

'Sure,' Jade said easily, and followed her inside. 'How are things?'

Toni walked back round her desk and sat down. 'Not bad. Chloe's home.'

'You don't sound very happy about it.'

'Oh, I am. It's just . . .'

'You're not looking forward to telling her you're leaving.'

Toni threw her pen on to the desk and looked miserably at her friend. 'I'm dreading it, but I've decided to wait until after she gets her results.'

'You're just finding reasons to put it off, Toni. Are you sure you *want* to leave?'

'Yes! That is, I'm sure I want to leave Theo, but I wish it didn't mean leaving Chloe too.'

'She might decide to move in with you.'

'Over Theo's dead body,' Toni said darkly. She could think of nothing that would enrage him more than for his daughter to choose her over him.

'He'd get over it.'

'Anyway, that's not what I wanted to talk to you about.'

'Oh?'

'It's Vicky.'

Jade groaned. 'What now?'

'She's asked for a few days off.'

'*What?*' Jade exploded. 'She can't! That's not on, Toni. Anyway she's just back from a long weekend.'

'Yes, I know that, but she says she has problems at home.'

'Yeah, right.'

'Look, I can't call her a liar, can I? I'll phone the agency and get someone in to cover for her.'

'Good, because I'm not going to.'

'Okay, okay. Keep your hair on.'

'Sorry. It's just that she's always taking advantage. We'd be better off without her.'

'The thought had occurred to me,' admitted Toni, 'though I'm not sure Robert would agree.'

'Tough.'

Toni put her head on one side. Jade had a point. Hiring and firing *was* her responsibility, once she'd agreed it with Daniel. 'You're right, Jade, but I'll have to go through the proper channels first. I need to give Vicky a formal warning in writing. Can you put together a note detailing any cock-ups she's been responsible for? I'll go through her attendance record.'

Jade was smiling broadly now. 'It would be my pleasure.'

Toni's phone rang. 'Hello? Toni Jordan.'

'Hi, Toni. It's Ian.'

'Oh, hi.'

'I'll go,' Jade mouthed, and left the room.

'Toni?'

'Yes, sorry. There was someone with me. What can I do for you?'

Ian laughed. 'Well, I'm not looking for a nose job, if that's what you're asking.'

'Oh, I don't know. A nose job might not be such a bad idea.'

'Cheek. I have a Roman nose—'

'Roaming all over your face, yeah, I know. Lord, your jokes don't get any better, do they?'

'But I made you laugh.' Ian's voice was soft and warm.

Toni held the phone tight to her ear and closed her eyes. 'I'm sorry I was a bit narky with you the other night. It was very nice of you to give me a lift.'

'I'm a very nice guy.'

'Yes, you are.' Toni's voice was barely a whisper.

'I want to see you, Toni,' Ian said quickly.

'Oh, I don't think—'

'Don't *think*, Toni, just say yes. Please?'

'Yes.'

'What?'

'I'll meet you.'

'The Beachcomber, tomorrow night?' Ian said.

Toni looked at the diary in front of her. 'No, I can't. Look, what about lunch on Friday? One o'clock?'

'Fine. See you then.'

Toni put down the phone. What on earth had she done? A shiver of excitement ran through her, quickly followed by guilt. What was she doing meeting her ex? 'It's only lunch,' she murmured, in an effort to calm herself. 'There's nothing wrong with having lunch with an old friend. As long as it's all above board.' But she knew she wasn't going to tell anyone she was meeting him. Not even Jade.

After Ian's call Toni threw herself into researching Vicky's attendance records. She was shocked at the pattern that emerged. Maybe it was because she was so preoccupied lately but she hadn't realised how often the girl had been off sick without medical certificates. She should have paid more attention to Jade. The report she'd put together on Vicky was even more incriminating.

'It's a bit drastic, isn't it?' Daniel stared at Toni. He'd been about to head home when she'd come to him with her findings.

'Read it, Daniel. The girl has screwed up a number of times – she could even have put lives in danger. She's always late and her attendance record has been getting steadily worse.'

Daniel sighed. 'What do you want me to do?'

'Nothing.'

'Oh?' Daniel looked relieved.

'I just need your agreement. I want to have a chat with her. Present her with a written warning and give her a month to sort herself out.'

Daniel stroked his beard. 'Seems reasonable.'

'Right.' Toni stood up. 'I'll talk to her as soon as she gets back.'

'Did you enjoy that?' Mark held Chloe's hand tightly as they walked out of the cinema.

'Not really.' It had been her idea to go and see *The Patriot*. She thought it would take their minds off the exam results. It hadn't worked: she couldn't concentrate on the story at all. 'Did you?'

'Mel Gibson was good,' Mark replied, without enthusiasm.

'What time are you going in tomorrow?' Chloe returned to the subject preoccupying them both.

'First thing. I couldn't wait any longer.'

'I know what you mean. Will you meet me afterwards?'

'Of course! But won't your dad expect you to come straight back?'

'He'll be at work. I have to phone him. *And* Toni. *And* Alice.'

'Yeah, I have to call Mam and Dad too,' said Mark.

'Do you think you did well?' Chloe hadn't asked before. Mark was so clever and he'd worked hard.

'I think so. Whether it will be good enough to get me a place to do computer science at UCD is another thing.'

'You'll get in,' Chloe told him confidently, 'though I wish you'd applied to Trinity. That would sort out all our problems.'

Mark laughed. 'Some chance! I'll be bloody lucky if

I get enough points to make UCD. I wouldn't have a hope of getting into Trinity. You're the brainy one in this partnership.'

'Rubbish.' Chloe punched his arm lightly.

'It's true. And it's nothing to be ashamed of, Chloe.' He hugged her affectionately. 'I'm proud of you.'

Chloe smiled. 'I'm not sure there's anything to be proud of. Sometimes I feel really confident that I did well, and then I start to have doubts.'

'That's only natural. Look, let's go for a beer and then I'll bring you home.'

Chloe glanced at her watch. It was only ten o'clock. 'Okay. Just one, though.'

After a solitary dinner Toni sat down in front of the TV and flicked idly through the channels. Thankfully Theo had taken himself off to his study some time ago and she was able to relax. Although now that Alice had gone home and Chloe was out most nights she felt a bit lonely. She'd grown to quite enjoy having Alice around. She chuckled softly. Who'd have thought it?

Theo put his head round the sitting-room door. 'Isn't Chloe home yet?' His voice was cold and accusing.

'No.' Toni didn't take her eyes off the TV screen.

'Well, where is she? Didn't you ask where she was going?'

Toni wondered when his daughter's whereabouts had become her sole responsibility. 'She and Mark went to the cinema.'

Theo snorted. 'She spends too much time with that boy.'

'He seems very nice.'

'I don't care how nice he is. He's a distraction. She's too young to be in a serious relationship.'

'So you'd prefer her to be out clubbing with a different guy every week like Ollie?'

'Chloe would never do that.'

Toni switched off the TV and stood up. She wasn't going to have yet another pointless argument. 'Look, Chloe will be out celebrating with her friends tomorrow night so I was going to organise a family dinner for Friday. Do you think you could squeeze that into your busy schedule?'

Theo smiled broadly. 'How could I resist a cosy dinner with my daughter and my loving wife? Of course I'll be there. But please leave the cooking to Alice.'

'I'm booking a restaurant,' Toni said stiffly, resisting his attempt to draw her into a slanging match. 'Alice deserves a night out too.'

Theo stared at her. 'Why the hell would we bring her?'

'Because Chloe wants her there and it's her night. Now I'm going to bed.'

'Shall I come with you?' He moved closer to her, tucking a tendril of hair behind her ear and running his fingers down her neck.

Toni shivered. 'Go to hell.'

Theo tut-tutted. 'My dear Toni, be careful, you might hurt my feelings.'

'What feelings are those?' Toni walked out of the room, his harsh laughter ringing in her ears. 'Sick bastard,' she muttered, as she climbed the stairs. She went into her room and, after a moment's hesitation, turned the key in the lock. Sometimes, she realised, he actually scared her. She hoped he didn't sense it. That would give him a real kick. She took off her clothes, tugged her hair out of its tight little bun and massaged her neck. She froze as she heard him come upstairs then quickly pulled on her pyjamas. She held her breath when his step paused outside her door and watched the door handle nervously. But moments later she heard his own door closing. She fell back against the pillow and closed her eyes, pulling the duvet around her protectively. It seemed unbelievable that she was lying here trembling, her door locked against her husband, a man she'd once loved but now despised and feared. She turned off the light, buried her face in the pillow and banished Theo from her mind.

Instead, she thought about lunch on Friday with Ian. She was looking forward to it, as a teenager would to her first date. But it wasn't a first date. She had a long history with Ian Chase. And it seemed that all she could think about today – when she wasn't trying to bury Vicky Harrison – was the love she'd shared with him. The incredible, fierce passion when they'd first met that had them pulling off each other's clothes almost as soon as they touched. There had been one occasion – which still made her blush to think of it – when they were having dinner together at the Grand Hotel in Malahide. They had barely eaten anything because they couldn't keep their eyes and hands off each other. Finally, Ian excused himself and came back a few minutes later with a key.

Wordlessly, Toni had stood up and taken his hand. She laughed as she remembered them calling Room

Service several hours later when their appetites had mysteriously returned.

Long after she heard Chloe come home she tossed and turned. Her thoughts tumbled between Theo and Ian, one moment guilty, then sad, and angry. Finally, exhausted, she drifted into a fitful sleep, her dreams as troubled as her thoughts.

Wednesday, 16 August

Chloe went round to Ollie's house first thing the next morning and they trudged off to school together. Many of their classmates were there before them and they soon lost each other in the hustle and bustle. Chloe had only just opened her envelope when Ollie came shrieking towards her.

'Chloe! Chloe! I did it! I can't believe it!' She danced Chloe around the corridor.

Chloe pulled away laughing. 'That's great, Ollie.'

'What about you?'

'Not bad,' Chloe admitted shyly. 'I haven't figured out the exact number of points yet so I'm not sure if I've enough for Trinity.'

'You will,' Ollie said confidently. Then understanding dawned as she saw the look on Chloe's face. 'You were *hoping* you'd only have enough for a place at UCD, weren't you?'

Chloe grinned sheepishly. 'Well . . .'

'You know you were kidding yourself, don't you?' Ollie said matter-of-factly. 'Even if they hadn't offered you a place immediately, you'd definitely have been included in the second round.'

'I suppose.'

Ollie shook her head at Chloe's downcast expression. 'For God's sake, Chlo, look around you! There are girls devastated because they didn't do well and you're moaning because you did *too* well!'

'Sorry. It's just that—'

'You want to be with Mark. I know, I know.' Ollie grabbed her arm and led her out into the sunshine. She was heartily fed up of Chloe going on and on about her beloved boyfriend. 'But it's unlikely that that's going to happen. So forget about it and let's concentrate on where we're going tonight.'

'I need to ask Mark—'

'Give me a break, Chloe!' Ollie exploded. 'Tonight is a girls' night. Anyway, I'm sure Mark will want to be out with his own friends.'

'I'll check. I'm meeting him in town in an hour.'

Ollie sighed. 'Well, okay, then. I have to go home now anyway. Mum will be in a tizzy wondering what's happening.'

'You can use my mobile to call her if you want,' Chloe offered.

'Nah.' Ollie grinned wickedly. 'I want to see the look on her face!'

Chloe watched her friend bounce off towards the bus stop and sighed. Ollie was going to Dublin City University to do a BSc in multimedia. 'Next stop, day-time TV. Then, I think, my own talk show,' Ollie had told her.

Chloe didn't doubt it. With Ollie's personality and extraordinarily hard neck, success was a certainty. Chloe phoned her father's office and waited for Emma to put her through. With Ollie in DCU in Glasnevin and Mark in Clonskeagh, she was going to be lonely.

'Hello, Dad? Yeah. I got it.'

Mark stared moodily into his coffee while his mother and Chloe exchanged worried looks.

'I'm sure you'll get in, Mark,' Chloe repeated desperately.

'Of course he will,' Meg Wheeler said smiling. 'Daniel says it's a given. You have four hundred and twenty points—'

'Four hundred and fifteen,' Mark corrected her.

'I'm sure that's enough to get you a place,' Chloe assured him.

Mark glowered at her. She'd have been desolate if she was in his position.

Chloe saw his expression and hurriedly changed the subject. 'Where are you going tonight? Ollie says all the girls are heading for the Red Box.'

'I don't think I'll bother.'

'Don't be ridiculous,' his mother said briskly. 'Justin and Luke will be expecting you to go out with them.'

'I'm looking forward to it,' Chloe lied. 'There should be a great atmosphere in town.'

Meg nodded approvingly. Thank goodness Mark was going out with such a nice girl. Daniel wasn't too keen on her because she was Theo French's daughter, but Meg thought they made a lovely couple. She sighed. Mark was still so young but she had only been seventeen when she had started to date his father. 'You listen to Chloe,' she told her son gently. 'There's no point in worrying until the places are offered next week. You may as well enjoy yourself tonight.'

Mark smiled reluctantly. 'Okay, Mum. But when the cops haul me home for being drunk and disorderly, remember it was your idea.'

Meg tousled his hair affectionately. 'Tell them to keep you in a cell till morning. I need my beauty sleep!'

Chapter Twenty

Friday, 18 August

Toni sat listening with only half an ear as the account-ant droned on. All she could think about was Ian and their proposed lunch meeting. She had been crazy to agree to it in the first place. Between worrying about that and the cosy little family dinner that she'd planned for tonight it was no wonder she couldn't concentrate on her work. When the meeting was over she escaped to the privacy of her office but within seconds there was a tap on the door and Sandra was smiling down at her. 'I have some messages for you.'

Toni took the page. 'Thanks, Sandra.'

'So, does Monday suit you?'

Toni looked blank. 'Sorry?'

Sandra sighed. 'For our night out.'

'Oh, eh, I'm not sure. Chloe's all worked up about her college applications and the first offers come out on Monday. I'd better not make any plans.'

'Okay, then, how about Tuesday? Jade said either Monday or Tuesday was good for her.'

Toni stood up abruptly. 'I just don't know, Sandra. Why don't you and Jade go ahead? If I can make it, I will.'

Sandra stared after her. Every time she thought she was getting close to Toni, the shutters came down again.

'What's up?' Jade put down a pile of files on Sandra's desk.

'Oh, nothing. I was just asking Toni about going out next week.'

'Is Monday okay with her?'

'No, and she's not sure about Tuesday either. She said we should go ahead without her.'

Jade frowned. It had been Toni's idea to invite Sandra out with them again. Surely she wasn't still annoyed about the business with Aidan. 'I'll have a word with her. Why don't you go ahead and book the restaurant?'

'China World?' Sandra asked, knowing it was Jade's favourite.

Jade thought of her bank balance. 'Yes.' She crossed Reception to Toni's office, tapped perfunctorily on the door and walked in.

Toni looked up irritably. 'What is it, Jade?'

'Just wondering about dinner next week.'

Toni looked pointedly at her watch. 'I told Sandra I'm not sure if I'm free. Look, I have an awful lot to do—'

'Have I done something? Is this about Aidan?'

'No, of course not. Honestly, Jade, I just have a lot on my mind at the moment.'

Jade wasn't entirely convinced. 'Want to talk about it?'

'No, look, I just need some space.'

'Fine. You know where I am. See ya.' Jade closed the door behind her with an angry snap.

Toni flung her pen on to the desk. She hadn't meant to be ratty. She picked up the phone and dialled. 'Mr Ian Chase, please.'

'I'm afraid Mr Chase isn't in today,' the receptionist replied pleasantly. 'May I take a message?'

'No, I'll call again.' Toni put down the phone and stared at it. Then she picked it up and dialled Ian's home number. After two rings she got the answering-machine. She thought of leaving a message but what if Carla heard it? She hung up and looked at the clock on the wall. Midday. She'd have to meet him. But she wouldn't stay: she'd just explain and apologise and get out of there as quickly as she could.

'I wish Mark was coming with us tonight,' Chloe said moodily, as she watched Alice put the soda bread in the oven and wipe her hands on her apron.

'Don't be silly, love,' Alice said, ignoring the girl's sulky pout. 'There's a time for boyfriends and a time for family. Anyway, I doubt he'd enjoy it much. Your father would probably spend the evening grilling him about his intentions.'

Despite herself Chloe giggled. 'Yeah. Poor Mark gets an earful every time Dad answers the phone. He saw him in the hospital last week but he scarpered down the corridor before Dad could collar him.'

'Sensible lad,' Alice said drily and then, remembering her position, added, 'although it's only natural that your father wants to get to know him.'

'I suppose. But I still don't think tonight's going to be much fun.'

Alice eyed her over her glasses. 'Of course it will. Won't I be there?'

Chloe hugged her. 'Yeah, sorry. And at least we're not going to one of Dad's fancy restaurants.'

'Where are we going?' Alice had been told the name of the restaurant but her memory wasn't what it used to be.

'Jasko's Bistro in Dame Street. You'll love it, Alice. There's a great atmosphere. Ollie's folks took us there a couple of times.'

'Sounds fancy,' Alice said dubiously.

'Fish is their speciality,' Chloe assured her.

'I do like fish,' Alice admitted.

'There you go. Now I'm going to call Ollie. She's going out tonight too. Maybe we could all meet up afterwards. That would be cool,'

Alice smiled as she watched her leave. It was unlikely that Mr French would think it 'cool' to meet up with Ollie and her family. Although, given how bad things were between him and Toni, he'd probably welcome the distraction.

'Are you sure this is a good idea?' Alice had asked Toni, as they strolled home from Mass the previous Sunday. Toni had just told her of the dinner she was planning.

Toni had linked her arm through Alice's as they came to some rough pavement. 'Probably not, but what choice have I? We must celebrate Chloe's exam results and it might be easier in a restaurant.'

'Where everyone's forced to be on their best behaviour?'

'Exactly.'

'You're going to have to talk to her soon. She's already suspicious.'

'I thought I calmed her down on that. Do you think she's still concerned?'

'I know it. And once all the fuss about college has died down she's going to start asking questions.'

'Then I'd better figure out some answers,' Toni said worriedly.

'You're definitely going, then?'

'I don't see what else I can do, Alice. Things have gone from bad to worse.'

'Then you must do what you think best, dear, and don't let anyone tell you otherwise.'

'Thank you, Alice. You've been a tower of strength these last few weeks.'

'Sure what have I done?'

'Well, I'm going to Mass again – and I haven't done that in years.'

'You only started because I couldn't walk and you brought me in the car. And I'm very grateful.'

'You're welcome – and maybe that was true to begin with, but now I enjoy it.'

'The Lord works in mysterious ways.' Alice had smiled knowingly.

'My mother would be amazed.'

'How is your mother?'

'We haven't spoken in a while,' Toni had admitted.

'That's a pity.'

'Alice, how come you can be so noncommittal and

still make me feel as if you're scolding me?'

'That's not me, that's your conscience talking.'

'You're wasted on housekeeping, Alice Scully. You should have your own chat show. Or, at the very least, be writing a problem page for one of the tabloids.'

Alice had allowed herself a small smile. 'I just speak as I find.'

'I must introduce you to my friend Dotty Price. You two would get on like a house on fire.'

Toni walked into the pub and blinked as her eyes adjusted to the gloom after the bright sunshine outside.

'Toni? Over here.'

She swung around to see Ian sitting in 'their' corner, at the table where they had sat the first time he had asked her out. She stared at him and, for a moment, considered turning tail.

Ian stood up and came towards her. 'What can I get you?'

'I'm not sure . . .'

'It's only lunch, Toni,' he said gently, leading her to the table. 'I'm not going to eat you. Unless you ask me to.' He grinned wickedly at her.

'Ian!' Toni looked around nervously.

Ian held up his hands. 'Sorry, sorry. Just a joke. Now, come on, what would you like?'

'Eh, a ham and cheese sandwich and a mineral water.' Toni lowered herself into a chair.

Ian watched her perch awkwardly on the edge of the seat, as though she might take flight at any moment.

'Wouldn't you like something a bit stronger?'

'I have a lot of work to do this afternoon,' she said curtly. 'In fact, I can't stay long. I shouldn't even be here.'

'I'm very glad you are,' Ian said, dropping a light kiss on her cheek before going up to the bar.

Toni touched the spot where he'd kissed her and stared after him. He hadn't changed, still charming, still funny and still so handsome. Grey hair at his temples was the only indicator of his age. His body was still lean, his eyes sparkled with the same good humour and his voice, if anything, had got deeper and sexier.

Toni tore her eyes away from him and began to shred a beermat. *Stop it, he's attached. This is just a friendly lunch between two old friends.* She jumped as Ian placed her glass in front of her and took the chair opposite. She tried not to look disappointed. He had always sat beside her. Very close beside her. Sometimes he'd even—

'Toni?' Ian was staring at her.

'Sorry! I was miles away. Just thinking about work.' She picked up her water hoping she could trust her trembling fingers.

'How is everything at the Blessington?'

'Good.' She sighed. 'Well, no, to be honest. Things aren't going well just now.'

'Oh?'

She explained Daniel's new procedure and Robert's feelings about it.

'It's a difficult one,' Ian said, when she'd finished. 'Your patients are paying a lot of money and they don't want to have to wait weeks for their operations.'

'But don't you see . . .' Toni paused as their food

arrived. An unimaginative sandwich for her and a cottage pie with chips for him. She looked at his plate longingly.

Ian grinned at her. 'Would you like a chip?'

'No, thank you. As I was saying, I think the problem is – especially with some of our younger patients – they haven't really thought it through. Often it's just an attempt to quick-fix something else. A husband has walked out or is suspected of having an affair. A girl is teased at school. Surgery isn't going to solve their problems.'

'But that's not *your* problem,' Ian pointed out. 'I hate to say it but Robert is right. They're adults and it's up to them to take the decision. All you can do is make them aware of the dangers.'

'But what about Robert operating on overweight people and diabetics?'

Ian sobered. 'That's not on. If I were Daniel I'd tell him he was out the next time he stepped out of line. There are plenty of surgeons who'd jump into Robert's shoes. The Blessington is a cushy little number, especially given its central location.'

Toni nodded thoughtfully.

'Aren't you going to eat that?' Ian looked at her untouched sandwich.

'No. Maybe I'll have a chip after all.'

Ian laughed. 'This is like old times, sitting here putting the world to rights while you eat my chips.'

'It seems like a lifetime ago,' Toni murmured. When they had started seeing each other, they'd agreed to keep it quiet. The hospital was a hotbed of gossip and a senior doctor dating a secretary would have set tongues wagging. The Beachcomber had become their hideaway: it was far enough from the hospital to avoid meeting anyone, but near enough to allow them to escape for brief lunches.

'I miss you,' Ian said suddenly, his grey eyes intent.

'What about Carla?'

'Carla has nothing to do with us.'

Toni was bewildered. Where was he going with this? What did he expect? 'I doubt she'd see it that way,' she said, in an effort to break the spell he was casting over them.

'I don't want to talk about Carla,' he murmured, taking her hand and kissing the tips of her fingers. 'I want to talk about you. About us.'

Toni snatched away her hand, alarmed at the effect he was having on her. 'There is no us.'

'Isn't there?'

'No, there isn't. I'm married.' *Just about.* 'And you're attached. We were over a long time ago.'

Ian sat back in his chair. 'Okay, then. We'll just be friends.'

Toni looked at him suspiciously. 'What?'

'What's to stop us keeping in touch, having a bite of lunch occasionally? Let's be friends again, Toni. I miss talking to you.'

'We could never just be friends. We have too much history—'

Ian looked at her with raised eyebrows. 'Don't you trust yourself? Are you afraid that you won't be able to keep your hands off me?'

Toni sat on her hands, her cheeks red. 'You should be so lucky.'

'Then there isn't a problem, is there? Come on, Toni.'

Toni's resolve weakened. 'Okay, then. Friends.'

That evening, dressed in a simple blue cocktail dress, with her hair hanging loose around her shoulders, Toni paced the living room waiting for Theo and Chloe. She couldn't stop thinking about Ian and the mixed emotions that had engulfed her when he'd suggested they be friends. If she were to be completely honest the overriding emotion was disappointment. Why had he given in so easily? And why had she played hard to get? Her marriage to Theo was over and she didn't owe Carla any favours. But she knew that she wouldn't have been happy to share Ian. *So instead you're going to settle for friendship?* she taunted herself.

'Come on, Toni.' She started as Chloe appeared in the doorway. 'Dad's waiting in the car.'

'Coming.'

'I wish I had more time before college started,' Chloe complained, putting down her knife and fork. 'I really could do with a rest.'

Alice laughed. 'You're only just back from holiday.'

'That was hard work, Alice.'

'And you never enjoyed a minute of it,' Toni chimed in, with a tolerant smile.

Chloe grinned at her. 'Yeah, well, I suppose I might have.'

'You should count yourself lucky, young lady,' Alice

said gravely. 'There are plenty less fortunate than you.'

Chloe rolled her eyes at Toni. 'Yes, Alice.'

'Look at that poor woman who was in that terrible accident last night.'

'Where?' Chloe asked.

'Oh, I don't know, somewhere around Mount Street. It was on the news. The car was in a terrible state.'

'Yes, I heard about that,' Toni said. 'It's a wonder she got out alive.'

'She's alive?' Theo said faintly.

'Yes. Serious but stable, whatever that means. Apparently she just ploughed into a parked car.'

'She was probably pissed,' Chloe said knowingly.

'You don't know that, Miss,' Alice said reprovingly.

'No, sorry,' Chloe said meekly. 'How's the hake, Alice?'

'Lovely. Everything's lovely.' Alice looked appreciatively round the restaurant.

'What about you, Dad? Are the scallops good? Dad?'

Theo looked blankly at his daughter. 'Sorry?'

'Your dinner? Is it okay?'

'Oh, yes, fine.' He picked up a forkful distractedly.

'What about more wine?' Toni suggested hopefully. Dinner hadn't been quite the trial she'd expected but she could still do with another drink.

'Of course.' And, to Toni's surprise, he signalled the waiter to bring another bottle.

'So, what about it, Alice? Shall we go dancing?' Chloe swayed in her seat and giggled.

'I think I might slow you down just a bit. You should meet up with Ollie and go on somewhere with her.'

Chloe shot her a grateful look.

'Where were they eating?' Toni asked.

'The Clarence,' Chloe said eagerly. 'And then they were going on to the Shelbourne for drinks.'

Clever Chloe, Toni thought. Theo loved the Shelbourne Hotel. 'What do you say, Theo? Shall we go to the Shelbourne and meet Ollie and her parents?'

Theo watched the waiter top up their glasses and took a long drink.

'Theo?'

'Sorry, what was that?'

'I was suggesting that we meet Ollie and her parents in the Shelbourne for a drink.'

He looked momentarily disconcerted, then managed a polite smile. 'You go, but I'm afraid I must leave early.'

'Oh, Dad!'

'I'm sorry, Chloe, but I have a very early start in the morning.'

'But tomorrow is Saturday!'

'Sorry, darling, but I have to go to a conference in Oxford this weekend.'

Toni looked vaguely surprised. She didn't remember him saying anything about a conference. Still, she cheered up, it would be a lot easier for her if he did go home early. 'You go on home, Theo. We can get a taxi.'

'I'll escort you to the Shelbourne first and say hello to Ollie and her family.'

That was big of him, mused Toni. The wine must have gone to his head.

∞∞

An hour later they left for the Shelbourne. Then, after Theo had made a little small-talk and bought a round of drinks, he made his excuses.

'Thanks, Dad. It was a lovely evening.' Chloe reached up to kiss his cheek.

Her father held her to him tightly. 'I'm very proud of you, Chloe,' he said gruffly. 'Never forget that.'

Chloe looked up, and was startled to see tears in his eyes. 'Thanks, Dad. I love you.'

Theo gave her another quick hug, pecked his wife's cheek and left.

Toni relaxed visibly when he'd gone and chatted animatedly to Ollie's parents while Chloe and Ollie gabbled nineteen to the dozen. Alice took a sip of her port, and within seconds was dozing peacefully.

Chloe nudged Toni with a giggle. 'Maybe we won't go dancing after all.'

'Maybe not,' Toni whispered back.

Chapter Twenty-one

Monday, 21 August

Toni stared at the phone. Emma might think there was a reasonable explanation but Toni certainly couldn't think of one. Theo had disappeared into thin air and she had no idea where he'd gone or why. Despite their recent hostilities Toni was worried. Theo never let anyone down – he certainly never let Sylvester's down and if he was delayed he would always phone. She shook her head in an effort to clear it. She should do something, but what? Should she call the police, or was that going too far? There was no point in calling anyone at Sylvester's. If Emma didn't know where Theo was no one else would. She decided to call Alice. If there was a problem Theo would have rung home first. The phone rang until the answering-machine cut in. 'Alice, hi, it's Toni. Would you give me a call when you get in? Thanks, 'bye.' She hung up and stared at the phone accusingly. *Damn you, Theo, where are you? What are you up to?*

She thought about ringing Chloe on her mobile, but if she hadn't heard from her father she would worry. No, best not to phone her yet.

'Hey, what's happening?' Jade breezed in.

Toni looked up at her. 'Theo's gone.'

Jade sank into a chair. 'What? He's moved out?'

'No, well, I don't think so – oh, I don't know. He seems to have disappeared into thin air.'

'Okay, slow down. When did he leave?'

'Saturday morning. He was supposed to be going to a conference in Oxford but he never got there.'

'And he hasn't been in touch?'

'Nope. His secretary was expecting him in this morning as usual. He might have called Chloe, but I'm afraid to ring and ask her in case—'

'Yes, of course. Where is she?'

'I'm not sure. The college places came out this morning so she's probably with Ollie or Mark.'

'He might have phoned home.'

'I've been trying to reach Alice but she's not there.'

'Why don't you go home and check? You're not going to get anything done here until you get to the bottom of this.'

Toni glanced at her watch. 'I was supposed to have a meeting with Daniel in an hour.'

'I'll tell him you had to go. Do you want me to explain why?'

'I don't mind. With a bit of luck Theo will either be at home or he'll have been in touch and we'll all be laughing about this tomorrow.'

'Yeah, I'm sure he's fine. Go on, you take off. I'll fill Daniel in and keep an eye on Sandra.'

Toni smiled gratefully. 'I don't know why your title is nurse. It should be chief all-rounder!'

'Hey, whatever your needs, Jade Peters can take care of them.' And, with a little bow, Jade was gone.

⚭⚭

Alice looked up in surprise when Toni walked into the kitchen. 'That was a short day,' she joked, then saw the look on Toni's face. 'What is it? What's happened? Is it Chloe?'

'No, no, nothing like that. Have you heard from Mr French today?'

'Well, no, but I've been out for most of the afternoon.'

'And did you check the answering-machine?'

'Yours was the only message. I was just about to ring you – why, Toni? What's wrong?'

Toni steered her towards a chair then sank into the one beside her. 'It's Theo. He's . . . missing.'

Alice took off her glasses and wiped them absently on her apron. 'What do you mean he's missing? Isn't he in Oxford?'

'No. Well, at least I don't think so. Apparently he never went to the conference.'

'But he told us on Friday night he was going to be there.'

'Yes, I know. It's all a bit of a mystery. I just hope there hasn't been an accident.'

'Now, don't think like that. I'm sure there's a reasonable explanation.'

'That's what Emma said,' Toni said grimly, 'but I don't know what it could be.'

'Look, why don't you check his study and see if you can find any clues? I'll look in his bedroom if you like.'

'Good idea, Alice,' Toni said, and hurried off.

The first thing that struck Alice about Theo's room was the untidiness. She hadn't been in there for a while as Toni had banned her from cleaning upstairs until her leg was better. But, even so, Mr French was a tidy man and usually she had only to flick a duster over the furniture and Hoover the carpet. She looked around her for clues. There was nothing on the dressing-table or bedside locker but something wasn't right. Alice couldn't figure out what it was. She slid back the mirrored door of the wardrobe and gasped. Half of his clothes were gone – much more than he'd need for a weekend away. She moved on to the chest of drawers. His sock drawer was almost empty and his best ties were missing too.

Then Alice realised what was different about the room: all the photos of Chloe and Marianna were gone. She checked the dressing-table drawers but the only photo she found was the one of him and Toni taken on their wedding day. The glass was cracked and the frame marked. Alice set it down and went out into the hallway. 'Toni?' she called. 'I think you'd better come up here.'

When she heard Alice's voice Toni stirred. She looked back at the letter in her hand. Alice didn't have to tell her what she'd found in Theo's room. Toni knew already. Theo had left her. But why?

'What on earth are we going to tell Chloe?' Alice asked yet again, as she sipped the brandy Toni had shoved into her trembling hands.

Toni stared into her own glass. 'I don't know. I could show her the letter, I suppose.'

'But that makes it look like you're to blame,' Alice protested.

'Maybe I am.'

'Rubbish! This has nothing to do with you, Toni, you know it doesn't,' Alice said vehemently, and read out the note again. Characteristically it was short and to the point.

> *Toni*
> *I've decided I can't live like this any longer. Tell Chloe*
> *I'm sorry and I'll be in touch as soon as I get settled.*
> *Theo.*

'Settled where?' Toni wondered aloud. Surely he wouldn't leave Dublin. She couldn't imagine him walking away from his high-powered position at Sylvester's. But, then, she couldn't understand why he'd left his daughter or his home either: after all, she had told him she'd be leaving soon. She was baffled.

'Live like what any longer?' Alice asked. 'Is he talking about the pressure of work or your marriage? It's a cryptic note. And it's out of character for Mr French to act on impulse like this.'

'You're right. He plans everything. And this couldn't have been planned. Why would he leave without knowing if Chloe got into Trinity? That was so important to him. Oh, Alice, maybe something *has* happened to him.'

'How could it have?' Alice said reasonably. 'Wasn't he able to write that note?'

'Someone might have *made* him write it.'

'And allowed him to pack his bags and take his photographs? I don't think so.'

'No. You're right, of course. I'm being melodramatic. But what the hell am I going to tell Chloe?'

'Did I hear my name mentioned?' Chloe pushed open the door and dumped her bags on the sofa. 'I'm knackered. Any chance of a cup of tea?' She noticed the empty brandy glasses on the coffee table. 'My, you two are hitting the bottle early, aren't you?'

Alice and Toni looked at each other bleakly.

'What is it? What's wrong?'

'Sit down, Chloe. We have something to tell you.'

'We've got to do something,' Chloe said again, some hours later. 'Why don't you call the police?'

'As I said, love, there's no point,' Alice said gently. 'They can't do anything about it. Your dad has left of his own free will.'

'I'm sure he'll call you tomorrow,' Toni tried to reassure her. 'He can't have gone far. He has his work to think of.'

'What did you do to him?' Chloe flung at her angrily. Against Alice's advice, Toni had shown her Theo's note. 'Are you having an affair or something?'

'No, Chloe, of course not!' She reached out a hand to her stepdaughter but Chloe had turned away.

'You're both upset,' Alice said gently. 'I think we should get some sleep. I'm sure your father will be in touch tomorrow, Chloe. Now, go on up and I'll bring you some hot chocolate.'

'You shouldn't be using the stairs,' Toni said automatically.

'Oh, don't be silly.' Alice flapped her hands and went out to the kitchen while Toni steered an unresponsive Chloe towards her room. She helped her to undress and put her to bed. Chloe begged her to stay, her earlier animosity forgotten. 'He'll be okay, won't he, Toni?' she asked tearfully.

Toni stroked her hair. 'Of course he will, love. He'll be fine. And he'll be so proud that you got offers from both colleges.'

As Chloe drifted into sleep, thanks to Alice's heavily laced hot chocolate, Toni tucked the duvet around her and tiptoed from the room. Please, God, let Theo call tomorrow. If he didn't, she didn't know what Chloe would do. Thank God she hadn't told her that she, too, had been planning to leave. Maybe that's why Theo had gone. Perhaps he was playing games, knowing full well that Toni would never leave Chloe alone.

She went into her own room and flopped on to the bed. Why was she trying to make sense of anything that Theo French did? The man was a law unto himself. No doubt he had his reasons for leaving. And he would make them known in his own good time and not before.

Chapter Twenty-two

Tuesday, 22 August

After a restless night, Toni crawled out of bed and stood for a good ten minutes under the shower. It wasn't true that old saying about things looking better in the morning. She was still baffled by Theo's behaviour and at a loss to know what she should do next. When she'd dressed she went downstairs and put on a large pot of coffee. They were all going to need it. Thankfully Chloe was still asleep and Toni could have some time to herself before she went into her reassuring mode. She'd better call the clinic later and tell them she wouldn't be in. Although there wasn't much she could do here. She had finished her toast and was on her second cup of coffee when Alice arrived.

'Any more news?'

Toni shook her head.

'How's Chloe?'

'Still asleep I think.'

'Good. I'll make a nice breakfast for you both.'

'Not for me thanks.'

'Nonsense. It will set you up for the day.'

The phone rang and Toni hurried out to answer it.

'Mrs French?'

'Speaking.' Toni frowned. Only someone from the hospital would call her Mrs French. To the rest of the world she was Toni Jordan.

'Mrs French, this is Mary Legge, Mr Allen's secretary.'

'Oh, yes, of course, Mary, how are you?' Toni wondered why Sylvester's general manager was phoning her. Unless, of course, they'd heard something from Theo.

'Very well, thank you,' the secretary continued politely. 'I wonder could I speak to Mr French?'

Toni gulped. 'Eh, well, I'm afraid he's not here.'

'Do you know where I could reach him? His mobile is off.'

'Sorry, I'm afraid I don't.'

'Well, this is odd. He was supposed to attend a board meeting here at ten.'

Toni looked at her watch. It was almost eleven. 'I see.'

'And you've no idea where he might be?' the secretary persisted.

'No. I'm very sorry I can't be of more help, Mary.'

'Maybe you'd ask him to call as soon as he gets in?'

'Yes. Yes, of course. Goodbye, Mary.'

'Goodbye, Mrs French.'

'Was that Dad?' Chloe ran downstairs and rushed to her side.

'No, sorry. Come on, let's have a cup of tea.'

Chloe followed her into the kitchen where Alice was ironing.

'Don't worry about that now,' Toni told her.

'I have to keep busy,' Alice said distractedly.

'Where is he, Alice?' Chloe said desperately. 'Is there

anyone he might go to? Someone from his past? A friend of Mum's?'

'I'm sorry, love,' Alice replied, 'I've been racking my brains but I can't think of anyone.'

'Maybe Robert Perkins would know something. They're friends, aren't they?' Chloe looked hopefully at Toni.

'I'll call him.' Toni went out to get the phone. She didn't think Robert would know anything. He and Theo weren't that close. That was the problem – Theo wasn't close to anyone, including his wife and child. 'Sandra? Hi, it's me.'

'Toni, we were worried about you. Is everything okay? Are you sick?'

'I'm fine, but I won't be in today. Is Daniel or Robert there?'

'Daniel's in theatre but Mr Perkins is free. Would you like me to put you through?'

Toni sighed. 'Yes, please.'

'Okay, then. See you tomorrow.'

The phone clicked, then Toni heard Robert's throaty voice. 'Robert Perkins.'

'Robert, it's Toni.'

'Yes, Toni?'

'I just wondered . . .' Damn! She hated having to tell him anything but Chloe was standing beside her, waiting expectantly.

'Yes?' Robert prompted impatiently.

'Well, it seems Theo has gone away. I wondered if he'd said anything to you.'

'Gone away? Where?'

'That's just it,' Toni admitted, with difficulty. 'I don't know.'

Robert burst out laughing. 'Well, that's a turn-up for the books.'

Toni bit her lip. 'So he didn't tell you he was going?'

'Not a word. Has he left the hospital? Don't tell me he's gone abroad.'

'I really don't know,' Toni cut him off abruptly. 'Sorry for bothering you, Robert. If you do hear from him please ask him to call home. We're very worried.'

Robert laughed again. 'I'll bet.'

Toni hung up angrily. 'He doesn't know anything,' she told Chloe.

'This is crazy! Somebody has to know where he is. Call Emma again. He has to let the hospital know where they can get hold of him.'

Toni dialled the number obediently. 'Emma? It's Toni. Any news?'

'Not a dicky-bird,' Emma said irritably. 'And a lot of people are looking for him. He was supposed to attend a board meeting at ten. They're not impressed.'

'So I gathered. Mary Legge phoned here too.'

Emma's voice softened. 'I realise how worried you must be. I'll call as soon as I hear anything.'

'Well?' Chloe asked impatiently.

'No news yet, I'm afraid. Look, I need to go out for a while. I'll call you if I hear anything.' She grabbed her keys and bag and left before Chloe could offer to come with her. She drove to the shops and when she'd parked she pulled out her mobile and dialled.

'Hello? May I speak to Mr Ian Chase, please?'

At exactly midday, Ian walked into the pub and strode

towards Toni. 'This is nice. I hadn't expected to hear from you so soon.'

'What would you like to drink?'

'Coffee for me too, I'm afraid. I have an operation in an hour.' He signalled the waitress and ordered for them both. 'You sounded a bit tense on the phone.'

'Theo has left me,' she blurted out.

Ian stared at her. 'What?'

'He's gone. He said he was attending a conference in Oxford at the weekend but he never turned up.'

'Perhaps he's had an accident.'

'No, I found a note in his study saying he couldn't live with me any more.'

Ian stood up as the coffee arrived, pulled some change out of his pocket and threw it on to the girl's tray. 'Thanks.' He waited for her to leave, then turned back to Toni. 'I don't know what to say, Toni. Are you . . . upset?'

'I don't know. I'm furious with him for walking out on Chloe and I'm baffled as to why he's gone now. Why would he leave Chloe? Why would he leave his work?'

'Why would he leave you?' Ian countered.

'We haven't been getting on very well. A few months ago I told him I wanted a divorce.'

'And what did he say?'

'That I could whistle for it.'

'Then it doesn't make much sense for him to leave you, does it?'

'Nothing makes sense, Ian. You know how much his position at Sylvester's means to him. Why would he walk away from that?'

'Maybe he's moved on to something better.'

'If that's the case then why do it in such a cloak-and-dagger manner?'

'So what are you saying?'

'He didn't plan this. He couldn't have. He was expected at that conference. He was due at a board meeting in the hospital this morning. Emma hasn't a clue what's going on either. Why would he keep us all in the dark? Unless . . .'

'Unless?'

'Unless he has something to hide.'

'What are you suggesting?'

'Maybe he was afraid of being fired. Afraid of being disgraced.'

Ian held up a hand. 'Hold on a minute, Toni. Don't you think you're jumping to conclusions?'

'Have you a better reason?' she snapped back.

'Okay. What do you think he might have done to disgrace himself?'

'Well, I don't know, I haven't figured that out yet. Maybe he botched an operation or something.'

'For God's sake, Toni, you can't go around saying things like that. You could ruin the man's reputation.'

'And God forbid I do that! He's only trying to ruin my life and his own daughter's!'

Ian put a hand on her arm. 'Look, Toni, you've had a shock and you're upset. I think you need time to cool down before you do anything.'

Toni shook her head in disbelief. 'I should have known it. It's like some kind of old-boys club. Any sign of trouble and you all stick together.' She jumped to her feet and grabbed her bag, knocking over her cup. 'Well, thanks a lot, Ian! It's so good to be friends again.'

She almost ran out of the pub, and pulled out of the car park with a screech of gears. She was about to head for home but the thought of Chloe staring at her mournfully made her change her mind. She'd go in to work after all. At least she'd be able to make some calls without Chloe listening in to every word.

Sandra looked up and smiled as Toni came through the door. 'Toni! I wasn't expecting you.'

'Change of plan,' Toni said briskly. 'Is everything okay?'

Sandra nodded. 'Have you thought any more about going out tonight? I heard that the college places came out yesterday so I—'

'It's out of the question,' Toni snapped.

She had just closed the door of her office when her mobile rang.

'It's me. Is there any news?'

Toni's heart almost broke when she heard the hope in Chloe's voice. 'Sorry, love, nothing.'

'We can't just do nothing, Toni! We have to try to find him.' Chloe's voice was rising.

'Calm down,' Toni said firmly. 'I've no intention of doing nothing. I'm in work and I have a list of people to call this afternoon.' She stared at the blank page in front of her.

'Who?' Chloe demanded.

'Well, his solicitor, his bank manager – maybe his doctor—'

'Oh, Toni, you're a genius! Thank you. I'm sorry for being bitchy – it's just that I'm so worried.'

'I know, love, but I'm sure your dad is fine, wherever he is. I'll call you later. Toni put down the phone and pulled out a telephone directory. She had been bullshitting about the calls she was going to make. But maybe it wasn't such a bad idea to call the bank and Theo's solicitor. She found the solicitor's number first and dialled.

'Mr Stringer is not available,' his secretary told her. 'Would you like to leave a message?'

'Please ask him to call Toni Jordan . . . French.'

'Certainly, Mrs Jordan-French, and your number?'

'No, it's just Jordan. But my husband's name is French. Theodore French.'

'Oh. Right, Mrs Jordan. And your number?'

Toni sighed and gave it to her. Then she called the bank. She wasn't sure who to ask for. Although Theo had given her access to all his accounts she rarely used them. Her salary was still paid into her own current account and she used that to cover her day-to-day expenses. Theo took care of Alice's salary, the housekeeping account and any bills that came in.

'I wanted to talk to someone about my husband's accounts. His name is Theodore French.'

'One moment, please.'

Toni listened to 'Für Elise' and tapped her fingers impatiently.

'Mrs French? I'm putting you through to the manager, Mr Shilling.'

Mr Shilling! She giggled. What a name for a bank manager.

'Mrs French? This is Tom Shilling, how can I help you?'

Toni thought quickly. 'I was wondering if my husband had been in touch with you. We've been thinking of opening an account for our daughter now that she's starting college.' It was pretty lame, but she could hardly tell him she was trying to find her missing husband.

'An excellent idea, Mrs French, but, no, I haven't heard from Mr French in quite some time.'

'I see.' That had to be good news, Toni thought.

'If you would like to make an appointment to come in and discuss the matter I'd be more than happy to take you through the options. I'm very glad that you want to do business with us again.'

Toni closed her eyes. 'I'm sorry?'

'I'm referring to Mr French withdrawing most of your funds.'

Toni's stomach lurched. 'Of course. When was that again?'

'Just let me check on the computer ... the fifth of June.'

'Ah, yes, I remember. Remind me, Mr Shilling, how much is left in our accounts.'

'Let me see. There's a balance of fifty-three pounds in the current account and twenty-one pounds and seventy-three pence in the savings account.'

'Great,' Toni said grimly. 'Well, thank you for your help, Mr Shilling. We'll be in touch.'

Chapter Twenty-three

Tuesday, 22 August

Toni flipped through the calendar on her desk until she found June. She had a habit of making small marks or initials against days where something personal was happening. As she'd expected there was a D beside Friday, 2 June. She picked up her pen and started to jot down some figures on her pad but they were as depressing as she'd feared. Still, she had a good salary and there were the dividends from her Blessington shares.

She was sitting at her desk with her head in her hands when Jade came in.

'Toni?' Jade took in at a glance her friend's faded blue jeans, T-shirt and trainers. Her hair was pulled back in an untidy knot. 'Toni, what is it?'

Toni looked up vacantly. She'd been sitting there in a daze for over an hour.

'What's happened now? Have you heard something?'

'Yes.'

'It's not good, is it? Has something happened to him?'

'Other than that he seems to have gone out of his mind, no.'

'Tell me.'

'There was a note in his study. It said he couldn't live

like this any longer – whatever the hell that meant. We checked his bedroom and he's taken a lot of clothes and some photos with him. It doesn't look like he's planning on coming back soon.'

'Jesus! How's Chloe taking it?'

'She's in a terrible state. And it should be such a happy time for her. You know she got places at UCD *and* Trinity?'

'No surprise there.'

'No. Oh, and there's more. Theo's cleaned out our bank accounts.'

'Oh, Toni! So he must have planned this.'

'No, he did that a while back – the Monday after I asked him for a divorce.'

'The bastard!' Jade gasped. 'But there must be more money somewhere. Theo has to be loaded.'

'All tied up in bonds, shares, pension plans.'

'Don't you have money of your own?'

'There's a couple of hundred in a building society and whatever is in my current account, but that's it. I always let Theo take care of our finances.'

Jade sighed. That's exactly what she'd done and look where it had got her.

'Oh, why did he do it, Jade? I don't understand.'

'Maybe he just wanted to dump you before you dumped him.'

'I don't buy that. He wouldn't have chosen to leave now, just before the college offers were made. No. He didn't plan it.' She stood up and started to pace. 'It has to have something to do with the hospital, I don't care what Ian says.'

Jade stared at her. 'Ian?'

Toni was too preoccupied to care about her friend's questioning look. 'I talked to him earlier. I thought he might be able to help.'

'And?'

'I was wrong,' Toni said abruptly.

'So, what now?' Jade asked.

'I'm going to phone John Allen to see if he knows anything.'

'If his secretary doesn't it's unlikely that John will.'

'But I'm going to have to tell him what's going on, Jade. I'm surprised he hasn't called me.'

'Yes, they're going to have to find a replacement for Theo,' Jade agreed. 'Maybe you should go and see him. It's not really a conversation for the phone.'

Toni picked up her keys. 'You're right.'

'Is there anything I can do while you're out?'

'Actually, there is, if you can spare the time.'

'I'm free for the next hour or so. What do I do?'

'Theo's solicitor, Timothy Stringer, is due to return my call. Pretend you're me and find out if he's had any dealings with him recently.'

Jade's eyes widened. 'Concerning wills and things?'

'You never know. And could you phone Bill Thompson, Theo's GP? Just in case there's a medical reason for his behaviour.'

'He's not going to tell me – that is, you,' Jade pointed out.

Toni grinned. 'You'll figure out a way to extract the necessary information, Ms Peters.'

Toni walked briskly down the long corridor leading to the administration area, her trainers making no noise on the pristine tiles. The hospital had changed a lot since she'd worked here and the administration department had doubled in size. Three young girls were typing diligently at computer screens when she walked in and Mary Legge was at her desk in the corner, the phone to her ear. She looked up in mild surprise when she saw Toni. Toni waited patiently for her to finish her call. 'Hello, Mary, I'd like to see Mr Allen please.'

'Well, I'm not sure that's possible at the moment—'

'It's very important,' Toni said firmly.

Mary shot her a worried look and stood up. 'I'll just go and see if he's free.'

Toni perched on the edge of a chair and waited. After several minutes, Mary emerged from the chief executive's office. 'Mrs Jordan?'

Toni took a deep breath and went inside. It didn't take long for her to tell her story – she had so little information.

'Well, this is all very strange.' John Allen shook his head worriedly. 'I had no idea that Theo had gone away. He has given no notice to this hospital. It leaves me in a very awkward position.'

Toni glared at him. 'Well, I'm afraid I'm more concerned about the effect this is having on his daughter than how it's affecting your schedule.'

'Of course. It must be distressing for you both.'

'It is.' Toni was slightly mollified. 'Maybe you could talk to his colleagues and see if anyone can shed some light on this mystery.'

John nodded emphatically. 'I can assure you I will leave no stone unturned. If Theo's departure has anything to do with this hospital I'll soon know what it is, you can depend on that.' He stood up, indicating that the interview was at an end. 'I'll call you later, Toni.'

When she got back to the office, Jade had left a note on her desk: '*In theatre until five. I'll drop back then to fill you in. J.*'

So, Toni interpreted, Jade had discovered something and she had thirty minutes to wait to find out what it was.

Sandra pushed open the door and carried in a tray with a large pot of tea, a plate of sandwiches and a packet of chocolate biscuits. 'I doubt you've eaten all day,' she said, as she put the tray on the desk, 'but you have to keep your strength up and a nice cup of tea always makes me feel better.'

Toni looked at her curiously. Surely Jade hadn't told her what was going on?

Sandra saw the look. 'Chloe was on. She told me about her dad. She's terribly upset, poor girl.'

'Yes.'

'But I told her he'd turn up when he was ready. Maybe a patient died on him or something and he flipped. Sure don't we all crack up from time to time?'

'You may have something there, Sandra. And thanks for being so kind to Chloe.'

Sandra smiled shyly. 'Not at all. Now I'll go and leave you in peace. You make sure and eat some of those sandwiches.'

'I will. Thanks.' Toni bit into a sandwich and poured a cup of tea. She was surprised to find that she was hungry.

She'd started on the biscuits by the time Jade arrived. Her friend grabbed one, sat down and said, 'Well?'

'No luck,' Toni reported. 'It was a total surprise to John. He's going to suss out the other staff to see if anyone knows anything. Did you talk to Stringer?'

Jade cocked her head on one side. 'I don't think I talked to him. It was more like he talked at me.'

'Solicitors!'

'Indeed. Well, he admitted that Theo was in touch with him on Monday.'

'So he's still in Dublin?'

'I don't know about that. Stringer wouldn't say if he made a personal appearance or not. He did tell me that letters were on the way to you and Chloe.'

Toni brightened. 'Well, that's got to be good news, hasn't it?'

Jade was sceptical. 'I wouldn't get your hopes up.'

'What about the doctor?'

Jade shook her head. 'Hasn't seen Theo since they did his annual check-up back in April when he was in perfect health.'

'I didn't really expect anything else. Sandra said something that made sense, though.'

Jade raised her eyebrows. 'You told Sandra?'

'Chloe did. Sandra thought that maybe one of his patients died and it upset him.'

'Well, it should be easy enough to find out. Get Emma to check.'

Toni picked up the phone and dialled. 'Good idea. It'll give her something to do. I think the poor girl is going round the bend without Theo belting out orders at her every five minutes. Emma? It's Toni.'

'Has he been in touch?'

'Nope. Anything at your end?'

Emma lowered her voice. 'Well, I've overheard some stories. They're probably not true but I thought you should know about them.'

'Go on.'

'Not over the phone. I could drop over to the house on my way home.'

'No, Chloe will be there. How about we meet at seven in the Gresham for a quick drink?'

'Fine. I'll see you then.'

When she hung up Toni was frowning. 'There's some gossip doing the rounds,' she said.

'Glad to hear nothing's changed,' Jade responded.

'Yes, but the problem with gossip is that usually there's a tiny percentage of truth in it.'

As Toni walked to the Gresham she made bets with herself as to what the rumours were going to be about. She was pretty sure that Theo botching an operation would be at the top of the list, but although this had seemed like a possibility before, Toni now thought it unlikely. Theo would stay and brazen it out. If he had made a mistake he would find a way to shift the blame to someone else. It would be the outdated equipment he had to work with or the limited staff available to him – Toni had no doubt he would come up with a reason why he was not responsible. God, she needed a drink. She had expected by now to have heard something from

Theo but she was still completely in the dark. Maybe Emma would be able to shed some light on the mystery.

Emma was waiting for her when she arrived and Toni quickly beckoned a waiter. After he had returned with their drinks, Toni lifted her glass to Emma. 'Thanks for coming.'

Emma gulped her gin and tonic. 'I hope you're still saying that when you hear what I have to tell you.'

'I've no intention of shooting the messenger, Emma. I want to know what people are saying. I talked to John Allen but he seemed to be in the dark.'

'Oh, I don't know. He probably wouldn't tell you anything anyway. You know what they're like.'

'Maybe you're right.' Toni thought of Ian's reaction when she'd said that Theo's disappearance might be connected to Sylvester's. 'So, tell me what you've heard.'

Emma shifted uncomfortably in her seat. 'The sources aren't exactly reliable—'

'Just tell me, Emma.'

The other girl sighed. 'Well, the first one I heard – but I don't believe it – is that he botched an operation and is afraid of being struck off.'

Bingo, Toni thought. 'Well, it's easily checked. Anything else?'

Emma looked down. 'There's a horrible rumour doing the rounds – I'm so sorry, Toni. They're saying he was on drugs.'

Toni laughed. 'Rubbish! Theo wouldn't touch them. It's hard enough to get him to have a few drinks, for God's sake. He's always preaching about the importance of moderation.'

Relief flooded Emma's face. 'Yes, of course.'

'Next?'

'There's another story going around that he might be involved in some kind of fraud.'

'Why?' Toni was genuinely surprised.

'Well, he was always going on about his shares and investments.'

'I don't believe he'd get involved in anything dodgy,' Toni murmured. 'His position in the medical community was too important to him.'

'I suppose. Well, I'm afraid the only other story is that he . . .' Emma paused to take a sip of her drink '. . . ran away with another woman.'

'You know your boss, Emma,' Toni said. 'Do you think the woman has been born who'd be able to drag Theo away from his beloved career?'

Emma smiled. 'I suppose not. He'd only leave Sylvester's if he had a much better position to go to or—'

'Or?'

Emma's smile faded. 'Or if he had no other choice.'

Chapter Twenty-four

Tuesday evening, 22 August

What had possessed Toni to come all the way up here? She should have phoned Jade first. She might be out or maybe even entertaining someone. It had been a bit silly to dash up here from the Gresham but Toni had been dying to talk to someone and she was also loath to go home to her stepdaughter. Chloe had kept looking at her as if she had all the answers and the sad truth was she had none. Anything she had managed to find out she couldn't tell the girl – it would only make things worse.

She wandered distractedly up the dark narrow street. She must have got the address wrong: there was no way Jade could live here. She paused outside number sixty-seven. It was the last house in the terrace and looked as uninviting and bleak as all the others. A light was on in the front room and Toni decided to admit defeat and ask for directions. She walked up the uneven path and pressed the bell. When there was no response she banged the knocker, sending a flurry of dead paint to the ground.

'What is it? I've no rooms, can't you see the sign?'

Toni looked from the tiny wizened woman to the

yellowing sign in the front window. 'Em, I'm not looking for a room and I'm sorry to disturb you. I'm looking for an address. I wondered if you could help me.'

Patsy Stewart inhaled deeply on her cigarette then threw the butt into the garden. 'Where was it you were looking for?'

'It's an apartment block on Manor Court. Number sixty-seven.'

'This is it.' Patsy cackled. 'Apartment block, is it?'

'I must have made a mistake. Sorry.'

'Who are you looking for?' Patsy asked, as Toni turned away.

'A Mrs Peters,' Toni said politely.

'Jade? You've come to the right place, love. Apartment block,' she muttered, with a broad grin. 'Maybe one day, love, when I win the lotto.' She hollered up the stairs, then went back to her sitting room.

Jade leaned over the banisters. 'Toni!'

'Hi.'

Jade gazed down at her friend. 'You'd better come up.'

Toni climbed the stairs and let out a gasp as Jade led her into the cold, shabby little room. Jade faced her, eyes defiant. 'Well, now you know. Welcome to my luxurious pad.'

Toni sank down on the edge of the bed. 'Why didn't you tell me?'

'Because it's my business and I don't want pity from you or anyone else.'

'Jade, I'm your friend.'

Jade looked away. 'Do you want a drink? I can offer you black tea, coffee or,' she reached into the press, 'a sniff of vodka.'

'Yes, I do want a drink, but I need a large one. Let's go down to that pub on the corner.'

'In case you hadn't figured it out yet, Toni, I can't afford to go out drinking every night.' Jade's voice dripped with sarcasm.

Toni's eyes flashed. 'Then you're just going to have to accept some charity, aren't you? Now, come on. I'm not in the mood for an argument.'

Toni marched out of the room and, after a moment, Jade picked up her bag and followed.

Toni bought the drinks and carried them over to the corner table where Jade was sitting.

'Any news? Had Emma heard anything?' Jade asked.

'Not from Theo, but she's heard plenty from everyone else in the hospital. But never mind that. I think you should be doing the talking.'

Jade seemed almost relieved that Toni had found her out. 'Well, the reason for my salubrious surroundings is simple. I'm broke.'

Toni blinked. 'I don't understand. You must have got a fortune for your house.'

'Well, the banks did. Aidan and I were up to our eyes in debt when we separated. I'm still paying off some of the bills now, though I should be in the clear soon.'

Toni was flabbergasted. 'But you never said anything. All this time, Jade – I can't believe it. Why didn't you tell me? I would have helped.'

'I know, and I would have been grateful, but I'd have hated you too. I couldn't risk that, Toni. Your friendship is the one thing that's kept me going. I'd go nuts if we didn't have our nights out.'

Toni drained her glass. 'Let me get a refill and then you can tell me all about it.'

'No, I'll get this,' Jade protested.

'Shut up, Jade,' Toni said equably, and went to the bar.

'It all started a couple of years before we separated,' Jade began, when Toni returned, 'although I didn't know it at the time. Aidan had been going through a rough patch. He was building this amazing house out in Malahide for a couple, but they broke up and neither wanted the house. Anyway, to cut a long story short, Aidan was never paid. He got a bit depressed and started to slack off work – though I didn't know that then. To cheer himself up he started going to the bookie's or the racecourse.'

Toni gazed at her, horrified. 'Oh, my God, how did you find out?'

'I was in his study one day and I found all the unpaid bills. I couldn't believe it. Aidan had never owed anyone a penny in his life. When I confronted him he told me he was owed money by a major developer and he was strapped for cash.'

'And you believed him.'

'Of course I did. We talked to the bank, worked out payment plans and cut back on all the non-essentials.'

'But he did it again?'

Jade's eyes were dark with sadness. 'I don't know that he ever stopped. But one day I found out how much he was lying to me and I knew I couldn't live with him any more.'

Toni took her hand. 'Oh, Jade, why did you go through this all alone?'

'I was embarrassed. I felt ashamed of Aidan. And I was furious that I'd been taken in so easily. How could I have been so stupid?'

'Because you loved him and he loved you.'

'He couldn't have loved me,' Jade spat out. 'You don't do that to someone you love. Take away their home, their life, their good name.' She rummaged in her bag and pulled out a crumpled packet of cigarettes.

'Can I have one?' Toni asked. What on earth had they done to deserve men like Aidan and Theo? Didn't trustworthy men exist any more? Did they all lie and cheat?

'You don't smoke,' Jade pointed out, as she lit their cigarettes.

'No.' Toni inhaled deeply and coughed until tears streamed from her eyes. She stubbed out the cigarette. 'Maybe I'll have another drink instead.'

Jade stood up. 'I'll go. I think I can just about afford one round.'

'I'll buy the fish and chips on the way home,' Toni offered.

While Jade was at the bar she dialled home. 'Chloe? Have you heard anything?'

'No, where are you? I've been worried sick.'

'I'm still at work,' Toni lied. She didn't think Chloe would understand if she said she was in a pub.

'Did you talk to Dad's solicitor?'

'No.' At least that was the truth, Toni thought. 'He's to call me. I got hold of Theo's doctor but he hasn't seen him in ages. And he says your dad is as fit as a fiddle.'

'Well, I suppose that's something.'

'Is Mark there with you?'

'Yes.'

'Good. Ask him to stay until I get home. I'll pay for his taxi.'

'Thanks, Toni. Will you be late?'

'Jade and I were just going to grab a bite to eat. Is that okay?'

'Sure. See you later.'

'Who was that?' Jade set down the drinks.

'Chloe. I've just told her I'm still at work and then I'm going for something to eat with you.'

'Well, that part is true. But why the lies?'

Toni looked grim as she remembered her talk with Emma. 'Because I can't face her just yet.'

Jade put down her drink. 'What's happened?'

Toni bit her lip and pushed a curl off her face. 'I'm not sure, Jade, and I don't know what to believe.'

'Just tell me,' Jade said gently. 'You'll feel better.'

Toni's eyes glistened with tears. 'I doubt that.' But slowly, her voice trembling, she related the rumours Emma had heard.

'There's no foundation behind any of these stories. If he screwed up an operation or did anything dodgy in connection with the hospital John Allen will soon hear about it,' Jade said.

'Yes, but will he tell anyone?' Toni asked. 'The reputation of their precious hospital is more important than anything or anyone.'

'You can't sit on a story involving your chief of surgery, Toni,' Jade pointed out, 'especially when he's done a bunk.'

'I suppose.'

'And as for the other stories, they just don't make sense. Theo is as straight as they come.'

'That's what I thought, Jade, but something made him leave in a hurry.'

'Maybe when you get his letter it will explain everything.'

'Jade, do you think he's been seeing other women?' Toni asked suddenly.

'Probably,' Jade answered, without hesitation. 'Oh, come on, Toni, you weren't born yesterday. His beautiful young wife wants a divorce and you're surprised that he might be seeking comfort elsewhere? I'll be amazed if he doesn't replace you with a younger model.'

Toni digested this in silence.

'Toni? Am I being too blunt? It's your own fault, though. Three vodkas on an empty stomach bring out the honesty in me.'

'No, it's okay. Poor Chloe. At this rate she could end up with someone younger than she is as a stepmother.'

'They'll be able to watch *Top of the Pops* together.'

'Jade!'

'Ah, Toni, if you don't laugh you cry.'

Toni saw the sadness in her friend's eyes. 'Come on,' she said. 'I'll buy you that supper. Now, do you have any bread in your flat or are you too poor to buy even that?'

Jade pondered the question. 'I have a couple of slices. But no butter.'

'Eh, lass, in my day if yer had a piece of dry bread, ye thought all yer birthdays had come together.'

'That's nothing,' Jade scoffed. 'We used to have to

wait until our da ate his dry bread and we'd be lucky if we got a bit of the crust.'

Toni linked her arm through Jade's. 'Come on, you daft old bat, let's go.'

Toni climbed into the cab and gave her address to the driver. Then she changed her mind. 'No, actually, can you bring me to Ashgrove in Beaumont?'

'Is that the posh apartments off Shantalla Road?'

'Yes.' Toni stared blindly out of the window. Why on earth was she going to Ian's apartment at this time of night? He was probably asleep in bed with Carla. Shit, this wasn't a good idea. 'No, take me to Griffith Avenue.'

'Look, love, make up your mind, will ye? Now is it Beaumont or Glasnevin?'

Toni took a deep breath. 'Okay, Beaumont. But I want you to wait for me. I'll just be a few minutes and then you can take me to Glasnevin.' She ignored the driver's muttered expletives, tidied her hair and straightened her T-shirt. She didn't want to look pissed and emotional when Ian answered the door. Five minutes later, the taxi pulled up. 'I won't be long,' she promised.

The driver pulled out a newspaper. 'Take as long as ye like, love. You're paying.'

Toni stood in the doorway, her finger hovering over the button.

'Are you going to stand there all night?'

She jumped as Ian loomed out of the darkness behind her. 'Ian! God, you scared the hell out of me!'

'Sorry. Here, let me.' He leaned across her to open

the door, so close that she could smell the familiar tang of his aftershave.

'I can't stay long,' she said shakily.

He took her hand and pulled her towards the lift. 'Oh, and I hoped you were spending the night.' He swayed slightly as he stepped into the lift.

'You're drunk!' Toni exclaimed.

Ian gave her a broad grin. 'You've had a few yourself, Toni. There's tomato ketchup on your chin.' He leaned forward and licked it off, his tongue hot on her skin.

'Ian, don't!'

The lift doors slid open silently on the next floor and he pulled her towards the door of his apartment. 'Come on, Toni, you know you want to.'

'No, Ian!' Toni slapped his face and pulled away.

'Jesus, Toni! What the hell did you do that for?'

'You said you were my friend.' Toni jumped back into the lift and pressed the button. As the doors closed she saw the baffled expression in his eyes as he held a hand to his cheek. When the lift opened again she ran out to the waiting taxi.

'Hey, love, is everything okay?'

'Fine,' she gasped then collapsed in a corner and cried all the way home.

Chapter Twenty-five

Alice continued to peel the potatoes and tried to ignore the tense atmosphere in the kitchen. Since Chloe had woken up she'd been like a coiled spring, asking questions that Alice had no answers for and wondering aloud about Toni's involvement in Theo's disappearance. Alice had spoken reassuringly though firmly. Chloe had no reason to harangue Toni and that poor girl had enough on her plate at the moment without having to deal with a moody teenager. She'd been relieved when Mark had arrived but even he hadn't been able to cheer Chloe up. After several terse exchanges and awkward silences Alice took pity on the lad and dragged him into the kitchen for some tea. Chloe followed.

'I wish Toni would stop treating me like a child. He's my dad, for God's sake. I've a right to know what's going on.'

'I'm sure she'd tell you if there was anything to tell,' Mark insisted, as Alice put a mug of tea in front of him.

Chloe was pacing the kitchen. 'No, she's keeping something from me. They must have had a row. Why else would Dad just up and leave like that?'

'I'm sure it would take more than a row with Toni to make your dad leave,' Mark said matter-of-factly.

Alice agreed. 'Quite right, Mark. I'm sure your dad had his reasons for going, Chloe, and he'll tell you soon enough. It's only been a few days.'

'But I'm so worried, Alice. What if something terrible has happened to him?' Chloe sniffed.

Mark gathered her into his arms. 'Don't cry, Chloe.'

'I think I heard the post,' Alice murmured, and left the room discreetly. She shuffled out into the hall and bent slowly to pick up the letters. Perching her glasses on her nose she flicked through them. Three junk mail, two for Mr French, one for Toni and one for—

'Oh!' Alice threw the other letters on the hall table and hurried back to the kitchen. 'Chloe! There's a letter for you.'

Chloe pulled away from Mark and wiped her eyes. 'It's probably from one of the colleges.'

'I don't think so.' Alice held it out to her.

'It's from Dad!' Chloe tore it open and pulled out a single sheet of paper.

'Well?' Mark prompted anxiously, after Chloe had read it several times and still said nothing.

'Here.' She shoved it into his hand.

Mark read it aloud.

My dearest Chloe,
I'm sorry to leave so suddenly and without saying good-bye. Things were becoming unbearable and I just had to get away.

I hope you will forgive me for leaving at such an important time in your life but I know that you are strong and well able to stand on your own two feet.

I have set up a standing order for you that will sustain you through university – Tim Stringer will be in touch with the details. And, of course, you will have your mother's inheritance in October.

Use it wisely, my dear, and study hard.

Make me proud.

Love,

Dad

'Well, at least he's all right.' Alice smiled reassuringly at Chloe.

'Yes, he is, isn't he?' Chloe said fiercely. 'God, what could be so bad for him just to take off like that? How could he leave me? He's been moaning on and on at me about exams and college but now, when I need him most, he disappears.'

'You don't need anyone, Chloe. You're strong, intelligent, beautiful, and apparently rich too.' Mark grinned at her.

Chloe smiled reluctantly. 'I suppose you're after me for my money now.'

'Hey, I'm a poor student. I need all the help I can get. If it wasn't for you I'd probably have to become a toyboy.'

'Why don't you two go for a walk and I'll have a nice lunch ready when you get back?' Alice suggested.

Mark took Chloe's hand. 'How about it?'

'Yeah, I could do with clearing my head.' She bent and hugged Alice. 'What would I do without you? Promise you won't ever leave me.'

Alice swallowed the lump in her throat. 'Not a chance.'

Toni was doing her damnedest to forget about the whole situation but failing miserably. When she wasn't trying to figure out where Theo was visions of her stepdaughter's miserable face swam before her eyes. She took a deep breath and went back to scrutinising the outstanding accounts list.

'Toni, could I have a word?'

'What is it, Sandra? I'm busy.' Toni did not look up from her work.

'It's about Mam,' Sandra murmured timidly.

Toni's head jerked up. 'Is she sick? Sit down, Sandra. Sorry for snapping.'

Sandra smiled gratefully. 'Oh, that's okay, Toni. You have a lot on your mind.'

'Never mind me. Tell me what's wrong.'

'Well, Mam won't admit it, but she isn't at all well. Her speech is slurred when she's tired and her balance isn't great either.'

'Has she seen the doctor?'

'Oh, yes. I asked him about putting her on this new drug, but apparently it's only proven to be effective in milder forms of the disease. He said he'd change her medication and see if that helped. But, Toni, I don't think I should be working full-time at the moment.'

'No problem, Sandra. I told you that before. You can take a few weeks off, if you like, or I could get someone in to job-share.'

'Oh, that would be great,' Sandra said. 'The job-share, I mean. Mam would be furious if I gave up work. She feels guilty enough as it is. If I could just be there in the mornings to help her wash and dress and make some lunch . . .'

'No problem. I'll call the agency today. In the meantime, I can sit at your desk in the mornings and I'm sure Jade will help out too.'

Sandra beamed at her. 'Oh, thanks, Toni. I really appreciate it.'

'Family comes first.'

Sandra noticed the dark misery in Toni's eyes. 'Is there no news?'

Toni shook her head. 'It's Chloe I feel sorry for. She's so worried.'

'But at least she's got you. If there's anything I can do . . .'

'Thanks, Sandra, but I think you've got enough on your hands.'

'Well, I'm still on for going out some night. A break would do us all good.'

'Yeah, I'd like that. Maybe next week if things have settled down . . .'

Sandra headed for the door. 'Whenever. See ya later, Toni.'

When the door had closed the smile faded from Toni's lips, and she slumped back in her chair. It was only two days since they'd learned of Theo's disappearance but it felt like months. Jade kept pestering her to do something about her financial situation but Toni couldn't summon up any interest. All she could think about was the look on Ian's face when she'd left him last night. He had been completely out of line in accusing her of going there for just One Thing. Toni sighed. Or had he? Maybe she was kidding herself that she'd gone there to talk. Maybe she wanted to feel his arms around her, his lips on her skin. She shuddered. She'd made a fool of herself and he would probably never talk to her now. Although he had been drunk. Maybe he wouldn't remember what had happened.

The phone on her desk rang, making her jump guiltily. 'Hello, Toni Jordan speaking.'

'Toni? It's Alice.'

'Is there anything wrong? Have you heard something?'

'Not directly.'

'What do you mean?'

'Chloe got a letter from her father.'

'Oh, thank God. What did it say?'

'Much the same as the first note and that he's set up a standing order for her.'

'That's something, I suppose. Is she happier?'

'She's gone for a walk with Mark. She was a bit upset.'

'Well, I suppose the relief—'

Alice sighed. 'I'm afraid it's not relief she's feeling, Toni. She's angry with him for leaving her.'

'She's not the only one. Poor Chloe. I think I'll take her out to dinner tonight. We need to talk.'

'Why don't I make you something before I go home? Then you'd have more privacy.'

'You're an angel, Alice.'

‿‿‿

It was nearly three when Chloe finally managed to

persuade Mark to leave. He was really getting on her nerves today, echoing everything Alice and Toni said. Why didn't he understand how she felt? When he was gone she took the phone into the conservatory. 'Ollie? Can you hear me?'

'Chloe? What's wrong?'

'It's Dad. He wrote me a letter and it sounds like he's never coming back.'

'Crikey. Where is he?'

'He doesn't say.' Chloe sniffed. 'He says he left because life was unbearable.'

Ollie whistled. 'What on earth could be unbearable in his life?'

Chloe bristled. 'What do you mean?'

'Well, he's got everything. A big job, lots of money, a gorgeous wife and a clever daughter.'

'Maybe he was under a lot of pressure. Stress does funny things to some people.' Chloe didn't really believe that her dad was one of them. He always seemed in control.

'Nah, he must have run off with someone else.'

'Why would you say that?' Chloe protested.

'Stands to reason. But he doesn't want you to hate him so he's lying low for a while. He'll probably call you in a few weeks and tell you. Then you'll be so relieved that he's okay and he's coming home you won't mind getting a new stepmother.'

Chloe chewed her thumbnail. She hated to think there might be any truth in Ollie's dramatic version of events but something weird was going on.

'Chlo? Are you still there?'

'Yeah.'

'Do you want to come over to my place?'
'Maybe later.'

'I'm not hungry.' Chloe pushed away her plate.

Toni tucked into her *coq au vin* with false gusto. Chloe had been positively hostile since she'd got home. Toni wondered wryly why it was that when Theo did something she was the one who got the backlash. But then Chloe was no fool and she knew that Toni wasn't being entirely honest with her. The trouble was Toni wasn't sure Chloe could cope with the full truth. She smiled cheerfully at her stepdaughter. 'It's a pity you're not hungry. Alice has outdone herself tonight.'

Chloe sniffed appreciatively. It did look good. She should probably have some. Just so Alice wasn't offended.

Toni suppressed a smile as Chloe served herself from the casserole. 'I'm so glad your dad wrote to you. It's wonderful to know he's okay, isn't it?'

'Wonderful,' Chloe said sarcastically.

'Chloe, I know you're angry.'

'Why would I be angry? I'm getting my own allowance. I'll have my mother's legacy in a few weeks. I'm free.'

'I'm sure it must have been hard for your father to leave you.'

Chloe looked her straight in the eye. 'Why did he leave? You know, don't you, Toni?'

Toni held her gaze. 'No, Chloe, I don't.'

'Had you had a row?'

'No, but we have been going through a difficult patch.'

Chloe put down her knife and fork and pushed away her plate. 'How bad?'

Toni was tempted to tell Chloe she'd asked Theo for a divorce but decided against it: the girl had enough to cope with. 'We've just been getting on each other's nerves. It happens.'

'I think you know something you're not telling me,' Chloe accused. 'I'll find out sooner or later so you might as well spit it out.'

'Okay. A lot of nasty rumours about your dad are doing the rounds. They're all rubbish, of course.'

'What kind of rumours?'

Toni sighed. 'Oh, the usual. He ran off with a patient, he was involved in fraud, someone died on his operating table—'

'That's a load of crap,' Chloe said angrily.

'I'm sure it is and you must ignore it all. It's nothing but vicious gossip.'

'But why did he go, Toni? Was it because of you?'

'I don't believe that either.'

'But what other reason could there be? Why has he left me, Toni?'

'I wish I could answer that, love. But I'm sure he will be in touch. In the meantime why don't you fill out your college application and send it back? He'll be thrilled to hear all about it when he does phone.'

'I'm not going,' Chloe said stubbornly.

'I know you'd prefer to go to UCD, and if you really want to—'

'I'm not going to either of them. I don't want to be a doctor. I'm going to take a year out, see the world and think about what I want to do with my life.'

'I don't think you've thought this through, Chloe,'

Toni said gently. 'It's a big decision and not one you should make lightly.'

'Hell, my dad made a decision to walk out on me pretty lightly, why should I be any different? He doesn't care so why should I?' And she ran from the room, crying.

Toni pushed aside her plate and rested her head in her hands. This was so unfair and so selfish of Theo. What kind of man was he to leave his own daughter like that? *A guilty one,* an ominous voice answered in her head. She stood up, poured herself a large Scotch and drained it in one gulp. Ignoring the dishes, she went out into the hall to set the alarm and lock up. She was too tired to think any more about this tonight. What she needed was a nice long bath.

As she reached up a hand to turn off the light, she noticed the envelope on the hall table. She peered at it in the gloom. Yes, it was for her. She tore it open as she went up to her room and turned on the bedside lamp to read it. The thick paper looked expensive and official. She scanned the printed name at the top. Timothy Stringer, Theo's solicitor. She started to read, and stopped half-way to turn on the main light. She reread the document several times before it sank in. 'You *bastard*, Theo.'

Chapter Twenty-six

Thursday, 24 August

Jade paced Toni's office in cold fury as she read the letter. 'God, he's a clever bastard.'

'He certainly has had the last laugh.'

'But how did he get everything organised so quickly?'

'I've no idea. What am I going to tell Chloe?'

'The truth,' Jade said firmly. 'You can't protect her from everything.'

'Oh, right. Let me see, how does this sound? "Your dad's taken all our money and put the house up for sale. Oh, I nearly forgot, he's filed for divorce on the grounds of irreconcilable differences." Yes, that should go down well.'

Jade sat down and stared at her. 'I'm not saying it will be easy, Toni, but you have to tell her. An estate agent is going to turn up on your doorstep any day now. You need a solicitor. You live in the house and possession is nine-tenths of the law.'

'I haven't got time for solicitors and all of that bureaucratic nonsense. I need to get to the bottom of this. Maybe if I find out the real reason why Theo did a runner it will help in the divorce courts.'

'The divorce courts won't care,' Jade said cynically.

'Well, sod them and Theo. I've got a job, and Chloe has her money. We'll survive.'

'What about the clinic?' Jade asked.

'What do you mean?'

'Well, Theo is a major investor – or was.'

Toni stared at her. 'Jesus! I'd forgotten. I wonder has he sold out to Daniel? No, he couldn't have. Daniel would have told me.'

'Oh, bloody hell,' Jade muttered. 'You know what he's done, don't you?'

'What?'

'Well, think about it. How does he get more money and get back at you at the same time? He sells his shares to Robert.'

'But that would make Robert the majority shareholder – oh, shit!'

'You may not have a job, after all,' Jade added.

'No way! Why would Robert fire me? What would be the point?'

Jade shook her head. 'This is silly. We don't even know that Theo *has* sold his shares.'

Toni stood up. 'There's only one way to find out.'

Jade's eyes followed her to the door. 'Just keep your cool,' she cautioned.

Toni paused in the doorway. 'Sorry? Is that Jade Peters telling *me* to keep my cool with Perky?' She chuckled mirthlessly and went on down the corridor to Robert's office. She knocked and walked in. 'Robert? Could I have a word?'

Robert beamed at her. 'Toni, my dear, of course you can. Do sit down. Have you heard anything from the Scarlet Pimpernel?'

Toni bristled at the amusement in the surgeon's eye. He's enjoying all this, she realised. He thinks it's funny. Or maybe he's happy because he's just become the majority shareholder. 'Not directly, Robert,' she said. 'He wrote to Chloe but that's all.'

Robert frowned. 'Didn't he write to you?'

Toni watched him carefully. 'No, he let his solicitor do that.'

Robert laughed, then stopped abruptly. 'I'm sorry, my dear. I'm not being very sensitive. It's just that you've got to hand it to the man. He really knows how to make an exit.'

'Have you any idea *why* he left?'

'I'm afraid not. If there's another woman, I haven't met her.'

Toni ignored that. 'Something must have happened at the hospital. There have been a lot of rumours flying around.'

'There's always talk at Sylvester's.'

'But there must be some truth in it for Theo to leave,' Toni persisted.

'Maybe he got a better offer,' Robert suggested. 'A lot of other countries would welcome a surgeon of Theo's calibre.'

If Robert knew anything, he obviously wasn't going to tell her, Toni decided. 'Did Theo sell you his shares in the Blessington?' she asked bluntly.

'Now, what makes you ask that?'

'That answers my question,' Toni said tightly. 'Does Daniel know?'

'I leave paperwork to solicitors but he has probably received notification by now.'

Toni walked to the door. 'I doubt it. If he had, I'm sure he'd have been straight up to congratulate you.' She banged the door behind her, and walked down the corridor, Robert's booming laughter in her ears. Even if he didn't fire her, Toni couldn't see herself staying on with him at the helm.

She went straight to Daniel's office, tapped on the door and walked in. The first thing she noticed was the pile of untouched mail on his desk. Daniel was engrossed in an article in the *Lancet*. 'Hi, Toni,' he said vaguely, and waved her to a chair.

'For God's sake, Daniel, don't you ever open your post?' she said, exasperated.

Daniel looked faintly surprised at her tone. 'There's plenty of time. Do you know there's the most amazing research going on in Wales—'

'Daniel! Theo has sold his shares to Robert.'

Daniel put down the magazine. 'What shares?'

'His shares in the Blessington, of course.'

'What are you talking about?'

'Chloe got a letter from Theo. It doesn't look like he's coming back. Then I got a letter from his solicitor and he wants a divorce. And he cleaned out our accounts and I think he's sold his shares in the clinic to Robert and – and—' Toni's eyes filled with tears of frustration.

Daniel came round to sit on the front of his desk and took her hand. 'Oh, Toni! I'm so sorry. What on earth has possessed him? I always thought he'd a screw loose – sorry, my dear – but this is a bit extreme even for him.'

Toni blew her nose. 'I'm convinced this has something to do with Sylvester's, Daniel, but I can't find out anything. Would you try?'

Daniel squeezed her hand. 'Of course, my dear. Did you talk to Francis Price? He is on the board, after all.'

Toni jumped up and kissed him. 'Of course! Why didn't I think of that?'

Daniel walked back to his chair, pulling his post towards him. 'Well, you telephone him, my dear, and I'll try to find out if we still have jobs.'

'Do you think Robert will want to get rid of us all, Daniel?'

Daniel chuckled. 'Not until it suits him.'

Toni felt guilty. 'I'm so sorry, Daniel. This is *your* clinic and you're going to lose it because of me.'

'Don't be silly, my dear. It's just business.'

As Toni walked back to her office she thought about those words. They were the ones Theo had used. 'It's just business.'

'Well?' Jade jumped to her feet and looked at Toni anxiously.

'You were right. Robert's grinning like the cat that's got the cream. I've just broken the news to Daniel.'

'How did he take it?'

'Remarkably well.'

'Oh, well, at least if Perky wants to get rid of us, we could always start again somewhere new.'

'Do you think so?' The idea hadn't occurred to Toni.

'I don't see why not. Daniel must have a few bob tucked away by now. And Robert would probably pay a good price just to get him out.'

'I can't imagine us leaving the Blessington,' Toni said sadly.

'It's only a building,' Jade retorted. 'It's people that make a place, not bricks and mortar.'

The rest of the day went by in a bit of a haze for Toni. Sandra had managed to delete several spreadsheets that Toni had been working on and Toni had spent hours trying to recover the information. For once she was almost grateful for Sandra's computer illiteracy. It had been a welcome distraction. But now that the work was finished and everyone had gone home, Toni's thoughts returned to her immediate problem. She felt the need to talk and the person she wanted to talk to was Ian. But how could she call him after the way she'd behaved the other night? She closed her eyes as she remembered the imprint of her hand on his cheek. She had really overreacted. Not giving herself time to change her mind, she picked up the phone and dialled his apartment. As the phone rang she started to regret her impetuousness. But maybe he wouldn't be in. Maybe she'd just hang up.

'Hello?'

'Ian, it's me.'

'Toni?'

'Look, I'm sorry about the other night. I overreacted.'

'I was a bit out of order myself,' Ian admitted. 'I'm afraid I'd had one too many.'

'Me, too. So, are we still friends? I could really use one right now.'

'Theo hasn't turned up, then?'

'No, not personally, but he sent Chloe what seemed like a goodbye letter. And he's been talking to his solicitor. He wants a divorce.'

'How strange,' Ian murmured. 'I wonder what happened to change his mind.'

'God knows,' Toni said, tiredly. 'Nothing's making sense. He never even let the hospital know that he was going. John Allen's in shock.'

'Our John is a very organised man. Having his chief of surgery disappear is enough to put him on the operating table himself.'

'There's more, Ian. I haven't told Chloe this. He's taken all of our money with him. And he's sold his shares in the Blessington to Robert. He also wants to sell the house so that he can have half of the proceeds.'

'Oh, Toni, I'm sorry. This is turning into a nightmare for you.'

'It wouldn't be so bad if I could understand why he did it. As it is, I don't know what to think and I haven't a clue what to say to Chloe. And there are some horrible rumours doing the rounds.'

'I've heard them,' Ian said grimly. 'I wouldn't pay any heed to them, if I were you. Theo's disappearance is as big a mystery to everyone in the hospital as it is to you.'

'I'm sorry about what I said,' Toni mumbled. 'About the old-boys' club.'

'Don't worry about it.'

'Oh, Ian, what should I do? I seem to be going down a blind alley.'

'Well, it's interesting that Theo needs cash. He's wasting no time in realising all of his assets, which means he's in some kind of trouble.'

'I hadn't thought of that. I just thought he was out to get me.'

'That's possible too. Look, why don't I do a little detective work? I could talk to the other doctors who got involved in the same investment schemes and brokers, that sort of thing.'

'I'd be grateful for anything you could do,' Toni said fervently.

'Leave it with me. I'll call you when I get news.'

Chapter Twenty-seven

Thursday night, 24 August

'This is nice.' Aidan smiled at Jade and looked around the busy pub.

'It's okay.' Jade was wondering why they were here. When Aidan had phoned and asked her to meet him she'd refused instinctively – he might try to tap her for more money. However, Aidan hadn't mentioned money, and he had bought the first round too. Also he was looking rather nice in his black chinos, a new blue shirt and his trusty leather jacket. 'How's the job going?' she asked.

'That's what I wanted to talk to you about.'

Here we go, thought Jade.

'It's going well. In fact, Dave is so pleased he's given me a raise.'

Jade gawped at him, then collected herself. 'I'm very happy for you.'

'Be happy for *us*.' Aidan reached into his jacket and pulled out an envelope. 'This is for you. It's only a fraction of what I owe you but it's a start.'

Jade stared at it. 'Oh, I don't know, Aidan. Maybe you should keep it. If something were to go wrong . . .'

His smile faded. 'You mean, if I were to start gambling again.'

'I didn't say that—'

'But it's what you meant,' he said harshly. He was silent for a moment. Then he said, 'Sorry. I know it must be hard to believe I'm back on the straight and narrow. All I can do is try to prove it to you. This is the first step.' He pushed the envelope towards her. 'Please take it, Jade.'

Jade picked it up and slipped it into her bag. 'Thank you.'

'Why don't we go and get something to eat?'

'I'm not sure I have time. I was expecting Toni to drop round.'

'Just a quick bite in the steakhouse on the corner,' Aidan said persuasively.

Jade smiled suddenly. 'Why not? I haven't had a thing since breakfast. I'm starving.'

Aidan's brow furrowed. 'You're very thin. I hope you're taking care of yourself.'

'I'm fine,' she said breezily. 'In fact, at the moment I'm probably the most trouble-free person in that clinic.'

'Toni must be in a bad way. I can't believe Theo would just leave like that. He was always a bit weird but this is strange even for him.'

'Chloe's taking it very hard – and she doesn't know the half of it. Toni hasn't said anything about the money or the divorce, so Chloe thinks it's all Toni's fault and is taking it out on her.'

'Toni just happens to be in the firing line. You always hurt the one you love.' Aidan's eyes held hers.

Jade coughed. 'Must just nip to the loo.'

Friday morning, 25 August

Ian shoved Carla's makeup bag out of the way and reached for his shaver. He hated the way she took over the place when she stayed the night. In fact, everything she did set his teeth on edge. Especially the way she hung on to him in public. He wasn't against holding hands or even the odd kiss, but she was like an extra limb.

'Ian, honey? Are you nearly ready?'

And he hated her calling him honey.

'I've got a meeting at Sylvester's later. Shall we have lunch together?'

He scowled at his reflection. He also hated her spending so much time at the hospital. 'No, I'm going to be tied up.'

Carla walked in then and slipped her arms around him from behind, her face appearing beside his in the mirror. 'Couldn't you get out of it? For little me?' She planted a kiss on his cheek.

'Afraid not.' Ian smiled apologetically, and went back into the bedroom to put on his shirt.

'Not to worry.' Carla followed him. 'I'll take Lynn out instead and get all the juicy gossip about Theo French.'

Ian groaned inwardly. The Sylvester's buyer was a nosy loudmouth and the last thing he needed was for Carla to team up with her. 'I wish you wouldn't talk to that cow. She's just a vicious gossip.'

'There's no smoke without fire,' Carla told him, as she put on a stocking.

Ian said nothing. If he made too big a deal out of this he would arouse her curiosity. Instead he sat down on the bed beside her and ran a finger playfully around the top of her stocking. 'You smell gorgeous,' he murmured, and kissed her neck. 'Maybe I *could* get away at lunchtime. We could come back here for a' – he nibbled her earlobe – 'bite to eat.'

Carla twisted her head round and kissed him hungrily. 'That would be nice.'

Ian pushed her back on the bed and began to kiss her throat.

'I'm going to be late,' she groaned.

'Then I'll see you at lunchtime?' Ian's lips moved down to trace the lacy edge of her bra.

Carla shivered. 'I'll be here at one.'

'I'll be waiting,' he promised, and watched as she finished dressing.

The things he did to protect Toni, Ian mused, as he watched Carla dress. But she didn't need the likes of Carla sniffing around. If anyone was likely to beef up the rumours it was her. He looked on objectively as she put in her contact lenses. She was a tough businesswoman, who had got to the top because she wasn't afraid of making enemies and stepped on anyone who got in her way. Carla had joined the sales team at Medway, the large pharmaceutical distributor, at twenty-eight. Just five years later she was head of sales for the Dublin area. And a year after that, when her boss had joined that big sales team in the sky, she was made sales director.

There was no reason for her to involve herself so deeply in the Sylvester's account – Ian knew she didn't pay half as many visits to the other hospitals in the city and was convinced she was keeping tabs on him. It was irritating – he disliked possessive women – but it was also hilarious. He didn't have time to see other women – he didn't even get a chance to eat most days.

Carla slipped on her suit jacket and came over to kiss him goodbye. 'See you later, honey.'

Ian pasted on his face what he hoped was an enthusiastic smile. ''Bye, Carla.'

When she'd left he finished getting dressed, collected a can of Coke from the fridge, his battered briefcase from the hall, and went out to the car. As he pulled into the early morning rush-hour traffic his thoughts turned to Theodore French.

When he'd offered to help Toni he hadn't figured out how he'd go about it. The more he thought about what Toni had told him the more likely it seemed that Theo had got himself into some kind of trouble. The question was, what? He drummed on the wheel thoughtfully as he drove up the North Circular Road. The man needed money, that was for sure. Did he owe someone? Was he being blackmailed? Did he have expensive habits? He didn't believe Theo would be taking such drastic action because of Toni. He would have been a lot more organised if that was the reason and he certainly wouldn't have been the one to leave. No, if he was out for revenge he would have kicked her out of his house then ensured that she was forced out of the clinic too. Ian had decided to concentrate for the moment on Theo's penchant for the stock market, and that Stuart Beecher was the man to talk to. Like Theo, the cardiologist loved to dabble in stocks and shares, and took some amazing risks. He and Theo shared information and brokers, so if anything was going down he would know about it.

Ian blasted his horn at a guy in a Honda who cut in front of him. The other driver gave him the finger and sped away into the distance. Ian sighed. In his younger days he'd probably have torn after him like a madman but now he couldn't be bothered. 'You're getting old, Chase. You're not up to it any more. No wonder Carla's fed up with you.' He knew his advances this morning had taken his girlfriend by surprise. He'd surprised himself too. He'd never seen himself as an actor. But once he started to make love to Carla his body took over. She was a beautiful woman and damn sexy. Once he forgot what a total bitch she could be, he quite enjoyed himself. But tricking her like this just to keep her away from the hospital was a bit cheap. Especially if it got her hopes up that their relationship was going somewhere.

Ian pulled into the hospital car park. She'd probably start talking about moving in together again. Damn it, maybe he'd ring her later in the morning and tell her he couldn't make it at lunchtime. But he wanted to keep her away from Sylvester's as much as he could. It was only a matter of time before someone told her he was asking questions about Theo. And it wouldn't take long for Carla to work out that he was back in touch with Toni. And then she'd want to know why he was going to so much trouble for his ex. And he wouldn't be able to answer that question honestly, because if he said he was just helping a friend it would be a lie. He grabbed his briefcase and got out of the car. He didn't want to dwell on his reasons for wanting to help Toni. It was better to concentrate on the job in hand and worry about that later.

Chapter Twenty-eight

Friday night, 25 August

Toni wandered listlessly from room to room. She was glad Chloe had gone to bed early – it was easier on her nerves when the unhappy girl wasn't around – but she couldn't relax even then. There had to be something useful she could do. She toyed with the idea of housework but dismissed it with a wry grin. She wasn't that desperate. She picked up a novel that Chloe was reading but found herself reading the same page several times over. Finally she decided to phone and see how Dotty was doing.

'Hello, Toni. How are you?'

'I'm okay, Francis, but how's Dotty?'

Francis sighed heavily. 'Not good.'

Toni clutched the phone tighter. 'Can I come and see her?'

'Not just now, my dear. She's in a lot of pain so she's sedated most of the time.'

'Oh, my God, I had no idea . . .'

'That's the way she wanted it, Toni,' he said gently. 'Everything was to be as normal as possible for as long as possible. You know how she loves a laugh. And she said that if everyone started creeping around her with long faces she'd go mad.'

'She's so brave. You must tell me, Francis, if there's anything I can do.'

'Thank you, dear, but the nurses are very good and Mrs Caulfield, our housekeeper, has been marvellous. Did you want me for something in particular?' he asked, ever the gentleman.

'Eh, no, Francis, I just called to say hello.'

'Well, it's always nice to hear—' Toni heard Dotty's frail voice in the background. 'Sorry, my dear, I've got to go. Thanks for phoning.'

'Tell Dotty I was asking for her,' Toni said softly. She put down the phone and crossed the conservatory to stare out into her garden. Poor Dotty. Poor Francis. She felt so helpless. It was difficult to stand back and watch someone you loved slip away. When Dotty was gone Francis would probably go to pieces. And that's when she would be able to help. She tidied the kitchen, locked up and was just going upstairs when the doorbell rang. She went down again and peered through the window beside the door. 'What is it?' she called nervously.

'Mrs French? Police.'

Toni threw open the door. 'Is it Theo?'

The older of the two men stepped forward and showed her his badge. 'I'm Detective Inspector Morrisey. And this is Sergeant Doyle. Is your husband in?'

'No.'

'May we come in?' he said, and stepped into the hall before she could reply.

'Of course,' Toni said faintly, and brought them into the living room. Well, Theo was obviously all right because it was him they wanted to talk to. 'Why do you want to talk to my husband?'

'Where is Mr French?' Morrisey asked, ignoring her question.

'I don't know.' Toni watched the sergeant wander round the room looking at photographs.

'Do you expect him home this evening?'

'No. He's left me.'

The two policemen exchanged a glance. 'I see,' Morrisey said. 'When was this?'

'Monday – no, Saturday.'

'Which was it, Mrs French? Monday or Saturday?'

'I didn't find out until Monday but he'd been gone since Saturday.'

The sergeant smirked. 'Didn't you notice he was missing?'

Toni glared at him. 'He left early on Saturday morning to attend a conference in Oxford. When he didn't return on Monday we started making enquiries. It turned out that he never went to the conference.'

'And weren't you worried about him?' The DI studied her with razor-sharp eyes.

'Of course I was worried,' she snapped. 'But then I found a note in his study saying he'd left me.'

'May we see his study?'

'No, you may not. Not until you tell me what this is all about.'

'Sergeant?' Morrisey nodded to his junior, who flipped open his notebook.

'We would like to interview Mr French about an accident that took place at approximately one o'clock on the morning of Friday, the eighteenth of August last.'

'*What?* Theo wasn't in any accident.'

'You were with him on that night, Mrs French?'

264

Toni cast her mind back. 'Yes. He was at home. I remember because it was the night before we went out to celebrate our daughter's Leaving Certificate results.'

'And he stayed in the whole night?'

Toni hesitated.

'Well, Mrs French?'

'I'm sure he must have—'

'You don't know?'

'Well, we have separate bedrooms.'

'So he could have gone out after you were asleep?'

'I suppose, but I'm telling you he couldn't have been in any accident. His car is in the garage and there isn't a mark on it. Take a look at it, if you don't believe me.'

'It wasn't his car that he crashed,' the sergeant informed her.

Toni looked from one to the other in confusion.

'Do you remember what time you went to bed, Mrs French?' the DI persisted.

'About eleven.'

'So he could have gone out and you would never have known about it?' the detective said solemnly.

'I would probably have heard him.'

'You sleep in separate bedrooms, Mrs French. It is possible that he went out and you never heard a thing, isn't it?'

'Well, yes, but I'm sure he wouldn't have—'

'We have a witness who says otherwise, Mrs French.'

'Who?'

The detective did not answer her. 'And he went away on Saturday morning?'

'Yes. I heard the taxi collect him at about six.'

'I see. And you have no idea where he might be?'

Toni shook her head.

'He hasn't made any contact since he left?'

'Well, yes. He wrote to his daughter, and he was in touch with his solicitor to instruct him to begin divorce proceedings.'

'Did that come as a shock to you?'

'Yes – no. Look, I don't see what this has to do with you. You're only investigating a car accident. You don't need to know all the ins and outs of my marriage to do that.'

'That's not necessarily the case, Mrs French. Other charges may follow.'

'Charges?'

'Mr French was the driver of a car in which a woman was badly injured. He had no insurance, is believed to have been under the influence of drink and drugs at the time and he left the scene of an accident. Quite a few charges are stacking up against Mr French.'

Toni stared at them. 'You're making a mistake. Theo is a surgeon. He's very careful about drinking, and he'd never touch drugs.'

'Really?' The detective studied her pityingly. 'I have the feeling that Mr French got up to a lot more than you know about.'

'Who is this woman? Is she all right?'

'I can't tell you her name, Mrs French, but suffice it to say she is well known to the Gardai. And, yes, she is going to be all right – no thanks to your husband, who left her for dead.'

Suddenly Toni had a flashback to the conversation at dinner that night. 'This was the accident on Mount Street? The woman was in a coma?'

'That's right. But, unfortunately for your husband, she's now very much awake and has a perfect recollection of the events of that night.'

'Is she a . . . prostitute?'

'Yes, Mrs French. And apparently your husband was one of her regulars.'

'I can't believe it. Theo would never—'

'If I had a fiver for every time a wife told me that,' the detective said, with a melodramatic sigh.

Toni stared blankly at him. Theo had been with a prostitute? He was a regular client? God, she'd felt she'd been living with a stranger lately but how could she know so little about a man that she'd lived with for six years? She thought of those nocturnal drives and cursed her naïvety . . .

'Now, Mrs French, may we have a look around Mr French's study? We don't have a search warrant but if you insist we will get one and be back in the morning.'

Toni stood up. 'There's no need for that. But please be quiet. Chloe is asleep upstairs.'

'That's your daughter?'

'Stepdaughter,' Toni corrected him automatically.

'Best prepare her for the shock, Mrs French,' the sergeant said kindly. 'You don't want her to read about this in the paper.'

'But surely you won't release his name?' Toni stammered. 'I mean, you haven't even talked to him yet. It's not as if he's under arrest.'

'Only because he isn't here,' the detective said drily. 'Now, I'll need something with Mr French's fingerprints on it. The sergeant will issue you with a receipt, Mrs French, and you can have it back in a couple of days.'

Toni led the way into the study. While they looked around she picked up the silver letter-opener she'd bought him for their first wedding anniversary. 'His prints should be on this.'

The sergeant produced a bag and wrapped it carefully before stuffing it into his pocket. Then he wrote her a receipt and tore it from his notebook. 'You should know, Mrs French, that once we have established that his prints match the ones in the car it will be public knowledge that we're looking for Mr French to help us with our enquiries.'

Saturday morning, 26 August
Mark rang the doorbell twice before a dishevelled Toni came to answer it. 'Thanks for coming, Mark,' she said, with a ghost of a smile, and led the way into the kitchen.

When eventually she had gone to bed the night before, Toni had tossed and turned all night. When she slept she saw Theo in her dreams with various women, in all sorts of positions. When she lay awake she wondered how long her husband had been going to a prostitute. Had it been in the last few months or had he been carrying on like this before? His solitary drives seemed to suggest the latter. While she might have believed he had a mistress she would never have thought he'd have gone to a prostitute.

'Toni?' Mark was looking at her worriedly.

'Sorry. Would you like some coffee?'

'Yeah. What's happened, Toni?'

Toni poured the coffee and handed it to him. 'Sorry

for getting you over here so early but I wanted you to be here before Chloe woke. The police were here last night, Mark. They came to arrest Theo.'

'Jesus! Why?'

'He was involved in an accident, but I won't go into the details now. You'll hear soon enough. I'm sorry to drag you into it, Mark, but Alice isn't due till this after-noon – she has an appointment with the physiotherapist and I didn't want to do this on my own.'

'That's okay. Are you going to wake her?'

Toni glanced at the clock. 'I'll give her another few minutes,' she said, knowing she was postponing the inevitable. 'God, I don't know how she's going to take it.'

'I'm sure it'll be all right, Mrs French. The police have probably made a mistake.'

'I don't think so, Mark.'

When Chloe came downstairs, she stopped short when she saw Mark. 'What are you doing here?' She turned to Toni. 'God, what's happened now?'

Toni led her to a chair and knelt at her feet. 'The police were here last night, Chloe.'

'Oh, God, has something happened to Dad?'

'No. They came to see him. They wanted to question him about an accident that took place last week.'

'He never said anything about being in an accident.'

'No,' Toni said quietly. 'He didn't tell anyone, Chloe. That's part of the problem. He left the scene of the accident and a woman was seriously injured.'

Chloe gasped. 'He knocked her down?'

Toni wished she could let Chloe believe that, it would be a lot simpler, but the sergeant had warned her that soon every detail would be spread across the newspapers. 'No, he didn't knock her down. She was in the car with him. It was her car, apparently.'

'I don't understand.' Chloe looked at her, scared eyes in a pale face.

Toni held her hands. 'I'm sorry, love. I don't know all the details but your dad was driving and she was in the passenger seat. He lost control and drove into a parked car.'

Chloe gasped. 'That was the accident Alice was telling us about.'

'Yes, that's right.'

'But they never said anyone else was in the car.'

'They didn't know until the woman woke up from her coma yesterday.'

'But who is she?'

Toni glanced at Mark. 'I don't know.'

Chloe frowned. 'The accident happened in the middle of the night. What was Dad doing out at that hour? And why wasn't he in his own car?'

'I don't know.'

'Was he having an affair?' Chloe thought about what Ollie had said.

Toni took a deep breath. 'No, Chloe. She's a prostitute.'

'Don't be ridiculous! What would Dad be doing with a prostitute?'

'I'd say that was pretty obvious,' Mark said drily.

Chloe shot him a venomous look. 'How dare you? Dad would never do anything like that, would he, Toni?'

Toni did not reply.

'Toni?' Chloe pulled her round and looked anxiously into her face. 'You don't believe this, do you?'

'Why would the woman lie?'

'God knows! She's a prostitute! How can you believe her over Dad?'

'We'll know for sure very soon,' Toni said quietly. 'The police are checking his fingerprints.'

'Jesus,' Mark breathed. 'He could be in serious shit here. He's lucky she didn't die.'

'There you go again, presuming he's guilty,' Chloe cried. 'Why are you both so ready to believe the worst of him?'

'Because he's left the country, Chloe. Because he's taken all our money with him. Because he's sold his shares in the clinic.'

'You never told me,' Chloe faltered.

'I didn't want to upset you, and I was hoping I could figure out why he'd left. I thought it had something to do with Sylvester's. I never imagined it would be anything like this.'

'He won't be coming back now,' Mark warned Chloe. 'He'd be arrested as soon as he set foot in the country.'

Tears were rolling down Chloe's cheeks. 'It can't be true.'

'It doesn't look good,' Toni told her. There was no point in trying to shelter Chloe from this. 'And it will be all over the papers before long.'

Saturday afternoon, 26 August

Toni sat at the kitchen table staring into space. The house was quiet except for the muffled sound of music coming from Chloe's room. She'd been up there for hours now but Toni was afraid to go near her. She felt that every time she opened her mouth she made things worse. It had probably been a mistake to blurt out about Theo taking the money but she just couldn't let Chloe fool herself that it was all some terrible misunderstanding. Theo was obviously guilty. Toni was glad when Alice arrived later although she was not looking forward to telling the poor woman the latest news.

'Oh, dear God!' Alice said when she'd finished.

Toni patted her hand. 'I'm sorry, Alice.'

'I just can't believe it's true. What kind of a man does something like that?'

Toni didn't reply. She had thought she knew every evil twist of her husband's mind but obviously not.

'So, what happens now?'

'Once the police have established that Theo was driving the car there will be a warrant out for his arrest and his name will be released to the papers.'

'Oh, poor Chloe. Is there anything I can do?'

'Keep an eye open for journalists and send them packing before they get to her,' Toni said. 'Other than that, Alice, I don't think there's anything we can do to protect her now.'

Chapter Twenty-nine

Saturday evening, 26 August
'Chloe, what's going on? I saw the six o'clock news. They said the police are looking to talk to your dad in connection with an accident last week.'

Ollie had got through to her friend on her mobile. Toni had taken the home phone off the hook hours ago after the first journalists had called.

'Oh, Ollie, it's a nightmare. They're making Dad sound like a dangerous criminal.'

'But why?'

'They said he was driving the car in that accident on Mount Street last week. They said he left her for dead.'

'Chloe, I'm sure it's not true,' Ollie said, with uncharacteristic sensitivity. 'They must have got the wrong man.'

'The journalists don't think so,' Chloe told her shakily. 'God, Ollie, you wouldn't believe the questions they asked.'

'It's not often they get such a juicy story,' Ollie said blithely, forgetting to be diplomatic. 'And your dad is well known, which makes it even better. But don't worry, Chlo, it'll be forgotten in a couple of days.'

'I don't know about that.'

'Are you going to stay holed up until it calms down?'

'I suppose we'll have to. Toni says it's only a matter of time before the press set up camp on our doorstep.'

'Look, why don't you come round here for a while? If it's going to be that bad you should get out while you can.'

'I don't know.'

'Oh, go on. Take a taxi. You need a break.'

'Yeah, you're right. Just let me check with Toni – I don't like leaving her. I'll call you back in five.'

Toni was sitting in the conservatory, staring blankly out at the garden, when Chloe came to find her. 'Toni, would you mind if I went over to Ollie's for a while?'

Toni summoned up a smile. 'No, of course not, but take a taxi. There's a twenty-pound note in my purse.'

Chloe bent and kissed her cheek. 'Thanks. I won't be late.'

Toni was relieved that Chloe wanted to go out – Mark had asked her this morning but she'd said no, and Toni had been afraid that she would go into her shell and talk to no one. Time spent with the down-to-earth Ollie would do her good. But would it be enough to get her through the awful time ahead? Toni dreaded the thought of the press harassing her. And the idea of Chloe reading sordid details about her father's secret sex-life in the newspapers didn't bear thinking about. If only she could get her away from here for a few days. On impulse she picked up the phone. 'Hello, Mum? It's me.'

Sunday morning, 27 August

Toni glanced around the bright sitting room. It had changed since she was last here. The sofas were covered in heavy dark green brocade and the curtains and carpet were a pale cream. The bookcases, however, still stood against the wall and were as stuffed with books as they'd always been. Toni fingered her school copy of *Hamlet*.

'Here we are,' her mother announced, as she arrived back with a tray.

'I could have come out to the kitchen,' Toni protested.

'Oh, no, it's a mess out there.'

'Where's Dad?'

'Pottering around somewhere. We didn't think you'd be down quite so early.'

Toni glanced ruefully at the clock. It wasn't even nine yet. 'Sorry. I just wanted to get back before Chloe woke. She's a bit nervous.'

'I'm not surprised. And how are you?' Mary asked gently.

'Fine. No, Mum, actually I'm not fine at all.' She put down her cup and burst into tears.

Mary Jordan sat down next to Toni and took her awkwardly in her arms. 'Oh, Toni! My poor girl. This is so unfair.'

Toni clung to her and breathed in her perfume, the wonderful scent that had always made her feel safe as a child. She closed her eyes and willed it to work its magic now. Mary smoothed the dark hair off Toni's face and looked into her troubled hazel eyes.

'Aren't you going to say "I told you so"?' Toni pulled out a tissue.

Mary stared at her. 'Of course not! My God, Toni, we thought he was too old for you. We never for one moment thought that he was capable of . . .' words failed her.

'I have a feeling that this is just the tip of the iceberg,' Toni said miserably. 'From what the detective told me, Theo was involved with some very strange people. And it's been going on for quite some time.' Toni's voice turned into another sob. 'That's something else you don't know,' she said. 'I had asked Theo for a divorce.'

'But I thought you were happy.'

'I haven't been for a long time. You and Dad were right,' she said. 'I should never have married him.'

'Oh, love, I'm so sorry. I've missed you so much and the only thing that kept me going was the thought that you were content.'

'I should have kept in touch more. My God, you're only an hour's drive away – and at this hour on a Sunday morning only half that,' she added tremulously. 'I'm sorry, Mum. I should never have let him come between us.'

Mary clasped her fiercely to her breast. 'Nothing and no one can ever come between us, Toni.'

'I just wish I understood why he did it.'

Mary's mouth set in a grim line. 'Some men have strange . . . needs.'

'Maybe I drove him to it.'

'Don't talk nonsense. What he did has nothing to do with you.'

Toni glanced nervously at her watch. 'I should get back soon. If those bloody journalists get to Chloe I think I'll strangle them.'

'Why don't you send her to stay with us?' Mary suggested. 'No one knows her down here and it would be a break for her. And it would mean one less thing for you to worry about.'

Toni considered the idea. Chloe had got on well with her parents on the few occasions they'd met, and she loved the old house in Skerries. 'Are you sure you could cope with her?'

'After all my years as a district nurse I think I can cope with one teenager. Especially one who is hurting as much as she must be.'

Toni hugged her. 'I don't deserve you. I've been a lousy daughter but as soon as I turn to you for help you're there for me.'

'We've always been here for you, Toni. I'm just glad you've finally realised it.'

'I don't think you can speak for Dad,' Toni said bitterly.

'You and your dad are too alike, both as stubborn as mules. I should have bashed your heads together a long time ago and made you see sense. Now, why don't you go and find him?'

'Oh, I don't know—'

'Toni Jordan, you are not leaving this house without speaking to your father.'

Toni knew her mother wasn't going to let her off lightly this time. 'Okay, Mum – but I'm not staying if he starts going on at me.'

'He'll be delighted to see you.'

'Right,' Toni said doubtfully, and followed her out to the kitchen.

'Try the shed,' Mary suggested. 'He usually ends up

in there fixing things.' She chuckled. 'Or reading the sports pages.'

Toni went out into the garden. It was months since she'd seen her father – the obligatory Easter visit, all polite conversation and awkward silences. She had hated those occasions, with Theo politely complimenting her mother on her fruit cake and her father asking him stiffly about the hospital. The last real conversation Toni had had with her father had been during the week before her wedding when he'd refused to give her away.

'Give you away to a man nearly as old as me? I'd cut my own arm off first!'

And no matter how much her mother had pleaded with him, he'd stuck to his guns. Toni had stared at him defiantly. 'Fine, Dad. It's your decision. But if you don't give us your blessing then I don't want you at my wedding.'

Her mother had been horrified. 'Toni!'

'Sorry, Mum.' She'd given her a quick peck on the cheek and run out of the house. And that had been that. The wedding in the register office on Stephen's Green had been a sad little affair, with only her mother, Jade and Aidan there to wish her well. She knew Mary hadn't approved either, but there was no way she would stay away from her own daughter's wedding. Even though it had caused a huge row with her husband.

Toni walked slowly down the path towards the shed and paused with her hand on the door handle.

'Looking for me?'

Toni swung round to see her dad standing behind her, a pair of clippers in his hands. She smiled weakly.

'I was but I'd feel happier if you put *them* down.'

Peter Jordan looked at the clippers thoughtfully. 'They're so rusty they wouldn't cut butter.'

'The garden looks well.' Toni looked around at the neatly manicured flowerbeds and the tightly clipped lawn.

'Your mother says you can tell I was an actuary just by looking at this garden. All the flowers are colour-coded and lined up like columns of figures.'

Toni's laughter was genuine. It was true that her father had always been a precise man and her mother had always teased him about it. 'I like it,' she said shyly.

Peter looked up at the house. 'Are you on your own?'

'Yes. It was just a spur-of-the-moment thing. I wanted to see . . . how you both were.'

His short laugh was bitter. 'Still alive, I'm afraid.'

'Dad!'

'Sorry, but it's hard to believe you give a damn, these days. We haven't set eyes on you in months and you never pick up the phone.'

'The phone works in both directions,' Toni shot back angrily.

Peter held up his hands. 'Okay, okay. Don't get on your high horse. I don't have the energy for a row.'

Toni sneaked a look at him as he hung the clippers on a nail in the shed. He looked older and greyer. And he'd lost weight. 'You're all right, aren't you?' she asked gruffly.

'Fine.' Then he switched to a subject they could

usually discuss without fighting. 'How's young Chloe?'

'Not great. But she did brilliantly in her Leaving Certificate.'

'She's left school? I can hardly believe it. The years have flown by. What's she going to do now?'

'Probably medicine at Trinity.'

'I should have guessed,' her father said drily.

'Actually, she's talking about taking a year off first.'

'And what does Mr French think of that?'

Toni stared at him. 'Mum hasn't told you?'

'Told me what?'

And, with a heavy heart, Toni sat down on the edge of his bench and told him her story.

Sunday night, 27 August

It was a long and difficult day for Toni and Chloe. Once Alice had made them all some lunch – that was hardly touched – she went home. With the phone off the hook the house was eerily quiet. Toni tried to do some work in the garden but Chloe's prowling around unsettled her. At eight o'clock Toni ordered in a pizza and opened a bottle of wine. She said nothing when Chloe polished off her glass and held it out for a refill, a rebellious look in her eye. It was a relief when she announced she was going to bed. Toni tidied up, took her glass into the living room and called Jade. As usual, Jade was full of down-to-earth good sense and by the time Toni hung up she felt marginally better. She was just locking up when the phone rang again.

'Toni?'

'Ian?'

'Yeah, sorry for ringing so late. I did try earlier but I couldn't get through.'

'We left the phone off the hook all day. There are only so many times you can say "no comment". And I was talking to Jade for the last hour.'

'So, is it true?'

'It seems to be. We'll know for definite after the police have checked fingerprints.'

'I just can't believe it. I knew there had to be a serious reason to make him leave in such a hurry – but this!'

'It is a bit hard to take in.'

'And is it true that she – that this woman is a prostitute?'

'Oh, yes. The police told me that. And they say that Theo was one of her regular clients. And I can believe it. Theo had a habit of going out driving late at night.'

'Didn't you ask him where he was going?'

'He said he just drove,' Toni said, feeling foolish, 'that it relaxed him. Lord, I was terribly gullible, wasn't I?'

'Just trusting,' Ian corrected her. 'Why would you suspect him? I can't believe the man went to a prostitute when he had you at home.'

'Well, thanks, but you don't have to worry about my ego, it's reasonably intact. I'm more shocked that Theo left her to die. He's a doctor, for God's sake. How could he do that?'

'Shock? Panic? Think about it. A respected surgeon found drinking and driving, possibly even under the influence of drugs, with a prostitute. His reputation would be in tatters, his career over.'

'Well, it's over now anyway, isn't it?'

'In Ireland, maybe. But there's nothing to stop him starting again somewhere else.'

'But how? Wouldn't he need papers and a visa to work abroad?'

'You're probably right. And, of course, that's why he would need the money. Well, it looks as if my job as a detective is over before it even started. The professionals have taken over.'

'I hope they find him,' Toni said grimly. 'He shouldn't get away with this.'

'But it would be terrible for Chloe if they did catch up with him and drag him back in handcuffs.'

'Yeah, you're right. But the least he could do is call her and explain himself.'

'Maybe he doesn't know that the cat is out of the bag yet. He could be anywhere in the world by now.'

'Yeah, but I bet he's keeping in touch with someone. He'd want to know if she died, wouldn't he? Because if she had, without regaining consciousness, then he'd be off the hook.'

'True. Maybe he calls the hospital.'

'Or maybe he just keeps in touch with Mr Stringer,' Toni mused.

'Who?'

'His solicitor. He's the last person Theo talked to.'

'Did you tell the police that, Toni?'

'Yeah. Would he have to tell the cops everything he knows or is there such a thing as client confidentiality?'

'I think there might be. Maybe I shouldn't hang up my deerstalker just yet.'

'What do you mean?'

'Why don't we try to track him down?' Ian suggested.

'Do you think we could?'

'You know his family, I know his medical background – we must have as much chance as the police, probably more so.'

'Then let's do it. I'll start by writing to him,' Toni announced. She felt better now that they'd decided to do something.

'I don't understand.'

'I'm going to write to him care of Timothy Stringer. If we're right and they're keeping in touch, Theo will get it eventually.'

'And what are you going to say?'

'I'm going to tell him that he's destroyed his daughter's life, that she's talking about bunking out of college and that the least he owes her is an explanation.'

'There's no harm in sending it,' Ian agreed. 'Let me know what the solicitor says when you give it to him.'

'Will do.'

'How come you're able to talk so freely, Toni? Where's Chloe?'

'Out cold. I poured a couple of glasses of wine into her over dinner and gave her a sleeping tablet before she went to bed.'

'Not a bad idea. Maybe you should take one too.'

'Maybe. But first I'm going to write this letter.'

Chapter Thirty

Monday, 28 August

'Toni! I wasn't expecting you in.'

'Hi, Daniel. I've been here since six thirty. I figured journalists wouldn't be up that early.'

'You shouldn't have come in at all. It's been a lousy weekend for you.'

'I have a lot to do, Daniel, and it keeps my mind occupied.'

'Have the police been in touch since?'

Toni shook her head. 'No, but they probably will be before the day is out. I must say, your son has been great, Daniel. Chloe would have cracked but for him.'

'They seem pretty close, don't they?'

Toni smiled. 'That's an understatement.'

'They're very young to be so serious but Meg keeps reminding me how young she was when we married.'

'And they're both so level-headed. I don't think either of them would rush into anything before they finish college.'

'I hope you're right. Look, I'd better go and scrub up. Talk to you later.'

Sandra walked into Reception. 'Morning, Sandra,' Toni called.

'Toni! How did you get past that lot?' Sandra indicated the throng of press at the gates.

'I got up early. Please don't put anyone through who phones from the papers or TV stations,' Toni begged.

'Should I call our security firm and ask them to put a man on the gate?'

'That's a great idea,' Toni said warmly.

Sandra flushed with pleasure.

When morning surgery was finished, Jade arrived with sandwiches and coffee. 'I didn't think you'd want to go out to lunch today.'

'Thanks.' Toni unwrapped a salad sandwich and took a bite.

Jade settled herself in a chair and took a sip of her coffee. 'I expect the police will be talking to staff at the hospital today,' she said.

'I suppose so. They asked me for a list of friends and relatives – anyone Theo might have gone to stay with or might know where he'd gone.' Toni gave a wry smile. 'It was a very short list.'

'Has he any family?' Jade asked.

'He had an older sister but she died a couple of years ago. His parents are dead too. Apart from that there's only Marianna's family and they haven't seen him.'

'And you have no idea where he might have gone?'

Toni shook her head. 'I'm pretty sure he's left the country, though. He took his passport.'

Jade noticed the faraway look in her eye. 'What are you thinking?'

'I want to talk to her,' Toni said.

'Who?'

'That woman. She's the only one who can tell me what really happened that night.'

'The police have told you what happened.'

'They said as little as possible.'

'Is she in Sylvester's?' Jade asked.

'Yes.'

'Then not only will the place be crawling with police but the staff know you.'

'Only some of them do,' Toni argued. 'I could go in after visiting time tonight when it's quiet.'

'It's a mistake,' Jade told her.

'Are you telling me that you wouldn't do the same?'

'I would have been up there first thing Saturday morning,' Jade admitted.

Toni knew she was taking a huge chance going to Sylvester's but she had to see this woman. How else would she find out what Theo had really been up to? Of course the woman was a prostitute and might lie – the more she embellished the truth the more she'd get from the tabloids for her story. Still, Toni had to try to get to the truth. She walked to the hospital, and hugged the collar of her trench coat to her face as she walked briskly through the foyer. Taking the lift to the fourth floor she turned left and walked down the long corridor only to find that she was in the cardiac unit.

'Can I help you?' a young nurse asked pleasantly.

Toni glanced around nervously but there was no one else around and this girl hadn't a clue who she was. 'Yes, please, I'm visiting my aunt. I think she's in St Gabriel's ward.'

'That's on the second floor. Turn right when you get out of the lift.'

Toni looked confused. 'But I thought—'

'They've moved around some of the wards,' the nurse explained, 'although I've no idea why.'

Toni smiled and hurried back to the lift. God, if she didn't get caught now it would be a miracle.

The ward was in darkness when Toni stepped out of the lift. She made her way quietly down to room four and put her head round the door. 'May Darcy?'

The woman in the bed lifted her head. 'Who wants to know?'

Toni closed the door quietly. 'Theo French's wife.'

The woman looked her up and down. 'So, you're the little wife, are ye? Yer not a bit like I was expecting.'

'Likewise,' Toni said faintly. She'd been expecting a skinny little blonde, someone not much older than Chloe, but May Darcy was at least fifty, probably weighed in at fourteen stone and had a mop of dyed auburn hair.

'I suppose yer here to warn me off.'

'Sorry?'

'Well, it's too late, love, I've told the police everything. I wouldn't have said a word if the stupid bastard had at least called an ambulance for me. I'm loyal to me regular punters, ye know, but the bloody fool just left me there.'

'I know. I'm sorry. How are you feeling?'

May looked taken aback. 'Eh, all right. I won't be working for a while.' She indicated her left leg, which was encased in plaster. 'But me 'ead's all right. A tough nut to crack, that's me.'

Toni smiled faintly.

'He should pay through the nose for this, ye know. I'm going to be out of pocket and I'll probably lose some punters. They're not going to sit playing with themselves for a couple of months until I'm ready to do business again.'

'You should be able to make a claim. You need to get yourself a solicitor. And the papers would pay you for your story.'

'Are you for real?' May was astounded.

'Yep. You see, I was planning to divorce him anyway.'

May threw back her head and laughed. 'Well, that's a good one. Yer divorcing him?'

'I've wanted to leave for months now. But after what he's done to you . . . I didn't think he could sink this low.'

'He probably just panicked, silly bugger,' May said generously.

'You're very forgiving.'

May shrugged. 'Life's too short. So, tell me, was he terrible to live with?'

'Recently, yes.'

'I'm not surprised. He's a bit of a weirdo, if ye ask me.'

'How long have you . . . known him?'

May screwed up her face. 'It must be nearly eight years now.'

Toni gasped. 'Eight years?'

'Yeah. He first came to me when his wife got sick.'

'Oh, my God. And, eh, how often?'

'Sometimes every week, then I wouldn't see him for a couple of months, then he'd be back again.' She paused. 'Some fellas are like that.'

'Did you do it – in the car?'

May laughed at her. 'We did it everywhere, love. Ah,

no, I'm just kidding ye. We usually went back to me flat. And sometimes I brought him to parties.'

'Parties?'

May nodded. 'Very select, only regulars – people ye could trust. Theo only came along a couple of times a year, he was very careful. He wouldn't go unless I knew everyone who was going to be there.' She chuckled. 'But they weren't half as exciting as it says in the papers. There was never more than six or eight people and most of them just wanted to get high or drink.'

'What did Theo want?' Toni asked quietly.

'He did a little coke and had a few drinks.'

Toni nearly fell off her chair. 'He was always giving out about drugs – he even hated smoking. And he never drank more than a couple of glasses of wine when we were out.'

'A lot of punters are like that,' May confided. 'They're like naughty schoolboys with me and like priests at home.'

Toni heard voices in the corridor and stood up. 'I'd better get out of here.'

'The papers would have a field day if they caught ye up here with me.'

Toni smiled wryly. 'Wouldn't they just? Look, thanks for talking to me.'

'It's not yer fault he did what he did,' May told her. 'And if ye want my opinion yer better off without him. A fine-looking girl like ye – sure ye could have any man.'

Ian was walking out to the car park at the back of the hospital when he caught sight of Toni. He was about to call out but stopped himself in time. She would really have appreciated that! Instead he quickened his pace and within moments was walking at her side. 'Good evening, Ms Jordan. Can't keep away from me, eh?'

Toni kept walking. 'For God's sake, Ian, don't draw attention to me.'

'It's hardly the place to come if you're trying to keep a low profile,' he murmured. 'Why on earth are you here? Were you visiting someone?'

Toni shot him a guilty look.

'Toni? Oh, Jeez, Toni, tell me you didn't.'

Toni said nothing, just kept walking.

'Are you crazy? What if someone had seen you?'

Toni stopped at the exit and glanced around. 'They didn't.'

'Are you driving?'

'No, of course not. The press and the police know my car.'

'I'll give you a lift.'

'If I'm seen with you—'

'You can stretch out on the back seat. Now, let's get out of here.'

'I still can't believe you did that,' he said again, after draining the last of his pint.

Toni's lips twitched. 'I can't believe I didn't get caught.'

'So, what did this woman have to tell you?'

'Nothing much.'

'What was she like?' he asked curiously.

'I liked her.'

Ian stood up to go to the bar. 'Women! I'll never understand you!'

Chapter Thirty-one

Thursday, 7 September

'My goodness, did you see this?' Vicky pored over the paper. '"Prostitute tells of Surgeon's Kinky Habits."'

Sandra glowered at her. 'I don't think you should be reading that in here. It would upset Toni.'

'She isn't here, is she? Probably skiving off again,' Vicky remarked loudly.

Sandra was furious. Vicky had done that deliberately because Mr Perkins was passing. 'Of course she isn't,' she replied, equally loudly. 'Toni is in a meeting with Daniel.'

Robert halted and turned to Sandra, with a silky smile. 'Are they in Daniel's office, Sandra?'

Sandra could have bitten her tongue off. Whatever the meeting was about she knew that Mr Perkins' presence wouldn't be welcome. 'Yes, Mr Perkins. They should be finished any minute. I think they were just going through Daniel's schedule for next week.'

Robert carried on to his own office. Sandra sighed with relief.

'What are you up to, Sandra?' Vicky asked, suspiciously. 'Or, more to the point, what are Toni and Daniel up to?'

Sandra busied herself with the post. 'Nothing. Why would they be up to anything?'

'Because they're wondering how much longer they're going to have jobs.'

'I'm sure Mr Perkins will keep things the same as before,' Sandra said firmly. 'Why would he change anything?'

Vicky smoothed down her blue uniform and gazed proudly at her breasts. 'Why not? But don't worry, Sandra. I'll put in a good word for you if you like.'

Sandra bristled at her cocky tone. 'No, thanks. I'll let my work speak for itself.'

'Then you'd better start looking for a new job.'

Sandra was too choked to reply. What had she ever done to Vicky? Why was she always so bitchy and cruel?

'Jade can certainly start looking,' Vicky continued. 'I'm going to make damn sure she gets the sack.'

'And how can you do that?'

'Robert listens to me. He'll do whatever I ask him.'

'And why would he listen to you, you silly cow?'

Vicky stared at her, shocked. Timid Sandra had never been bitchy. 'How dare you?' she blustered.

'Because you're getting too big for your boots.'

'Well, your days are numbered, that's for sure,' Vicky said angrily.

'Whatever.'

Vicky stormed off. To hell with Sandra! To hell with them all! When they were gone, she'd be in charge and anyone she hired would damn well show her some respect. She marched straight up to Robert's office to discuss it with him.

When she barged in, Robert looked up and watched

as she perched on the chair in front of him, making sure to hike her skirt up a few inches. 'I just wondered, Rob,' she said, 'if you'd thought any more about staff.'

Robert sighed. Vicky had been going on and on at him since he'd bought Theo out. It was so tiresome – the perils of screwing someone you worked with. Perhaps he should do something about that. For the moment, though, he smiled charmingly. 'There hasn't been time, my dear. I've been so incredibly busy.'

Vicky's eyes wandered to the newspapers spread out on the desk. 'You *are* going to put me in charge, aren't you, Rob?' she persisted.

'Oh, my dear, you don't want to be bothered with all the humdrum work involved in running this place. You're much too pretty for such a dreary job.'

'You don't think I can do it,' Vicky accused.

'Of course I do,' Robert said placatingly. 'But I need to keep Toni on until I've got this place under control. Then we can start making some real changes around here.'

Vicky relaxed slightly. He'd said 'we'. She was being too paranoid. Of course Robert would look after her. Hadn't he always said he would? It was the one reason she'd stayed with him – it certainly wasn't for his body. Within a few months she'd be running the Blessington. And then, once she had some money and experience, she could wave Robert and the clinic goodbye. She stood up and came round the desk to plant a kiss on his cheek. 'We'll make such a wonderful team,' she murmured in his ear.

Robert fondled her bum and buried his face in her cleavage. 'We already do, my dear.'

Toni left Daniel's office and walked slowly back to her own. She didn't feel any better for the meeting, even though Daniel had assured her that Robert had no immediate plans to change anything. And it seemed Daniel had no immediate plans either: he was resigned to Robert being the boss now. Toni threw her pad on to the desk in frustration. She had hoped this meeting was about them joining forces either to ensure the continued integrity of the clinic or decide to start up somewhere else. But Daniel, like Jade, had suggested she concentrate on getting her personal life in order.

She had finally seen a solicitor – a girl from an old firm her dad had recommended. But her sympathy and kindness had got on Toni's nerves. She had explained her situation to Teresa Neil in a cool, calm voice and sat patiently as Ms Neil told her what she already knew. Divorce was a long, complicated business and it didn't help that her husband was not traceable.

'I'm sure his solicitor knows where he is,' Toni had said.

'I will write to Mr Stringer and let him know that I am representing you. Then we need to agree an official separation. That's only a formality as Mr French is the one who filed for divorce. We need details of his financial status, of course.'

'Well, I can supply part of that,' Toni had told her bitterly. 'He took most of the money in our joint accounts.'

'Right, then, that's about it for now.' Teresa had stood up and held out her hand. 'I'll set the wheels in motion and be in touch.'

❦

Toni didn't share Ms Neil's confidence that everything would be plain sailing. Theo had shown no sign so far of playing ball: he had not answered her letter and the discreet Mr Stringer wouldn't even reveal if Theo had received it. 'But why not?' Toni had demanded.

'It's my duty to keep my client's confidence,' Stringer had replied self-importantly.

'Fine!' Toni had slammed down the phone.

Now, as she stared out of the window of her office and watched a woman struggle with a brolly in the car park, Toni regretted her temper. She would probably get further with these people if she batted her eyelashes and wept prettily. That's what Jade would have done: she was one hell of an actress when the situation called for it – Toni had seen her in action. There had been the memorable occasion when Perky had accused her of deliberately not booking him into the black-tie dinner he attended every year along with the other ambitious movers and shakers. 'Oh, Robert, I'm so terribly sorry,' Jade had said, full of remorse, 'I must have forgotten. It was that time of the month, and you know what we women are like – completely unreliable when our hormones come into play.'

Robert had looked at her disbelievingly but Jade's expression was innocent. 'I'm so ashamed of myself,' she'd continued. 'If there's anything I can do to make it up to you . . .'

'Oh, forget it,' Robert had said, then strode back to his office.

After the door had shut behind him Toni and Jade

had burst out laughing. 'You didn't forget at all,' Toni had accused her.

'How can you say such a thing?' Jade had asked, but as she sashayed down the corridor she'd delivered over her shoulder a broad wink.

'Nutter,' Toni said now, thinking of her friend. Mind you, it would be great to be more like her. No one got the better of Jade, yet everyone liked her. Well, except Perky and Vicky, but that was almost a compliment.

The phone interrupted her thoughts and she was thrilled to hear her stepdaughter on the line. 'Chloe, how's life in Skerries?'

'Fine, did you hear the news? Mark got a place at UCD on the second round of offers on Monday.'

'Daniel told me. I'm delighted for him.'

'I miss him. I miss you too,' Chloe added hastily.

'And I miss you, love.'

'Any word from Dad?'

'No, I'm afraid not.'

'I saw the papers. Your folks didn't want me to but I needed to know.'

Mary Jordan had called to let Toni know that Chloe had seen every article there was to see about her father.

'Do you think it's all true, Toni?'

'No, love,' Toni said – quite honestly, thanks to May Darcy. The colourful details of the parties was fabricated at least.

'Me neither.' Chloe sounded relieved. 'Okay, then. I'd better go. I'll put you on to your dad. He wants a word.'

'Hi, Dad.' Toni couldn't get used to this new relationship with her father. In the past when he'd answered the phone they'd exchanged some stiff pleasantries and he'd passed the phone to his wife. At least some good had come of this sorry mess.

'Hello, love. Did you see that solicitor?'

'I did. She's going to get in touch with Theo's guy.'

'That's good. Now just try to put it out of your mind and leave it to her.'

Toni said goodbye and turned back to the files on her desk. Her dad was right: if she concentrated on the day-to-day running of the clinic and put Robert, Theo and Daniel out of her mind she'd be a lot better off.

She had just got down to work when the phone rang again. 'Toni, it's Francis Price.'

Toni's heart skipped a beat. 'Francis? Is everything all right?'

'I'm afraid not, my dear.' His voice shook. 'We're at the hospice. Do you know where that is?'

Toni swallowed back the tears. 'I'll be there in half an hour.'

Toni tried to smile at the tiny shape in the bed, but it didn't matter – Dotty's eyes were closed. She glanced up in alarm at Francis. He came over to her and kissed her cheek. 'She sleeps most of the time now, but she isn't in any pain. Do you mind if I pop out for a moment?' He squeezed her hand and left the room.

Toni sat down by the bed and took Dotty's thin hand.

Dotty's eyes fluttered open.

'Sorry, Dotty. I didn't mean to disturb you.'

Dotty grinned and, for a moment, looked just like her

old self. 'I'll have plenty of time to sleep, love. Help me sit up a little. It's good to see you.'

Toni fixed some pillows and eased her up carefully. Dotty lay back. 'I don't suppose you've heard from the old sod yet.'

'If you mean my dear husband, no, I haven't. Anyway, let's not talk about him. Tell me about you.'

'I'm in a bloody hospice, Toni. What do you want me to say? That I'm feeling much better?'

Tears pricked Toni's eyes and she bowed her head to hide them from her friend. 'I'm sorry.'

'Oh, don't be,' Dotty said impatiently. 'It's actually very nice here, and at least Francis isn't fussing around so much.' She realised he wasn't in the room. 'I suppose he's off having a smoke?'

Despite herself Toni grinned. 'I think so. Are you in any pain?'

'No. To be honest I feel as high as a kite most of the time. If only I'd had these drugs in my student days.'

'Dotty Price! Shame on you.'

'Ah, you've got to laugh, haven't you? How's Chloe holding up?'

'She's with my parents at the moment.'

Dotty's eyes sparked with interest. 'You're kidding?'

'Nope. I took your advice and went to see Mum. She's been wonderful.'

'And your father?'

'We've managed to have several conversations without rowing.'

Dotty clutched her hand. 'Oh, I'm so glad, Toni. You need your family at a time like this. And I'm sure they've missed you terribly.' She closed her eyes again.

'Do you want me to go?'

'No, dear. I'm always dozing off these days. But I'd like you to stay for a while, if you don't mind. It's nice to know you're there.'

Toni kissed her forehead. 'I'll be here as long as you like.'

Chapter Thirty-two

Sunday, 10 September

Three days later Dotty passed away with her husband at her side. Toni had gone home for a shower, remarkably cheered by how bright and lively Dotty had been that afternoon: she had entertained Francis and Toni with stories of her student days, although Francis insisted she was making most of it up. 'It's hard to believe now, Toni, but Dotty was a shy, timid girl when I met her first.'

Dotty had winked at Toni. 'That was all technique. Francis was terrified of women and I knew I'd have to play the meek little girl to get him.'

'So you set your cap at him?'

'Absolutely! We were meant for each other. But the silly man would never have realised that. I had to nudge him along.'

Francis smiled. 'You were so pretty.'

Dotty snorted. 'It's a wonder you noticed. He always had his head buried in his books.'

'Ian used to be the same.' Toni had laughed.

'Ian Chase?' Francis looked vaguely surprised. 'Lord, I'd forgotten that you two had been an item. Nice chap.'

Toni stared at her hands. 'Yes.'

Dotty regarded her speculatively. 'How do you feel about fulfilling an old woman's dying wish?'

'Dotty!' Toni was appalled. 'Please don't talk like that.'

'Oh, don't be so silly, girl. It won't be long now. So, will you make me a promise?'

Toni didn't trust herself to speak so she nodded. She knew Dotty didn't have long but it was just so hard to accept. Especially when she was as animated as she was today.

'I want you to go and see Ian Chase and have a nice long chat.'

'Now, Dotty . . .' her husband warned.

'I'm not asking her to jump on him, Francis,' Dotty protested.

Toni giggled. 'Actually, Dotty, we've already made our peace. Ian has been a tower of strength over the last few weeks.'

'Excellent! Will you be moving in together?'

'Dotty!'

'Oh, leave me alone, Francis! I'm not going to be here to see it all played out. I'm entitled to a preview.'

'You are,' Toni confirmed, 'but I'm afraid Ian already has a girlfriend.'

'I wouldn't worry about her,' Dotty said dismissively. 'He'd go back to you like a shot if he had the chance.'

'We'll just have to wait and see,' Toni said.

'If only,' Dotty said, with a wistful sigh. 'Now, off you go, Toni, and let me and my fella have a kiss and a cuddle before I nod off again.'

Toni collected her coat and went to the door. 'I'll bring you back some marshmallows.'

'Lovely,' Dotty said, though her bedside table was full of tempting treats that she hadn't touched.

And when Toni returned a couple of hours later it was to be told by a nurse that Dotty had slipped away twenty minutes earlier and Francis was still with her. Toni sat in the waiting room, not wanting to intrude on such a private moment. When he finally came to her she took his hands and kissed him. 'I'm so sorry, Francis.'

Francis smiled through his tears. 'It was very peaceful. She told me what suit and shoes I should wear for the funeral, who I should invite back to the house and then she just said, "I love you," and she was gone.'

Tears rolled down Toni's cheeks.

A nurse appeared in the doorway carrying a tray. 'I thought you could do with some tea,' she explained. 'We're all very sorry for your loss, Mr Price. Dotty was a lovely woman. She was a pleasure to look after.'

When they were alone again, Toni handed him a cup of tea and he looked at her worriedly. 'Dotty has given me instructions about the funeral and she wants me to have people back to the house. Lots of them. She said it should be like a party.' No surprise there, Toni thought. But it was a shame Dotty would not be able to enjoy it.

'I don't know if I can cope with all that,' Francis said, distraught. 'I want to follow her wishes but I just don't know if I'm up to it.'

'Why don't you let me organise it all?' Toni said. 'You take care of the church and the service and leave the rest to me. Between us we'll make sure it's a credit to Dotty.'

The funeral went off exactly as Dotty would have wanted, Toni thought, as she looked around the large living room full of people talking and laughing. There were a few people from the hospital, but most of the guests were Dotty's friends and relations and there were – not surprisingly – a large number of them. Dotty had left lists of people to be informed of her demise. Some of the comments she'd scribbled beside certain names had had Toni rolling around laughing. Beside Ivy O'Brien's name she'd read: 'Nosy old cow who'll be trying to figure out how much the coffin cost. Make sure she sees all my best silver.'

Much to Francis's embarrassment, she had even left instructions for 'My Way' to be sung when she was being carried out of the church.

Toni watched him now, surrounded by friends and family. There was a polite smile on his face but a distant look in his eye. He had, as Dotty had stipulated, worn his new tweed suit with a garish tie she'd bought for him some time ago. 'You've never worn it,' Francis said she'd complained from her sickbed, 'so it's the least you can do for me.'

'But it's so . . . inappropriate.'

Dotty's eyes had twinkled mischievously. 'It will give them all something to talk about.'

Toni smiled to herself.

'A penny for them?' Ian said quietly.

Toni swung round. 'I was just thinking how much she

made me laugh – no matter how miserable I was. Poor Francis looks so lost without her.'

Ian moved closer. 'It can't be easy for you either – especially after all that's happened.

Toni blinked back tears. 'I'll miss her advice,' she admitted. 'She never steered me wrong. Do you know that one of the last things she said to me was that I should make my peace with you? She was thrilled when I told her we were friends again.'

'I'll take that as a compliment.'

'You can,' Toni assured him. 'She liked you. And Francis does too.'

'He's a good man. Look, Toni, I know this isn't the time or the place but I just wanted you to know that I'm getting close to a lead.'

'I thought you'd forgotten. It's been a while since I've heard from you.'

'I had to go away for a couple of days.'

Toni had a mental image of him rubbing oil into Carla's back.

'A conference down in Cork. Total waste of time.'

Toni smiled broadly. 'Oh, well, no problem.'

'Anyway, I hope to have some news for you soon.' He lowered his voice as he saw Francis approaching. 'I think you're needed. I'll call you.'

'Hello, Ian.'

'Francis.' Ian shook hands with the older man. 'How are you holding up?'

Francis flourished his glass. 'As long as I've got one of these in my hand I can cope,' he joked. But he was only a shadow of his former self: his shoulders drooped and there were dark circles under his eyes.

'Have you had anything to eat?' Toni asked him.

'I had a sandwich.'

'Let me get you some smoked salmon and brown bread,' she offered. 'It will soak up some of that Scotch.'

'That would be a shame,' he said. 'I'd prefer it if you filled up your own glass and joined me for a chat in the library.'

'I'll leave you to it.' Ian moved away to join his colleagues.

'Thank you for all your help, my dear.' Francis handed her a Scotch, took his own glass and went to sit at his desk. 'I just wanted to have a word with you before I get too squiffy to talk. Dotty left me very specific instructions about a lot of things, as you know.' A sheaf of paper lay in front of him covered in Dotty's slanting scrawl. 'She wanted me to distribute some of her personal items – ornaments, jewellery and the like. She wanted you to have this.' He took a black velvet box from the desk drawer and handed it to her.

Toni opened the box and gasped. 'Oh, Francis! I can't take these.'

'You must, my dear, or I'll be haunted until the day I die.'

'But . . . but . . .'

Francis looked at the heavy ruby earrings and matching necklace. 'She loved them and she loved you. She wanted you to have them, Toni. Please don't argue.'

Toni stood up to hug him. 'Thank you, Francis. It's nice to have a keepsake.'

'Toni, I wonder if I could ask you to do me yet another favour?'

'Anything.'

'Well, Dotty left some gifts for the nurses at the hospice. And although I'm extremely grateful to them, I just can't face going back . . .'

'I'll take care of it.'

There was a brief silence, then Toni asked, 'What will you do now, Francis?'

He stared into his glass. 'I don't know. I suppose I'll muddle along somehow.'

'You must take care of yourself.'

'I don't have a choice. Mrs Caulfield shoves food down my throat every chance she gets.'

'And you must get out and about too. Dotty wouldn't want you moping around in the house on your own.' Toni saw the bleak look in his eyes. How could she talk such crap? The man had just lost the love of his life, his partner, friend and confidante. If he wasn't so polite he'd probably tell her to bugger off – and rightly so! 'Don't mind me, Francis. I don't know what I'm talking about. All I can tell you is that there's always an ear at the end of the phone if you want it.'

'What about a drinking partner?' Now Francis had a twinkle in his eye.

Toni raised her glass. 'Need you ask?'

Chapter Thirty-three

Friday, 15 September

Chloe pulled on a sweatshirt and went out to the garden. 'Hi, Mr J,' she said shyly.

Peter Jordan turned. 'Hello there. Have you come to help?' He waved towards the flowerbeds where he was digging up bulbs and placing them carefully in crates.

'I think I'd be more of a hindrance than a help,' Chloe said. 'Toni's tried to get me interested in gardening but I'm just no good at it.'

'Toni has green fingers all right,' Peter said proudly.

'Yes, you should see our garden. It used to be a wilderness but now it's gorgeous.'

Peter had fallen silent. Although he'd grudgingly accepted Theo French into his home, he had always vowed that he would never step inside the other man's. And he'd been proved right about him. When Toni had told him what Theo had done he had felt sick at the idea of his daughter being married to him.

'Are you okay?' Chloe looked at him, concerned.

'Just daydreaming, love. Why don't you pick a few flowers for Mary? Lots of pink.'

He watched her go to the shed for the secateurs. She was a pretty girl and, no doubt, would become a beautiful woman – a strong, kind, intelligent one at that. It was hard to believe she was French's daughter, though there was no denying she had his eyes. But she had a gentle, sweet nature and loved a laugh. In fact, she could almost be Toni's own daughter. Although, he chuckled, Toni was a lot more stubborn. She got that from him. He sighed heavily. So many years had been wasted because of Theo French, who had hurt not only Toni but his own daughter too. It was time Peter put the past behind him to look after his daughter – and his step-granddaughter. He was chortling to himself as she approached.

'What is it?' she asked shyly.

'I was just wondering if there's such a thing as a step-grandfather.'

'Sure there is. His name's Peter Jordan.'

Peter felt as if he'd been given another chance. He'd messed things up with Toni but maybe he could make up for it by looking out for Chloe. The girl needed a father figure in her life. His heart had nearly broken as he watched her read the details of her father's accident and, worse, his weird sex-life.

It couldn't be easy for Toni either: the shame and embarrassment were overwhelming. But all she seemed bothered about was Chloe. He swallowed the lump in his throat and bent over the flowerbed. He was proud of the way his daughter was handling this situation. Very proud indeed.

Jade was rushing back from the bank when she saw Ian climbing into his car outside the clinic. 'Ian, what on earth are you doing here?'

Ian got out and hugged her. 'Jade, great to see you. How are things?'

'Fine. Were you here to see Toni?'

Ian grinned. 'Actually, Robert. We're organising a rota of anaesthetists for the clinic.'

Jade knew that Ian had refused point blank until now to have anything to do with the clinic and they'd had to use anaesthetists from a hospital across town. 'Well, that's great. Toni will be pleased.'

'How is she? She was very upset at Dotty's funeral on Tuesday.'

'Oh,' Jade said, surprised. Toni hadn't mentioned that Ian was at the funeral but, then, she'd been walking around in a daze since Dotty's death. 'Yeah, they were close. But you know Toni, she's getting on with things.'

'I was sorry to hear about you and Aidan,' he said suddenly. Jade started. 'Sorry.' He fumbled for words. 'It's just I've never had an opportunity to say that before. I've missed you both. We had some good times. Do you keep in touch?'

'We didn't, but that changed lately when Aidan's mother died.' In fact, she hadn't seen Aidan since the night they'd had dinner together. 'He's got a new job so that's probably a good distraction.'

'Isn't he working for himself any more?'

Jade bit her lip. It wasn't like her to slip up. 'He was fed up worrying about accounts and tax. He wanted to get back to doing the job he was qualified for.'

'Sensible man. Give him my best. Good to see you, Jade.'

'You too.' He was such a nice man, she thought. She reached up to give him a friendly peck on the cheek.

'Goodbye, Jade.'

Jade hurried inside. It was such a pity Toni had broken up with Ian. He was still good-looking too – although he had a slight beer belly but that was to be expected at his age. She knew he was seeing Carla but from what she'd heard from her sources at the hospital, the relationship didn't seem to be going anywhere. Maybe there was a chance that he and Toni would get back together . . .

'That bitch has been driving me mad.' Sandra banged the filing-cabinet drawer.

It wasn't often that Jade had heard Sandra curse. 'Let me guess. Are you talking about my lovely colleague Vicky Harrison? What's she done now?' She took off her coat and sat down beside Sandra.

'Oh, nothing . . . Everything. She's acting as if she owns the place. It makes my blood boil. She doesn't do half as much work as you do.'

Jade smiled. 'Is Toni in?'

'You just missed her. I think she had another meeting with the solicitor.'

'She seems to spend her life in meetings these days.'

'We ought to organise another night out to cheer her up,' Sandra said brightly.

'You're becoming quite a party animal, Ms Tomkins.'

'That's what Mam says. She's delighted.'

'How is she?'

Sandra's eyes danced and Vicky was forgotten. 'Steadier on her feet than she's been in years and her speech is perfect – unless she's very tired.'

'Any reason for the improvement?'

'Nothing I can put my finger on. Her medicine is the same. Her diet is the same. But she's been going out more to social events in the parish. One of our neighbours started taking her along.'

'Maybe she's got herself a fella,' Jade suggested.

'Don't be silly.'

'She's not that old, Sandra.'

'And she's great company,' Sandra said thoughtfully. 'I often thought she must be lonely. It's almost fifteen years since Dad died.'

'She was a very young widow.'

'She never looked at another man though – and plenty were interested.'

'Maybe she's ready for companionship now,' Jade suggested. 'And if she thinks your social life is improving she probably feels more comfortable about going out.'

'Oh, Jade! Do you think she's been staying in just because of me?'

'Sandra, your mother's been very sick. All I'm saying is that she'll enjoy herself more if she knows you're having a good time too.'

Sandra thought about this for a moment.

Jade looked at her worriedly. What had she started? 'Sandra?'

'There's only one thing for it,' Sandra said firmly. 'We're definitely having a night out. And it's going to be a late one!'

'Mr Stringer still hasn't supplied me with financial statements,' Teresa Neil told her client.

'Because the money is all in offshore accounts.' Toni tapped her nails impatiently on the arm of her chair.

'Have you any proof of that?' Teresa had asked.

'Of course not. He'd hardly call me with the account numbers.'

Teresa put down her pen and fixed her with a cool stare. 'Ms Jordan, this isn't an easy time for you, and separations can get ugly and costly. It would help if you remembered that I'm on your side.'

'I'm sorry, but surely it's a clear-cut case. He stole all of my money.'

'No, he didn't. He withdrew money from your joint account. You could have done the same. There was nothing illegal about it.'

Toni pinched the bridge of her nose between her thumb and forefinger. 'Well, if Stringer won't co-operate what do we do?'

'Mr Stringer is co-operating as far as he can, but he says he cannot contact his client and his hands are tied until Mr French contacts him.'

'He knows where Theo is. I'd stake my life on it!'

'Be that as it may, Ms Jordan, I can't call the man a liar. It was Mr French who asked for the divorce. We have to assume he will be in touch with his solicitor to progress matters.'

'And until then we just twiddle our thumbs?'

'No. I have written to Mr Stringer and told him that we will not agree to the sale of the house until financial arrangements are in place.'

'Oh.' Toni was mollified.

'Like I say, Toni. I'm on your side.'

Chapter Thirty-four

Saturday, 16 September

Jade sipped her wine and looked around her appreciatively. It was so nice to sit in Cooper's café instead of her usual Chinese restaurant. Cooper's was in one of the nicer parts of the city and populated in the evenings by Beautiful People. It was also nice to look at the menu without worrying about the prices – although, of course, she'd still be careful in her choice. And it was a definite plus to be able to order a glass of wine while she waited for Toni and Sandra. She glanced at her watch. It had only just gone eight so they weren't exactly late. Anyway, Jade didn't mind if they were: she was enjoying people-watching and soaking up the atmosphere.

'Jade!' Sandra handed her coat shyly to a waitress and hurried over to the table. 'Sorry I'm late. It's very posh here, isn't it?'

'You're not late, I was early,' Jade said as Sandra sat down. 'You're going to have to learn to stop apologising all the time.'

'Sorry . . . oh!' Sandra giggled.

'Let me get you a drink. What would you like?'

'Whatever you're having.'

'This chardonnay is nice, so why don't I order a bottle?'

'Lovely.'

Jade beckoned to a passing waiter and gave him their order. 'I'm sure we'll get through it,' she said to Sandra, and winked, as Toni appeared and sat down.

'Hi, Toni. Jade's trying to get me drunk.'

'Well, she'll have no problem getting *me* drunk,' Toni said drily. 'I'm ready to drown in the stuff.'

The waiter appeared with the wine and filled their glasses.

Jade raised hers. 'Here's to forgetting all of our problems.'

'I'd have to get completely rat-arsed to manage that,' Toni assured her. 'But I'd like to make a toast to you two. Thank you for putting up with me these last few weeks and for talking me into coming out tonight.'

'You're welcome.' Sandra sipped her wine. 'This *is* nice. And this place must be *very* expensive.'

'This is on me, Sandra.'

'Jade?' Toni looked at her enquiringly.

'Aidan's doing really well in his new job. And he insisted on giving me a little . . . present.'

'I'm delighted for him, but you shouldn't be spending your money on us,' Toni remonstrated.

'Absolutely not,' Sandra agreed stoutly.

'Rubbish! And, anyway, I'm entitled to a little treat.'

Toni laughed. 'Well, okay, then. But at least let me buy the next bottle.'

'*Another* bottle!' Sandra gasped. 'Oh dear.'

'I'm afraid you're in very bad company, Sandra,' Toni told her.

'True,' Jade agreed. 'You'll learn nothing but bad habits from us.'

'And how to screw up your life,' Toni added.

'Oh, stop that,' Sandra protested. 'I didn't have a life at all until you two took pity on me.'

Toni tossed back her hair. 'Sandra, you're a tonic.'

'You should wear your hair loose more often – it's gorgeous like that.' Sandra would have killed for Toni's silky mane.

'But not very practical.'

Jade made a face at her. 'Who cares about practical, Toni? You're not at work now.'

'And I probably won't be at work at all soon, if Robert has his way.'

Sandra's smile disappeared. 'You don't believe that, do you?'

'Of course she doesn't,' Jade said quickly. 'She's just feeling sorry for herself.'

'Don't mind me, Sandra.'

'I suppose Vicky will get promoted,' Jade added morosely.

'Well, put it this way,' Toni said, 'I don't think I'll be giving her that formal warning.'

Sandra's eyes were on stalks. 'You were going to give Vicky a formal warning?'

Toni knew this was unprofessional but it probably didn't matter any more. 'She's been messing us around so much lately. Her attendance record is lousy—'

'And when she's in she makes mistakes all the time,' Jade chipped in.

'It's a wonder she hasn't killed someone,' Toni added.

'Oh, well. She'll probably be running the place soon. She might have to do some work for a change.'

Jade's eyebrows disappeared under her fringe. 'No chance. She'll just sit in your chair and bark orders all day.'

'She's welcome to my job and all of the hassle that goes with it. I bet her little affair with Robert won't last long once she starts to ruin his business.'

Sandra choked on her wine. 'Mr Perkins and Vicky are having an affair?' she gasped.

'Oh, Sandra!' Jade groaned. 'Where have you been?'

'In a different world by the sound of it. I've seen the way she flirts with him but I had no idea they were at it!'

'And how!' Toni said wryly.

Sandra shuddered. 'How can she?'

'I wonder will Daniel start again somewhere else,' Jade mused.

'Oh, wouldn't it be lovely if we could all stay together?' Sandra said wistfully, as the waiter arrived with their starters.

'It certainly would.' Toni raised her glass to her friends. It was nice to get out of the house for a while. Chloe was still with her parents and Alice was only coming in once a week so Toni found the place more depressing than ever.

'So, Sandra, what's new in your life?' Jade asked. 'Any men?'

'Don't be silly, Jade. Where would I meet *men*?'

'You do work in Reception,' Toni pointed out.

'Yes, and the men I meet are either coming to get tummy tucks or hair implants. Very attractive.'

'Well, maybe it's not the best place to get a date,' Jade conceded. 'You should let us set you up.'

'We've been through all this and I'm still not interested,' Sandra said firmly. 'I'm quite happy as I am. Anyway, I don't have time for a boyfriend, even though Mum's so much better.'

'The herbal tea must be doing her good.' Jade winked at Sandra.

Toni looked puzzled. 'Herbal tea?'

'Absolutely! Oh, look, here's our food. Shall I order that second bottle?'

'Why not?' the others chorused.

'Another Irish coffee?' Toni waved her empty glass. It was a good thing Chloe wasn't here to see the state she was in.

'Not for me,' Sandra said, and hiccuped. 'Excuse me,' she said, with a giggle. 'I think I'm a bit tipsy.'

Jade looked at her stretched out on Toni's sofa, one foot waving about and her skirt riding up her hips. '*No!* Are you?'

'How about it, Jade?' Toni asked.

'Just a little one.'

Toni picked up the glasses and wove her way out to the kitchen. There was only a little cream left so she made Irish coffee for Jade, straight coffee for Sandra, poured a large Scotch for herself, and put them on a tray with a packet of chocolate biscuits.

'Oh, yummy.' When she spied the biscuits Sandra pulled herself up.

Jade eyed the Scotch. 'You shouldn't mix your drinks,

Toni. You'll be dying in the morning.'

'So? God, you sounded like Ian there. He was always giving out to me for mixing drinks.'

'Ian Chase never gave out to you in his life,' Jade retorted.

Toni collapsed into an armchair. 'He didn't, did he?'

'Maybe you two will get back together,' Jade said lightly. Toni still hadn't told her there was anything going on but Jade had a feeling . . .

'There's no going back after all these years.'

'Why not?' Sandra asked curiously. She might be drunk but she was still capable of sniffing out gossip, and it was great to hear Jade and Toni talk openly about their love-lives. 'I think life's too short for that kind of attitude.'

'Well said, Sandra.' Jade applauded her.

Toni scowled at them. 'Stop ganging up on me. I've enough on my plate at the moment. Romance is the last thing on my mind.'

'*Really?*' Jade said, but before Toni could answer she turned to Sandra. 'I think you and I should be making a move.'

Sandra snuggled into the sofa. 'But I'm so comfortable.'

Toni stood up. 'I'll phone for a taxi.'

'That's pushing the boat out a bit,' Jade said.

'Maybe you could make it home,' Toni said drily, 'but there's no way this girl can walk to Kilmainham.'

'Maybe not,' Jade conceded. God, it was good not to have to worry about money. If only she could believe it would always be like this. But it would be a long time before she could trust Aidan again. He'd hurt her too badly and the wounds hadn't healed yet. But they were improving, she acknowledged. And given time . . .

'I think I'm going to be sick,' Sandra moaned.

Jade jumped up and hauled her out to the bathroom. 'Come on, I've got you. Let's go talk to God on the big white telephone. Back in a mo,' she called to Toni, who was standing in the hall with the phone in her hand.

Toni gave her address and hung up. When Jade reappeared, she said, 'Is Sandra okay?'

'No, but she'll live. I just hope she doesn't throw up in the taxi.'

'Maybe I should get her some water.'

'Good idea – and a couple of painkillers. In fact, I'll have some too.' Jade yawned widely and looked at Toni's rumpled hair and smeared mascara. 'You should join us. I don't think any of us is going to feel too bright in the morning.'

Chapter Thirty-five

Saturday, 23 September

Mark was watching the train pull into Connolly station. He couldn't wait to see Chloe again. It had been almost a month since they'd met although they'd spoken nearly every day. He scanned each carriage as the train slowed and then there she was, waving at him from behind a young family unloading buggies. She hopped from one foot to the other impatiently, then moved past them and ran into Mark's arms.

'I thought you were never going to get off,' he said, his eyes caressing her beautiful face. 'Your hair's longer.'

Chloe made a face. 'I was going to get it cut but then I thought maybe you'd prefer it long again.'

'I'd like you if you were bald,' he assured her. He took her backpack, slung it easily over his shoulder and led the way to the car. 'So, did you have a good time?'

'I actually did. I thought it would be quiet and boring but Mary and Peter socialise more than we do.'

Mark laughed. 'One of the perks of being retired. Money.'

'It's a nice thought, isn't it?' Chloe said dreamily. 'To be that old and still enjoying life. Still enjoying each other.'

'That's the way we'll be. We'll have his-and-hers zimmer frames and we'll roll down to the pub together. I'm so glad you're back. I didn't know what to do with myself while you were gone.'

'But it won't be for long, Mark.'

'What do you mean?'

'I'm going to travel. I told you that.'

Mark's smile faded. Chloe had talked about taking a year out to travel but he'd thought she'd change her mind. He hadn't expected her still to be talking about it after her break in Skerries. 'I thought you were just saying that because you were upset.'

'I still am upset,' Chloe said, a steely note in her voice.

'Of course you are,' Mark said. 'And that's all the more reason why you should stay with the people who love you. Don't run away, Chloe. It won't solve anything.'

'I'm not running away,' she said angrily. 'I'm taking a year out to weigh things up and decide what I really want.'

'But now that you don't have to worry about your dad's opinion you could come to UCD with me.'

Chloe wavered for a second, but then her mouth set in a firm line, very like her father's. 'No. It just doesn't feel right. I've got to get away and clear my head. And I need to stand on my own two feet for a change. I've been dependent on Dad for too long.'

'Well, that won't change,' Mark pointed out. 'It's his money you'll be using to travel. Poor little rich girl.'

Chloe stopped in her tracks and slapped his face,

then stared at him in horror as his cheek reddened. 'I'm so sorry!'

Mark touched his face with a rueful smile. 'Me too. Look, I don't want us to fight, Chloe, it's just that I don't want to lose you. You've only just got back and you're talking about leaving again.'

'Please don't make it any harder than it already is, Mark. I have to do this.'

They were half-way home when Mark had plucked up the courage to ask the question uppermost in his mind. 'When will you go?'

Chloe had thought about this a lot. 'After my birthday. It would upset Toni and Alice if I went before then.'

Mark swallowed. 'That's only a few weeks away.'

She nodded and stared out of the window, her eyes bright with tears.

Mark squeezed her knee. 'Then we're going to have to make it one hell of a birthday, aren't we?' he said, with forced enthusiasm.

When they reached the house Alice had laid on a huge spread.

'Roast stuffed chicken,' Chloe squealed in delight. 'And peas and gravy – oh, Alice!'

Alice blushed. 'It's nice to have you home, love. We've missed you.'

'It's great to see you moving around so easily.'

'Oh, I'm fine now. I might even enter the Marathon!'

'Toni isn't home, then?' Chloe had expected her stepmother to be there. It was six o'clock on a Saturday, after all.

The hall door banged and Toni hurried into the kitchen, laden with bags. Mark rushed to help her. 'Oh, thanks, Mark. Chloe!' She threw her arms around her stepdaughter.

Chloe allowed herself to be hugged. 'Hi, Toni. You're only just in time. Alice has made us a lovely dinner.'

Toni heard the reproachful tone and decided to ignore it. 'Sorry, Alice. It took longer than I thought.'

'Shall I get the glasses?' Alice queried.

Toni nodded and produced a bottle of champagne. 'This is what kept me. I couldn't get the damn cooler to work.'

Alice arrived back with champagne glasses just as Toni popped the cork.

'Welcome home, love.' Toni handed Chloe the first glass.

Chloe flashed her a guilty smile. 'Thanks, Toni. This is great.'

Mark took his glass and clinked it against hers. 'Cheers, Chloe.'

Alice took a small sip. 'I think it would be safer if I saved mine until I've served up the dinner. This stuff goes right to my head.'

'I don't think I've ever seen you drunk, Alice,' Chloe teased her.

'Well, today might be the day,' Toni said, and pulled out a second bottle. 'I figured you're nearly eighteen, so what the hell?'

'And what's in here?' Chloe inspected another bag. 'Oh, Toni! Cheesecake – gorgeous!'

'Don't expect this treatment every day,' Toni warned, but she was delighted to have Chloe home.

'Come on, everyone, sit down,' Alice called, as she carried the plates to the table.

'This looks great, Mrs S.' Mark eyed his plate hungrily.

'I hope your mother won't have anything prepared for you,' Alice said.

'He'll eat it as well,' Chloe said. 'He's like a dustbin.'

'Excuse me, I'm a growing lad,' Mark protested.

Toni attacked her plate enthusiastically. She hadn't been eating well while Chloe was away and it was so nice to sit down to a home-cooked meal in a relaxed atmosphere. She raised her glass to Alice. 'God bless the cook.'

'Hear, hear!' Chloe cried.

Alice took a sip of her champagne. 'Ooh, this is nice,' she said.

'Get used to it,' Toni told her. 'You'll be drinking buckets of it when this lady turns eighteen.'

Chloe's smile froze. How could she tell them that she didn't want a party any more? And that she'd be leaving home soon after.

Mark shot her a meaningful look but she pretended not to notice. Toni saw the exchange and had a pretty good idea of what it meant. Though she and Chloe hadn't discussed college since Chloe had gone to Skerries, her mother had told her she was still adamant that she wanted a year off. Toni wondered how soon she planned to leave. They hadn't even discussed where she would go.

Later, Toni shooed Chloe and Mark from the kitchen, and made Alice sit down with a cup of tea while she stacked the dishwasher.

'She seems happier,' Alice remarked.

'I must phone Mum and Dad and thank them. I'm not sure what they did but it worked.'

'The poor girl just needed some time to herself. Now she'll be ready to start college.'

'She doesn't want to start college. She wants to take a year out to travel. I just wish I could believe that she's doing it for the right reasons. I think she sees it as a way of getting back at Theo.'

'Damn that man!' Alice stormed.

Toni's eyes popped.

'He's ruined that poor child's life. I'd dearly love to give him a piece of my mind.'

'I'm going to find him, Alice, if it's the last thing I do. I don't care if he never comes back to Ireland but he should keep in touch with Chloe.'

'She may not want him to any more.'

'She should at least have the choice.'

Chloe let her head slide on to Mark's shoulder. 'It's so nice to be home.'

'I think you'd be better off in bed,' Mark murmured. 'That champagne has gone right to your head.'

'I feel wonderful,' Chloe said sleepily.

'You look beautiful.' Mark bent his head to kiss her.

When they came up for air Chloe smiled shyly at him. 'Mark, there's something I wanted to ask you.'

'Oh?' He tucked a tendril of hair behind her ear and kissed the tip of her nose.

'Before I go away I want you to . . .'

'What?' He looked into her wide blue eyes.

'I want you to make love to me. Properly.' Chloe's face reddened but she held his gaze, her eyes full of love.

'Are you sure—'

She pressed a finger to his lips. 'I've never been more sure of anything in my life. But I don't want it to happen in the back of your mother's car.'

'We could go somewhere,' Mark said, racking his brains.

'No. We'll do it here. In my room.'

Mark stared at her as if she'd taken leave of her senses. 'And will Toni bring us some hot cocoa afterwards?'

Chloe giggled. 'No, silly. Toni goes out nearly every week with Jade and Sandra. We'll plan it for one of those nights. Then we'll have the whole place to ourselves until at least eleven.'

'Oh.' Mark could hardly believe that after all this time they were finally going to do It. 'And you're sure?'

'I'm sure.'

∞∞

Alice tied a headscarf under her chin. 'I'll be off now, love. It's wonderful to have you home.'

Chloe jumped up from the sofa. 'We'll drop you home, won't we, Mark?'

'I've already offered,' Toni told them, 'but apparently Alice has a hot date.'

'Go away out of that!' Alice rolled her eyes. 'Don't mind her, Chloe. I'm just going to bingo and Mr Reilly said he'd give me a lift.'

Chloe remembered the skinny little man who lived down the road from Alice. 'So you and Tommy Reilly have finally got together.'

'I hope I've better taste than that.' Alice sniffed. 'He wouldn't even keep me warm at night.'

'Alice!' Toni was scandalised.

A horn beeped outside. 'That will be him,' said Alice. 'Goodnight, everyone. Wish me luck.'

After Alice had left Mark went in search of his jacket. 'I should be making tracks too.'

'It's only eight thirty!' Chloe exclaimed.

'I've got football training,' he explained.

'I don't know how you're going to run around a football pitch after one of Alice's dinners,' Toni said.

'And drinking all that champagne.' Chloe giggled.

'I'll probably get thrown off the team. Or throw up!'

Chloe walked him to the door. 'I hope the next night Toni goes out there isn't football practice,' she said lightly.

Mark pulled her to him. 'I don't care if Man U want me to try out for them. If it's a choice between them and you, you win every time.'

Toni was watching television, smiling at the romantic mumbling punctuated by long silences in the hall. Maybe Mark would persuade Chloe not to take a year out. She seemed so crazy about him, it was hard to imagine her leaving him. He might not be willing to wait for her. After all, he was only nineteen and he was a handsome lad.

Finally the hall door closed and Chloe wandered back in. She curled up on the sofa.

'Glad to be home?' Toni asked.

'Oh, yes.'

'Well, I'm glad you're back. I've missed you.'

'I've missed you too, although I'm glad I went to Skerries. You're so lucky, Toni. Your parents are great.'

'I didn't always think so.'

'Was it because of Dad?' Chloe asked.

Toni looked up sharply. Surely her folks hadn't said anything to Chloe. 'Why do you say that?'

Chloe looked at her candidly. 'Well, he was a lot older than you. There can't be many years between my dad and yours.'

'Seven,' Toni admitted. 'My father was furious.'

'And now?' Chloe prompted.

'Now we're okay,' Toni said, and knew it was the truth. 'Chloe, about this travelling—'

'Oh, please, don't start, Toni.'

'Will you hear me out, please?'

'Sorry.'

'I won't object to you going if you really want to but I have an alternative suggestion.'

'I'm listening.'

'I understand why you don't want to go to college at the moment – it would be impossible to concentrate, and even though things have quietened down in the press it might still be awkward for you.'

'Yeah, kids pointing at me saying, "There's the daughter of that sick surgeon."'

'Whatever. But I think you need your friends and family right now. I hate the thought of you in some crummy hostel in the middle of nowhere all on your own.'

'I'll make friends,' Chloe said, more confidently than she felt.

'Of course you will, but I'd still like you to postpone

the trip for a few months. Sandra is only working part-time at the moment. How would you feel about helping her out at the clinic?'

'What?'

'Well, think about it. You'd have a salary – not an enormous one – and you'll get some work experience. You'll be able to see Mark and Ollie, and you'll have your year out to think about what you want to do.'

'And I could go abroad later?'

'If you wanted to,' Toni agreed. 'I just hate the idea of you going right now, Chloe. It's been an unsettling time. I'd feel happier if you were here with me.'

'Can I think about it?'

'Of course. There's plenty of time.'

Chapter Thirty-six

Monday, 25 September

Jade bit back a smart retort as Vicky put on her coat and tottered out of the room on those silly heels she insisted on wearing. The girl was enjoying winding her up at every opportunity, and Jade was doing her best not to retaliate.

But it wasn't easy. She was finding it hard to keep her temper in check. In fact, she had been feeling down lately and she'd no idea why. She didn't owe anyone any money – Aidan had paid off all of their outstanding debts last week – and she could probably afford to find herself a nice little flat now, but somehow she couldn't summon up enough enthusiasm. Maybe she'd get Toni or Sandra to come flat-hunting with her: it would be more fun than doing it alone. Jade smiled wryly, thinking of how much she'd changed in the last few months. There had been a time when she insisted on doing everything alone, shunning any intervention or offers of assistance from her friends.

The phone buzzed and she picked it up. 'Yes?' she said briefly.

'Jade, could you drop in to me, please?' Robert asked.

Jade raised an eyebrow at his polite tone. 'Certainly.' She hung up, walked down the corridor and tapped on his door. 'What can I do for you, Robert?'

Robert gestured for her to sit down. 'It's a bit delicate, Jade,' he said, steepling his fingers and looking serious.

'Oh, yes?' Jade said calmly. *This is it. I'm getting the push.*

'There have been a lot of slip-ups lately. Files misplaced, case-notes missing . . .'

'I hope you're not pointing the finger at me,' Jade said hotly.

'Oh, no, not at all, my dear.'

My dear.

'I'm afraid it's Vicky who has let us down.'

Jade was astonished. 'Vicky?'

'I'm sure you'll agree that she hasn't been pulling her weight recently.'

'I can't say she ever did,' Jade said bluntly.

'Quite. Well, I think Daniel has probably been too soft on her.'

Jade blinked.

'Toni too,' Robert added. 'But now that I'm in charge I think it's time for a clean sweep.'

'Clean sweep?' Jade echoed faintly.

'Indeed. There's no room in my clinic for layabouts. I've looked at Vicky's file and her attendance record has been abysmal lately. She's got to go.'

'Oh.'

'I need to know, Jade, if you'll be able to manage until we find a replacement. Of course I'll ask Toni to organise a temp in the meantime. What do you think?'

Jade gaped at him wordlessly, and felt a rush of pity for Vicky. The bastard was dumping her. And how! 'I, eh, it's up to you of course, Robert. I'll manage the workload no problem.' *I always have before.* 'Once I get some kind of back-up.'

'Well, then, I'll discuss the matter with Toni and set the wheels in motion. Needless to say, Jade, keep this to yourself for the moment.'

Jade stood up and flashed him a false smile. 'Of course.' *You cold, conniving bastard,* she thought, as she walked back to the office she shared with Vicky. The poor bitch thought she was going to be running the place and he had been planning her downfall. Though it was hard to feel truly sorry for Vicky: she was a lazy, two-faced cow and they'd be better off without her. She'd pick up work easily enough: there was a shortage of nurses in Dublin and some unfortunate was bound to offer her a job. But Robert's ruthlessness had taken Jade's breath away. Maybe she was next for the chop.

She was still musing over the sudden turn of events when Toni walked in.

'You'll never guess.' Toni shut the door and sat down, her eyes sparkling.

'Perky's sacking his girlfriend?'

Toni looked disappointed. 'You know?'

'He just told me. Poor bitch.'

'I can't believe you! You've never had a good word to say about her.'

'Still,' Jade looked uncomfortable, 'to be fired by your own boyfriend.'

'I suppose. I wonder what she'll do.'

'Probably take a knife to him. I can't imagine her going quietly, can you?'

Toni chuckled. 'No, I suppose not. But I thought you or I would be the first ones he'd get rid of.'

'Robert's a businessman first,' Jade said shrewdly. 'As long as we keep this place running smoothly and he keeps making money, he'll be happy.'

'You're right. I never thought about it like that before. Thank God that's one less thing to worry about.'

'Any news?' Jade asked, noting the dark circles under her friend's eyes.

'From Theo? Not a word. But Chloe's in much better form.'

'Is she still planning to go away?'

'Hopefully not. I've suggested that she come and work here instead.'

'Doing what?'

'Helping Sandra. She can't be any worse than the temps we've had.'

'That's a great idea, Toni, and it would still give her a year to think about college.'

'That's what I said but she hasn't said yes yet.'

'She will. She must be upset about leaving Mark.'

Toni shrugged. 'It seems serious between them.'

'There you are, then. She's probably looking for a reason to stay but she's too stubborn to back down and admit defeat.'

That made sense to Toni. Chloe could be as stubborn as her father – or even her stepmother. 'You should set up a counselling service.'

'I might have to when Robert gets round to firing me.'

Toni paused in the doorway. 'You know? I don't think

that's going to happen. I've a feeling everything is going to work out just fine.'

After her conversation with Jade, Toni couldn't wait to get home to talk to her stepdaughter. She was delighted to find a good-humoured Chloe in the kitchen with Alice who was putting the finishing touches to a casserole for their dinner.

'Hi, Toni.' Chloe blew her a kiss.

That was a good sign, Toni thought. 'That smells lovely, Alice. Are you staying to eat with us?'

'I promised to drop in and see my neighbour. She hasn't been too well. I thought I'd bring her some of this,' she gestured to a smaller dish, 'and keep her company for a few hours.'

'Well, then, I'll drop you home.'

'Thanks, love,' Alice said gratefully. 'Now, Chloe, turn the temperature down in about ten minutes.'

Chloe hopped off the counter. 'Will do. See you tomorrow.'

Over dinner Toni entertained Chloe with the tale of Vicky's impending departure.

'What a horrible man he is,' Chloe said.

'Have you thought any more about my suggestion?' Toni asked lightly.

'A bit,' Chloe mumbled.

'Wouldn't you miss Mark if you went away?'

'He could come with me, but he wants to start his course.'

'You can't blame him for that.'

'If he loved me he'd come,' Chloe said sulkily.

'And if you loved him, you'd stay. Don't be silly, Chloe.'

Chloe looked slightly shame-faced.

'Why not compromise?' Toni suggested, and stood up to clear away their dishes.

'How?'

'You take the job at the Blessington and when Mark gets his holidays you could go away together.'

Chloe brightened. 'I suppose, but he doesn't get that long a break.'

'No,' Toni agreed, as she scrubbed the casserole dish. 'Well, it's just an idea.' Deciding not to push her luck any further, she changed the subject. 'We need to plan your birthday party soon.'

'I don't think I should have one.'

'Why on earth not?'

'Well, on top of this whole thing with Dad it just doesn't seem right. And it would probably bring the journalists back in droves.'

Toni's eyes hardened. That man was not going to screw everything up. She wouldn't let him. She came back to the table and sat down. 'They won't know about your birthday, Chloe, and you can't let your dad affect all your decisions. It's time we got on with our lives.'

'That's not so easy for me,' Chloe said sadly. 'No, I've decided. No party.'

Toni saw the determined look in her eye and decided not to argue. 'It's up to you. Let me know if you change your mind.'

'You're not annoyed with me, are you, Toni?'

Toni paused to give her a quick hug. 'Of course not, love. Maybe we'll just have a quiet dinner.'

'We'll see,' Chloe said evasively.

Toni threw down her dishcloth. 'Okay, I'm going to have a soak in the bath. I'll be down in time for *Who Wants To Be A Millionaire?*.'

'I think I'll go over to Ollie's.'

'Don't be too late.'

Toni went upstairs wondering if she'd made any headway. At least she'd got Chloe thinking. Maybe it was best to leave it at that for now. But it was an awful pity about the party. Damn Theo! She'd murder him if they ever met up again.

The phone rang just as Toni was about to step into the bath. Luckily she'd brought it upstairs with her but where she'd left it was another matter. 'Yes?' she said breathlessly, after finding it under the towel.

'Hi, Toni. It's me.'

'Ian?' Toni tightened the towel around her.

'I was talking tó a few people about Theo's old college buddies. One name came up that I thought might interest you. Eric Levinson.'

'Eric! Of course – the New Zealander. He was at our engagement party. God, do you think Theo might have gone over to him?'

'It's worth checking,' Ian said. 'I'm afraid I've found no one else who hails from far-off climes.'

'Then it must be Eric.'

'Don't get your hopes up too soon, Toni.'

'I won't.'

'So do I get a reward for my good work? How about dinner?'

'Oh, I suppose so,' Toni said teasingly. 'And I suppose it should be on me.'

'Well, if you insist! How about next Friday?'

'Fine. Where shall we meet?'

'The usual place at eight?'

Chapter Thirty-seven

Tuesday, 26 September

'There's a new nurse starting today,' Jade told Sandra. 'What time is she due in?' Sandra asked, with an eye on the clock. It had just gone eight.

'He,' Jade corrected. 'Matthew Little. And he's due at eight thirty.'

Sandra's eyes were like saucers. 'A man?'

'I'm willing to give him a go if he's got half a brain. We're desperate. I just wish we had someone suitable to help you out, Sandra. Although I have a feeling that Toni has someone in mind.'

'Bev was great,' Sandra said. 'It's a pity she had to go. Why is it whenever we find anyone decent they leave?'

'Maybe it's us!' Jade joked. 'Listen, I'm just going in to see Toni. Give me a shout when Matthew gets here.'

Left to herself, Sandra turned her attention to sorting the post and was engrossed in it when there was a polite cough behind her. She swung round to look at the large, clumsy-looking man in front of her. 'Yes?'

'Hi, I'm Matthew Little. The agency sent me.'

His eyes were huge and very dark brown. Like a faithful dog, Sandra thought dreamily. In fact, everything about him was big. He was built like a rugby player and had hands like shovels. She giggled. 'Sorry, it's just your name . . .'

Matthew gave a wry grin. 'Yeah. Everyone says that.'

'I'm Sandra. I run Reception.'

Matthew nodded shyly. 'Nice to meet you.'

'I'll just get Jade Peters. She's the senior nurse.' Sandra buzzed through to Toni's office, her eyes never leaving his face. He was gorgeous. Everything about him seemed brown and fluffy. His hair was brown and stood on end in soft curls. He wore a brown leather car coat that looked years old, teamed with faded brown cords. Sandra figured he must be about her age.

Jade came out a couple of minutes later. She stopped dead in her tracks half-way across Reception when she saw the mountain of a man. Collecting herself, she stuck out her hand and adopted her professional smile. 'Matthew? I'm Jade Peters.' Her hand disappeared in his huge one. 'Why don't you come down to my office and we'll have a chat?'

Matthew ambled down the corridor after her. 'I'll bring you some tea,' Sandra called after them eagerly. 'Matthew,' she breathed, and went off to the kitchen to put on the kettle. 'What a nice name!'

'So, Matthew, you seem to have all the relevant experience. Do you mind me asking why you're temping?'

Matthew's face clouded. 'I gave up my permanent job to look after my dad. He had cancer.'

'Oh, I'm sorry. Is he . . .' Jade searched for the right words.

'He died last month,' Matthew said simply, 'but I

haven't done anything about getting a permanent job yet.'

'There's plenty of time for that,' Jade said gently. 'When could you start?'

'Right away,' he assured her, the nice smile returning to his eyes. 'I can't wait, and any overtime that's going, just throw it my way.'

'I think you're going to fit in very well here,' Jade said, pleased.

'I hope so.'

'Here we are.' Sandra bustled in and set a tray on the desk.

'Meet our latest recruit, Sandra.'

Sandra beamed at him. 'Oh, congratulations, Matthew. Welcome to the Blessington.'

Matthew grinned back. 'Thanks.'

He was blushing! Jade realised. And Sandra was positively *glowing*. Wait until Toni heard about this. Jade sent up a silent prayer that Matthew would work out. Sandra would probably throttle her if she let him go.

'You're kidding?' Toni goggled at her. 'Love at first sight, eh?'

'Looks like it,' Jade chirped. 'Sandra's floating around the place. And it's all "Any questions, Matthew, you just come to me."'

'And what's this Matthew like?'

'He's got a gorgeous, sexy Donegal accent, he's quite shy, nice-looking and very big. And get this, his surname's Little.'

Toni laughed. 'It sounds like they're made for each other.'

'Except we'll have to get her a box to stand on when she's kissing him.'

'Oh, I do hope he works out,' Toni fretted, 'for our sake and Sandra's.'

'And his,' Jade added, and told Toni about his background.

Toni shook her head in wonder. 'He took care of his father and she's looking after her mother. This is uncanny.'

'Maybe there's such a thing as fate after all,' Jade observed. The phone buzzed and she picked it up. 'Yes, Sandra?'

'Aidan's in Reception for you. Can you come down?'

'Eh, right, yes. I'll be there in a moment.' She hung up and stared at Toni. 'It's Aidan. I wonder what he wants.'

'Perhaps it's just a social call.'

'I don't know. It's all been going a bit too well lately. I've been waiting for reality to return.'

'That's a bit harsh. He's done well. Look at all the money he's given you.'

'It's just hard to trust him after all that's happened.'

Toni patted her hand. 'Just go and say hello and stop reading so much into it. Maybe he's got another brown envelope for you.'

'You're right. I'm too bloody suspicious. If Perky's looking for me tell him I won't be long. We have surgery in thirty minutes.'

Jade hurried down to Reception, straightening her uniform and slicking back her hair as she went. 'Hi, Aidan.'

They stood awkwardly, looking at each other.

Sandra watched them as the silence lengthened. 'I've just got to go and show Matthew where, eh, where we keep the cups and things.' She hurried away.

Aidan laughed. 'So discreet.'

'She thinks we want to be alone.'

Aidan smiled into her eyes. 'Clever girl.'

Jade looked away. 'What can I do for you?'

'Well, I was looking for a favour,' Aidan admitted.

A knot formed in Jade's stomach. 'Oh, yes?' she said.

'It's not about money, Jade.'

Jade looked down at her hands. 'So what is it?'

'I wanted your opinion on something.'

'Are you sure?'

'I think so. I'm going to look at an apartment this evening and I wanted you to come too.'

'Are you selling your mother's house?'

'No, but Ann's got a man in her life and it's looking serious. I'm in the way.'

Jade bristled inside at the thought of him moving into a fancy new pad while she still lived in a hovel. 'So where's the apartment?'

'Clontarf.'

Jade's blood boiled. 'Clontarf? That's an exclusive area. Apartments must be expensive there.'

'I'd get a good deal. I know the estate agent. So, will you come?'

'When?' Jade was curious despite herself.

'I could pick you up at six thirty.'

'Okay then.' Jade stood up and stalked off down the corridor, leaving Aidan staring after her, baffled.

⚭⚭

'The cheek of him!' She stormed up and down Toni's office.

'I don't see—'

'I'm living in dire poverty and he wants to show off the swanky new apartment he's buying himself.'

'You could afford to move too,' Toni reminded her.

'That's not the point.'

'Oh.' Toni was confused. 'What exactly *is* your point, Jade?'

'He's being irresponsible,' Jade said stubbornly. 'He's only just getting back on his feet and he's throwing all his money away on a fancy bachelor pad.'

Toni's lips twitched as realisation dawned on her. 'How much is it?'

'I don't know.'

'You're not worried about the money. You just don't want him setting himself up as an eligible bachelor.'

'Rubbish!'

'Is it?'

'Of course. I just wish he'd be more practical. If he's not careful he'll end up in the gutter again.'

'But he ended up in trouble because he was gambling. He's not doing that now, is he?'

'Well, no, I don't think so,' Jade said reluctantly.

'Then why don't you just wish him well instead of waiting for him to fall flat on his face?'

Jade looked at her, horrified. 'I'm not!'

'Aren't you?' Toni said softly. 'Leave the past in the past, Jade. Go along and see the flat and wish him luck. Hasn't there been enough heartache?'

'It's not that simple.' Jade flopped into a chair, feeling sad and defeated.

'I think it's up to you how simple it is.' Toni stood up. 'Anyway, enough of this preaching. I'm beginning to annoy myself!'

'Only beginning?' Jade enquired.

Toni hit her with her pen as she left the room.

Jade sat staring into space long after Toni had left. Was there any truth in what her friend had said? Did she begrudge Aidan happiness? A future? That wasn't like her. Usually. But the circumstance of their separation was still a raw memory. Damn it, she'd do her best to rise above it. She was forty-three, not some naïve teenager. She would go with Aidan tonight and wish him well. She knew he wanted nothing but happiness for her.

'Jade?' Robert barked, as he stuck his head round the door. 'Are you planning to assist me or shall I call Sandra?'

'Sorry, Robert, I got sidetracked.' Jade followed him hastily to the theatre.

'Don't you start letting me down too, Jade.' The threat in his words was implicit.

'Of course not,' Jade said tightly. 'It won't happen again.' There might come a time when she had enough of Perky and his silly ways but she was damned if she'd give him reason to fire her.

Aidan picked her up at six thirty sharp and they chatted amicably as they drove to Clontarf. But when Aidan turned off the Howth road and guided the car in through the security gates of an exclusive apartment block Jade had to swallow hard. How could he bring her here knowing the way she lived?

Aidan, seemingly oblivious to her dark mood, led the way to a discreet doorway on the side of the building and pressed a button. Jade heard the estate agent greet him and buzz the door open. Inside, Jade was immediately aware of the silence created by the thick carpeting. Guiding her into the lift, Aidan pushed the button for the fourth floor. 'Well?' he said excitedly.

'It seems very nice so far.'

'Wait till you see the view, Jade. It's amazing.'

Jade didn't doubt it. And she expected that the price was equally so.

They got out of the lift to be met by a man standing outside a door. 'Aidan! Good to see you.' They shook hands warmly. 'And you must be Jade.'

'Jade, this is Alan Kiely.'

'I'll go outside – I've a couple of calls to make – and leave you two to wander around in peace.' He gave them a set of keys and got into the lift.

Aidan unlocked the apartment door and they went inside.

'He seemed to be expecting me,' Jade remarked, and wandered over to the window to inspect the 'amazing' view.

'I told him I was bringing you. Come on. You have to see the kitchen.'

It had been decorated, rather unusually, in dark greens and browns. The effect was warm and sophisticated and Jade loved it. She ran her hand along the tiled worktop.

'Well?' Aidan said expectantly.

'It's beautiful.'

'Okay, now the bathroom. There are two *en-suites* as well.'

Jade followed him into the blue and white bathroom and stared at the expensive tiles, the power shower and the jacuzzi switch by the bath. 'Don't you think this is all a bit . . . much?' she said, unable to keep her feelings to herself any longer.

'Maybe . . . for one.' He crossed the room, took her hands and gazed down into her eyes. 'But not for two. Share it with me, Jade. Let's start again—'

'No!' Jade pushed him away. 'What are you talking about? You want me to move in with you as if the last two years haven't happened? You think that a flashy apartment with amazing views and fancy tiles is going to wipe the slate clean?'

'But, Jade—'

Not trusting herself to say any more without bursting into tears – which she would never do in front of him again – she ran from the apartment and stabbed the button for the lift.

In the lobby Alan Kiely moved forward, smiling until he saw the look on her face. 'Thanks for your time,' she said coldly, 'but it's not my style.'

Chapter Thirty-eight

Wednesday night, 27 September

Toni and Chloe sat watching television in companionable silence, but Chloe wasn't taking in the storyline of the medical drama. She couldn't stop thinking about Toni's proposition. Now that Mark had started college she saw less of him and it was killing her. If she was finding that hard to cope with how would it be if she were in a different country with only the occasional telephone call to look forward to?

'Toni,' she said, as the credits rolled, 'is that offer still open? You know, the job at the clinic?'

'It certainly is.'

'Then I'll take it. When do I start?'

'Tomorrow morning?'

Chloe grinned. 'I'll go and phone Mark and tell him.'

'And then go straight to bed. You've got work in the morning!'

When Chloe had gone Toni poured herself a large Scotch to celebrate. Looking at the golden liquid in her glass reminded her of Francis. Maybe she'd give him a call – she hadn't talked to him for a few days. She carried her drink back into the study and dialled his number. It rang for some time before he answered. 'Hello?'

'Francis? It's Toni.'

'Toni, my dear, how nice.'

'Did I wake you?' Toni asked anxiously. He sounded rather groggy.

'Not at all, my dear. I was just going through some old photo albums.'

'That's nice.'

Francis sighed. 'I'm not so sure. It just reminds me of what I've lost.'

'Poor you,' Toni said inadequately, and wished she could think of some words of comfort.

'How are things with you, my dear? Any word from French?'

At least she'd be able to distract him with her story, she thought. 'We're trying to track him down, Francis.'

'We?'

'Ian Chase is helping me,' she admitted.

'Well, he's a sensible chap. I'm sure if anyone can find French it's him. Just make sure that when you get hold of him you get some money out of him.'

'Well, the solicitor says he'll have to give back half of what was in our accounts,' Toni said.

'No, no, my dear. I'm talking about *real* money. Theo was a great one for the stock market.'

'Yes, I know that. It's a pity I can't prove he made some successful investments. It would be useful when we're sorting out the financial arrangements.'

'That should be easy, my dear. Ask anyone who

worked with him. He was always boasting about his success on the market.'

'That wasn't very discreet.'

'Bloody stupid,' Francis agreed, 'but he couldn't resist it. He wanted everyone to know how brilliant he was. The man has an incredible ego.'

Toni smiled as she remembered that Dotty had said the same thing about Francis.

'Now, keep me posted, Toni. I want to know all the details.'

'I promise. And you look after yourself, Francis.' When Toni hung up, she took a long drink, then phoned Ian.

'Hi, I wasn't expecting to hear from you tonight. You're not cancelling our dinner, are you?'

Toni smiled at the warmth in his voice. 'Of course not. I just have another job for you.'

'Slavedriver! What is it now?'

'Remember you were going to check out Theo's pals in the stock market? Well, I'd really appreciate if you did that. According to Francis Price, Theo made quite a lot of money. If I had any proof of that it would help my solicitor a great deal.'

'Leave it with me.'

Toni smiled as she hung up. It was amazing how quickly she and Ian had settled back into such an easy friendship. But then the tumultuous events of the last few weeks had helped. Toni had needed him and he'd been there. She wasn't sure how she would have coped without him. Somehow having Ian to lean on made it easier to deal with the sordid mess that was her husband's life. It still hurt of course. To think that Theo was seeing that woman even when they were dating. But then how could she complain? He was seeing May when his first wife was on her deathbed. The man was undoubtedly sick. Though Ian hated Theo, he had said nothing as the press uncovered the various hidden layers of Theo's life. He had offered no opinions or comments. He had been fantastic. She couldn't have got through it all without him. *And he has a girlfriend*, a little voice reminded her. *Don't forget that.*

Thursday morning, 28 September
'Sandra? I'd like you to meet your new assistant.'

Sandra wondered how long this one would last. Then she looked up. 'Chloe!'

'Reporting for duty – if you'll have me.'

'Of course I will! How marvellous! But I thought you were off on your travels soon.'

Chloe and Toni exchanged a smile. 'I've put that on hold for the moment. So, tell me what to do.'

'Right, then.' Sandra steered her towards the canteen. 'Let's start with the most important job.'

'I'll leave you to it,' Toni called after them and went into her office.

A few moments later Jade stuck her head around the door. 'Did I just see what I thought I saw?'

'If you mean Sandra showing her new assistant the ropes, then yes.'

'So Chloe isn't going away?'

'Not yet. She probably will at some stage and then, hopefully, it will be for the right reasons.'

'I'm delighted things are working out for you both.'

'They're not working out too bad with Robert either, are they?'

'Only because he still needs us. As soon as he's got into a routine he'll start looking for replacements.'

'Oh, I don't know.'

'Do you think Daniel will stay?' Jade asked.

'Probably. As long as Robert lets him get on with his job without too much interference. If he wants him to take on some of the cosmetic stuff I'd say Daniel will be out the door before you can say collagen.'

'Perky won't ask him to do that. Daniel would spend all of his time trying to talk the patients out of it.'

'True. And Robert will probably be happy to let Daniel get on with it. He lends a certain . . . credibility to the clinic. But what about Aidan?' Toni asked. 'Did you go and see that apartment with him?'

'Oh, yes. And it was amazing. Perfect for a rich young architect about town.'

'Why are you so angry with him, Jade?'

'*Why?* You have to ask that after everything he's put me through? I know you think I should put it all behind me, Toni,' she said, as Toni tried to interrupt, 'but it's easier said than done. The man is living in Cloud Cuckoo Land.'

'Did you tell him that?' Toni felt a bit sorry for Aidan.

'I was too angry to say anything much. Especially after he . . .' Jade trailed off.

Toni's ears pricked up. 'Especially after he what?'

'Asked me to move in with him.'

'But that's wonderful, Jade. You still love him, don't you?'

'I'm not sure what I feel, Toni, other than anger. After all we've been through . . .'

Toni was bewildered. 'I'm sorry, Jade, I'm not sure what I'm missing here. I just don't understand.'

'Okay. If he'd asked me if we could make another go of it, then I might well have said yes. If he'd suggested then that we look at apartments together, I might have agreed. But to go from being practically on the streets to something so plush, present me with a *fait accompli* – it's ridiculous. He's being completely unrealistic. He wants to make up for the last two years in a couple of weeks. I'd prefer to keep things on a more down-to-earth footing. How can I trust him like this? He's behaving like Donald Trump!'

'Did you tell him this?'

'I just got the hell out of there. I thought I might hit him.'

'Maybe you should have. It might have brought him to his senses. Look, promise me you'll talk to him,' Toni pleaded. 'It would be a shame to let things go back to the way they were. You could still be friends at least.'

Jade searched Toni's face. 'Do you *really* believe that? That it's possible to be friends with a man you once loved? Once shared a bed with?'

Toni felt the colour rise in her cheeks. 'It's worth a try.'

Chapter Thirty-nine

Friday evening, 29 September

'What are you up to?' Ollie asked curiously, as she watched Chloe try on her clothes.

Chloe tugged at the hem on Ollie's skimpy psychedelic shift dress. 'What do you mean?' she asked innocently. She pulled it off in disgust: Ollie was much smaller than she was and on Chloe the dress had looked indecent. Mark would be shocked if she wore that.

'You heard,' Ollie persevered. 'You go out with Mark most nights of the week. What's different about tonight?'

'He's taking me somewhere special,' Chloe improvised.

'Where?'

'It's a surprise. He just said I should dress up.'

'Well, it's not long till your birthday,' Ollie said thoughtfully. 'Oh!'

'What?'

'Maybe he's going to ask you to marry him.'

'Don't be ridiculous!'

'It's not ridiculous,' Ollie said sulkily. 'He's crazy about you.'

'Mark couldn't afford a ring, never mind a wedding and a mortgage.'

'The bride's family pays for the wedding,' Ollie reminded her. 'And you're going to be rich very soon.'

'Mark is *not* going to propose,' Chloe said emphatically.

'You sound very sure.' Ollie looked at her curiously.

Chloe reddened. 'I am.'

'So what *is* going to happen? And why are you picking all of my sexiest clothes – oh, my God! You're going to do It, aren't you?'

'Ollie!'

Ollie fell on to her bed and rolled around laughing uproariously. 'Finally Miss French is going to lose her virginity!'

'For God's sake, Ollie!' Chloe hissed, mindful of Mrs Coyle hoovering outside the door.

'Oh, don't worry about Mum. She can't hear a thing when she's got that thing on. So, are you going to seduce him?' Ollie hopped off the bed and started to scan the pile of clothes with a critical eye. 'You need something sexy but subtle.'

'Then I won't find it here.' Chloe gazed at the flimsy garments that made up Ollie's wardrobe.

'Cheeky! You'd better be nice to me or I won't help you.'

Chloe sighed. She wasn't sure she wanted Ollie's help but she had to talk to someone. Suddenly she felt nervous about the whole thing. A night of passion with Mark before she went away had seemed romantic at the time but now that she wasn't going anywhere it didn't seem quite so momentous. And what if she was disappointed? Or, worse, what if she disappointed him? What if she was no good at sex? She was tempted to ask

Ollie about it but she knew her friend would tease her mercilessly then pester her for details afterwards. Mind you, that would happen anyway.

'So where are you two going?'

'My place,' Chloe mumbled. 'Toni's going out.'

'Excellent! So you need to set the scene. Music, lots of booze and some nibbles.' She giggled. 'Although Mark will probably be happy with just you!'

Chloe put her head in her hands. 'Oh, why did I tell you? I knew you'd be like this.'

'Like what?' Ollie asked innocently.

'Smartassed.'

'Oh, come on, Chlo. I'm only having a laugh.'

'At my expense.'

'Will you lighten up? I'm not as dumb as you seem to think, you know. I realise this is a big deal for you.'

'Honest?'

'Of course. But you'll feel a lot more comfortable if you plan it all and if you feel sexy. Jeans and trainers just won't cut it.'

'That's why I came over here. Nothing in my ward-robe seems . . . right.'

'More suitable for a convent than a club,' Ollie agreed.

'But I don't want to go overboard either. I'm not going to be comfortable if I'm tarted up to the nines. It's just not me.'

'I've got the very thing. You know your black velvet hipsters?'

Chloe nodded.

'Well, how about this to go with them?' Like a

magician, Ollie produced a black, sparkly top from the wardrobe. It had a round neck – quite demure by Ollie's standards – but at the back it was nothing but thin, lacy straps.

'Gosh!' Chloe breathed.

'Gorgeous, isn't it?'

'Yeah, but I'm not sure I could get away with it.'

Ollie sighed. There was no point in telling her friend that she'd look good in a sack. 'Just try it on.'

'Okay.' Chloe knew it was easier to give in. But there was no way she'd wear it. 'Wow!' she squeaked when Ollie spun her in front of the mirror.

'Wow is not the word,' Ollie said. 'You look sensational.' The plain top emphasised Chloe's long neck and the narrow sparkling straps revealed the perfect creamy skin of her back.

'It is nice,' Chloe acknowledged.

'Nice!' Ollie was exasperated. 'You're wearing it.'

'Do you think I should?'

'Yes.'

'But it's brand new, Ollie. It must have cost you a bomb.'

'You can make it up to me when you're rich.'

'Deal,' Chloe said, and meant it. She'd bring Ollie on a shopping day to remember when she got her inheritance. 'I hope Mark doesn't think it's too much.'

'Mark will love it.'

'You think so?'

'I know so.'

'. . . and Mrs Dunne's bandages need to be changed.'

'Right,' Matthew scribbled on his pad, his large hand almost obscuring the page.

'You don't have to write everything down.' Jade was amused.

'Oh, I always do for the first few days,' Matthew said seriously. 'I don't want to forget anything.'

'Fair enough,' Jade said, impressed. 'You can assist Daniel in surgery on Monday.'

'Really?'

'You have assisted in the theatre before, haven't you?'

'Oh, yes. I just didn't think you'd let me jump straight in.'

'I wouldn't with Perky – Mr Perkins. But Daniel is a lot more patient. Just do as he tells you and you'll get along fine.'

Matthew continued to write furiously in his notebook.

'I think that's everything. I'll be here for another thirty minutes – excuse me.' Jade broke off to answer the phone. 'Jade Peters.'

'Jade, I have Aidan for you.'

'No, Sandra, don't—' But the phone clicked as Sandra put the call through. 'Hello?'

'Jade? Hi, it's me.'

'Yes?' Jade said coolly, turning slightly away from Matthew.

'Jade, I'm so sorry about the other day. I can see it was bloody insensitive of me—'

'Aidan, I'm very busy.'

'Then meet me tonight. Give me a chance to explain.'

Jade hesitated. It wasn't as if she had anything else to do when her shift finished. 'Okay, then. Where shall we meet?'

'Why don't you come over here? Ann's going out. I could cook.'

'If you make threats like that I'm definitely not coming.'

'Fair enough. We'll order in. See you about eight?'

Jade looked at her watch. 'Make it half past. 'Bye.' She hung up and turned back to Matthew. 'Now, where were we?'

Toni got out of the car and let herself into the silent house. Chloe had gone straight to Ollie's after work and probably wouldn't be in before Toni left, and Alice was off today. She had the place to herself. She checked her watch as she threw her coat over the banisters and went upstairs: six thirty, and she was meeting Ian at eight. She went into her bedroom and sat down in front of the mirror, looking critically at her reflection. There was no chance of Ian getting any romantic ideas – at least, not if he saw her like this. Her grey suit and white blouse drained her face of colour. Her hair was pulled back in a tight, unbecoming knot and there were bags the size of suitcases under her eyes. 'You're getting old, Jordan.' She went into the bathroom, turned on the taps, then looked idly through Chloe's range of Body Shop bath products. Lavender to help you relax. That would do. She poured a large dollop into the running water and breathed in the scent.

Back in the bedroom she took off her suit and blouse, and opened her wardrobe to search for something suitable to wear. Every instinct screamed that she should make herself look feminine and attractive. But what if he got the wrong idea? Maybe she should wear jeans. But Toni had never been a jeans person. She pulled out a red wool dress with a high neck. It always looked well, if a little on the formal side. 'And old,' Jade would probably say. She thought Toni dressed much too old for her age. 'You've got a beautiful figure, Toni,' she was always saying. 'For God's sake, show it off while you can!'

Toni laid the dress to one side and rummaged deeper in the wardrobe. Her hand came to rest on a warm rich fabric. She pulled out the pair of black suede trousers she'd bought last year and hardly worn. She'd forgotten all about them. She went over to the chest of drawers and pulled out a thin chocolate-brown sleeveless top. She had always loved it and knew it made the best of her hazel eyes and dark hair. But Theo hadn't approved of it. 'You should give it to Chloe,' he'd remarked scathingly, when he first saw it. 'It's more her age group.'

Toni's lips settled into a firm line. This was the outfit for tonight. She hurried back into the bathroom and turned off the taps. She dropped her underwear on the floor, lowered herself into the hot water and closed her eyes. She couldn't believe the excitement bubbling up inside her. The thought of spending an entire evening with Ian, looking into his fathomless grey eyes . . . She shivered despite the warmth of the water. She had forgotten what it was like to feel turned on. And that was just from thinking about dinner. She sat up abruptly and reached for the soap. This was ridiculous. She was behaving like a sex-starved nympho. And it wasn't as if she had a chance with Ian. He had the lovely Carla to keep him warm at night. How could she compete with her? The woman oozed sex, from her long red fingernails to the legs that went all the way up to her armpits. And Ian was a leg man. Toni stretched one of her legs out of the water and scrutinised it. Ian had always said she had lovely legs. In fact, he complained that she didn't show them off enough with her long skirts and tailored trousers. Well, he wasn't going to see them tonight. Unless, of course . . .

By the time Chloe got home Toni had left. She showered and dressed and was just putting on some lip-gloss when the doorbell rang. Her stomach churned and panic filled her. The bell rang again. 'Oh, God!'

'Hi.' Mark smiled into her eyes.

'Hi.' It was only Mark, for God's sake. Why was she getting herself into such a state? Chloe wondered.

'Can I come in?'

'Oh, yeah, sorry.' Chloe turned and led the way in. She stopped when she heard Mark gasp. 'What is it?'

'That's some top.'

Chloe pulled at the neckline.

'You look wonderful, Chloe,' he said, running his hands up and down her arms. 'Just beautiful.'

'Thanks. I'll go and get some drinks. Do you want Coke or something stronger? There's no beer, I'm afraid.' She was aware that she was prattling but she couldn't seem to stop herself.

'Coke will be fine.'

She escaped into the kitchen, grabbed two cans of

Coke from the fridge and held them against her burning cheeks. Oh, God, what was she doing?

'I brought a video with me,' Mark said calmly, when she returned with the drinks. '*Sliding Doors.* You wanted to see that, didn't you?'

'Oh, yeah. Great.'

Mark set up the video and sat down on the sofa next to Chloe. She snuggled up against him and allowed herself to relax. It wasn't until it was over and the credits rolled up that she stiffened again.

'Just relax, Chloe.' Mark had sensed her withdrawal. 'We don't have to do this if you don't want to. I'll understand. I love you.'

'I love you too. And I do want to . . . It's just that I'm a bit nervous.'

'I promise I'll be very gentle and if you want me to stop it's no problem.'

Chloe put a finger to his lips. 'Let's go upstairs.'

Mark bent his head and kissed her. When he pulled back he looked into her eyes. 'I want you so much.'

They climbed the stairs in silence, their hands tightly entwined.

'That was lovely.' Jade pushed away her plate and smiled at Aidan.

'Yes, there's nothing quite like a number twenty-six with fried rice.'

Jade stood up to clear the plates.

'No, you sit down,' he said. 'I'll have those done in a jiffy.'

Jade watched as he carried the plates to the sink,

dumped the empty cartons in the bin and put on the kettle. 'I'm afraid I can only offer you instant coffee.'

'That's terrible! You know I'm used to better than that, Aidan,' Jade teased.

Aidan's eyes were sad. 'I'm only too well aware of the life you've become used to.'

Jade bent her head and twirled her glass between her fingers.

'That's why I wanted to do something about it,' Aidan continued. 'Although I made a total botch of it.'

'You did,' Jade confirmed, but there was no longer any anger in her voice.

'I've no excuses. I suppose I was just looking for a quick fix to blot out the past.'

'That's not possible.'

'I realise that now – but, God, did you ever see anything like that apartment?'

Jade burst out laughing. 'It was a bit . . . much.'

'I'd have been afraid to walk on those cream carpets.'

'They were very suitable for a man who spends most of his time wandering around building sites,' Jade said drily.

'I don't know what I was thinking of.'

'You meant well,' Jade said kindly.

'Yes.' He set a cup of coffee in front of her and sat down. 'And though I got the location wrong, Jade, the proposal still stands. I want you to move in with me. We'll find somewhere together, a flat, a house, whatever you want. And if you don't want to share a bedroom, I'll understand.'

'That would never work.'

'Which bit?'

'The last bit . . . all of it . . . Oh, I don't know.'

Aidan reached out, took her hand and kissed the palm, his lips soft and warm. 'I'd prefer you to share my bed. I've missed you so much, Jade.' He leaned across the table and kissed her hungrily.

This was madness, Jade thought. There was no way she was getting back with Aidan. She certainly wasn't going to bed with him. 'No, Aidan, we can't . . .'

'Why not? We're married, aren't we?' Aidan's lips descended on hers once more.

Jade gave herself up to the sensations that were engulfing her. She wound her arms around his neck and moulded her mouth to his. Maybe this wasn't the answer, maybe she'd regret it tomorrow, but right now she knew exactly what she wanted.

Chapter Forty

Still Friday evening, 29 September

'I never talked like that!' Toni protested, laughing.

'Oh, yes, you did,' Ian told her. 'It was your telephone voice when you first started in admin. Very mid-Atlantic indeed.'

'Oh, leave me alone. I was young and trying to make an impression.'

Ian's eyes twinkled. 'You made an impression on me.'

This wasn't going at all as Toni had imagined. They'd hardly mentioned Theo all night. In fact, all they'd done was reminisce about old times and, she realised, with pain, that those had been very good days indeed.

'You're not eating,' Ian remarked.

Toni flashed him a smile, then turned her attention to the enormous steak in front of her. 'I'm struggling. I shouldn't have had those chicken wings to start with.'

'Nonsense. You can't come to Sale e Pepe and not have the chicken wings.'

Toni had been delighted when he'd told her that he'd booked a table in the cosy Malahide restaurant. 'Then I should have had a salad for my main course,' she replied.

'Toni Jordan eating rabbit food! Hah!'

'I eat healthily.' Lord, Theo would laugh his head off if he heard her!

'You do,' Ian agreed, munching steak. 'And there's nothing healthier than a fine piece of Irish beef.'

'Well, maybe I could eat a little more.'

'You just need to wash it down with plenty of red wine. It helps the digestion.' Ian caught the waitress's eye and held up the empty bottle.

'It's just as well I took a taxi,' Toni said. She was feeling more than a little tipsy already.

'When did you ever drive when you were out with me?'

'Well, I didn't, but that was usually because I was staying over . . .' Her voice trailed off, and she kept her eyes firmly on her plate.

Ian smiled lazily. 'Oh, that's right. I'd forgotten.'

The waitress brought the wine. 'Just pour it,' he told her. 'I'm sure it will be fine.'

'So, have you any news for me?' Toni asked, after the waitress had gone.

'I do. First, good old Francis was quite correct. Theo had a major windfall at the beginning of the year, and he talked to a few doctors about it so I suppose that's proof. I also managed to track down Eric Levinson.'

Toni put her glass down with a clatter. 'You didn't?'

Ian grinned. 'I did, although we haven't spoken yet. He's no longer in New Zealand. He's in Cape Town.'

'The man gets around. Do you know where?'

'I don't know where he's living but I do know the hospital he's working at. I'll call him on Monday.'

Toni frowned. 'What are you going to say?'

'I was wondering about that. What could I say that wouldn't frighten Theo off – if he's there?'

'And?' Toni prompted impatiently.

'Maybe I'll tell Eric that it's Theo's broker calling with news on some shares.'

'Will he believe you, though?' Toni agonised. 'I mean, would they go to the trouble of tracking him down? What's in it for them?'

'Fees,' Ian said, clearly pleased with himself. 'It's a gamble, yes, but Theo is probably greedy enough to take the bait. Especially if he needs money.'

'But he has plenty,' Toni protested. 'I'm the one who's broke.'

'It takes a lot of money to buy your way into a new practice. Especially if you don't have the correct papers.'

'God, you've got it all worked out,' Toni gasped.

'A lot of it is guesswork. I could be wrong.'

'We'll know on Monday, won't we?'

'Maybe. I wouldn't expect to get much out of Eric straight off. But if I'm right, either he or Theo will be in touch very soon. What you have to decide is what then?'

'I don't understand.'

'Are you going to tell the police?'

Toni swallowed. She knew she should, and that she wanted to, but—

'Toni?' Ian's voice was sharp.

'How can I do that to Chloe?'

'Don't then. I will.'

'Oh, Ian, *please.*'

'Please what? Protect your beloved husband?'

'You know that's not what I mean.'

'I'm beginning to wonder, Toni. Why do you really want me to track Theo down? Is it getting lonely in that big old bed all on your own?'

'Ian, listen to me. The only person I care about is Chloe. She has been – no, is going through hell. Hardly a day goes by without another nasty story appearing in the paper. The journalists still call. She has opted out of college because she can't face being laughed at. Now, do you think she needs to see her dad brought back here in handcuffs?'

'Maybe that's *exactly* what she needs to see. If he came back, he'd be tried, sentenced, and that would be an end to it. At the moment she's in limbo. She doesn't know where he is, and when or if he'll ever come back.'

'I suppose you're right,' Toni admitted. 'But promise me something, Ian?'

He eyed her warily.

'Before we tell the police, let me talk to him.'

'I don't know, Toni.'

She took his hand. 'Please, Ian. Trust me.'

Ian studied her silently, then nodded. 'Okay, Toni. We'll do this your way.'

'Thank you. I promise it's only Chloe I'm interested in.'

'Your marriage is over?'

'It's been over a long time, Ian. It was a mistake from the beginning.'

'I'm sorry.'

'Are you?'

'I suppose that was a lie. Was it my fault you married him?'

Toni looked startled. 'No. Why would you say that?'

'Well, I thought we'd been getting on fine. I obviously missed something. Had you got bored with me?'

'Not with you, with us. We'd settled into a predictable pattern and there was no sign of that changing. Theo came along and he was so different, so vibrant. When he looked at me I felt as if I was the most important person in his world.'

Ian winced.

'Sorry, you don't need to hear this. Anyway, why are we raking over the past?'

'So that we can have a future, Toni.' He stroked the back of her hand.

'How can we? I may be free but I don't believe you are. What about Carla?'

Ian had forgotten about Carla: in his mind they were finished. But there was a minor complication in that he hadn't told *her* that yet. 'Ah,' he said softly.

'I'm not into playing the part of the other woman, Ian. My life has been complicated enough,' Toni said stiffly.

'I'll sort it out,' he assured her.

'Don't do anything on my account. After all, who are we kidding? We can't just turn the clock back. We've had fun tonight after too many glasses of wine. It doesn't mean we have a future.'

'Doesn't it?'

Toni had to look away from the intensity and warmth of his eyes. 'No, it doesn't. Now I think we should go.'

'Fine.' Ian signalled the waitress and, after a brief argument with Toni, settled the bill. 'You can pay for the taxi,' he told her.

Toni stared at him.

'Oh, for God's sake, Toni. It would be ridiculous to get separate taxis when we live so close by.'

Toni flushed. He was hardly likely to jump on her in the back of a cab. She'd be so lucky!

They got their coats and went downstairs to find a fleet of cabs at the rank outside the door. Ian gave a wry smile. 'One of the advantages of going home early on a Friday night.' It was only ten o'clock.

Toni said nothing but got into the car. Ian climbed in on the other side and gave the driver directions. She was a bit put out that he told the man to drop him off first. Fine, she was paying, but whatever had happened to seeing a lady home after a date? But this isn't a date, she reminded herself. Not unless you're willing to share him with Carla. God, he had some nerve, coming on to her when he was still involved with someone else!

'It's over between Carla and me, Toni,' Ian said, as if reading her thoughts.

'Does she know that?'

Ian slid his arm across the back of the seat. 'No, she doesn't. But I'll tell her on Sunday. I won't see her before then. She's been away for a few days.'

Toni digested this piece of information in silence, conscious of Ian's fingers fiddling with her hair. 'How can I trust you?'

Ian put a finger under her chin and turned her to face him, his eyes only inches away from hers. 'Have I ever given you reason not to?'

Toni's eyes dropped to his lips. No, Ian had been the honest, faithful one. Yet he was ready to give her another chance.

'Well?' he said softly, then bent to drop a gentle kiss on her lips. 'Have I?' He kissed the tip of her nose.

Toni closed her eyes and leaned into him.

He kissed her eyelids. 'Do you trust me, Toni?'

She breathed in the scent of him, the familiar wonderful smell.

'Toni?' His lips touched hers, teasing.

She opened her eyes and looked straight into his. 'I trust you.'

The cab pulled up outside Ian's apartment. 'We'll both be getting out here,' he said, his eyes not leaving her face.

The driver grinned at him in the mirror. 'Whatever you say, boss.'

Toni stumbled out of the car, too shocked and aroused to notice that Ian was paying off the taxi. He took her firmly by the hand and led her to the door, kissing her while he fumbled for his key. They practically fell into the hallway, and Ian tugged her into the lift where he pinned her against the wall then jabbed the button for the second floor. Toni moaned as his hands moved under her coat and touched her through the thin fabric of her top.

When the lift door opened again, Ian propelled her towards the flat, pulling her coat from her shoulders as they swayed wildly around the hall.

Toni giggled. 'For God's sake, open the door before one of your neighbours comes out to see what's going on.'

'Fuck the neighbours,' Ian muttered, opened the door of the flat and practically lifted her inside. 'I don't give a shit who sees us. I want you and I want everyone to know that I want you.'

Toni stepped away from him and slowly removed her top. Ian gasped at the sight of her in the skimpy black bra. He groped for her but Toni sidestepped him, and reached behind her to open the hooks.

Ian was mesmerised, his breathing heavy. 'Jesus!' He stepped forward but Toni backed away again and found herself pressed up to a table.

Ian moved closer. 'I've got you now.'

Toni watched him through a haze as she slid her bra off her shoulders. 'Then take me,' she murmured, allowing herself to fall back on the table.

Ian bent to kiss her breasts, his hands busy with the zip of her trousers. 'God, I want you, Toni!'

'I've wanted you, too, for so long.'

'We'd probably be more comfortable in the bedroom.'

'Who wants to be comfortable?'

Chloe lifted her hand to stroke Mark's face. He turned his face to kiss her palm.

'Was I . . . okay?' Chloe asked anxiously.

'You were fantastic!'

She settled back into his arms happily.

'And?' Mark prompted.

'And what?' Chloe replied innocently.

Mark started to tickle her mercilessly.

Finally she wriggled out from under him. 'Oh, stop, please.'

'Say it.'

Chloe gave an exaggerated sigh. 'Yes, well, you were quite good too.'

Mark resumed the tickling. 'Only quite good? Bloody cheek!'

'You were brilliant! Now please stop tickling me.'

'That's more like it.'

Chloe planted a tender kiss on his chest. 'I meant it,' she said softly. 'But now you have to get dressed. Toni could be home at any minute.'

'It's only five past ten.'

'You don't have to go home yet – I'd just feel a lot more comfortable if we were downstairs and fully dressed.'

'Okay, then, but give me one more cuddle first.'

'Just a quick one then,' Chloe said, and he pulled her back under the duvet.

Chapter Forty-one

Early Saturday morning, 30 September

Jade let herself out of the house as quietly as she could and almost ran down the road. Aidan would be disgusted that she'd crept out while he was asleep but she just couldn't face him. And she certainly couldn't face Ann. There had been no sign of her when they'd got in last night but Jade knew Aidan's sister would be there this morning and the thought of her knowing, cheesy grin made Jade cringe. She reached the bus-stop just as a bus pulled up. She flung herself on to it gratefully, flopping into the nearest seat.

No, Aidan wouldn't be impressed with her but she didn't know what to make of last night and needed time to think. The sex had been amazing – just as it always had been. Aidan was a sensitive lover and she'd been thrilled that he'd remembered exactly how and where she liked to be touched. She'd often wondered if he'd had any other women while they'd been apart but usually dismissed it as highly unlikely. Aidan's mistress had been the gambling.

She'd never gone out with anyone else either. She'd been so hurt and shocked by Aidan's behaviour it was as if she'd gone into a stupor for the last couple of years, concentrating all her energies on paying off his debts and living as cheaply as possible. There had been no time for other men. And she was too wary to let anyone so close again.

And now she'd slept with Aidan again. She shook her head as the bus pulled into her stop. She jumped off and walked the short distance to her bed-sit. It was as if the last two years had just been some kind of nightmare. Spending last night with Aidan had felt right. Their lovemaking had been sweet, passionate and forgiving. It was like they'd been trying to purge themselves of the bitterness and hurt that had grown up between them. And, Jade admitted, as she let herself in to the dreary old house, it felt good. She'd got precious little sleep but she felt full of energy and . . . happy. Yes, she actually felt happy. So what now? She went into her room and put on the kettle. It was only six o'clock but she was much too hyper to sleep. What she needed was a large mug of creamy coffee. She went to the fridge and smiled as she took out the carton of cream – a luxury she would never have allowed herself a few short weeks ago. She made the coffee and carried it and a packet of biscuits to her chair. How much longer would she spend in this hellhole? she wondered. Should she agree to get a place with Aidan? Could they really start again, could she trust him? She sighed as she bit into a biscuit. She wasn't getting any younger and she had no interest in looking for a new partner but she didn't want to end up alone. And she did love Aidan. And, whatever his faults, she knew he adored her too. 'So why not, Jade?' she murmured. 'What have you got to lose?'

Chloe snuggled deeper under the covers and closed her eyes. She'd heard Toni going downstairs but she couldn't face anyone just yet. She wanted more time to herself to think about last night. She smiled a secret smile. She was a woman now, Mark's woman. And it had been so right – not sordid or dirty, just perfect. They were meant for each other. And she was glad she'd decided not to go away. As Toni had said, there was plenty of time for that. When Mark was on holiday from college she could treat them both to a little break. Maybe in Amsterdam. Because, in a few weeks, she would be a rich woman.

Ian rolled over in the bed, burying his face in the pillow. He sniffed appreciatively at the faint traces of Toni's perfume – evidence that last night had happened. What a pity she couldn't have stayed the night. It would have been wonderful to wake up beside her. But she'd had to rush back to Chloe. 'I can't stay out all night, Ian. What would she think?' Toni had insisted, as he'd tried to pull her back into bed.

'I suppose she'd think you've got a life of your own.'

'She's just a kid, Ian, whose dad has done a bunk, in case you've forgotten. The last thing she needs is for me to leave her too.'

'But you're not leaving her.'

'That's what she'd think, though.' Toni had wandered around the apartment collecting her clothes.

Ian hadn't thought he'd ever see Toni Jordan walking

naked around his apartment again, and enjoyed watching her.

She dressed hurriedly, gazing anxiously at the clock. Ian picked up the phone by the bed and dialled the local taxi firm. 'They'll be here in five minutes.'

Toni sat down beside him. 'Thanks.'

Ian held her hand tightly. 'When will I see you again?'

'I don't know.'

'How about lunch.'

'Today?' Toni stared at him.

'Why not? It's Saturday.'

'Well, I'll have to see what Chloe's doing.'

Ian sighed irritably.

Toni glanced at him sharply. 'There's one thing you've got to understand, Ian. I have responsibilities. If you want me back you have to accept that my stepdaughter is part of my life. Theo's daughter.'

'She's almost an adult. She'll be going her own way soon.'

'Maybe. But she will always have a home with me.' Toni gave him a quick peck on the cheek and stood up. 'I'll wait downstairs for the taxi.'

'I'll call you later.'

'No,' Toni said quickly. 'I'll call you.'

Ian frowned now as he remembered their conversation. He had been surprised by how devoted Toni was to her stepdaughter. It looked as if he'd have to get to know her too if he was going to see anything of Toni. A cosy threesome, he thought, with a sigh. Not quite what he'd had in mind. It wasn't going to be easy: the girl was sure to resent him. She might even blame him for the break-up of the marriage. And then there was Theo. He wouldn't want his daughter anywhere near Ian. Although, Ian chuckled, there wasn't much he could do about it if he was in South Africa. He jumped out of bed and headed for the shower, whistling. Once he'd explained things to Carla. Shit! Carla! He'd forgotten about her. He'd have to finish with her tomorrow and it was not going to be pleasant. Carla was the kind of woman who did the dumping and would be furious that he wanted to break up with her. Maybe he could do something to make her walk out on him. 'You wimp,' he berated himself, and turned the cold tap on full. Carla would have to be told and he would have to take the consequences.

Feeling like a young girl in love and unable to keep it to herself, Toni phoned Jade and asked if she could come over. Jade was delighted. They could wander down to the pub and have a nice lazy lunch.

When Toni arrived, bright-eyed and bushy-tailed, Jade was immediately suspicious. 'You seem in a very good mood.'

'I am. I had a date last night.'

'With— Crikey! It was Ian, wasn't it? I just knew you were seeing him again.'

Toni flopped down on Jade's lumpy mattress. 'I wanted to try to track Theo down and he's been helping me.'

'That was nice of him but I'm sure he's not doing it for the good of his health. So are you back together or was it just a one-night thing?'

Toni sighed. 'He seems to think everything's back on.'

'And you don't.' Jade leaned against the fridge and studied her friend's face.

'Things are so complicated, Jade. How can I possibly think about a new relationship at a time like this?'

'But it wouldn't really be new, now, would it?'

'And that's another thing. How can we pretend nothing's changed?'

'You can't. But you can't let something really good slip through your fingers either.'

Toni gazed at the tender expression on Jade's face. 'Is there something *you* want to tell *me* by any chance?'

'Let's say that while you and Ian were in the throes of passion, Aidan and I were . . . getting reacquainted too.'

'You're kidding!' Toni hopped off the bed to hug her. 'Oh, Jade, I'm delighted for you.'

'Why?'

'Well . . . because you belong together. You love each other.'

'Does that sound familiar to you?' Jade enquired.

'Oh, stop trying to trick me!'

'I'm just pointing out the obvious.'

'Except you don't have a stepdaughter to worry about.'

'Chloe will get used to the idea. Eventually.'

'I'm afraid I might be collecting my pension by then.'

Chapter Forty-two

Sunday lunchtime, 1 October

Ian looked at his watch. Nearly two. Carla would be here at any minute. He looked around the busy restaurant. It had been his idea to meet at Giovanni's: there was less chance of a scene. Although being in a public place probably wouldn't deter Carla, who had a fiery temper. She'd been surprised by his call. Normally she just dropped over to his place on a Sunday, they read the papers then went out for a pub lunch. He'd noted the curiosity in her voice at this change of arrangement. Carla was no fool. She'd probably figured out what he was up to.

He was on his second glass of wine when she arrived, breathless and smiling. Ian watched the waiters' appreciative glances as she peeled off her leather jacket to reveal a slender figure in black jeans and tight red top. 'Sorry, hon,' she said, and planted a long kiss on his lips, leaving a crimson stain. 'I didn't realise the time. Have you been waiting long?' Her eyes went to the wine bottle.

Ian knew she liked to think of him sitting around waiting for her. 'Not long.' He poured her a glass of wine.

Carla had a quick look round the restaurant and

turned back to him once she'd assured herself that no one more important was there. 'So, how are things, hon? Did you miss me?'

'The place is never the same without you,' Ian said honestly.

'Oh, hon! You say the nicest things,' she purred.

Ian gritted his teeth. Had she always been so false? How had he stayed with her so long?

Carla watched him from under her lashes. 'So what have you been up to while I was away?'

Ian swallowed. 'Eh, nothing, working, the usual.'

'Poor you, always working.'

Ian smiled guiltily.

'Any more on Theo French? Have they found a body in his back garden yet?'

'I don't read the rubbish they print. And I certainly don't listen to the bloody gossips in that hospital. They're worse.'

'Okay, okay, keep your hair on. I was just making conversation.'

'Sorry, it's just that I'm sick of hearing about Theo French. Now can we change the subject?'

'Sure.' Carla smiled into his eyes. 'What would you like to talk about?'

Two hours later Ian was sipping the last of a second bottle of wine, his jacket on to cover the red wine stain spreading across his denim shirt.

'Can I get you anything else, sir?' the waited asked sympathetically.

Ian smiled at him bravely. 'No, thank you. I'm fine.'

The waiter left him to his drink. Ian sat staring out of the window hardly able to accept that he was free.

And despite the wet shirt and the string of abuse Carla had just hurled at him he felt happier than he had in months. He couldn't wait to talk to Toni. Maybe she'd meet him for a drink this evening – dinner even. Perhaps there would be a repeat performance of Friday night. His spirits soared as he remembered the feel of Toni's bare skin under his hands. He pushed away the wine and laughed. He didn't need alcohol. He was high on life. 'The bill, please,' he called, and paid in cash, incorporating a large tip. 'Thanks very much. Everything was lovely,' he said to the waiter, and strode out, oblivious of the curious stares from the other customers.

Toni was delighted, and a little irritated, when Ian called late on Sunday to tell her that it was all over with Carla. Evidently he thought that once Carla was out of the way they could take up where they'd left off all those years ago. 'Let's have dinner,' he said. 'Let's celebrate.'

'I can't,' Toni hissed. She was standing in the hall and Chloe was close by in the living room. The house was too quiet for confidential conversations. 'It's just not possible.'

'Oh. Okay, then. I'll call you after I've talked to Eric Levinson.'

'Okay, good luck. 'Bye.'

'Who was that?' Chloe asked, when Toni walked back into the room.

'Oh, just work,' she said vaguely, and buried her head in a newspaper.

Chloe left it at that and went back to staring blankly at the television. She was feeling decidedly left out because neither Ollie or Mark wanted to go out tonight while she was still full of energy and excitement from Friday night. She had spent most of yesterday and today with Mark but when she'd tried to persuade him to go out he had said, 'I've got work to do for tomorrow, Chloe. I haven't picked up a book all week-end.'

'But it's only the beginning of term,' Chloe had wheedled.

'Yes, and I'm starting as I mean to go on. I'll call you tomorrow night.'

For once, Toni was heartily glad that her stepdaughter was in a bad mood. There were so many things flying around inside her head that she didn't think she was capable of intelligent conversation.

'I think I'll go to bed.' Chloe stood up.

'Good idea, love. An early night will do you good.'

'Whatever.'

Toni dropped her paper into her lap, rested her head against the chair back and closed her eyes. Now she could think about Ian in peace and she didn't have to worry if there was a silly smile on her face.

Monday afternoon, 2 October

Ian took a deep breath. 'Eric Levinson? Hi, how are you? Stuart Beecher, Sylvester's Hospital in Dublin.'

'Stuart! Good to hear you.'

Ian smiled with relief: thankfully, it seemed Eric's memory for voices wasn't too good. 'Eric, I wonder if you can help. I've lost contact with a colleague and I need to get hold of him.'

'If you're referring to Mr Theodore French, you've found him.'

Ian gulped. He hadn't expected it to be so easy. 'Eh, he's there, then?'

'Certainly is. Oh, it took me a while to persuade him to sign on the dotted line. He insisted he was only here on holiday, but I knew he was ready for a change.'

'That's great.'

'Look, he's not here right now. I could get him to phone you back.'

'No! Eh, no, I won't be here. Can you tell me when would be a good time to call again?'

'Sure, Stuart. Try between six and seven in the morning. He has surgery at seven thirty so he should be around.'

'That's great, Eric. Thanks.' Ian hung up and flopped into his chair. He'd found Theo! The urge to pick up the phone and call the police was almost too much to resist. But he'd promised Toni. He picked up the phone again and dialled. When the receptionist had put him through he didn't bother with the niceties. 'I've found him, Toni.'

'You're kidding!'

'No. I just spoke to Levinson. Theo is working at the same hospital in Cape Town. Eric just persuaded him to sign up. We should tell the police.'

'I want to talk to Theo first.'

'But what if he takes off? You could be in big trouble, Toni, if the cops ever hear about it.'

'Please, Ian, for Chloe's sake, I have to give him the opportunity to do the decent thing.'

Ian doubted that French was capable of that but he didn't want to lose Toni a second time.

'You should be able to get him between six and seven in the morning. I'll give you the number.'

Tuesday, 3 October

'May I speak to Mr Theodore French, please?' Toni asked, hoping her voice wasn't trembling as much as her hands.

'One moment, please.'

Toni listened to a series of clicks and then music. She hoped fervently that he was available. She wanted to finish this conversation before Chloe woke.

'Theodore French here. Hello?'

Toni took a deep breath. 'Hello, Theo.'

'Toni!'

'Surprised to hear from me?'

'How did you find me?'

There was something different about his voice. He sounded frightened. 'It wasn't difficult.'

'Have you told—'

'The police? No, not yet. I want you to do that.'

'What?'

'For Chloe.'

'How is she?'

'Not good at all.' Toni crossed her fingers. 'She's not eating, stays in her room most of the time and is refusing to go to college.

'But she must go!'

'I'm afraid there's no hope of that. She's decided to

leave home. She's planning to work her way around the world.'

'What? But that's ridiculous! She's too young to do that alone. Or is Mark Wheeler behind it?'

'No, Mark has started his course at UCD. He's tried to persuade Chloe to stay but she won't listen to him either.'

'You have to make her see sense, Toni,' he insisted.

'I've tried. But she says she wants to get as far away from Ireland and the Irish press as possible. She's fed up reading sick stories about her father every day. They upset her too much.'

This was greeted with silence.

'Why don't you come home, Theo?'

'I can't.'

'So what are you going to do? Spend the rest of your days alone in a strange country?'

'It's better than spending them in jail.'

'If you handed yourself in, I'm sure it would reduce your sentence. And it would mean you'd see your daughter.'

'But she's going away.'

'She wouldn't if she knew you were coming back.'

'But after all I've done, surely she wouldn't have anything to do with me any more.'

'You're her father, Theo. It won't be easy but she'll learn to forgive and forget.'

'It was an accident, Toni. You do know that? And I panicked. I thought she was dead.'

'I believe you. But I'm afraid it's the reports on your sex-life that you're going to find harder to explain to Chloe.'

'God, no, I can't face her.'

'If you care about her you will, Theo. You're the only one who can help her now.'

'I don't know.'

Toni took a deep breath. 'Let me make the decision easier for you, Theo. If you don't agree to come back I'll tell the police where you are.'

'I need time to think.'

'To think or to run? Look, Theo, it's only a matter of time before they catch up with you. Do the decent thing. Wouldn't you like to win back the respect of your daughter?'

'Can I talk to her?' His voice was barely a whisper.

'Not now. I don't want you making things worse. If you agree to come back I'll let you talk to her. Otherwise I will make it my life's work to make sure you never get near her again.'

'You've grown very hard, Toni.'

'I wonder why?'

Chapter Forty-three

Thursday evening, 5 October

It was two more days before Theo agreed. Ian was frantic, convinced that he was using the time to plan his escape but Toni begged him to wait. And then Theo called. 'I need to give Eric notice here and book my flights, but I should be back in Dublin before the end of the month.'

'For what it's worth, Theo, I think you're doing the right thing.'

'Can I speak to my daughter now?'

'Let me talk to her first. Call back at ten.' She hung up and went in search of Chloe, who was lying on her bed listening to music.

'Hi, Toni. What's up?'

'I have some news.' Toni sat down on the side of the bed and began to explain. 'I know it's probably a shock, Chloe,' she said, when she was finished and Chloe hadn't said a word, 'and you don't have to talk to him yet, if you don't want to.'

'Of course I want to, I suppose – oh, I don't know!' Chloe tugged nervously at the dark wisps of hair fanning her face. 'Why now? Why hasn't he been in touch before?'

'He didn't make contact with me. I found him.'

'When is he going to call?'

'At ten.'

'I think I'd like to be on my own for a bit.'

Toni stood up. 'Will you be okay?'

'Sure.'

After Toni had left, Chloe curled up into a ball and tried to figure out how she felt about her father. The reports of his other life in the paper had disgusted her, and although she knew that parts of it had been fabricated she knew there was some truth in it. She was ashamed that he had left that woman to die, but Mark had said he must have panicked, which made sense. Also, she was disappointed that he hadn't come back of his own accord. And she was still angry that he hadn't thought of her before running away. At least he could have said goodbye. Even her mum had done that.

She remembered that day so clearly. She had been sitting up on the bed, wearing her favourite blue dress while her mother gently brushed her long hair. As she brushed, she had explained that she had to go away.

'Don't go, Mummy,' Chloe had begged tearfully.

'I must, love.'

'Then take me with you.'

'I can't do that. Anyway, you have to stay here and mind Daddy.' And she'd turned Chloe round to face her, gazing tenderly into her eyes. 'But I'll always be with you, Chloe. Whenever you look up into the night sky, I'll be up there among the stars watching over you.'

Chloe wiped away a tear as she remembered her mother's words. 'Mind Daddy,' she had said. Maybe that's why he'd left. Maybe she hadn't looked after him properly. Maybe she'd let him down. Maybe he'd gone because of her. When the phone rang she jumped. Moments later, Toni walked in and handed it to her.

'Daddy?' Chloe said faintly, gripping it with trembling fingers.

It was more than an hour later when she went downstairs to Toni, who was pacing the kitchen, pausing only to gulp mouthfuls of coffee. 'How did it go?' she asked anxiously.

'Okay,' Chloe said, but the tears were already falling.

Toni held out her arms and Chloe rushed into them. 'He's going to come home and face the music. He kept asking me not to go away,' she added, sounding confused.

Toni suppressed a smile. 'I told him you were thinking of travelling. It's going to be hard for him when he gets back, Chloe. Do you think you can be there for him?'

'I know the papers will be all over us again and we'll have to go to court and he'll probably end up in jail—' Her voice cracked. 'But I suppose I'm proud that he's coming back to face up to what he's done.'

'You know he'll be arrested as soon as he steps off the plane, Chloe? And it's unlikely they'll give him bail.'

'He said that.' Chloe wiped her hand across her face and took a couple of shaky breaths. 'You know, you're right. He *is* going to need support. I don't suppose there's any chance of you two getting back together—'

'None.'

Chloe nodded. 'I can't blame you.'

Toni took a deep breath. 'Look, there's something you should know, Chloe. I asked your dad for a divorce a few months ago.'

Chloe sank into a chair. 'So you knew what he was up to all along?'

'No, amazingly, I didn't. We had grown apart and I wanted to put an end to it. I had planned to leave after you finished your exams but then Alice had her accident so I stayed.'

'I see.'

'I'm sorry, love. I wanted to make it work for your sake.'

'Are you involved with anyone else?' Chloe asked, in a small voice.

Toni pondered the question. 'Yes and no.'

Chloe looked alarmed.

'I didn't lie to you, Chloe, when I said I never had an affair. But since your dad left I've started seeing someone I knew a long time ago.'

'An old boyfriend?'

'That's right.'

'And are you going to marry him?'

Toni laughed. 'My God, Chloe, it takes four years to get a divorce, so it's a bit soon to talk about marriage. I've no plans to rush into anything. I'm going to move into an apartment in Clontarf. It has two bedrooms and I'd like to think that you would look on one of them as yours.'

'What about this house?'

'That's up to your father. He may want to sell it.'

'And Alice?'

'I think it's time she retired, don't you? Anyway

she's part of the family, Chloe. We're not going to lose touch with her simply because she doesn't work for us any more.'

'I'm so glad you two are friends now.'

'Me too. She's been so good to me over the last couple of months.'

'And you've been good to her,' Chloe pointed out.

'God, we sound like *The Waltons*! Enough of all this, I'm starving. How about we go down to the take-away and buy lots of unhealthy food?'

'I *am* hungry,' Chloe realised, with surprise.

'Good.'

'Just let me go and wash my face.'

Toni let out a sigh of relief as Chloe disappeared. Thank goodness the young were so resilient. She went out to the garden and phoned Ian on her mobile. 'It's all going to be okay, Ian. Theo just talked to Chloe. He'll be home in a couple of weeks.'

'Do you think you can trust him?'

'Yes.'

'You should probably tell the police, Toni.'

'I will, closer to the time.'

'Toni—'

'Oh, please, Ian, leave it at that. It's going to be all right.'

'I just don't want you to get into any trouble.'

Toni smiled in the darkness. 'I know, and I'm grateful.'

'Can I see you tomorrow?'

'I think I can slip out for a quick lunch. Usual place?'

'Usual place.'

Friday morning, 6 October

The next morning, Toni was up early, scribbling on a notepad when Alice arrived. 'Hello, Alice. Beautiful morning, isn't it?'

Alice eyed her curiously as she took off her raincoat. 'Morning. Aren't you going to work today?'

'Later, but first I wanted to talk to you about Chloe's birthday.'

'A little dinner party you were saying.' Alice put the kettle on and dropped two slices of bread in the toaster.

'No, Alice, we're going to have a party – a huge party. In fact, you can bring all your bingo buddies if you like.'

Alice frowned. 'But didn't Chloe say she didn't want a big do now that her father has gone away?'

'Ah, but that was before she talked to him.'

Alice sank down on a chair. 'No.'

'Yes, Alice. It's all over. Theo's coming back and he's going to hand himself over to the police.'

'But how? Why?'

'Let's say that when he heard how devastated his daughter was he decided it was the right thing to do.'

'You found him.'

'With a little help from a friend.'

'Where is he?'

'South Africa. He has a friend there.'

'And how did Chloe take the news?'

'Unbelievably well. I wouldn't say she's forgiven him but she's ready to stand by him.'

'She's a good girl,' Alice said lovingly. 'And she wants to have a party?'

'We haven't discussed it. It's going to be a surprise.'

Alice looked dubious. 'Is that wise?'

Toni nodded confidently. 'I think so. When Theo gets back we're going to be skulking around trying to avoid the press again. I think we're entitled to one big bash before that happens. We'll have it next Saturday.'

'We don't have much time to organise everything,' Alice said. 'We have to decide on the food and then there's the cake to make.'

'You don't have to worry about a thing,' Toni promised her. 'I'm going to get caterers in.'

'Oh, but I could manage—'

'Absolutely not, Alice. You're going to be a guest at this party. And we're not going to breathe a word of it to Chloe. We'll go along with the quiet-dinner story and I'll get Mark and Ollie to arrange for all of her friends to come along.' Toni stood up, took a slice of toast and her mug of tea, and headed for the door. 'I'll make some phone calls right now. If Chloe comes down keep her away from the study.'

'Leave it to me.'

Toni put down the phone and ticked another item off her list. She was almost half-way through it. The food was sorted – good old Liz Connolly never let her down. Ollie was in charge of inviting all of Chloe's friends. Mark was charged with keeping Chloe out of the house all day. Next, Toni decided, she'd phone her parents. They could stay the night – for the first time – and go home the next day. That way they'd both be able to enjoy a drink. It was so good to have them back in her life, she thought. She phoned them at least twice a week now, and her mum had been up for a day's shopping. Even conversations with her father were no longer stilted. In fact, when Toni had told him about her conversation with Theo he had been very supportive: 'You're handling all of this very well, Toni. I'm proud of you,' he'd said gruffly. Until then Toni hadn't realised how much her father's approval meant to her.

Mary Jordan told her daughter they'd be delighted to come to the party and started to quiz her about what Chloe would like as a birthday present. After a long chat Toni put down the phone and went back to her list. She planned to invite everyone from the clinic and their partners, although she was hoping that Matthew wouldn't bring anyone. He and Sandra seemed made for each other. She wondered if Jade would bring Aidan. She'd love to invite Ian, but that was out of the question. Although Chloe didn't know him so maybe – she'd have to think about it. Next, Francis Price. It might be rather unseemly to invite someone so recently bereaved to a party – but Francis and Dotty had never been 'ordinary' people. And Francis would tell her if he didn't want to come.

'Lovely, my dear!' was his delighted reply. 'I shall bring the Scotch. I know the youngsters won't want it but we'll probably need it if we have to listen to their ridiculous music.'

Toni laughed. 'Good idea. I'll provide the paracetamol!'

Chapter Forty-four

Friday, 13 October

'I can't wait for this party, can you, Jade?' Sandra asked excitedly.

'Shush, Sandra, what if Chloe hears you?'

'She and Toni have gone out to lunch. So, are you going?'

'Wouldn't miss it. Is Matthew coming?'

Sandra shuffled the papers in front of her. 'How would I know?'

'Would you like me to find out for you?'

'Jade!'

'Oh, come on, Sandra, there's nothing wrong with me asking him if he's coming to Chloe's party. And, anyway, you know you fancy him. It will be a great opportunity for you to get to know each other outside work.'

'I do *not* fancy him.' Sandra looked anxiously over her shoulder.

'You like him, though,' Jade persisted.

'He's very nice,' Sandra agreed lamely.

'He likes you too, you know.'

Sandra stared at her. 'Don't be silly. What makes you say that?'

'Because he watches you when you're not looking. Just the way you watch him.'

'I do not – oh, okay. I do. But I'm sure you're wrong. He's not interested in me. He probably has a girlfriend.'

'I doubt it. I'm sure he would have mentioned her by now. I'll tell you what, I'll ask him.' Jade stood up and stretched.

'You can't do that!'

'Why not? I'll just tell him that Toni says we can bring our partners to the party, if we want to.'

'Oh, right,' Sandra said miserably. Matthew was bound to have a partner. How could someone so handsome and nice not have one? And he'd bring her along to the party and Sandra would have to watch them being lovey-dovey all night.

'Stop worrying,' Jade said, as she walked across Reception. 'It's going to be a great night.'

Sandra watched her retreat down the corridor. If only she had Jade's confidence, then maybe Matthew would be interested in her. He was always very nice to her but then, Sandra thought, with a tender smile, he was nice to everyone.

'Penny for them?' Daniel asked, as he breezed in the door.

'I was just thinking about the party.'

'Oh, young Chloe's eighteenth? Should be a good night, although I'm sure Mark would prefer it if his folks weren't there.'

'You probably won't even see each other in the crowd. Toni seems to have invited just about everyone,' Sandra said.

'Good on her. I think it's just what's needed after all that's happened. And now, Sandra, give me five minutes to sort myself out, then send in my first patient.'

'Yes, Daniel.'

Toni and Chloe were strolling back to the clinic after a sandwich and some shopping when Toni saw Ian striding towards them, shoulders hunched, hands deep in the pockets of his jacket. She considered walking past him. If he kept his head down—

'Toni!' Ian's face lit up when he spotted her. 'Hi.'

Chloe, who'd fallen a step behind as she rummaged in her bag, came up beside her stepmother and stared at him curiously. 'Hello.'

Ian's smile faltered. 'Oh, hi.'

Toni looked awkwardly from one to the other. 'Ian, this is Chloe, my stepdaughter. Chloe, this is Mr Chase. He's consultant anaesthetist at Sylvester's.'

Chloe smiled warily. 'Hello, Mr Chase. You must have worked with my dad.'

'Eh, yes, I did. And Toni, of course, before she became such an important person.'

'Wow, that must have been years ago! I never knew her when she worked at Sylvester's.'

'I barely remember it myself,' Toni said. 'We'd better be going. Good to see you, Ian.'

Ian frowned at her cold formality. 'And you. Nice to meet you, Chloe.'

'Yeah, you too. 'Bye.'

They walked on in silence for a moment, then Chloe stopped. 'That's him, isn't it?'

'Sorry?' Toni did her best to look as though she didn't know what Chloe was talking about.

'That's your old boyfriend. I'm right, aren't I? He was beaming at you before you introduced me.'

'Okay, Chloe, that was him.' Toni started to walk again.

Chloe hurried after her. 'Were he and Dad friends?'

'Hardly.'

'Why not?'

'Because I was going out with Ian when I met your dad. I left Ian to be with him.'

'And now you're sorry you ever broke up with him, aren't you?'

Toni sighed miserably. Just when things were getting back to normal. 'I have no regrets, Chloe.'

'The day Dad disappeared I asked you why you had married him.'

'I remember,' Toni said softly.

'It was a mistake from day one, wasn't it?'

'No, of course not,' Toni said, but she couldn't look Chloe in the eye.

'I don't believe you,' Chloe said, on the verge of tears.

Toni put a hand on her arm. 'Chloe, you mustn't think—'

Chloe shook it off. 'I've got to go. Sandra will be wondering where I am.'

Toni watched her almost run the rest of the way back. 'Shit, shit, shit.'

When Toni walked into Reception, Chloe kept her head

bent over her desk. She went into her office and shut the door, wondering what to do next. The surprise party didn't seem such a good idea now. Chloe would probably walk out. The phone rang.

'Hello, Toni Jordan speaking.'

'Hello, Ms Jordan. This is Mr Chase.'

'I'm so sorry, Ian. It was such a shock bumping into you like that.'

'I could see that.'

'Chloe guessed who you were.'

'I take it she's not too happy?'

'That's putting it mildly,' Toni said grimly.

'Look, I can't talk now, Toni, I have an operation in five minutes. Meet me this evening for a drink.'

Toni thought of all the things she had to do for tomorrow night's party but she wanted to see Ian. 'Okay then. The Beachcomber at eight?'

'Eight it is.'

Minutes later she was staring into space when Jade walked in. 'Hi, Toni – what's the matter?'

'Nothing.'

'It looks like it,' Jade said, sitting down on the edge of the desk. 'Let me guess. Ian?'

'Yes and no.' Suddenly Toni felt close to tears. 'Chloe and I bumped into him on the way back from lunch. She guessed who he was.'

Jade frowned. 'But you told her about him, didn't you? I thought she was okay about it.'

'I think she was, in theory. But when she saw him in the flesh . . .'

'What are you going to do?'

'I'll have to stop seeing him for the moment. Even

if Chloe learned to accept him, Theo will do every-thing he can to turn her against him when he gets back.'

'Chloe's not that stupid. You can't lose Ian again, Toni, you've got a life too. Chloe is eighteen and she'll just have to learn to deal with it.'

'But what if she doesn't want anything more to do with me?' Toni said glumly. 'Whatever I do or say I'm going to end up losing someone I love.'

'You should have more faith.'

'In whom?'

'Both of them. If Ian loves you he'll learn to accept Chloe, and if Chloe loves you she'll want you to have a life of your own.'

'You really don't know the first thing about kids, do you?' Toni said drily.

Jade winced. 'Probably not.'

'Oh, Jade, I'm sorry, that was a horrible thing to say.'

'But it's true.'

Toni grabbed her hand. 'It was thoughtless and hurt-ful. I'm sorry.'

'Forget it.' Jade flashed her a broad smile. 'I'd better get back to work. Best of luck, whatever you decide to do.'

'Thanks.' Toni watched her leave. How could she have been so tactless? Jade and Aidan had always wanted children but for some reason it was not to be. Toni didn't know why and it was pointless asking Jade. It was a subject about which she was determinedly tight-lipped.

'Toni? Sorry to bother you but I've been going

through these figures and I just can't seem to make things add up.'

Toni looked up into Sandra's apologetic face. 'Let's have a look then.'

'This is nice,' Ian said sarcastically, after they'd sat in silence for what seemed like hours.

Toni looked blank. 'Sorry?'

'What's going on, Toni?'

Toni sighed. 'I'm sorry. I need to say something to you but it's not easy.'

Ian's face darkened. 'Then don't say it, Toni. Please don't say it.'

'I have to—'

'No, you don't! You don't.' Ian lowered his voice as Toni looked round uneasily.

'It's not going to work.'

'But you're not giving us a chance! Can't you even do that? Do I mean so little to you?'

Toni looked at him desperately. 'You mean everything to me. I love you.'

Ian's expression softened. He took her hand and held it between his. 'Then let's give it a go, Toni. Chloe will learn to accept it.'

Toni smiled through her tears. 'I'll talk to her.'

Oblivious to their surroundings, Ian gathered her into his arms and kissed her. 'I love you, Toni. And I'll do whatever I have to do to make Chloe like me. I'll even bring her to the zoo.'

'I think she might be a little old for that. Now if you were to bring her to a nightclub . . .'

'Anything.'

'Don't even think about it,' Toni warned, with a shaky laugh.

'It will be all right,' Ian said softly.

Toni gripped his hand and wished she could believe him.

When Toni got home Chloe was in bed. She tapped on the door, went in and sat on the side of the bed. 'Chloe? Are you awake?'

'Did you have a nice evening?' Chloe asked pointedly.

'Please, Chloe. Try to understand.'

'I understand and, hey, why do you care what I think? You're moving out and starting your new life. Now that you've persuaded Dad to come back you can go off into the sunset with lover-boy.'

'Is that what you think? You think I only tracked down your father so I could turn my back on you?'

'It's true, isn't it?' Chloe challenged.

Toni stood up wearily. 'No, Chloe, it isn't. But there's no point in talking about it. You've obviously made up your mind.'

Chapter Forty-five

Saturday, 14 October

Alice walked over to the table, sat down and dumped her dusters in front of her. 'What is it now, Toni?'

'Sorry?'

'You've been polishing that glass for the last five minutes. What's wrong?'

'I had a row with Chloe.'

'What about?'

'I told Chloe about—' Toni stopped, remembering that Alice knew nothing about Ian either. She got up and went to fill the kettle. 'You'd better sit down. It's a long story . . .'

Three cups of tea later, Alice said, 'She'll see sense when she calms down.'

'I'm not so sure. She went out very early this morning without even talking to me. Oh, God, Alice. What if she doesn't turn up for the party tonight?'

'Of course she will. Mark will see to that.'

'But what if she doesn't want it? She'll probably be furious with me.'

'Maybe,' Alice replied calmly. 'But your friend Jade is right, Toni. You're entitled to have a life.'

'But it's all so soon to be throwing this at her.'

'You didn't tell her you were getting married, did you?'

'No.'

'Or that you were moving in together?'

'Of course not!'

'Then I don't think you've anything to apologise for. You were just being honest with her. You told her you wanted to start seeing this man again. It's probably a bit of a shock, but she'll get used to it.'

'I'm not so sure. I think Theo has suddenly become the victim in her eyes.'

'Well, that's just silly and I shall tell her so.'

'Oh, no, Alice. Keep out of it. I want her to have at least one person she can talk to. I wonder where she's gone.'

'She's probably with Ollie.'

'Yes, you're right. Should I call her?'

'Why don't you just polish those glasses, Toni?'

Chloe spent the day wandering around town looking absently into shop windows. By the time she turned up on Ollie's doorstep her friend was almost frantic. 'Where the hell have you been?'

Chloe shrugged.

'Everyone's looking for you. Well, Toni and Mark are. You should give them a call and tell them you're okay.'

'But I'm not,' Chloe said grumpily, as Ollie led the way up to her bedroom.

'What's wrong?'

'Toni's involved with someone. It's the guy she was going out with before she met Dad.'

Ollie's eyes were round. 'Way to go, Toni!'

'Ollie!'

'Sorry, Chlo, but it's kind of romantic.'

'What about Dad?'

'What about him? Jeez, Chloe, I know he's your dad but he's not exactly saint material! I think you should be happy for Toni. You don't expect her to spend the rest of her life on her own, do you? I mean she's not that old. She could still have kids.'

Chloe paled. 'What about me?'

'What about you? Just cos she's dating someone doesn't mean she won't want anything more to do with you.'

Chloe scowled. 'I just think it's all a bit convenient. Probably the only reason she tracked Dad down was so she could go off with this other man and not worry about me.'

'Chloe, you're eighteen tomorrow, you don't need a guardian. She could walk away from you any time she likes. But she hasn't and she won't.'

Chloe chewed at a nail. 'She's bought an apartment. It's two-bedroomed and she says the other room is mine.'

'There you are, then,' Ollie said triumphantly. 'I'm right, aren't I?'

'Oh, I don't know. It just all seems a bit quick.'

Ollie sat down and put an arm around her friend. 'Look, I know it's sad for you to see them split up but you knew it was going to happen. The fact that Toni is seeing someone else is incidental. Though I think you should wish her luck. The last few weeks must have been hell for her. Imagine finding out all those horrible things about your husband. Imagine the embarrassment.'

'I suppose.'

'It won't be long before your dad finds himself a new girlfriend. Some women are really attracted to jailbirds.'

Chloe's dismay was written all over her face.

'Sorry, just kidding. I know it's not easy to take, Chlo, but things change. People change.'

Chloe's eyes filled with tears. 'But I don't want them to, Ollie. I want everything to go back to the way it was.'

'Not possible, my friend.'

Chloe sniffed. 'No, it isn't, is it?'

'No, Mark, she still hasn't been in touch. Try Ollie again and phone me if you catch up with her, will you? And remember, back here for nine. Okay, Mark. Thanks. 'Bye.'

Toni hung up and went into the kitchen. Liz Connolly had arrived with two waitresses, and gorgeous aromas were now emanating from the oven.

'Any luck?' Alice asked, as she put on her coat and scarf.

Toni shook her head.

'Don't worry.' Alice patted her arm. 'She'll be here. Now, I must go and get my glad-rags on. See you later. Good luck.'

'Thanks.' Toni turned to Liz. 'Anything I can do to help?'

'No thanks, Toni.'

'I'll go and get ready then. Shout if you need me.'

Toni went into the dining room, poured herself a whisky and took it upstairs. She was tempted to bring the bottle but she couldn't hide behind booze tonight. Whether or not the guest of honour turned up, she had nearly eighty guests arriving in two hours. Show-time.

'Toni, you look fabulous!' Jade twirled her friend around in the hall, taking in the knee-length black cocktail dress, with its low neck and clinging folds.

'Thanks.' Toni smiled vaguely. 'You too.'

Jade was resplendent in a green silk trouser suit that made her eyes even more brilliant than usual.

'You're the first,' Toni told her, leading her into the sitting room. 'Isn't Aidan coming?'

'Yes, but I told him I wanted to be here early in case you needed any help.'

'Liz seems to have everything under control.' Toni went to the drinks table at the end of the room and poured Jade a large vodka.

'What's wrong?' Jade asked, as she took the glass.

'It's Chloe. We had a row last night and I haven't seen her since. She went out first thing this morning.'

'Was it about Ian?'

Toni nodded. 'I wish I'd kept my mouth shut.'

'Don't be silly. You can't live like a nun for ever.'

'Maybe not for ever but I should have waited a bit longer. I was silly thinking she'd be able to handle it so soon.'

'Oh, shut up, woman. You're talking cobblers. It's not as if Chloe's a child and you're her only parent.

Thanks to you she's going to have her father back in her life. And you'll always be there for her too. I think she's doing pretty well, considering.'

'Considering what?'

'Considering the way Theo's treated you. Toni, most women would have walked away from such a mess but you've been there for Chloe through all this shit.'

'Chloe's like my own daughter. I couldn't ever leave her.'

'I know that and so does she, deep down. You have to toughen up, Toni. Chloe is out of order. She seems to have forgotten that Theo is both a pervert and criminal—'

'Jade!'

'It's true. You're a better parent to her than Theo has ever been. You've put her happiness first every time.'

'I couldn't have done anything else,' Toni protested.

'No, you couldn't,' Jade said softly. 'Because you're a good mum.'

The doorbell rang, echoing through the quiet room, and Jade smiled at her. 'Now, it looks as if your guests are arriving. Why don't you go and let them in and I'll put on some music?'

'Great food,' Aidan said, through a mouthful of vol-au-vent.

'Thanks.' Toni gazed around the room, which was almost full. But it was ten past nine, and there was still no sign of Chloe.

'She'll turn up,' Aidan said kindly.

'Oh, God, Aidan, I hope so. I'm going to look very silly if she doesn't.'

Jade appeared at her side. 'Mark just phoned. She's at Ollie's dolling herself up. She thinks they're going clubbing. He's on his way to pick them up.'

'Oh, God, I feel sick.'

'You'll be fine. Drink up.'

'I'll just go and check that they have the champagne and glasses ready,' she said, and hurried away.

'My, but she's a bundle of nerves,' Aidan remarked to his wife.

'I can't say I blame her,' Jade muttered. 'This could all go horribly wrong.'

Toni moved across the room, stopping occasionally to talk and smile.

'Toni?'

'Hi, Mum, is someone getting you a drink?'

'Your dad's gone to fetch me one although I don't know where he's got to. Where's the birthday girl?'

'Good question.'

'Is something wrong?'

'Can't go into it now, Mum, but we had words last night. I haven't seen her since.'

'Oh dear.'

'I'm not quite sure how she's going to react to this. Maybe a surprise party wasn't such a good idea after all.'

Mary hugged her. 'It was a lovely idea. Don't you worry. She'll be thrilled when she sees all her friends.'

'I hope you're right,' Toni muttered, and carried on

towards the kitchen, where she found her father and Francis deep in conversation.

'Hello, Dad.' She kissed her father's cheek. 'Mum was wondering where you'd got to with her drink. Hello, Francis.'

Peter rolled his eyes at Francis. 'Better get back. Nice to meet you.'

'And you,' Francis called after him. 'How are you, my dear? Looking lovely as ever.'

'Thank you, Francis. I'm so glad you came.'

'Wouldn't have missed it. Dotty would have loved this. She adored parties – as long as they had nothing to do with Sylvester's, of course.'

'Oh, I wish she were here,' Toni said, in heartfelt tones. 'I could certainly do with her advice at the moment.'

'Oh?'

'Trust me, Francis, you don't want to know. Look, I must go and stand by the door in case Chloe turns up.'

'Righto. See you later.'

'Can I have your attention, please?' Toni called, and the room quietened. 'A car has just pulled up outside and we believe it contains our guest of honour. So, quiet, everyone, and lights out, please.'

After several minutes, when nothing had happened, Jade slipped out of the back door and round to the side of the house. She could hear raised voices.

'I'm not going in now,' Chloe was protesting. 'I'll talk to Toni when I'm ready. You can't force me—'

'I can.' Jade pulled open the door and tugged at Chloe's arm.

'What are you doing here?' Chloe asked, puzzled.

'I'm one of the guests at the surprise party Toni is trying to give you. Now, please get inside before I lose my temper.'

'Party?'

'Yes. Party. And don't even think about not going in there. And when you do you'd better give Toni the biggest hug and kiss in the world.'

'And I suppose you expect me to kiss her boyfriend too.'

'Not possible because he's not here,' Jade said abruptly. 'Toni had too much respect for you to invite him.'

'Oh.'

'Yes. Oh. And another thing, Chloe, Ian was the one who spent all of his spare time trying to track down your dad. And they were doing it for you. If you'd stopped and thought about it, you would have realised that life would be lot easier for them if Theo stayed in Cape Town. But they put you first. Now, don't you think it's time you showed a little gratitude?'

After a moment Chloe nodded.

Jade beamed at her. 'I'll go in the back way. And remember, look surprised!'

Chapter Forty-six

Saturday night, 14 October

Toni held her breath as she heard Chloe turn the key in the front door.

'Surprise! Happy birthday!' everyone shouted, as Chloe reached a hand up to the light switch.

'Oh!' Chloe blinked as her schoolfriends descended on her with kisses.

'Happy birthday, love.' Alice fought her way through the crowd and hugged her.

'Oh, Alice, did you do all this?'

'No, Toni took care of everything. She's been running around all week trying to get everything ready on time. She wanted it to be a very special night for you.'

Chloe looked from Alice to her stepmother, who was standing at a discreet distance. She smiled tremulously and Toni smiled back. Alice squeezed her hand as she made her way over to Toni. 'Thanks,' she murmured, and kissed her cheek.

Toni hugged her tightly. 'Happy birthday.'

'Champagne!' Jade appeared beside them with two glasses, while the waitresses distributed it to the other guests. 'Happy birthday, Chloe!' Jade kissed her cheek. 'You look gorgeous, by the way.'

Chloe grinned sheepishly at her. 'My best friend insisted on dolling me up to visit some new club in town.'

'Well, this is it, love,' Toni said nervously. 'I hope you're not disappointed.'

Chloe's bottom lip trembled. 'No, it's great. Thanks.'

'Chloe? Happy birthday, dear.' Mary Jordan came forward to kiss her, with Peter hot on her heels.

'Hi! My goodness, you came all the way from Skerries!'

'It's not *that* far!' Mary laughed.

Ollie tugged at her friend's arm. 'Let's go and talk to the gang from school.'

Chloe looked at Toni.

'Go on, it's your party! Enjoy it.'

As Toni watched Chloe being swallowed up by the crowd Jade grabbed a bottle of champagne off a passing tray and refilled Toni's glass. 'Drink. Everything's going to be fine.'

Toni tried to stave off the tears that were threatening. 'I can't believe it! She seems okay.'

Jade smiled. 'Well, like I say, she's a sensible girl. She just needed time to think about things.'

Mark grinned at her.

'Shouldn't you be with your girlfriend, Mark?' Jade said pointedly.

'On my way.' He saluted, and went in search of Chloe.

⌒⌒

Toni sat slumped in a corner with her mother, Jade and Alice, who were all assuring her that everything was going to be fine. 'I can't believe that you and Ian are back together,' her mother said, for the third time.

'I can't believe I haven't even met him,' Alice chipped in.

'He's lovely,' Mary said fondly.

'He is,' Jade agreed, with a wink at her friend.

'I wish you'd stop talking as if I'm not here,' Toni murmured.

Jade pushed her glass towards her. 'You just drink up and don't mind us.'

'You should have invited him along tonight,' Mary continued. 'Your dad would have loved to see him.'

'Oh, yes, so would Chloe – I don't think!'

Jade stood up. 'Would you excuse me? I need to go to the loo.'

Toni got up too. 'And I need to circulate.'

Alice smiled as Toni moved away. 'She's gone to so much trouble to get everything just right and she still can't relax.'

'Well, it looks as if Chloe's forgiven her.' Mary's eyes followed her daughter anxiously.

'They're very close. Toni's been like a real mother to that girl. You should be proud of her.'

Mary smiled. 'I am.'

Aidan reached out and grabbed Jade's arm as she hurried past. 'Hey, I've hardly seen you all evening.'

'Sorry, Aidan, I'll be back to you in a minute.'

'Where are you going now?'

Jade grinned. 'Trust me.'

'Jade, there's something I wanted to tell you—'

'Later, Aidan,' Jade called over her shoulder, and hurried away.

Jade followed the noise, and finally found Chloe surrounded by her ex-school pals. 'Chloe? Could I have a quick word?'

Chloe eyed her warily as Jade led her to a quiet corner. 'Look, Jade, I'm sorry and I'll tell Toni so later—'

'Good,' Jade said, with a bright smile, 'but why not do something to show her just how sorry you are?'

'Like what?'

'Come with me,' Jade said mysteriously, and led her outside.

Toni was crossing the hallway as Mark opened the door to some late arrivals. 'Oh, my God!' She gaped as Robert Perkins stood there beaming down at Vicky Harrison. 'Sandra?' she hissed. 'Look what the cat's dragged in!'

Sandra's mouth fell open as she looked at the smug grin on Vicky's face.

Robert moved towards them. 'Good evening, ladies. Having a nice time?'

'Eh, yes, thanks,' Sandra said faintly.

'Glad you could make it, Robert.' Toni looked pointedly at her ex-nurse.

Vicky grinned at them victoriously. 'Hi, girls! Bet you didn't think you'd be seeing me again. Still sweating away at the clinic, are you? I couldn't stand another day of that job.' She shivered dramatically. 'And Robert was worried about all the stress I was under. He's such a honey.'

She planted a kiss on his cheek and Robert blushed. 'Well, come along, my dear. Let's get a drink.'

'Where's Jade?' Vicky looked around. 'Won't she be surprised to see me?' She giggled as she allowed Robert to lead her away.

'She'll be stunned,' Toni murmured, staring after them.

'I just don't believe it,' Sandra spluttered. 'How could she go out with him after he fired her like that?'

Toni laughed. 'I don't think he did fire her somehow.'

'But what's he doing?'

'I think it's called having your cake and eating it.'

'I'm back.' Jade appeared at Aidan's side and smiled apologetically. 'Sorry about that – oh, my good God, would you look at that!' She gulped as she saw Vicky and Robert laughing and joking by the bar.

'Jade, I—'

'Back in a minute, Aidan. I just need to talk to Sandra and Toni.' And she was gone again.

'Have you seen them?' Jade hissed in Toni's ear.

Toni turned away from the people she was talking to. 'I take it you're referring to Pinky and Perky?'

'The nerve of the woman,' Jade fumed. 'What the hell is Robert thinking of?'

Toni watched him fondle Vicky's bum. 'I think he's making the best of a situation. Oh, come on, Jade, you've got to laugh.'

'I suppose.' Jade smirked reluctantly. 'I always wrote her off as stupid but I'm beginning to wonder.'

'She seems to have got what she wanted,' Toni agreed. 'Toni?'

She turned round to see Chloe at her side. 'Yes, love?'

'There's another guest arriving.'

'I thought everyone was here,' she said, as she followed Chloe out to the hall.

Ian stood awkwardly in the doorway. 'Hi, Toni.'

Toni shot Chloe a look of alarm. 'Chloe, honestly, I didn't invite him here—'

'No, I did,' Chloe said quietly, and kissed her cheek. 'I'm sorry, Toni. I've been such a silly cow.'

Toni hugged her fiercely. 'No, you haven't. It's been a lousy time for you.'

'For both of us,' Chloe corrected, 'and I conveniently forgot that. But my friend and yours,' she nodded to Ollie and Jade, who were standing and grinning from ear to ear in the background, 'talked some sense into me.'

Toni looked from them to Ian and back to Chloe. 'I don't know what to say.'

'Well, you could offer him a drink,' Chloe suggested.

Ian came forward and held out his hand to Chloe. 'Thank you, Chloe. And happy birthday.'

Chloe took it shyly. 'Thanks. Now, I'd better get back to Mark.'

'I need to go to the loo.' Ollie disappeared.

'I'd better check on Aidan.' Jade sped away with a little wave, and Toni and Ian were alone.

'I can't believe you're here,' Toni murmured, as he took her in his arms.

'Me neither.' Ian chuckled. 'I nearly dropped the phone when she called. What caused the sudden change of heart?'

'I have no idea,' Toni said between kisses, 'but I'm not complaining.'

'Are you planning to stand still for a few minutes?' Aidan said sharply, when Jade reappeared at his side.

She stared at him in surprise. 'What on earth's the matter?'

'Nothing, it's just that I've been trying to talk to you all evening.'

'What about?'

He took a gulp of his drink and looked her straight in the eye. 'Well, you know we were talking about getting a place together—'

'Oh, don't tell me you've gone and rented somewhere without me? Really, Aidan, will you never learn?'

'Please, just hear me out.'

Jade's lips thinned to a narrow line. 'Go on.'

'The guy I sold our house to, do you remember him?'

'How could I forget him?' she said drily.

'Well, he was just buying it as an investment,' Aidan hurried on, ignoring her hostile expression. 'He let it to a few different people and, well, it's been nothing but a headache for him.'

'My heart bleeds.'

'The couple who are renting it at the moment, their lease is up in January and he's not going to renew it.'

'Why are you telling me all this, Aidan?'

'Because, love – if you agree, of course – I want to buy it back off him.'

'What?'

'Wouldn't it be wonderful to have our home back?'

'Well, yes, but how could we afford it?'

'It needs a lot of work done to it.' Aidan grimaced. 'Some of the tenants weren't exactly house-proud. And he's looking for a quick sale.'

'My God, I don't believe it.'

'It's true. Just say the word and we can move back in a few months.'

Jade threw her arms round him. 'Oh, Aidan, thank you!'

'Is it what you really want, Jade?'

Jade's green eyes sparkled. 'Oh, yes, love. It's what I want – it's what I've always wanted.'

Toni led Ian shyly over to her parents.

'Ian!' Mary blinked. 'You're here.'

Ian bent to kiss her. 'Hello, Mary.'

'Nice to see you, lad.' Peter pumped his hand.

Ian grinned. It had been a while since anyone had called him a lad.

'Does Chloe know he's here?' Mary whispered to Toni.

'It's okay, Mum, she invited him.'

'Oh, that's wonderful.'

'Do I get an introduction?' Alice eyed the tall, dark stranger.

'Sorry, Alice, this is Ian Chase.'

Ian shook her hand. 'I've heard a lot about you.'

'And I about you – although only since this morning.'

Ian laughed. 'It seems to have been quite a day.'

'You wouldn't believe.' Alice exchanged a look with Toni and they laughed.

'Hello.' Sandra advanced on them. 'You're Ian, aren't you? We've talked on the phone.'

Toni grinned. 'This is Sandra, Ian.'

'You work at the Blessington too?'

Sandra blushed. 'That's right. Nice to meet you.'

'And this is our new nurse, Matthew Little.' Toni drew him forward.

'How are you getting on, Matthew, surrounded by all these women?' Ian asked.

Matthew's blush matched Sandra's. 'Fine, thanks.'

'I'll go and get you a drink.' Toni smiled at Ian and took the long way round the room so that she could check on her guests. She was thrilled to see Jade and Aidan locked in each other's arms. And in another corner Chloe was standing arm-in-arm with Mark in kinks of laughter at a joke Ollie was telling.

'It's turned out a successful evening, I'd say,' said a voice behind her.

She swung round to see Francis smiling at her. 'Oh, Francis, it's like a dream. I'm just afraid of waking up.'

'There's nothing to be afraid of, my dear, just enjoy it.'

Ian was looking for the loo when he came face to face with Chloe. 'Hi.'

'Hi.'

'Thanks again for inviting me. How did you know my number?'

Chloe blushed. 'Jade told me. She told me quite a lot of things. One of them was that I was lucky to have Toni.'

'I'm sure you knew that already.'

'Yeah. She also told me that you were the one who found my dad.'

Ian shrugged uncomfortably. 'I was just helping Toni out.'

'And you didn't tell the police?'

Ian shook his head. 'Toni was sure that once he talked to you he would come back. She was right. He obviously loves you very much.'

Chloe smiled shyly at him. 'Well, I just wanted to say thanks.'

Ian grinned back. 'You're welcome.'

'Thanks for coming, Francis.' Toni kissed his cheek. Robert had offered to drop him home, though Vicky looked none too pleased at the idea. 'Goodnight, Robert, Vicky.' Toni forced a smile.

Vicky smiled sweetly. 'Bye-bye, Toni. I'll drop in and see you all sometime. We could do lunch.'

Over my dead body, thought Toni. 'Sounds great.'

'Goodnight, my dear. Lovely evening.' Robert patted her arm. And, with a wink from Francis, they were gone.

'I still can't believe it.' It was Sandra.

Toni smiled. 'It was a bit of a shock all right. Where's Matthew?'

Sandra blushed. 'He's just gone to the loo. He's going to take me home.'

'Really? So, are you going to see each other again?'

'I don't know, Toni. I hope so. I feel like I've known him all of my life. He's so easy to talk to.'

'I'm so happy for you.' Toni hugged her.

'Ready to go, Sandra? Thanks for a lovely evening, Toni.' Matthew smiled shyly at her.

'You're very welcome, Matthew. Safe home.'

Toni watched them leave. Matthew looked like a giant beside the tiny Sandra. She looked round, stifling a yawn. Apart from Jade and Aidan, the only guests remaining were Mark and his parents, Daniel and Meg. Ian was nowhere in sight. Probably still talking to her parents. They'd had him pinned in a corner most of the evening.

'We'll head off now, Toni.' Jade hugged her.

Toni smiled affectionately at her friend. 'I don't know what you said to Chloe, but thanks.'

'No problem.'

Toni watched as Aidan slipped an arm around Jade's waist. 'Oh, it's so good to see you two together again,' she said.

'We should try for a foursome,' Aidan said, kissing her cheek.

Jade glared at him. 'Aidan, don't interfere.'

'Yes, Aidan. You know your wife would never do such a thing!' Toni put in.

Jade made a face at her. 'Ha-ha, very funny. Night, Toni. I'll see you on Monday.'

Daniel and Meg came over, leaving Mark and Chloe alone to say goodnight.

'Thanks for everything, Toni.' Meg kissed her. 'Such a lovely evening.'

'Lovely,' Daniel echoed. 'Mark? Come on, lad. The taxi's here.'

'Goodnight,' Toni called, as they were driven away.

Chloe gave a final wave and walked back into the house, closing the door behind her. Then she turned and hugged Toni. 'Thank you. It was a great party. How did you manage to organise it so quickly? Alice said you only decided to do it last week.'

'It wasn't easy. Come on, let's go and have a last drink with my folks. If I don't sit down soon I'm going to fall over.'

They found Mary and Peter in the conservatory, with Ian in Toni's favourite chair.

'Is everyone gone, then?' her mother asked.

'Yep.'

'Except me.' Ian stood up. 'I'll head home and let you guys get some rest.'

'I was just about to make some tea,' Chloe said lightly. 'You're welcome to stay for a cup.'

When he'd had his tea, Ian said goodnight and Toni walked him to the door. 'This has been the strangest evening,' she said, leaning her head on his shoulder and looking up at the stars. 'I can't believe Chloe called you.'

'I was a bit dumbstruck myself.'

'It's probably just the calm before the storm, you know,' Toni warned. 'Teenagers can be unpredictable.'

'Oh?' Ian ran his fingers up and down her bare arm.

'When Theo gets back and the story hits the headlines she'll probably hate us both again.'

'I see.'

'I'm just preparing you,' she said gravely. 'If she moves into the apartment with me, well, you're going to be seeing a lot of each other, and she's bound to be upset when the trial is on. And then, of course, Theo will try to poison her against you.'

'You think?'

'Oh, yes. But you'll just have to keep your patience—'

'Toni?'

'Yes?'

'Shut up.'

And Toni had no choice as his lips came down on hers in a sweet and tender kiss. 'But I suppose we'll manage,' she breathed happily, when they came up for air.